Books by Talia Wall:

The Nightshades
The Bleeding Hearts
The Oleander

The Bleeding Hearts

Talia Wall

Trigger Warnings:

Violence, gore, and one reference to suicidal ideation.

For those who want to watch the world burn.

PART I

Clipped Wings

1

BRIAR

Those were the last words I heard before everything went mute. In my dreamless stupor, they echoed and clanged against the walls of my skull, like the boots that crunched against my ribs when I was snatched from the parking lot—

I woke up shivering against a dingy, white-tiled floor flecked with grey speckles. There was a quiet gasp, and my spine locked as I sat up. Two young girls, probably no older than fifteen, were huddled in a corner. I surveyed them with a frown, rubbing my eyes and blinking rapidly as they came into focus. The first thing I checked was their eyes, expecting to see crimson irises. To my relief, two pairs of dark russet irises gawked back at me.

"Where am I?" I breathed. The girl on the left, with a thicker figure and round face framed by bone-straight black hair, merely shrugged at me. The other girl—with a smaller, petite frame and tousled sandy hair—shrunk closer to her, hugging herself as her teeth chattered. I tore my focus from them to take in our surroundings.

The room was roughly ten feet wide and ten feet long, with only one door and not a single window in sight. Not even a vent to attempt climbing through. Four recessed lights hovered over us, but they were dim and one of them flickered. I tried to look around the room for something to use, but once again, I was left without any resources.

I eyed the door warily as I crawled closer to the girls.

"What is this place?" I whispered after a ragged breath.

"We don't *know*," the girl with black hair hissed. "We woke up here just like you."

I scoffed and pulled away from them, then rose to my feet and shuffled to the door and stood next to the frame.

"What is she doing?" the blonde's voice came out like a squeak.

"Getting us killed," the other girl droned. "Hey, Pinky, why don't you get away from the door?"

"My name is Briar," I snapped, just seconds before the door opened.

I swung my elbow into the shaft of light pouring into the room. It connected with something solid and triggered an angry yowl, but I didn't stop to inspect what I hit. I dove through the doorway as rough hands wrapped around my waist and fingers dug into my ribs. I shrieked and thrashed my legs until I was slammed into the cold floor. A blunt weight pressed into my back. I wheezed and went rigid, gazing down the bright white hallway with no end.

"We're not the Nightshades, girl," a deep and gravelly voice rumbled near my ear. "Don't. Make. Me. Angry," the man warned slowly through tight teeth.

A strained whimper was all I could give. He forced my hands behind my back, then jerked me to my feet.

"Grab the other two, we'll process all three of them," he ordered two other guards who wore half masks similar to the police officers. My heart sank as I immediately thought about Sterling.

Please... please find me.

"Who are you, then?" I rolled my jaw. It stung from striking the floor.

"We are White Fang, and my name is Cyrus. I am your Keeper. I am the head of all Keepers, and you will obey me at all times." He spoke in short, abrasive chunks, like a knife chopping through an onion.

"Am I going to die here?" It was the conclusion I came to since he'd freely given his name. I still hadn't looked at him—I was too busy observing the rooms we passed. Some had long display windows stretched across the top half of the wall, exposing exam chairs and large lights like dentist offices. Others were completely shut off, some with warnings and others with nothing.

Cyrus' chuckle interrupted my thoughts.

"If you keep that pretty little mouth shut, you just might stall your death a bit," he said.

I finally peered over my shoulder to face him. His left eye was a milky white and had a deep, gouging scar running from his hairline to his chin across it. His right eye was the color of tart cherries, and his skin was colorless like limestone, with hair to match aside from a single patch of black hair at the front. He gave a twisted, unsettling smile that struck me like a chord from an untuned guitar.

"At least she listens." Cyrus turned to one of the guards, who chuckled in response. I gritted my teeth. I had to remember I was surrounded by Vampyres.

I had to keep my rage under control. My fear needed to give me the common sense I'd lacked weeks ago when I kept breaking curfew.

We finally rounded a corner, then three more in a labyrinth of hallways until we stopped at an open bay of showers. I faltered a step, remembering the horrible cleansing I'd gone through at the Nightshades, where they scrubbed me so hard I thought my skin would peel off. The other two Keepers shoved the girls from my cell into the washroom. They had been so silent that I forgot they were there.

"Coming from the Nightshades, they probably already gave you baths. However, we don't fully trust them to do their jobs right. So, you gals will be doing it here." Cyrus and the other Keepers turned their backs against the window in unison.

"Go." He glanced at his watch. "You three have... one minute."

The two girls didn't think twice, they just ran. White scrubs sat on a small console table placed near the door, and the girls took the opposite ends of the shower room. They didn't turn their water on yet, just glanced at the window as if waiting for me to enter.

"Something wrong with your legs?" Cyrus sneered.

I remained silent but walked into the room. I kept looking over my shoulder to make sure the Keepers weren't watching. I tossed my scrubs on top of the girls' pile and padded to the showerhead in the middle, my icy hands tucked under my armpits. I stared at the chrome handle, took a shaky breath, and turned it on.

I screamed.

The water was so cold, so forceful, so *solid*, it felt like it instantly sliced me in half when it barreled out of the showerhead. I'd never felt water pressure like a fireman's hose meet my skin. I sunk to the tiled floor and curled over my knees, trembling violently until the water cut off on its own.

"Briar, is it?" one of the girls asked. "You better hurry, we only have fifteen seconds left."

My back ached as I peered up at her with chattering teeth. The blonde had a towel wrapped around her and was offering me a dry one. Just stretching my arm and fingers out to grab it sent lightning strikes through my body.

"Thank you," I croaked, and wrapped the towel around my body before standing. My knees trembled with each step, but the soft, warm fabric of the scrubs soothed my skin a little when I put them back on.

The door swung open to let us out, and each Keeper put us back in cuffs.

"How did you like the showers? Premium, aren't they?" Cyrus quipped. I only stared ahead blankly while my eyes burned. "I hope your tattoos haven't contaminated your blood."

I hope they did, I thought, and ignored the heat rising in my cheeks. The humiliation I'd felt when an officer dragged me out of a high school biology class for a mandated blood donation paled in comparison to this.

We continued down the corridor. I struggled to keep up with Cyrus' relentless shoving. My body felt covered in massive bruises.

"This is where you three will never see each other again." Cyrus smiled as the other two Keepers took the girls down a separate corridor labeled "West Wing." My blood ran cold as I watched them leave. Silence filled the space.

Cyrus gripped the top of my arm and resumed pulling me along until we reached another room, just as sterile and white as everything else. It had a salon chair and a tall, lithe woman standing behind it. Her placid face had minimal wrinkles. She stared blankly as we approached the doorway. I dug in my heels a little but Cyrus shoved me inside.

"The usual, Marg," he grunted, moving to stand at the doorway with his bulging arms crossed over his chest. I hesitantly sat in the chair. I only complied since my strength had gone down the drain with the painful water of the showers. For the first time in perhaps... two or three weeks, I saw myself in a mirror.

My cheeks were hollow, and my skin was pallid. My grey eyes were sunken and dull like ashes. I couldn't decide how much weight I'd lost in the short time I'd been captured. My eyes burned more as I watched the lady cut my shoulder-length hair to just above my ears, the short strands now in a sharp taper down my neck—a hacked up pixie cut. It wasn't done with care or purpose like at Sundance hair salon.

It was just to rob me of the last piece of my identity I clung to.

I peered down at the pink strands scattered around the chair, and then at the fresh scars strewn across my arms from the Nightshade Vampyres who had cut me. I'd never be able to get tattoos to cover these scars. Not like the others.

I raised my eyes back to the mirror, tears soaking my cheeks as I gazed at the shaven skeleton staring back at me.

❋

The rest of processing consisted of being medically assessed from head to toe. To my dismay, I was healthy enough for them to keep me rather than kill me. After the final assessment taking my blood-work, Cyrus pulled me to an elevator a few doors down from the exam room. I watched the numbers climb to the fifth floor and my knees locked when the elevator slid apart.

"No—"

My breath caught in my throat as Cyrus shoved me into the new corridor lined with barred cells. I immediately thought about the solitary, windowless cell at the Nightshades and my heart clenched.

"I can't be locked up again," I whimpered. My slippers sighed against the floor as Cyrus pushed me forward. "Please, I'll listen!"

"You need to earn that privilege, doll."

Cyrus dragged me to a cell, waved his watch over its lock, and threw me inside. I slid across the tile and jumped to my feet, running to the door just as he shut it. I gripped the bars, blinded by the tears cascading down my cheeks.

"I'm sorry! I'm sorry, I promise I'll listen, please just let me out! *Cyrus!*" My chest heaved as I tightened my grip around the bars. He smirked before sauntering away, dismissing my desperate cries. My words jumbled together, growing into a crescendo of unintelligible screams. I shook the bars like an ape at a zoo.

"It's no use, we've all done that and we're all still here," a breathy voice of ice dragged from across the hall. I sank to my knees.

"What is this place?" I whined, bracing my elbows over my knees and burying my forehead in my palms with a sniffle. The cold metal bars dug into my back as I leaned against them. I wondered if Vivian's chest tightened just as badly as mine every night she stayed in those cells at Black Bay County Prison.

"The end of the line," the tired voice responded. I lowered my palms and turned to peek across the hall.

"Who are you?" I asked, narrowing my eyes as I tried to make out the figure lying across their bed. A dry chuckle was my only response.

"Her name is Azha, she doesn't like names and she's the world's biggest pessimist," a smooth voice with the timbre of a jazz singer cut in.

"*Realist*," Azha hissed, and sat up from the bed with a huff. She emerged from the deep shadows of her cell and stood near the barred gate, revealing a warm complexion of mahogany, as if Autumn itself had birthed her. Her hair was shaved like mine, and tight onyx coils neatly blanketed her scalp. Her eyes, however, were cold. Narrow slits that either held judgment, disdain, or anger. Perhaps all three. Her spine was rigid, her feet spread shoulder-width. The stance of a confident warrior—or a mountain lion. I shifted my gaze from her to the cell adjacent, where the jazz singer had spoken from.

"What's *your* name then?" I asked. I was fine if Azha didn't speak to me anymore.

"Malachi. And you?" He lowered to the floor, leaning against the wall and propping a knee up. While Azha exuded cinnamon, apples, and brewed coffee, Malachi was deep, rich velvet. He was Gloaming and everything beyond it, the time of day I once called home. Looking at him made my chest squeeze as I remembered the clear night I spent with Draven at The Hole.

When I had thought everything finally fell into place.

His eyes held the warmth that Azha's lacked. For a second, I forgot that I was in a cage. For a fleeting moment, I was in my bedroom, gazing at Neoterra's skyline after Check-In.

"Briar," I said with a sigh, and hugged my knees to my chest. "What is this place?" I repeated the question since Azha's answer didn't exactly satisfy me.

"The Vampyres are testing on us for something, I don't know. I think they're trying to either cure themselves or make themselves stronger," Malachi shrugged.

"How long—" My breath hitched. "—have you two been here?" I wasn't sure if I wanted to hear the answer.

"Six months. Others haven't been so lucky," Azha said flatly as she picked her nails.

I closed my eyes and inhaled deeply once my head started to swim. My quiet exhale trembled and I rocked back and forth, tightening my arms around my knees. Two weeks at the Nightshades was already too much.

You can't fall apart now, Briar. Not yet. I sniffled and wiped my cheeks roughly, then stood from the floor. I felt like I was drowning by the second, but I had to keep my mind on the shore if I had any hope to get out of here. I took deep breaths to push the tears back into the ocean.

I wanted to ask what happened to those who didn't last six months, but I wasn't sure I had the strength to hear the answer yet.

※

Once I finally calmed down, I was able to observe my cell. There was a stainless steel toilet and sink in the far corner. There was even a light switch to turn on the recessed lighting above me. The bed was floating, bolted into the wall, and had a fluffier pillow. I eased onto the bed, the mattress sinking gracefully beneath me. At the very least, they made it more comfortable than the Nightshades.

I curled over my pillow in fetal position, holding it close to my chest like a stuffed animal. I hoped the Nightshades never found out about my family.

I wondered if Sterling was making any headway to find me. He was considered gifted on the police force. Perhaps he'd be able to use those gifts to find me. Then again, I'd completely disregarded every warning he gave me and we'd been fighting constantly. He could think I just left on my own.

And Astoria...

I hoped she knew I'd never just leave her without warning. Most of all... I hoped she'd learn to live her life without me.

※

Another week passed, which I only knew because Azha kept track on scrap papers. She and Malachi were released to eat in a cafeteria for dinner while I was given all three meals in my cell. According to Malachi, I was still in my probationary phase and wouldn't be allowed to eat with them until after my first experiment. They were also let out for an hour every day, where they were supposedly allowed to stand around in an outdoor courtyard with close monitoring.

It sounded like a myth, but their disappearances were in line with their claims. I couldn't stomach the idea of being docile for the sake of more privileges. It would've been an act of acceptance. But... maybe on a day I could roam for an hour, I could find a way out of this place.

As always, I slept fitfully with bombarding nightmares and flinched awake at the sound of the cell door sliding open. Half of the thin sheets were twisted on the floor.

"Rise and shine," Cyrus intoned as a woman in a white, faceless mask came inside. My eyes went straight to the fat syringe in her hand and I reeled on the bed, kicking the rest of the sheets at her.

"Let's play nice, now," Cyrus said coolly, still waiting by the bars. Just before I could jump off the bed, the woman grabbed my ankle with an iron grip and jammed the needle into my calf. She turned and gave Cyrus a nod, jerking her chin in my direction. My eyelids were rapidly growing heavy and I opened them wider in a lousy attempt to repel the oblivion trying to engulf me.

"Nighty-night," his silken voice crooned.

2
DRAVEN

Three weeks and I still couldn't figure out how I didn't see Wraith's hunting spree being a trap. I'd been staying in the chamber next to Briar's old one in Uriah's basement since that night. The feeling in my legs had yet to return from Larkin's poison, but I could at least pull myself around. I spent most of my days on the bed, savoring Briar's scent since they'd moved her pillow to my cell. Her smell was bittersweet. It reminded me of the moments I felt most alive with her, as well as my failures and the torture she could be enduring at White Fang.

The hardest part about being in the cellar wasn't the lack of nicotine or the inability to move. It was the Vampyres' curse of sleeplessness. I could have spent most of my time chasing dreams. Whenever I was sent down here in the past, I used my energy to work out. With the paralysis, I couldn't even do that much.

On top of that, there was the silence. I'd never cared much about having friends or socializing. Then again, I'd never realized how much I took it for granted until the shadows started talking back to me.

Uriah either forbade anyone to give me the antidote for the toxin or Larkin refused it himself. Caspian visited once a week, sneaking a few bags of blood into my cell. The blood was the only thing that allowed me to heal. At a much slower rate, but it was better than nothing. He was always so loyal to the Nightshades and their principles, yet he was willing to go against Uriah's orders so I wouldn't starve.

I was lying supine on the cool concrete when I heard the main cellar door slowly grind open. I twisted with a soft grunt and grabbed my pant legs to turn them with the rest of my body. I gripped the metal bed frame, hoisted myself onto the bed, and rolled onto my back. It was the same position they'd left me in the night they poisoned me, and it was the position I made sure they found me in so they wouldn't know I was healing yet. I didn't want Caspian implicated in helping me.

The metal door swung open and I squeezed my eyes shut from the brightness pouring into the dim chamber. Against the white light, there was an hourglass silhouette, until the figure took a step forward into my cell. My eyes focused on the witch.

"Delilah." I released a low, guttural growl.

"The one and only," she crooned, and sat at the edge of my bed. She traced her frigid fingertips along my shin, then up to my knee.

"What could ya possibly want after what happened?" I bared my dulled fangs.

"I wanted to tell you I'm sorry." Delilah placed her hand over mine and I almost snatched it back, but I had a role to play.

"*Sorry?*" I scoffed. Every decision she'd made wasn't born of impulsivity. She calculated every step, and the way I saw it... an apology could never cover it.

"Yes," she whispered, and lowered her lashes as she rubbed her thumb in circles over the top of my hand. "I just wanted Briar out of the picture so it'd be like old times."

"*Old times?*" I echoed, raising my voice with each word. "Ya mean the three-month fling we had? You attacked a woman who knew nothin' about you or this place!"

"Draven... she's *human*. You'd get executed and she would've been arrested if you two were caught together in public. I was doing you a favor." Delilah's thumb paused over my hand as she lifted her gaze to mine. I gnashed my teeth so tight, I thought my jaw would break. She raised my limp arm and pressed her voluptuous, coal-stained lips to my hand.

"Briar ain't deserve any of this." My voice cracked. "Don't... touch me."

It was an effort not to sit up and strangle her.

"You want to cling to your past in every way imaginable," Delilah sighed. She slowly rose from the bed, tugging at the waistband of her denim shorts to readjust. "A past that isn't even worth clinging to. Hanging around humans is just keeping you from progressing forward, and risks your life with the cops. They'll look away when we hurt our own, but dating the humans? There's not a bribe in the world that'll satiate them."

My lips curled taut as I bared my fangs. She headed back to the cell door, but stopped at the threshold as I loosed a malicious snarl.

"You know *nothin'* about my past. The second I get outta of here... I'll rip your throat out first," I warned.

"Hm. We'll see. I'm sure you'll change your mind," Delilah said with a small grin, then closed the door.

✳

I scowled at my cell door, fuming. I wished I could melt the door right off its hinges, level the entire city of Neoterra and purge it of the filth I'd groveled in all these years.

I expected Delilah to come back. I hoped for Caspian to finally visit so I could gain more strength, but there was just silence for one, two, maybe three hours.

Then I was blinded again... and it wasn't Delilah *or* Caspian behind the door. The first thing I noticed was a wry, shark-like grin emerging from shadow. Then, it split into two. My mouth went dry as Wraith and Larkin strolled into my cell like a pair of hyenas.

"First thing you do when you get your speech back is threaten Delilah?" Wraith tilted his head and clicked his tongue as he slowly shook his head. "Maybe we should wash your mouth out with soap."

"Should I give him another dose?" Larkin held up a small green vial, a small pearl of toxin oozing at the end of its needle like the sweat upon my brow.

"No, Uriah has something better for him," Wraith sneered.

"Did you come in here to talk about me as if I'm not here, or did ya have something to say?" I spat. As if seeing Delilah wasn't bad enough.

Wraith's smile widened as he scanned my chamber. "I'm proud to let you know that Uriah is officially done with you."

Larkin reached into his pocket and casually pulled out a stick of gum, tossing the wrapper onto my chest. I hissed, then reeled back. I had to keep in mind that they wouldn't hesitate to hurt me in such a defenseless state. At least Delilah respected a fair fight.

"What does that mean?" I mumbled, my eyes fixed on Wraith, who turned in small circles and kicked my empty bucket over.

He leered at me over his shoulder. "It means, my human-loving friend, that you will be joining them at White Fang."

"What?!"

In the blink of an eye, Larkin flashed to me with his needle, holding it just centimeters from my iris. Cool air brushed over my widened eyes as I froze. I didn't dare blink.

"Watch that tone of yours, Draven... I could still blind you and the White Fangs would be fine with it," Larkin warned. Beyond the needle, I could see Wraith smirking at the cell door. Larkin eased away from me and I blinked rapidly with a hard swallow. My palms were coated with sweat, but I resisted the urge to wipe them on the sheets.

"When is this supposed to happen?" I asked, lowering my tone so it'd appear steady.

"Whenever. Before the antidote will kick in, obviously." Larkin shrugged. He pulled out a needle with a pink vial the size of a fingernail, similar to the green vial. Without warning, he pricked me behind the ear. "Transporting a paralyzed Vampyre is a lot easier than a functional one."

I scoffed, ignoring the burn that swirled around the back of my head.

"Y'all planned this from the start... didn't you? This wasn't just because I let that cop get away!" I shouted after them as they ambled toward the door.

Wraith turned back with a twisted grin. "You know, Draven, you're a lot smarter than you look."

The door slammed shut, and my chest tightened so much that I fell into a coughing fit.

✳

My legs were burning and tingling within thirty minutes. Panic began to settle in my bones as I realized my transport to White Fang would be sooner than I thought. I sat up on the bed and scooted until my back hit the wall. I heard the cellar door open shortly after and cursed under my breath, knowing full well that whoever came in to bother me would see that I could move substantially better. They'd go running to Uriah—

The door cracked, then slowly opened to minimize the creaking. I sighed with relief as Caspian emerged with four bags of blood. His face was still hardened marble despite constantly looking over his shoulder.

"Good to see you can sit up now," Caspian whispered, tossing the pouches to me.

I caught them without hesitation, twisted the caps, and drained them in seconds. He rushed to grab the empty bags, but I gripped his arm tightly so he wouldn't leave just yet. He said nothing, but I could feel the subtle resistance of him pulling away.

"What are you doing?" he asked tightly.

"I got a huge favor to ask ya. I ain't got much time—"

Caspian had always been loyal to the Nightshades. Asking him for such a favor could potentially ruin Briar's family's life. On the other hand, he was the only Vampyre I could trust with my life. He had to draw a line somewhere for how far his loyalty to the clan would stretch.

Right?

"I don't have much time either, so out with it." His pale brows lowered.

"Briar's family. Remember her brother? His name is Sterling Shaw. Don't forget he's a cop and she's got a younger sister named Astoria. Please... *please* promise me you'll protect them from this place. I know it's a lot to ask and it's putting ya in the middle but—"

"Where is this coming from? Why are you telling me this?" He finally snatched his arm from my grip and it felt like it ripped my fingers apart.

"They're sendin' me to White Fang, man." My shoulders slumped with defeat. "They're sendin' me and ain't no tellin' what they'll do if they find out."

That marble mask cracked, Caspian's nose crinkling and eyebrows raising. If I didn't know any better, I'd say it was fear.

He looked away and mumbled something under his breath.

"Her family lives south of here, in a yellow house in the country and—"

"I told you she wasn't worth it," he grumbled. "Now look!" he shouted in a hushed whisper.

"I know, I know... but maybe if ya somehow get information to her brother without putting yourself in danger—"

"Shouldn't you be more concerned about becoming White Fang's guinea pig?" Caspian scoffed as he straightened the sleeve I'd ruffled earlier. "This is insane, Draven. Do you hear what you're asking me? Briar is gone! None of this would've happened if you just did what you needed to do from the beginning!" His whispers were becoming more strained by the second.

"Yeah, well, we're past that now," I breathed. "But if you save her... I'd owe ya one forever."

Caspian briefly poked his head out the doorway to check the cellar's hall. His expression hardened back to stone with resolve.

"Okay," he said coolly, as if a switch had been flipped back on.

"Promise me," I demanded through tight teeth. He took in a sharp inhale, then exhaled loudly through his nose.

"I promise."

3
CASPIAN

I INSTANTLY REGRETTED ALLOWING THOSE WORDS ESCAPE my lips. I stared at my friend sitting on that degraded mattress, his sickly ashen skin slowly deepening to a bronze. I dipped a glance at the blood bags in my hands, wondering if our friendship was truly worth the risk of losing a secure place here at the Nightshades. If it was worth potentially falling into the same trap Draven was in, after all they had done for me.

Briar wasn't a depraved Sun Dweller like most of them, but she wasn't enough for me to risk my life. I couldn't quite wrap my head around why Draven was so desperate to save her. Of all the humans we had to kill or capture in the past, not a single one had such a pull on his heartstrings like this woman.

Any time I couldn't understand his line of thinking, I brushed it off as a result of his Sun Dweller past.

"Thank you," Draven whispered, his voice subtly cracking. I gave him a stiff nod in response before shutting the door. I wanted to take the promise back.

But if there was anything positive I'd learned from my despicable father... it was that a man's word held the most value.

The Nightshades who volunteered to participate in White Fang's trials had yet to return home. With Draven going there—without anyone having reported their activities—they could be slaughtering us in disguised science experiments, and the rest of us would be none the wiser.

I felt like I was balancing on a tightrope hundreds of feet in the air, waiting for it to snap.

I stuffed the empty blood bags in the waistband of my slacks before I sped out of the basement. The cellar door was still groaning shut by the time I reached upstairs. I glanced at the wide picture windows lining the far wall and the French doors that led to the backyard. The crescent moon was a tiny smile in the sky, mocking me.

I stalked toward the front doors with the intention of disposing the bags far from the King Estate, but Larkin swept through the foyer and snapped his fingers at me as if I were a dog in the street.

"Where are you off to, Ghost Boy?" He poked my shoulder. I glanced at the spot he touched, and slowly lifted a disgusted gaze to meet his.

"You were never much of a talker, were you?" Larkin pressed. He took a step back and hooked his thumbs through the belt loops of his jeans, puffing out his chest like a proud state trooper.

"Not to irrelevant people," I said calmly, though I felt the beast begin to stir in the pit of my gut. I glanced at his throat, imagined ripping it out with my bare hands.

Larkin folded his arms with a proud smirk. "Irrelevant? Haven't you heard? Uriah's got me and Wraith as his top Watchmen while he's in Helios for the week."

I blinked, then turned to open the door again. Larkin rammed his shoulder into it, forcing it shut. I took a step back with a quiet inhale.

"This is the smallest amount of power I've ever seen get to anyone's head," I said, brushing a hand over my shoulder to wipe away the ghost of his finger poking me moments ago.

"Yeah? Well, I don't think you should be allowed to leave without telling me your whereabouts. Wraith would be interested to know too, seeing as how you're friends with a traitor."

Guilt by association already, but I saw it coming. I paused for a moment, thinking up a story that could be deemed satisfactory just to get him out of my way.

"Very well." I ran a hand through my hair. "I'm tracking down some potential test subjects. We're still keeping White Fang stocked, are we not?"

Larkin's eyes darkened as the corner of his mouth pulled into a sinister smirk.

"Of course," he said. "Just... let us know if you find anyone good. It'll be hard to top Briar's blood type."

"I'm sure," I said, and turned away to continue my path to the garage. My body was rigid as I expected Larkin to follow me or Wraith to wait around the corner and grill me about the same issue.

But I didn't feel or smell either of their presences once the garage door opened.

Nonetheless, I chose a blacked-out SUV and set the back seats down in case they decided to watch. Why would I choose a sports car with minimal trunk space if I was hunting for more Sun Dwellers? Perhaps I was being too cautious... but being that way was what had kept me in Uriah's good graces all these years. I wished Draven wasn't so careless.

As I climbed in the driver's seat, my eyes swept over a new motorcycle with LED lighting around the rims across. I frowned as I remembered Delilah once boasting that Briar's abduction had come with a bonus ride. Delilah never rode motorcycles, but it wasn't hard to assume she took it out of spite.

I kept an eye on every vehicle I passed and especially on any that found themselves snaking behind me. Even with enhanced Vampyric sight, blinding headlights at night concealed the vehicles' makes behind me. My mind would play tricks on me as I imagined clan members tailing my whereabouts.

I loosed a relieved breath each time the vehicles turned on a different street.

I drove further north, toward a gated apartment complex known as Crow's Nest. It resided on a hill overlooking the beach and was just one street away from the Nocturne District.

I approached the gate and triple-checked my surroundings before I punched in the four-digit code, then waited for the iron gates to slowly open. I drove through, glancing at the group of Vampyres lounging around a fire pit and several others swimming in the pool.

I could smell the grill and hear the laughter, and I sucked my teeth at their obliviousness to the world around them.

I went to my building at the back of the property and climbed the stairs to my fourth-floor apartment, hoping my nosy neighbor, Nadia, was buried in hers. She was always conveniently leaving when I arrived, and vice versa, or poking her head out her front door when she heard mine open.

I heard paper crinkle at my shoe as I worked to unlock my door and looked down to see a cupcake with a smiley face on a sticky note that said, "Hope you had a good night!"

I growled under my breath and picked it up, only to immediately toss both items in the trash when I went inside. I just wanted to be left alone.

As much as I wanted a high-rise, keeping a low profile was more important. This was the last place any of the Nightshades would be willing to look for me because Uriah detested the Nocturne District. I supposed I should've opted for a cabin in the woods to avoid people like Nadia.

I finally pulled the empty blood bags from my waistband and tossed them in the biohazard trashcan at the edge of my kitchen. With an exhausted sigh, I shuffled across the apartment and stepped onto the balcony. I peered down the rocky hills and at the black sea subtly glittering beneath the crescent moon. I listened to distant cries and car alarms, shutting my eyes. The sound reminded me of Briar's screams when I took her to be prepared for the White Fang transport. No one had ever been so desperate for my help before, not even Draven.

I pushed away from the railing and went back inside to research the yellow house on a satellite map.

For the past few weeks, I couldn't figure out how she ended up in Pelican's Crossing and witnessed our arson. Finding out that she lived on the south side of Neoterra only nourished my confusion.

I plopped on the couch and swiped through the map on my phone. Once I felt confident I'd found the right area, I switched to street view and followed the road until I saw the yellow house. I pressed my lips into a thin line and ran my hands through my hair.

Approaching the brother directly would be too risky. I would be implicated along with the entire clan, especially with his reputation of sharp investigative skills. There had to be a way to get the message to him without the Nightshades being exposed and there had to be a way to stop the White Fangs before they could hurt Draven and—free Briar. I stared at the ceiling with a developing headache until an idea hit me, and the corner of my lips ticked upward.

4
STERLING

Endless ropes of intestines wrapped around my hands and forearms. My uniform shirt was heavy with blood and clung to my skin. My chest heaved with ragged breaths. I lifted my gaze from my slick and sticky palms to a corpse whose abdomen was shredded. I expected to see Cyrene, but was greeted by a mess of matted cotton-candy hair stuck to my sister's lifeless face.

"Briar?" I whimpered and crawled to her with arms that could barely hold me up.

I screamed in anguish as I pulled Briar to my chest. I rocked back and forth as howling wails overwhelmed me.

"Some genius detective you are," a sultry voice spoke dryly behind me. I could barely hear her over my sobs until my cries turned breathless. Her voice sent ice to my veins, a calm rage stroking my bones. I slowly turned to look over my shoulder.

Lyra's jaw was covered in blood. She smiled widely, revealing hundreds of stained fangs like the beast that killed Cyrene. I dropped Briar and scrambled to my feet as Lyra burst into maniacal laughter.

"You're too late, Sterling," she sang. "You couldn't save her, and now you won't be able to save yourself."

I tugged my body forward to run, but my legs locked in place. Lyra's laughs turned to snarls before she lunged forward and sank her fangs into my throat.

✳

The sheets were drenched, and I could've sworn Briar dumped water on me again, but it was just another night riddled with cold sweats and nightmares. I gripped my comforter in a tight fist and began to count the ceiling fan blades, doors, and my own breaths.

I'm at home. Astoria is downstairs. That... that wasn't real...

I glanced at my hands to confirm the blood wasn't there. I sighed and fell back on my pillow, then turned toward my alarm clock.

It was three in the morning.

I sighed and kicked my feet over the edge of the bed, staring at the floor until my eyes adjusted to the brownish-black of my bedroom.

I stood and tiptoed to Briar's room across the hall. I cracked the door open to peek inside, hoping by some miracle that she'd snuck in. We'd argue, but then later apologize to each other, and everything would be back to normal—

Her room was still a mess from when I'd rummaged through it for clues three weeks ago. Her bed was still empty, and the hole in my heart was *still* there. I shut the door, then quietly shuffled to the kitchen for water.

I leaned against the counter with the glass, ruminating. With everything that had happened, I wasn't sure what to do with what I'd learned. The Vampyres at The Nightshade bar would've killed me if it weren't for the one with a half-shaven head. The very one I'd deemed my prime suspect.

I rubbed the bruise on my chest from when he kicked me and winced. Even after three weeks, the yellow splotch was still splattered across my sternum.

I remembered Lyra being there and the Nightshades letting her go, but I hadn't taken the time to ask her if she was okay. It hadn't crossed my mind until I was standing in that kitchen, alone with my thoughts.

I glanced at the clock above the dining table. It was inching toward three-thirty in the morning. My skin jumped when Astoria's sallow face emerged from the shadowed archway.

"Did I wake you?" I asked, visibly cringing.

"No, I never went to sleep," she answered dryly and padded to the cabinet for a glass. She opened the refrigerator and squinted at the light beaming back at her. I pursed my lips and looked down at my glass, gripping the edge of the counter.

"I'm trying everything I can to find her, Ria." I knew saying it wasn't enough. It never could be.

"Right," she said flatly, and shut the refrigerator after she poured herself a glass of water. Her slippers scuffed the floor as she moved to the dining table and plopped in the wooden chair. Its legs scraped brashly against the floor, then was instantly replaced by more silence. I sighed to break it.

"Did Briar ever mention anything about a boyfriend to you?" I tilted my head slightly. It was simultaneously late and early, but I didn't want Astoria to think I wasn't putting in any effort to find our sister.

"He wasn't a boyfriend, but I think she was interested." She cupped her hands around the glass, staring blankly at the still water within it.

"Did she ever say his name?" I stifled my heart's urge to jump at the possibility of a lead.

"No, just that she was upset that he probably had a girlfriend. Why? Did you find out some news?" Astoria straightened in her chair.

"I... can't say."

Rather, I didn't *want* to. I wasn't much closer to finding Briar now than when I started, and judging by the darkness under Astoria's eyes, she didn't need any more bad news.

"Can't or *won't*?" Astoria murmured. Her words reminded me of something Briar would've said, but gentler.

"Ria... I don't want to do this right now." I turned my back and leaned over the sink, suddenly feeling weak.

"She's dead, isn't she?" Astoria's voice cracked. "That's why you won't tell me, just like you did with Dad."

I spun around, nearly choking. "No! That's not true!"

"I'm not stupid. I know you're not on duty. You can't make this confidential like everything else. You didn't even report her missing, so it's not an official case." She stood from the table, the chair screeching loudly against the floor. "I don't know why everyone keeps turning their backs on me or treating me like I'm some... *fragile* thing."

I slumped, my mouth hanging open.

"What do you mean?" It was all I could manage to say.

"Briar didn't completely open up to me. You never talk about anything. I failed a test at school and now my friends don't want to invite me to study sessions because of it..." She stared blankly at the glass she left on the table. Her voice faded as her face finally twisted into a grimace, as if the words she spoke caused a delayed reaction.

"I don't think you're fragile," I said. "I just don't want you to try to help."

She finally met my gaze. There was a flash of heat, then her eyes went cold.

"Why."

"Whatever Briar got herself involved in—" I sucked in a breath, trying to piece together words that could be gentle. "—it's very dangerous."

Astoria nodded, considering. She clenched her fists, arms tight against her sides.

"I think I'm going to go to Helios tomorrow," she whispered.

"What? Why?" I asked quickly. "I don't think—"

"I need to clear my head," she said, then turned her back. The darkness beyond the archway swallowed her up.

I shouted after Astoria, then abandoned my water on the counter to follow her back to her room. When I reached for the doorknob, I realized she'd locked me out.

"It's not safe." I tried to steady my voice. "If you want to see Mom, that's not a good idea either."

"It's not like I'm breaking curfew." Astoria's voice was almost muffled. I figured she was already back in bed, probably picking up a book to immerse herself in another world.

"Nothing is predictable anymore," I pleaded. "Those men and women were still taken during the day."

"Sterling..." she started with a warning.

I wasn't going to be able to change her mind. I let my hand slip from the doorknob and took a step back with a shaky sigh. My palms were clammy as my chest tightened. If I lost her too...

No. I couldn't allow my mind to go to that dark corner. I trudged upstairs to my room and stripped the damp sheets. I replaced them with a spare set and started the shower just to lay on the tile.

The cold water pelted my skin, gradually warming to scalding heat. I contemplated going out to continue my search until sunrise. I doubted I'd be able to go back to sleep anyways.

That night kept replaying in my mind. From the Sundance stylists to the bartender to the group of Vampyres that stalked me and Lyra, and finally—

The prime suspect telling me to *run.*

I never bothered to consider why he let me go, especially with how I'd hassled him at City Hall. That alone would've made it the perfect opportunity to get back at me, yet he told me to run. He wouldn't have cared if it hadn't been for Briar... and he might've known we were related.

My mind shuffled through the memories like papers in a file cabinet. When it reached the folder with Lyra, I remembered how she'd admitted to knowing about the Nightshades and being unable to do anything about it.

I was so wrapped up in tracking down Briar's steps with Vampyres she'd come across that I didn't realize I had a lead—and possibly a potential suspect—right in front of me.

42

5

STERLING

The bathroom was a sauna by the time I got out. It was four-thirty in the morning, and if I had any chance of getting ahold of Lyra, I had better do it fast.

I dressed in an all-black sweatsuit and sat at the edge of my bed, already in sneakers with keys in hand. I stared at her number and name in my phone for a moment. My gut twisted as I dialed it.

It rang five times. It was easy to imagine her as a human until she answered.

"Hello...?"

I didn't realize she'd given me her cellphone number. If it were her work phone, she would've answered with her last name. Unless it was the wrong number to start with, which wouldn't have surprised me.

"Is this Lyra?" I asked with a frown.

"Who is this?" Her tone matched mine, sharpening.

"It's Sterling."

An audible exasperation.

"Yeah, it's me. Why are you awake and what do you want?" Her voice was flat, almost annoyed.

"I couldn't sleep. I have some questions for you and I want to ask them in person." I squeezed the keys, allowing them to dig into my palm.

"This can't wait until tomorrow?" Lyra huffed.

"Why, am I interrupting another outing at The Nightshade?" I scoffed.

She chuckled scornfully. "No. Let's get it over with. Meet me at Aurora's Diner."

"Alright." I jumped to my feet.

"*Don't...* keep me waiting," she snarked, then hung up without warning.

✳

Aurora's Diner was one of many restaurants sprawled throughout Neoterra's mainland. It wasn't part of downtown, but it was too far north to be part of Neoterra's countryside. It was strictly exclusive to Vampyres, so I assumed we'd have our conversation in the parking lot.

I wove my car over the cracked pavement, avoiding gouging potholes and bumps as much as possible as I searched for a parking spot. Lyra stood near the front doors, leaning against the dark brick with her arms and ankles crossed. Her jet-black hair was pulled back into her usual fishtail braid, roping down her shoulder. Vampyres entered and exited the diner without so much as acknowledging my presence.

"At least you were quick," she mumbled as I approached.

"You couldn't have picked a better spot to meet?" I grumbled, shoving my hands in my pockets with a slight shiver. My wet scalp had felt frozen the second I left the house, and my rust-colored hair hung in disheveled curls.

"That's one question. You have two more." Lyra opened the door and walked inside. I groaned, following closely behind her.

The hostess' smile waned when she saw me.

"Excuse me, sir—"

"He's with me," Lyra interjected. The hostess eyed her carefully before grabbing two menus.

"Don't worry, I don't want to be here either," I called out to her. Lyra hissed at me and I rolled my eyes.

The ceilings were bedecked with stars, planets, and nebulas with glow-in-the-dark paint. The booths were made of deer antlers and solid walnut wood, accented with candles. The walls were painted with murals of aspen forests. It was quite beautiful... for a Vampyric diner. It sickened me that as a police officer, I had the privilege to come here at any time, but my sisters—or anyone else—couldn't enjoy the building's beauty without risking legal trouble. It was another thing *they* claimed, another joy humans were deprived of.

Lyra sat across from me, the tangled antlers at the helm of her seat arching above her head like a throne. She picked up the menu and started browsing. I didn't touch it yet, as I was still deciding if the place was worth trying their food. I was more concerned about them spitting in or poisoning it.

"Why bother eating food when it has no nutritional value for your kind?" I blurted. I didn't mean to ask it aloud. Lyra flicked her eyes up at me without moving her head.

"Is that the question you want to ask? That'll bring you down to one." She returned her gaze to the menu. I shook my head and leaned back in the seat, pushing my menu away.

"Fine, don't answer that. I want you to tell me what you know about the Nigh—" I paused, observed the customers in nearby tables, and leaned forward as I dropped my voice to a whisper. Even at below-average volume, the Vampyres in the booths behind us could've heard. "That *group*."

"Not here." Lyra rested the menu down and looked around, I assumed for the waitress. I sighed frustratingly.

"What's your problem? First you're willing to help me find my sister, and now you're giving me a hard time." I crossed my arms over my chest. Lyra plastered a false smile across her face as the waitress approached.

"Good evening, Lyra! What can I do for you... both..."

The waitress took a step back and I gave her a tight grin, not realizing I was rolling a napkin between my fingers until I jerked my chin in Lyra's direction.

Lyra pulled out her wallet and flashed her badge at the waitress. "I won't say anything if you don't."

"Yes, ma'am..."

"I'll take a glass of blood—"

I reeled back, curling my lip with disgust. I ignored the rest of the order.

"A-and for you, sir?" The waitress' pen trembled as she waited for my answer. I just shook my head and waved my hand dismissively.

"Why are you so rude?" Lyra hissed once the woman hurried away.

"I asked you first," I retorted.

"Hm."

It was all she said for the rest of the stay in Aurora's Diner. I sat there, watching her eat the rarest steak I'd ever seen, my throat constricting each time she put a piece in her mouth to swallow my oncoming vomit. Of all the tragedies I'd witnessed over the years, I'd never once felt more repulsed than now.

I glanced at my watch, then out the window. The sky was turning into a lighter grey-blue as dawn crept closer. The diner was quickly clearing out until we were the only table left, and she had ordered a dessert.

"You're doing this on purpose, aren't you?" I sneered. She shrugged in silence. I sighed and shifted out of the booth, then stood up.

"Thanks for wasting my time." I started stalking away.

"Wait," Lyra called. I paused and turned to face her. She wiped cake from her mouth and slapped cash on the table before standing. "We'll talk in my car."

Lyra led me to a sporty black hatchback. I hesitantly climbed into the passenger seat as she got in the driver's side. She winced at the early light.

"So what's the problem?" I kept my gaze forward on the diner, watching the various waiters clean tables and mop the floor.

"You left me," she snapped. I could've sworn I heard her voice crack.

"Left you?" I scrunched up my nose and tore my focus from the waiters, back to her. "When?"

She released a dry laugh.

"I'm sure those Vampyres were Nightshades. They let me go when you got away, but... what if they didn't? Is getting abandoned by my own partner what I have to look forward to if I help you?" She narrowed her eyes.

Partner. I thought I'd really throw up then.

"Everything happened so fast. That guy told me to run, so I did. Besides, you're a Vampyre. I knew you could handle yourself a lot better than I could if *I* got caught."

Lyra just shook her head.

"Why do you hate us so much?" she murmured. I wasn't sure if I was meant to answer.

"Lyra—"

"If I'm going to help you, I need to know you have my back. I don't care if you're human. We're both part of the force, got it? I'm supposed to be blue before I'm a Vampyre." I winced at her words, remembering Cyrene's. She'd said something similar, and even promised me a date if I participated in our department's integration program. Only minutes before she was murdered in cold blood by the likes of Lyra's kind.

"Don't you think my sister's life is a little more important than the issues we have?" I tried to tone down the sharpness in my voice, but to no avail.

"Don't you think I need to be able to trust you in order to help you?" Lyra shot back.

The silence became tangible, almost choking me. I rubbed my palms along my sweatpants, tempted to open the door for fresh air. I suppose she had a right to be angry, but I still couldn't understand why she'd expect me to do *anything* when there were four of them against the two of us. One had definitely been armed, and they could've been immune to silver bullets like the Vampyre that killed Cyrene.

"The Nightshades aren't above killing cops." Lyra's voice cut the silence, but it didn't make the car any less suffocating. I gazed out the windshield, catching two men exchanging a brown paper bag on the side of the building. They looked over their shoulders.

"Hold on." I leaned in the seat and squinted. "Is that... what I think it is?"

Lyra leaned over the center console for a better angle, then quickly jumped out of the driver's seat. I followed suit despite being unarmed.

"Hey!" she shouted, snatching a pistol from her waistband. The two men whipped their heads our way and dashed in opposite directions, leaving their trucks behind. I skidded to a stop, kicking up rocks. I watched which Vampyre Lyra chose to pursue and ran back to my car to cut him off. Her shouts became indistinguishable with distance.

I sped out of the parking lot to catch up with them. I swerved through traffic, running red lights and narrowly missing bumpers. I watched Lyra leap over the entire street once the perpetrator disappeared into an alley. I jerked the wheel to the right at the last minute, rounded the left turn through a yellow light, and screeched to a stop on the other side of the alley. I flinched as my front bumper clipped the perpetrator's shins and he was thrown back. Lyra nearly teleported, immediately cuffing his hands behind his back before he could scramble to his feet. I jumped out of the driver's seat to examine him. Blood ran down his face, but it stopped flowing seconds later as he healed. He glowered at me, eyes full of malice. He didn't look away as Lyra yanked him to stand and dragged him to the back seat of my car.

"He can't know about this." I glanced at the dealer through my rearview mirror. He scowled at me through the plexiglass divider as Lyra sank into my passenger seat with a wince. The sun crested behind a towering skyscraper and small swirls of steam rose from her arms. Lyra examined the exposed skin and rubbed them with a sigh.

"It's fine, just hurry up and follow this route." She yanked a hood over her head and pulled out a pair sunglasses from her pocket.

I didn't want to say Chief Duncan's name in front of the suspect, but it seemed Lyra knew who I was talking about. I glanced at her phone once she mounted it on my dash. The GPS didn't lead to the police station. I eyed her warily, but didn't ask questions while I drove to the unknown location.

Tendrils of smoke floated from Lyra and the Vampyre suspects' skin. She sank in her seat and used her jacket to cover her face while the suspect lay across the back seat. The GPS led us across a highway that snaked through small rocky hills jutting out of the lush green landscape.

"Where are we going?" I grumbled after driving for an hour.

"Somewhere special," Lyra droned, her voice muffled behind the jacket. I groaned, but chalked up my frustration to her withholding information due to the suspect behind us.

We drove for thirty more minutes before cresting a hill, where a large square building covered in vines and cracks emerged at the bottom. A couple acres were paved but were worn from years of abandonment. There was an old wrought iron gate that encircled the perimeter.

"What is this place?" The Vampyre whimpered in the back seat as he briefly poked his head out. I gave a wary sidelong glance at Lyra as I drove into the lot and pulled as close to the building as possible. As soon as the car rolled to a stop, Lyra put her jacket on and jumped out of the vehicle, snatching the suspect and hauling him inside. I stepped out and rounded the hood, staggering from the gust of wind Lyra left behind. I straightened my jacket and hesitantly followed.

The roof was made almost entirely of glass. Several panels were knocked out, letting in shafts of light. Lyra avoided them, dragging the cuffed Vampyre behind her with one hand. She threw him ahead of her across the dusty floor and his body tumbled into a beam of light. He shrieked and quickly rolled out of it, his breath quivering as the burns on his face regenerated.

"Why am I here?" he cried as he flipped to his side. "Take me to the station!"

Lyra cracked her knuckles and circled him slowly.

"No, no. You won't be going there." She rammed her chunky boot heel into his stomach, forcing him on his back. "If you comply with our questions, I'll make this as painless as possible."

I raised an eyebrow, folding my arms and keeping a considerable distance. I didn't know how Lyra worked, and I wasn't sure how far she'd go to get whatever intel she was looking for. I crouched low and leaned against a dusty pillar.

"What's your name?" Lyra demanded.

"J-Jared..." he stammered.

"Which clan do you work for?" Lyra's voice reverberated against the walls and I glanced up at the glass ceiling to see if the bass in her tone was enough to make it collapse.

"Come on now, lady, you know they'll kill me if I tell you that." Jared's face crumpled, then he flinched to shield himself as Lyra snatched her pistol and aimed at him.

"Yeah? Well *I'll* kill you right here, *right now* if you don't." She bared her fangs, racking back her weapon. I straightened, debating whether or not this was the line I should draw. I wouldn't protest killing a Vampyre. If it were legal, I would've been shooting first and asking questions later since the day I joined the force to satiate the retribution I craved.

"Don't make me rip that shirt and search you for tattoos," Lyra growled lowly. She took a sharp step forward and Jared cried out, scooting away on his elbows.

"Crimson Daggers! I-I was just makin' an exchange with one of those Nightshade creeps," he said quickly.

"What kind of exchange?" I crept closer, closing the vast distance between us.

"They've been buying a lot of sedatives. I don't know what they're up to, man. I just deliver." Jared kept his gaze fixed on the stainless steel barrel pointing at him.

"You got another drop coming up?"

"What?" Jared's skin went ashen.

"We don't care about the drugs, we just need to get ahold of a Nightshade," Lyra said. "If you have a drop coming, we'll capture them and you're free to go."

Jared's eyes bounced between me, the barrel, and Lyra. Beads of sweat pearled on his upper lip as he swallowed.

"N-next week," he rasped. "Next week, Saturday, at midnight. Same place y'all caught me."

Lyra holstered the gun in her waistband, her jacket falling to conceal it once again. She unlocked his handcuffs, and Jared scrambled to his feet. She caught him by his shirt collar. Her eyes darkened with a smirk.

"If you skip town, I'll find you and you'll wish the Crimson Daggers killed you." Lyra whispered. For a moment, I forgot she was a Vampyre. It was... alluring. Chills rolled down my spine as she shoved him away and Jared scurried out of the warehouse in a blur of color.

Lyra loosed a shaky breath and glanced at me, turning my chills to rigid ice. I squinted, a bitter taste in my mouth, as I gazed into those rubies sitting in her head, reminded of what she was once again.

"You're welcome," she said, pushing past me with a sharp shoulder. She removed her jacket and held it over her head as she strode to my car. I stared after her for a moment. For the first time, we had a step toward progress.

I just felt too conflicted about how we'd gotten it to really celebrate.

6

ASTORIA

I had never been a night owl. My morning rituals consisted of opening the window once curfew ended, savoring the crisp morning air. I would do stretches on my yoga mat and watch the sunrise as its liquid gold light poured over the farmlands. Then I'd head downstairs for a hot cup of coffee to kick-start my day before getting ready for college classes or whatever else I had planned. I was my older sister's polar opposite. Briar was always sluggish and cranky throughout the day up until after Check-Ins, where she'd suddenly become lively. Sometimes, I worried if my sister was secretly a Vampyre because of how much she loved the night, but her grey eyes served as a reminder that I could have irrational thoughts at times.

But since her disappearance—since it began to feel like her presence had left my side for good—it seemed the days were running away from me, and the night was chasing me. I had never known what sleep deprivation looked like until I got my grade back on my final exam and the threat of failing a simple class like second-level chemistry loomed over my head.

I knew Mom couldn't help me. I knew Briar would've probably told me not to waste gas money on visiting her or asking for her advice, but I had no one else to talk to.

As I packed a small bag for the trip, I heard Sterling's keys jingle and the front door creak open. I watched the headlights flash through the window until they shrunk down the driveway, then disappeared into the night toward Neoterra's metropolitan area. I assumed our conversation in the kitchen had driven him to continue his search.

The silence in my room—no, the *house*—only grew louder.

I should've been studying, but all I could think about was Briar being holed up somewhere in chains, being tortured in ways unimaginable. Maybe she was already dead. Maybe we were chasing a ghost trail to a dead body.

I was placing granola bars in a side pocket when I glanced at my bookshelf, aching to pick a romance or comedic novel to soothe my headache. I shook my head and continued shoving supplies into pockets.

Perhaps Briar had run away, needed time to herself after so many fights with Sterling. Maybe she was in Neoterra having the time of her life among the very monsters we were taught to fear.

I cursed myself. I hadn't asked enough questions about her friend. I didn't ask about his name, what he looked like, what they did together, or where they went. At the very least, I could've tried tracing her steps during the day while Sterling worked at night.

What kind of sister was I?

I set my bag next to my bed and climbed under the covers, but kept the light on. The corners of my room warped into shadow people whenever I cut them off. I stared at the ceiling.

"I'm sorry," I croaked, my eyes burning. "Bri... please come back." I rolled onto my stomach and wept into the pillow.

✳

I cried myself to sleep at some point. I still probably only got two hours of slumber, and when I lifted my heavy head from the pillow, my temples throbbed. I squinted out my window, noticing Sterling's car was still gone. I took a deep, trembling breath.

Dawn was unfurling across the sky, painting pastels in the clouds. It was something Briar would've stared at, despite her preference for sunsets. Something I always took two seconds to observe before burying my head in a book. Briar kept her head in the clouds, but I loved her for it.

Getting ready for the day took a lot more effort than I expected. As I brushed my teeth, I inspected my frizzy hair and the dull circles under my eyes in the mirror. The circles were so dark that even concealer couldn't hide them without caking up, so I didn't bother with makeup. After dressing in a loose knee-length cardigan and jeans, I went downstairs to make a cup of coffee to bring with me. I tried to pick up the pace so I could be gone before Sterling returned, but every limb felt so heavy.

Once I finally got in my car, I drove the hour to the ferry slip in complete silence. No audiobooks, no music.

Just the thoughts that battered me day in and day out.

※

I had taken many trips to Helios by myself, but the last time I was here, I forced Briar along to visit our mother on her birthday. *Dragged* Briar to the very place she hated.

A horrible sister indeed.

The waves crashed against the shore. Farther out, surfers dominated them. I stopped at a bench to watch one slice through a wave, defying all laws of physics. I glanced at my phone for a time update, then set it aside. I still had thirty minutes.

I wondered if Briar ever came out here past curfew. If she'd been here when she was taken—*if* she was taken. This was the Nocturne District, after all. The most dangerous area in the city at night. I wondered if Sterling had begun his search here.

When the clock ticked to fifteen minutes left, I got up from the bench and trudged to the ferry slip. Ordinarily, the smell of popcorn, cotton candy, and smoked turkey legs would've left my mouth watering. Instead, the boardwalk was the blurred background of an unfocused photograph.

I reached for my necklace as I waited in a long line, sliding the opal teardrop pendant back and forth on the thin gold chain. My mind drifted across the ocean, nowhere to be found, until I finally reeled back and homed into a group's conversation in front of me.

"Have you seen the news lately?" a stocky boy in a snapback hat spoke around a freshly baked muffin.

"No, what about it?" A frail girl that didn't appear to have seen the sun at all this summer picked at her nails nonchalantly.

"Another girl is missing," he said in a bored tone.

A knot formed in my throat. How many victims did that make?

"Aren't like, twenty missing now? Who cares anymore at this point?" another girl with sun-bleached curls cut in.

I bit my lip as my cheeks heated from the shallow remark.

"You could be next, who knows?" the boy retorted. The sun-bleached girl scoffed and waved her hand. I gritted my teeth and stared daggers into her back.

The line eventually started moving steadily, the captain greeting each of us as he checked our tickets. I watched where the majority of people piled on and went where fewer of them would be. The last time I'd come with Briar, we were the only ones on the bottom deck, but it looked like I had to go to the top to avoid the crowd this time.

White leather benches wrapped around the perimeter of the top deck. I sat toward the back, watching Neoterra's shore shrink behind us. I clasped my cold hands tightly in my lap. I peered at the empty space next to me, imagining Briar peacefully gazing at the beach.

*

Cab drivers always seemed to take their time getting to the destination. I had never confronted any of them about it in the past, but I did question their methods. Today was different. Humans were holding up signs declaring Vampyres should be put away in prisons, made to work in camps, or wiped from existence in a parade that held up traffic. My driver tried his hardest to get out of it as quickly as possible. I sunk in the back seat to force myself to stop looking at the shouting, furious pointing, and spit flying from their mouths. I wondered if the abductions triggered the protests, or if something else was happening on the island.

Black Bay County Prison was a hundred-floor ivory tower, despite its name. There were some days when clouds would swirl around its peak, concealing how high it climbed toward the heavens. It was surrounded by impenetrable holographic fences.

I stepped out of the cab and gave the driver a tip along with a mumbled farewell, then stalked down the long drive toward the spherical gatehouse. It always reminded me of an oversized marble placed next to the tower, as if Helios were just a board game for invisible giants and Black Bay was the main game piece.

The closer I got to the gatehouse, the more I could hear the fence's thrum of power.

"State your business, miss." The correctional officer jumped from leaning back in a computer chair and fixed his patrol cap when I approached. I gave him a small smile.

"My name is Astoria Shaw. I'm here to visit inmate Vivian Shaw." I reached into my clutch purse and showed him my identification. The man nodded and took my card, then started typing on the computer. I'd gone through the process probably a hundred times and yet I still felt the skin around my neck go taut.

Once the officer returned my ID and gave me a visitor pass, the gates slid open and he gestured for me to enter. I had to go through a full-body search once inside, then another officer escorted me to the visiting room. The space was split by a long navy blue laminate counter, with plexiglass forming divided booths. Some people were already visiting with inmates dressed in either black or crimson jumpsuits. I'd never seen Vampyre inmates in the same room as human ones, but I supposed for visiting hours they had no choice but to share.

I eased into the metal chair and waited for my mother. I looked up at the television, where the news was showing footage of a riot in a distant southern city named Orion. Some of the signs were demanding freedom for Vampyres, others demanding genocide because of the abducted humans. I resisted the urge to reach for my necklace.

The world's gone mad today...

I forced a small smile as Mom sank into the seat on the other side of the plexiglass. She looked healthier than the last time I saw her. She'd still lost a lot of weight, but the rosy blush had returned to her formerly hollowed cheeks.

"Ria, my sweet baby," she beamed. "This visit's already made my week."

"I... wouldn't count on it this time." I hooked some of my hair behind my ear and sniffled as the threat of tears burned my eyes. "I have to tell you something about Bri."

My mother rolled her eyes with an exasperated sigh.

"What has that girl gotten herself into now?" she grumbled, leaning back in her seat and crossing her arms and legs.

"She's missing, Mom," I said, furrowing my brows at her calloused tone. For a moment, she stared at me like the words didn't quite flow through the holes in the plexiglass.

"Briar doesn't go missing, hon." Mom forced a laugh.

"What do you mean?" I asked.

"She's probably out on one of her stupid little adventures and didn't tell you or Sterling anything about it." She waved her hands dismissively.

"It's been three weeks, and she would *never* leave without saying anything." My voice rose and quaked. I slowly stood from the chair as my mother shrugged.

"I don't know what to tell you, Ria. She's probably safe and sound at some boy's house and you're just making a fuss. Wouldn't you rather that be the case?"

"No!" I snapped, and quickly looked around to see the warden tense at the door and a few conversations cease.

"Sorry" was all I muttered as I slouched in my seat again, my cheeks burning. I stared at my hands, afraid to look up as everyone's eyes continued to sear into my back.

"I'm sorry, honey," Mom leaned forward and pressed her palm against the glass. "I'm sure Bri will come around soon."

"You don't care," I rasped. "I know something's wrong. She wouldn't just leave. Not without telling *me*." I dropped my voice lower, saying it more to myself as I repeated it in my mind.

"I do care, but I know Briar is a twenty-three-year-old woman capable of making her own decisions. For what it's worth, if she did get in trouble, she'll fight tooth and nail to get out of it," she said.

I wiped away a tear before it could escape. I took a deep, ragged breath, and rose in the chair again.

"I need to go. I love you," I said, then turned away. For once, Mom didn't beg me to stay a little longer. She probably knew it was for the best.

✷

By the time the ferry reached Neoterra, it was mid-afternoon. I had to remove my cardigan and sling it over my forearm—my sable hair stretched to my lower back and absorbed more heat than necessary.

Before I took the trek down the boardwalk, I pulled it into a messy high bun.

After searching for where I'd parked for a solid ten minutes, I decided to do research of my own. I hoped Sterling wasn't home, because if I set foot anywhere near Briar's room, it would be a hassle to deal with him. Despite ransacking it to find a lead on her whereabouts, he didn't want it further desecrated. It wasn't quite an immortal shrine, but it wasn't a living space either.

My shoulders sank when I saw his car in the driveway. I avoided the crunching gravel as much as possible—even though my car rolled over it—and cut through the grass as I tread up the front porch. I held the keys in my fist to minimize any jingling, silently praying that Sterling was sleeping. The door whined as I crept into the living room and my eyes instantly checked his favorite recliner near the television.

Empty. Good.

I loosed a sigh and set my backpack in my room, then paused at the stairs. I removed my shoes for less sound before I snuck to Briar's room. The biggest threat was the fact that her bedroom was right across from his. My shoulders loosened once the wooden stairs transitioned to carpet at the top, and the soles of my feet inaudibly padded across it.

Judging by the silence of the house, it was safe to say Sterling was sleeping after all.

I carefully closed her bedroom door behind me, then took a moment to look at the clothes and papers strewn everywhere. Every drawer was left open. All I could imagine was Sterling frantically looking through all of her things for any sort of clue. I briefly closed my eyes with a deep, shaky breath as I tried not to get overwhelmed. My head swam each time I observed the room as a whole.

Where could I possibly look that Sterling hadn't already checked? Would he have taken the clue with him or left it behind? Every time I hit an empty space in her drawers or found irrelevant scattered items, I wondered if Sterling already had the evidence.

I checked under her bed, the mattress itself, and her nightstands. I checked her closet, vanity, and bathroom drawers. After ten minutes, all I had left to look through was her endless shelving of vinyl records. I flipped through them, wondering if she'd have a secret diary or photos sandwiched between them. Just as I reached the last shelf and was ready to walk away for fear of Sterling waking up, I noticed the corner of a crumpled sheet poking between two albums. I squinted and carefully pulled it out. My heart fluttered as I unfolded the paper and smiled at the heading.

Her offer letter.

Surely, Sterling came across it—

But I didn't want to face his wrath if I brought it up. I scanned the letter and learned the hair salon's name before carefully sliding the paper between the albums. I savored the silence the carpet provided until I reached the stairs and snuck back to my room, my heart slamming with each step.

I packed my laptop in my backpack, slung it over my shoulder, then left the house again. I loosed a breath once I got in my car, as if I had been holding it the entire time. I backed out of the driveway and drove north, toward Cypress Hill University's library.

Neoterra had a severe shortage of old buildings, but the library was one of the few they'd preserved from hundreds of years ago.

Built in grey Gothic style, it was once a cathedral and later converted into a library when the campus rose around it. I always marveled at its pointed arches, its ornate carvings along the ribbed domed ceilings and columns, and its sharp spires that jutted toward the skies like daggers. Formerly known as St. Brine's Cathedral, it became known as St. Brine's Bibliotheca.

Students from all walks of life milled about, flipping through books and browsing on computers. I scanned the tables for an empty one and plugged in my laptop. I wasn't a detective like Sterling—not even close—but I hoped I could find something significant. Studying for the next test in my other classes itched in the back of my mind, but the thought was easily forgotten once I typed "Sundance Hair Salon" in the browser. Bethany's Corner by day, Sundance by night, I saw there was no way I could ask them any questions since they were strictly a nocturnal business. Goosebumps prickled along my arms when I read up on the news articles detailing their robbery, shut down, and mysterious renovation.

"What kind of project are you working on?" a quiet voice sounded behind me.

I quickly shut my laptop before whirling around in the wooden chair. My cheeks instantly heated as I faced the most beautiful man I'd ever seen, with smooth skin of marble like a living Greek statue, spiked champagne hair, eyebrows and eyelashes of ice and snow, and dark brown eyes like a hazy night sky.

"I-I, um—" My lips tangled and I had to tear my gaze from him for a moment. I expected him to be gone the second I turned back to face him, like a phantom.

"Top secret?" he whispered, tilting his head with a subtle half-grin. I glanced at him, only to avert my eyes once more.

"I'm just... looking for someone," I mumbled, and grabbed my necklace charm. Sterling didn't want anyone to know about Briar's disappearance for fear of the department taking over and not making her a priority. I remembered him threatening Officer Kent, and with the stranger standing over me, I wasn't sure what connections this stranger might have.

"Do you mind?"

He extended a slender hand to the empty chair next to mine. I shook my head, hooking my hair behind my ear and shifting uneasily in my seat. I hesitantly opened the laptop again and continued scrolling through articles. I detected movement and peeked in the corner of my eye to see him set up his own computer.

"I'm looking for someone too," he whispered. I wanted to ask him who, but I didn't want to pry or open the door for him to ask about who I was looking for. Instead, I gave him a nod and returned to my computer screen, jotting down notes.

"Her name is Briar," he added. I dropped my pen. Time came to a halt.

"What... what's her last name?" My voice cracked and I forced a swallow. I began to wonder if he was the friend she referred to, the Vampyre escorting her past curfew—

No. He has brown eyes and there's no way he could be out during the day without turning to ash.

My breaths steadied as my racing thoughts slowed down. His nostrils twitched slightly.

"Shaw," he said. "Do you know Briar Shaw?"

I leaned away from him in my chair, my mouth going dry.

"Who are you?" I whispered harshly.

"An old friend of hers. You can call me Christian." His lips stretched into a thin smile, but it didn't reach his eyes.

"My sister doesn't have any friends," I said dubiously, my chin raised. "Not any human ones, anyway."

Christian shrugged.

"I don't know what to tell you. If she never told you about me, that's out of my hands." His tone remained flat as he pulled out a small notebook the size of his palm and jotted something down. He tore the paper out and slid it toward me. I read it before I picked it up. Neatly written was his name, phone number, and a time.

"Five-thirty for what?" I arched an eyebrow.

"If you want to help me find her, you'll meet me at Frankie's Café at that time." He clicked his pen a couple times before putting it away.

"That's too close to Check-In." I swallowed, suppressing the wave of nausea that overwhelmed me. Christian shut his laptop and stood up, slinging his backpack over his shoulder.

"It's the only time I'm available. If you show up, great. If not... good luck." He shrugged, then smoothly drifted out of the library like a gentle breeze. I still held his paper in my hand, stuck in place. His aura was so cold, as if he'd emerged from the depths of the Arctic tundra. How could he possibly know Briar, let alone be *friends* with her? He didn't seem like the type to be in her circle if she had one.

I shouldn't judge, though. Maybe she confided in him more than me, and we could combine our knowledge together. Even if he was a deadly psychopath disguised by a handsome mask, he was my only chance to find Briar so far.

67

7

BRIAR

Leather straps dug tightly into my chest, hips, and wrists when I regained consciousness. My head hung forward and it was a great effort to lean back against the headrest. As the blurred lines in my vision turned crisp, I realized I sat across from a man also strapped in a white leather chair, in a room with white walls and stainless steel baseboards. His piercing carmine eyes gazed back at mine hungrily.

They're testing on Vampyres too?

"Good morning, sweetheart," an olive-toned woman in a white lab coat said with a soft, rounded Slavic accent. Her black hair was dull like coals, pulled into a half-up, half-down style. She looked vaguely familiar, possibly the woman who stood at the front doors when I arrived, moments before I was sedated. She sat at a stainless steel table with a computer, monitors, test tubes, and a stack of papers.

I opened and closed my fists as I felt pins and needles shoot across my palms.

"What's going on?" I whimpered and yanked at the binds. The Vampyre across from me winked, his fangs much more blunt than the others I've seen.

"I'm Dr. Ivanov. Today is your first step toward the greater good." She stood and walked to the drip stand next to me. I followed her movements, and where I expected to see a saline bag, there was instead a bag full of my blood.

"Wait... wh-what are you doing to me?!" My voice cracked as I wriggled in the straps. I fixed my gaze on the IV in my arm.

"No worries, child. I will not drain you. This is only the first trial and you're much, much too valuable to go to waste." She removed the needle and patted my cheek before stiffly shuffling to the Vampyre.

"You're a lucky man. You're the first to try her AB negative blood as we enter the next phase of our trials." Dr. Ivanov put on a fresh pair of gloves, then connected my blood bag to his IV. I tried to predict what sort of experiment she was doing, why she would inject my blood through an IV rather than feed it to him. What purpose could it possibly—

The Vampyre's claws extended from his cuticles. His smile stretched wider, his cheeks growing rosy with excitement and his fangs sharpening.

"I think... I think it's working, Doc!" he exclaimed. "I can make my café twenty-four hours!"

Dr. Ivanov clicked her tongue and patted his shoulder. "Patience now, Frankie." She examined the blood bag hanging on the drip pole next to his chair. It was draining rapidly.

Dr. Ivanov crossed to my side of the room and I craned my neck to see what she was doing. She hummed quietly to herself as she adjusted a large dome-shaped lamp to point in Frankie's direction.

"What is that?" I mumbled. She ignored me, and sauntered toward the table with her laptop and a remote. She reached for a rack bolted to the wall above the stainless steel desk, then extended a thick plastic sheet over everything on it.

"What's happening?" I wasn't quite sure why I insisted on asking questions.

"Are you ready, Frankie?" she asked with blank expression. He didn't seem bothered by her lack of excitement. He nodded quickly, shifting in his seat as if preparing for the best news of his life.

"Yeah, come on!" Frankie demanded. My heart tried to break free from my chest, the strap squeezing against it.

Dr. Ivanov walked out of the room with the remote in hand. Only a few seconds passed before the whole room became a blinding star. I slammed my eyes shut.

Frankie screamed, and I flinched when something warm and slick hit me. Then it was silent.

I cracked open my eyelids.

What was once a purely white and grey room was now stained in chunks and splatters of blood. My eyes widened to the max, darting to every corner where the Vampyre now resided. Every part of him was *everywhere*, and as I slowly looked down at myself, I realized a lot of him had landed on *me*.

Something snapped in my mind, scrambled all my thoughts to mush. I shrieked with desperate terror. High pitched ringing pulsed in my ears as if a bomb had gone off, and everything muffled when more doctors flooded the room. They crowded around me, their lips moving, but nothing registered. My bottom lip trembled while tears mixed with the blood on my cheeks. Heavy breaths became hyperventilating hiccups as they stroked my hair, patted my shoulders, and tried to get me to calm down.

"If... calm... take... out..." I tried to force breaths through my nose and out my mouth, only to be met with more hiccups racking my body. I looked up at the faceless doctors, four of them splitting to eight as my vision blurred and shifted.

"If you calm..."

Their voices were slowly becoming recognizable English, but I was still trying to break out of the straps.

"Get away from me!" I cried, spit flying from my mouth like a rabid dog. I shook my head and slammed it back against the headrest repeatedly.

"If you calm down, we'll take you out of these binds!" one of them shouted.

"Don't make us sedate you in this state!"

"You still need to answer some questions!"

"Breathe!"

Too many voices. I couldn't process, couldn't keep up, couldn't breathe—

I picked one voice to focus on and avoided looking at them in their creepy masks—and peered at my lap. More people flooded into the room and started to clean Frankie's remains off the floor, windows, and walls. I let the doctors coach my breaths, and the scrambled parts of my brain slowly stitched themselves back together.

"Where are you right now, Miss Shaw?" Dr. Ivanov emerged from the hallway and approached me with her hands in her lab coat pockets. The doctors straightened and stepped away from me.

"Hell," I uttered. Dr. Ivanov chuckled softly, shaking her head.

"Perhaps to you. Where are you *really*?" She leaned in front of me, taking a flashlight and running its beam across my eyes.

"White Fang," I rasped.

"What's your full name?"

"Briar Leigh Shaw," I said slowly, to steady my quivering voice.

"What's your Keeper's name?"

"C-Cyrus." My eyes flicked to the door to see him standing there with a smirk across his face, like a crooked crack in marble.

"Good, good." Dr. Ivanov sighed and placed the flashlight back in her pocket. She crooked a delicate finger at Cyrus and he approached.

"You know the drill." Dr. Ivanov stepped aside to allow him to loosen my binds. I rubbed my wrists with a wince, weighing my options. Ordinarily I would've taken this opportunity to kick him in the face to buy myself a couple seconds to run. However, there had to be at least ten Vampyres in the lab room. I wouldn't even reach the door.

The blood was drying, flaking off my stiffened skin. My scrubs were destroyed and every time my stomach expanded with my breath, I felt the cold fabric cling to it.

Cyrus straightened and grabbed my upper arm, swiftly pulling me out of the chair. My legs wobbled and I grasped his arm for balance. His knuckles cracked as his fist tightened, but he relaxed once he realized I wasn't trying to pull any tricks. The tile was cold and slick against my bare feet and I searched for my slippers just to see they were bloodied and ruined. Cyrus led me out of the room and I felt vomit inch its way to the back of my throat as I padded over slippery pulp.

"Well, doll, it's safe to say that trial didn't go as planned." Cyrus clicked his tongue and bit his inner cheek as he escorted me to the showers. He peeked over his shoulder and I followed his gaze to see the bloody footprints I left behind.

"There should be a fresh uniform and shoes waiting for you. Assuming they did their jobs right..." He sniffed and tightened his grip each time we turned a corner. My mouth hung open, searching for the words that were still piecing themselves together.

"Weren't so brave after seeing a Vampyre blow up, huh?" Cyrus added with a smirk, the scar across his face shifting. I kept my silence, focusing only on the painful shower that awaited me. I welcomed the idea. Anything to get Frankie's blood and guts off of me.

Cyrus gave me ten minutes. It didn't seem like enough time, but it was certainly better than the one minute I had during processing. I scrubbed my skin and my hair and kept my eyes open despite the soap burning them to watch the water turn from crimson to clear. I even went as far as scraping under my fingernails and toenails. I didn't want any trace of Frankie anywhere.

I dried off and dressed in a fresh set of scrubs and socks with white grips on the bottom. Cyrus grabbed my arm again, leading me back to the lab room. Like magic, the floors were clean, and when we walked past it, there wasn't a speck of blood in sight. Like it was all a dream.

"Now, I'll let you off easy since that was your first experiment." Cyrus's voice punctured the silence. "But if you freak out like that again, I'm putting you to sleep and you'll wake up in a room worse than that one."

I nodded and watched him use his watch to open a set of double doors, revealing the cellblock beyond.

I closed my eyes briefly and followed the same breathing instructions those doctors had given me moments ago. I kept reminding myself that at least I wasn't in a sealed-off dungeon and there were people I could talk to through the open bars.

I opened my eyes and glanced at the cells we passed, then dug in my heels when I caught a familiar face.

He was sitting on the edge of his bed in the dark with his midnight hair buzzed to a half inch. The lights from the corridor gilded the curves of his muscled arms, braced over his knees. He wore a matching uniform to mine, exposing his collar of geometric shapes, skulls, and Nightshade flowers tattooed around his neck. The short sleeves exposed the spiraling dragon tattoos snaking up his deep amber arms. From the squeak of my thin, grippy socks, he raised his head and met my gaze. Those eyes of blood diamonds, of fiery sunsets and rose petals, paired with the mole over his upper lip—and those delicately curved lips that usually held a toothpick or cigarette...

He sprang from the bed and grasped the bars of his cell, eyes bulging with his jaw dropped as Cyrus shoved me ahead. Just as I caught my breath, I lost it again.

I never expected to see Draven again—least of all behind bars in the very place his people had sent me.

8
CASPIAN

The plan to pose as a human seemed much simpler in my mind than in practice at St. Brine's Bibliotheca. In the short minutes I'd spoken with Astoria, she appeared calculating and observant. A little skittish, but I often provoked that reaction from anyone who crossed my path. If it weren't for Draven giving me information about the Shaws, I would've been exposed in an instant.

Getting Astoria to agree to meet so close to Check-In was the biggest hurdle. I expected to fail, but to my surprise, she decided to meet. I wondered if it was partially because I chose a café close enough to her house that she could make it back home in time. I would've picked an earlier time if I could withstand the milder UV rays as the sun waned.

The smell of coffee and food mingled throughout the café. I sat in the back corner near the bathrooms. The occasional loud hissing of the milk steamer, the indistinct din among baristas and patrons, the oven beeps, and the clanging of dishware were all overstimulating at first, but I adjusted. I rubbed my eyes and blinked rapidly as I cupped my icy hands around a warm mug. These contacts were getting irritating fast.

I had never been much of a coffee or tea drinker, but the warmer I could make my palms appear—just in case we had to do a handshake for whatever reason—the more human I would seem. I watched Sun Dwellers of all backgrounds enter and depart the café, shuffle along the street, and talk among themselves. I never really took the time to watch them in their everyday lives. I only observed my targets.

I closed my eyes and it seemed to soothe the burning a little. I distracted myself further by listening to different heartbeat rhythms. Someone had a heart murmur. Another had a rapid pulse, possibly from too much caffeine, and another had the mechanical whir of an artificial heart—one of many revolutionary medical innovations from thirty years ago.

The front door chimed and a faint woodsy scent mixed with vanilla and salt wafted inside. I opened my eyes and carefully brought the mug to my lips, watching Astoria approach the front counter and nervously look around until her eyes landed on me. I forced a tight smile and she gave a stiff nod in acknowledgment. I curled my lip in mild disgust at the bitter black liquid I'd ordered and set the mug down.

Astoria stood at the counter for a few minutes before the barista handed over her drink with a tender smile. Steam wafted from the paper cup, indicating she'd asked for a to-go order. I pursed my lips tightly, realizing I'd failed to consider that requesting a porcelain mug showed I wasn't in a rush to get home for Check-In.

I cursed under my breath and hoped Astoria wasn't *that* observant.

She sat down across from me, looking over her tightly squared shoulders once more as she hooked her purse over the back of her chair.

I tilted my head slightly. "Are you avoiding something?"

"No, just... keeping an eye on when everyone starts leaving so I'll know when I should." She slumped back in her seat slightly.

I scanned the planes of her face as I brought the mug back to my lips and lightly slurped the coffee. Astoria's round brown eyes were the color of aged honey, her button nose was delicately sloped, and the pale freckles dotting her nose and cheek bones were like paint splatter.

Artfully made by a skilled potter.

"Christian, right?" Astoria asked. The mug paused midway back to its coaster. For a moment, I forgot I'd given her an alias back at the library.

"Yes?"

"How well did you know my sister?" Her eyes flickered like a topaz angled in sunlight. My lips twitched slightly as I searched for the right words. I thought about everything Draven told me about her and the long talks I'd had with Briar in her chamber while everyone was away. I was the only one she allowed to get close enough and help her out of her panic attacks. She still couldn't speak Draven's name despite the number of times I tried to convince her he'd had nothing to do with her misfortune—not directly, anyway.

"Well enough," I said curtly. The lies coating my tongue tasted even more bitter than the coffee. Astoria looked down at her cup for a few moments, as if she was also searching for the right words to say. As if she had a very limited amount of questions she could ask before I'd run away.

"Did she ever tell you about a boyfriend?" Astoria asked with wide eyes full of hope.

"She was single, but she had a friend..." I trailed and gazed out the picture windows behind her. The roads were dimming, the streetlights flickering to life.

This was the moment I kept replaying in my mind—whether or not to mention Draven's name. Wondering if it would lead to the downfall of my home or potentially save his life and Briar's. A gamble at best, because I was sure that he'd be the first suspect in Briar's investigation if I gave his name.

"Do you know his name?" Astoria pressed, leaning forward ever so slightly in her seat, as if at the precipice of a thriller movie. I never liked to gamble, but for my brother...

"Draven Hawthorne."

Astoria's eyes lit up as she quickly dug through her purse for a small notepad and a pen. I kept my gaze fixed outside. The passing vehicles were beginning to drive recklessly, the Sun Dwellers growing anxious to get home by Check-In.

"Can you spell that?" The tip of her pen pressed against the paper, pooling into a saturated dot as she waited for my answer. I spelled his name for her.

"Do you know his species? Is he dangerous? Have you ever met him?" Her voice was strained, a pressured whisper as if she only had seconds left.

"Vampyre. Not to Briar. I have and he's missing too." I answered every question in the exact order they were asked, each answer a sharper chop than the last like hacking wood.

Kernels of information. That's all she needs.

"So." Astoria cleared her throat, hooked her bangs behind her ears, then leaned in close to whisper even lower. I almost forgot to lean forward as well, to pretend that I needed to close the space to hear her better.

"What?" I muttered.

"Do you break curfew too?" Her eyes bounced around the café. I pursed my lips into a thin line. I felt like I was skating on thin ice, that whichever answer I gave could make this plan ten times easier or more difficult. I remained silent, but my lips twitched into a subtle smirk before I concealed them behind the mug. The mild summer tan in Astoria's face immediately drained.

"Are you *serious*?" she whispered harshly. I shrugged.

"Why not? And how else would I know Briar's friend?" I tilted my head.

"That explains why you wanted to meet so late. You don't care about the rules." Astoria glanced at her watch and nearly flinched out of her seat. "I gotta go. Can we continue this tomorrow at a *better* time?"

The baristas were beginning to sweep the floors and pile the chairs on top of the tables. We were the only ones left.

"Yeah, but, everything Briar did was after Gl—sunset," I sputtered quickly. Gloaming wasn't a term among her kind.

"What are you suggesting then?" Astoria's eyes were wide, as if she already knew the answer. I jerked my chin toward the door and started walking. She fell into step beside me, then lingered a foot behind as we walked out.

I slid my hands into my pockets, waiting. "I think you know what I'm suggesting," I finally said.

"No, absolutely not, Christian. Breaking the law is *exactly* what got Briar into this mess!" Astoria exclaimed, her knuckles whitening as she clenched her purse strap.

"Briar was by herself, probably leaving work when she disappeared." I tightened my jaw, cringing at the fact that all Astoria needed to know was that Briar was at White Fang. But I still needed to figure out the details on how I could "discover" that information without bringing the Nightshades into it—or implicating myself.

"You... you're proving my point." Astoria frowned with a quiet huff. I took a step toward her, and she took a half step back.

"My point is that you'd be with me, and I've been breaking a lot of rules long before Briar ever started. I know these streets better than your average person, maybe even better than the cops," I said. Astoria glanced at the deepening sky. Her pouty lips parted, then sealed back shut.

"I have to think about it," she mumbled, then rushed down the street to her car.

"You have my number!" I shouted after her, then ambled in the opposite direction.

So far, the plan was shaping up to be better than I expected, but I feared it wouldn't stay that way.

＊

I reached the King Estate just as my phone rang. I fought with my pants pocket to get it, and looked blankly at Uriah's name across the screen.

"Bishop," I droned, pinching the bridge of my nose.

"Cass! Good to hear your voice. Listen, son... are you at home right now?" Uriah's voice always had the warmth of a father and the hollow charisma of a politician.

"Yeah, what do you need?"

"Go to my office and let me know when you're at my safe," Uriah ordered. I rushed upstairs to the room behind the white lion statues and double mahogany doors.

I always tensed up when I was in here. The study was where most of us endured Uriah's wrath. There was an old blood stain on the floor, partially concealed by the Persian rug placed to conceal it. Draven's ghost lived there, but I was getting better at not looking at it each time I entered the study.

I curved around Uriah's desk and knelt at the stainless steel safe.

"Alright, I'm here," I said, staring before the combination lock.

"Now... I'm going to give you the code," Uriah said. I frowned and pulled the phone from my ear for a moment, processing his words. I never had an issue maintaining trust with anyone here—other than Wraith and Larkin—but I never expected *anyone* to have access to Uriah's precious safe. He had to be in a situation where he needed to confirm to someone that he had possession of its contents.

"Are you sure?" I whispered. "Didn't you assign Wraith and Larkin as your Watchmen?"

"You're the only one I trust there to do things the right way, and not get tempted. Being a Watchman doesn't count for anything. It's four-six-six-seven. Now hurry," he demanded. I turned the dial and the lock clicked. I carefully opened the door with clammy hands, only to see stacks of bills, a golden watch with a diamond-encrusted face, and Mr. Barnaby's phone.

Draven and I had killed him and his wife for that phone in front of the Solaris Theatre.

"What do you see in there?" Uriah asked, clearly a test.

"Money, your watch, and Mr. Barnaby's cellphone," I said flatly.

"Great. Take the phone and go to the address I have written inside the case," Uriah ordered. "Send a picture and call me back whenever you can."

"Yes, sir," I murmured, and pulled the phone out of its case, a small sheet of paper fluttering out of it. I picked up the address, studied it, then straightened from behind Uriah's desk. I had suspicion of where the address would lead. For the first time in years, I truly felt sick to my stomach because the rumors were getting closer to confirmation.

I stepped out of Uriah's office with the doorknobs already twisted to minimize any clicking noises. I carefully pulled the door closed, but my effort was for naught. Wraith was already slithering up the stairs, heading toward Draven's old bedroom—a place he eagerly took ownership of the second Draven became a prisoner.

"Whatcha doin' in Uriah's office?" Wraith tilted his head, and his black-and-pink eyes flicked to my hands on the doorknobs.

"He requested something from me," I said.

"Is that so? You ain't in there trying to find something to help your buddy, are you?"

I raised my chin, eyeing him carefully. I could feel the storm begin to churn within. I hated Wraith and his brother... possibly more than Draven or anyone else ever did. Ever since the day they took *her* away from me. Their only punishment was to spend their time in lovely Helios. It was Uriah's way of keeping the peace without losing two of his men.

"My *buddy*," I said coolly through a tight jaw, "is already at White Fang, and is more than likely a mutated monster by now." I stepped away from the double doors and headed for the stairs. Wraith lingered behind me.

"Aw, are you lonely now?" he pouted mockingly. I rolled my eyes.

"People come and go, live and die. Draven was weak and was doomed from the beginning. I always saw that," I said matter-of-factly. Wraith whistled and shook his head, weaving in front of me to block my path at the bottom step.

"You know, they always said you were cold. They never said *how* cold." His thin mouth stretched into a serpentine grin.

"Being too warm is how you'll get burned in this world." I pushed past him. Unlike his brother Larkin, he let me go without further question.

But between the two Kline brothers, Wraith was the craftiest. If I had to watch my back before, I definitely needed to do it now.

I had a feeling Uriah didn't want anyone to see what was at that address.

9

BRIAR

THE SECOND I RETURNED TO MY CELL, I RAN TO THE TOILET and hurled my guts up.

"Hey, Briar, you okay?" Malachi called from across the hallway.

"She had her first experiment, so she's probably fine." I could practically hear Azha eyeroll in her voice. I sunk to my knees, leaning over the bowl for fear another wave would come. I reached for a small tear of toilet paper and wiped my mouth. Despite the shower beating the sweat, blood, and dirt from my skin, I still felt the stickiness of it. The dried flaky parts caking up in the creases of my fingers. The slipperiness everywhere else. I kept picturing the spontaneous explosion of Frankie's body, his skin, bones, and everything else separating in every direction like the initial spark of a firework.

Then my mind went to Draven. Was that going to happen to him here?

"Hey, guys." My bottom lip trembled and I leaned further over the bowl with a string of saliva stretching from it. "Um…"

"What?" Malachi asked gently.

"I think I saw somebody I know here," I said.

"I wouldn't go around flaunting that," Azha warned. "The second the White Fangs know you've got some sort of connection with someone, they'll use that against you."

Seeing him here made me wonder if Caspian was telling the truth. If *Draven* was telling the truth. Perhaps he never meant to hurt me after all—maybe he'd even tried to help me. It made sense that the Nightshades would treat him as *my* equal instead of theirs and send him here.

"I need to try to get to him," I said. My heart fluttered with hope that he was truly my friend. Granted, it pained me to see him in that cell, and it was a nightmare thinking about him having a similar fate to Frankie… but it eased the void of betrayal in my soul.

"Why? That's literally the opposite of what I just told you," Azha said in a biting tone.

"Yeah, well, he might be able to help us," I whispered as I moved closer to the bars.

"Humans can't subdue Vampyres unless you're a well-trained cop armed with silver bullets," Azha said with a condescending scoff.

"He is human… right?" Malachi muttered.

"No. He's a Vampyre, actually." I shot Azha a derisive look, obliged to put her negative assumptions in their place. Instead, she laughed.

"There's no such thing as Vampyres helping humans unless they're getting paid for it."

"There is if they're friends." I gripped the bars angrily. "If you want to stay here, be my guest. But my fight isn't over yet."

A flash of Frankie reentered my mind and I sprinted back to the toilet.

"Yeah, you look like a real fighter," Azha chuckled. With my face still in the toilet bowl, I reached behind my back and flipped an obscene gesture in her direction.

The doors at the end of the hallway swung open. I flinched away from the bowl and wiped my mouth with more tissue before Cyrus reappeared at my cell. Two other Keepers trailed behind him to let Azha and Malachi out.

"Today's your lucky day, Shaw. Don't screw it up playing games," Cyrus hissed as he slid the door open. I scowled and rose to my feet. He tapped his foot impatiently as I stood there. I didn't want to go anywhere near him.

"Don't you wanna eat?" he snapped.

Honestly? Not really. Not after I'd *just* expelled my insides.

Nonetheless, I approached Cyrus and complied while he cuffed my wrists in front of me. Azha and Malachi didn't wear handcuffs and they fell into step with their Keepers with ease. Malachi gave me a gentle nod with a soft smile. Some of the tense muscles eased in my shoulders, but my legs remained rigid and primed to run if necessary.

We were led to the elevators and taken to the first floor, then down another hallway without windows. We stopped at a set of double doors and my mouth went dry as I glanced at Azha and Malachi. The former's face was blank, but the latter tried to give me another reassuring nod without the Keeper catching it.

"Since you haven't tried to escape after the first experiment, I'll introduce you to one of your privileges. Dr. Ivanov tries to make your last days as comfortable as possible for your great contribution," Cyrus explained casually.

My last days? How many do I have left?

I stared at the push bar on the double doors, my palms growing slick with a thin layer of sweat. A privilege was supposed to be a good thing, right? Azha was already hard to read, but Malachi didn't have a drop of fear anywhere on his face. I couldn't understand why the air was choking me when the others were so calm.

"You only get one warning before you're thrown in the Box," Cyrus said. I didn't bother asking what the Box was. I just forced a swallow and licked my dry lips before he pushed the door open. I was greeted by sweet, balmy breezes for the first time in days. They circulated through a large courtyard at the center of the entire White Fang facility.

Silky bluegrass blanketed the courtyard, a small stone path connecting the door I stood at to an angel fountain in the center. The path continued to another set of double doors on the other side, shielded by a mature, towering weeping willow. There were small iron bistro tables scattered around the courtyard, some occupied by Vampyres eating their dinner under the starlight and others by humans. None of them intermingled and they all sat as far away from each other as possible.

I lifted my chin and gazed at the sky through the wooden slats built halfway up the building like a cage. They stood just above the weeping willow, with vines of heart-shaped buds and deep green leaves woven through them. I'd never seen those flowers before, but they were gorgeous despite growing in such an evil place.

Most importantly, the glittering night sky beyond the cage brought on the first smile I had in weeks. The pale full moon hung above the courtyard in a near-perfect view if it weren't for the slats. I took off my socks and wiggled my toes in the soft grass, then closed my eyes with a deep inhale. I thought I'd never see the sky again.

I swept my eyes over the courtyard and my heart skipped a beat when I met an intense crimson gaze.

Draven sat under the willow tree with his arms braced over his bent knees. His face was fixed in a dark glower, refusing to look away even after I caught him. For a moment, I vaguely noticed the ball of his jaw feathering, but I brushed it off as the darkness playing tricks on my human eyes.

"Alright, time's up! Let's get to the cafeteria. You'll have your chance out here tomorrow," Cyrus shouted from the door. I tore my focus from Draven and whipped my head toward the door. I stalked toward Cyrus, clenching my fists at my sides as my stomach fluttered once again. The same kind of feeling I got when I nearly fell off a ladder helping my brother clean gutters, when Draven first slung his arm around my shoulders to get me inside The Nightshade bar, and when the music swept me off my feet at The Hole. I stopped at the doors' threshold and stole a glance over my shoulder. Draven was still watching.

Azha and Malachi were gone, probably taken to the cafeteria by their Keepers already. Cyrus shut the door behind me and eyed my movements warily. Perhaps I'd enjoyed being in the courtyard too much.

I squinted at the bright lights flooding the cafeteria. A lot more people sat at the long banquet tables, eating their slop. There were large signs inside at the head of each table, one that said "Vampyres Only" and another that stated "Sun Dwellers Only."

I scoffed under my breath. How was I supposed to get to Draven without getting caught? At least that part wasn't much different from the world outside of captivity. I was surprised the White Fangs would even schedule our meals at the same time.

I stood in the line for humans and fidgeted with my handcuffs' chain. The smell of the grey slop they always served us irritated my gut further. I gagged and coughed with a swallow, suppressing the nausea as much as possible. I peered at the other side of the cafeteria—at the Vampyre line—and noticed the vibrantly colorful, aromatic food on their trays. And *seethed*.

I was used to the curfews, the arbitrary registration and segregated residential zones, but this...

This was a blatant slap in the face.

I side-stepped along the line, sliding my tray over the metal counter. I watched the Vampyre workers slap beans all over the tray and pursed my lips tightly to hold my breath the rest of the way.

I scanned the cafeteria for Azha and Malachi. They sat at a round table with two other humans, but weren't sharing any words. I inched toward them, gluing my focus to the last empty chair. It was in a perfect view of one Keeper posted at the exit to the court-yard, and two more at exit to the hallway.

"Oh, nice to see you're joining us, Briar." Malachi grinned as I eased into the stiff plastic seat. I gave him a tight, fleeting smile as my eyes continued to observe every nook and cranny of the place. I ignored Azha muttering under her breath.

"Where else would I go? You're the only ones I'm comfortable with," I said.

"Apparently not so," Azha mumbled. I gnashed my teeth and drew in a sharp breath to give her a piece of my mind—

The double doors to the courtyard swung open. Draven shuffled in. His hands were shoved in his scrub pockets. He took a bee-line straight to the only empty table on the Vampyre side of the cafeteria and continued to stare at me. In the light, his features were softer. Sullen, with his brows low and weary. I didn't know how to read it—as a nonverbal apology or longing. Maybe it was neither.

I had been harsh to him... I never considered his side of the story, even when Caspian tried to defend him to soothe my rage.

We locked eyes. His nostrils flared, shadows fell over his eyes, and his jaw hardened to a quiet wrath.

Until it wasn't quiet anymore.

Draven rose from his seat and flipped the table, flinging it across the mess hall toward two Keepers. I felt the wind whoosh over us, my fellow human prisoners yelping as they ducked to the floor. I only leaned forward, instantly trembling when the table narrowly missed my head.

The Keepers fell back against the door. The one guarding the courtyard had already begun beating Draven with a baton in one hand. He electrified him with a taser in the other. Four more Keepers flooded inside while Draven lay prone, twitching from the surges. They piled over him, beating him mercilessly before he could fully recover from the taser.

Tears flooded my eyes and I forced myself to look away, biting my lip deeply to avoid crying aloud. Everyone rose from beneath the table. Azha pointed a finger at her eyes, signaling for me to stop crying. I wasn't sure if she meant it as Vampyres weren't worth our tears, or because it was a sign of care the Keepers shouldn't see.

Either way, watching them pummel Draven and drag away his lifeless form haunted the rest of my day and night, and like a parasitic worm, it latched onto my nightmares. At least by the time we were forced to get our showers for the night, I could cry wholeheartedly. I sat on my calves, hunched over my knees under the beating water.

Azha and other female prisoners looked the other way.

10
BRIAR

The next morning, I felt bruised as usual. Pins and needles spidered along my neck when I rolled over to my side and an earthquake rumbled behind my forehead.

"She finally rises," Azha taunted.

"Will you lay off, Z? Yesterday was rough for all of us," Malachi hissed.

"Can you guys please stop talking?" I asked, hoarse, as I forced myself to sit up. I didn't have the strength to brave their bickering. "What time is it?"

"I don't know, maybe noon?" Azha shrugged. "Maybe midnight."

I loosed a quiet, wry laugh and rolled my eyes. I cracked my neck and reached to the ceiling, stretching my arms. My throat constricted as flashes of Draven's incident flickered through my mind. Did he heal instantly? Was he *alive*?

I gripped the cool metal bars, running my thumb over a rough rust spot. I observed the keypads on our doors, imagining stealing a watch from one of the Keepers like an unstoppable ninja.

I flinched at the sound of the heavy doors swinging open at the end of the hall.

"Chow time, freaks!" Cyrus boomed. The Keepers clanged their batons against the bars as they marched down the hall. I shook my head at the notion that to them, *we* were the freaks.

I waited at my door with my arms folded, listening to their heavy boots draw near. The same boots I watched crush Draven's ribs and face last night. I glowered at Cyrus. He whistled and twirled a set of handcuffs on his index finger as he slid the door open.

"Dr. Ivanov decided to give you the day off, doll," he said with a smile. "Hope you're hungry, since you've skipped breakfast and lunch by sleeping all day."

I blinked. It was hard to believe I slept that long with all the nightmares. Their hold on me was so tight I couldn't even wake up.

I kept my mouth shut as I followed behind Cyrus. He led our little convoy with Malachi and Azha's Keepers in the back. I still felt hollow. I'd missed breakfast and lunch and I didn't mourn it—I just wanted to go back to sleep.

✳

"You get to eat in the courtyard today," Cyrus explained once we entered the cafeteria. I gave him a stiff nod and got in line, going through the motions. I looked for Draven, but he was nowhere to be found. My stomach squeezed tighter, snuffing out any hope of my appetite returning.

I couldn't understand why so many of the humans and Vampyres preferred to eat in the cafeteria when there was a beautiful place beyond these doors. The only beauty any of us had access to in this sterile environment.

Everyone was already a prisoner, whether they volunteered for the trials or not. Even a sliver of freedom was enough to bring back some sanity. All I needed was a taste.

The quiet din of the cafeteria was shut off once the door snicked shut behind me. I scanned the courtyard once more for signs designating areas by species. I didn't see any, so I headed straight for the willow tree and tried to resist allowing my heart to swell with hope.

The soft branches swept over me with a gentle caress and the grass rustled beneath my feet. Draven was sitting in the same spot, his buzzed head leaning against the tree trunk. He lifted his head for a heartbeat, then looked back down.

"Briar..." He spoke so low I barely heard it. "Did I hurt ya?"

I gripped the sides of my food tray tightly and inhaled sharply. I shook my head, at a loss for words as I scanned every detail of his chiseled, copper face like it was the first time. There wasn't a mark on him... but with his healing abilities, there was no telling what they did to him after his outburst.

"No, I'm fine," I mumbled.

"I see they cut your hair," he said tightly.

"Yours too." I jerked my chin. "Why did you do that yesterday? Do you know how stupid it was?"

"I was already thinkin' about cuttin' it myself, though." He pulled his knees closer to his chest and peered at the fountain, disregarding my remark. I set my tray on the grass and sat across from him. I glanced over my shoulder for Keepers looking in our direction, pursing my lips tightly.

"Is... there somethin' you wanna say?" It seemed like more of an effort to look at me than when we first saw each other. His eyes were dull, only catching small highlights from the dim sconces around the courtyard walls.

"You didn't answer my question." I tilted my head.

"Ain't the first time I got beat down. I wasn't thinkin' straight," he said flatly.

"I'm sorry." I wasn't sure if that apology was sympathy from yesterday, from how I treated him at the Nightshades, or from something else. Draven knit his eyebrows and met my gaze again.

The whites of his eyes glistened. "What for?"

"I'm assuming you're here against your will, right?" Draven only blinked.

"Well... I'm sorry for pushing you away and not trusting that you didn't set me up. If you were on the Nightshades' side, you probably wouldn't be here," I said. Draven chuckled softly and shook his head, returning his lost gaze to the fountain.

"There's plenty of Nightshade volunteers here." He tucked his chin and stared at his palms in his lap. "Everything you said... everything you probably think of me and the rest of my kind now... is true."

I frowned mildly. I'd never seen him so... defeated.

"So... you read minds now?" I laughed.

"No, but ya can't tell me that you'd still wanna be around Vampyres after all this."

I sighed and crawled closer to him. As I closed the distance between us, he straightened against the tree trunk. I reached for his hand and opened my mouth to speak—but Draven shoved me away and jumped to his feet. He roared as a thrum of electricity buzzed through the air. The energy threw him back to the ground.

I scrambled backwards as Cyrus towered over Draven with an electrified baton, all curled lips and bared fangs.

11
DRAVEN

The electric shock pulsed through every cell of my body. I bit my tongue as my jaw locked, blood filling every crevice in my mouth. The Keeper's alabaster skin and ivory hair was uncannily similar to Caspian's. The jagged scar stretching from the top of his forehead to the left side of his chin carried a blood-soaked story, and although his left eye was a foggy white, it somehow pierced through my soul just as strongly as the healthy one. He charged the baton again with a growl, daring me to move another muscle. I shifted my eyes to Briar without moving my head. Her mouth gaped open, eyes so wide her light grey irises appeared nonexistent.

"I'll give you the benefit of the doubt, Miss Shaw." The Keeper spoke through his panting and sucked a deep breath to regain control. He ran a hand through his hair, slicking back the strands that had broken free. "But in case you haven't noticed from the cafeteria, we like to keep Vampyres and Sun Dwellers separate."

Briar's eyes darted between me and the Keeper.

"Sorry, Cyrus. It won't happen again," she said without taking her eyes off me.

"Do you know this scum?" Cyrus kicked my foot as I leaned weakly against the tree. When Briar didn't respond right away, he snapped his head in her direction.

"Hello?" he snapped.

"No," Briar blurted, quickly tearing her gaze from mine. "I don't know him."

I felt a sting, but... she had to say it for both our sakes. She must've. A "yes" would've brought on more questions.

Or worse.

Cyrus straightened and whistled, summoning three other Keepers. He pointed the baton at Briar, but she didn't flinch.

"If I catch you around any more Vampyres, it won't be pretty," Cyrus growled. Briar bit her lip, stealing one more glance at me as he yanked her arm and dragged her from the courtyard. The three other Keepers forced me to stand.

"I can walk," I snarled as I snatched my arms from their grasps. I felt something solid poke into the small of my back and instinctively raised my hands as they led me inside and down the hall.

We took the elevator to the fifth floor. Relief washed over me at the thought of being left alone in my cell, but that dried out when we stopped in front of a door with a frosted window. The words "Dr. Ivanov" were plastered in black vinyl across it.

"She wants to speak with you, Mr. Hawthorne."

I groaned and planted my feet, but the Keeper nudged me roughly with the barrel of his gun.

The same woman that had given Caspian and me the cold shoulder when we delivered those humans sat behind a U-shaped wooden desk. Narrow tortoise-shell glasses rested at the tip of her slender, hooked nose. Her obsidian hair was pulled back into a flawless ponytail. She was looking through manila folders splayed across the desk, tapping her nails in a metronome rhythm. Dr. Ivanov gave me a tight smile, then gestured toward the claw-foot chair across from her. I slowly entered, shutting the door and scanning every corner of the room.

It was just as cold and sterile as the rest of the building—aside from the furniture that echoed Uriah's taste. There weren't photos of friends or family members, instead just a map of Neoterra, much like in Uriah's office. The periodic table was on the adjacent wall, sandwiched between two bookshelves. Every book was leather-bound and at least two inches thick.

"I've been meaning to talk to you since the day I laid eyes on you, Draven." Dr. Ivanov's accent was thick with intrigue. She removed her glasses, propped her elbows on the desk, and rested her chin on her laced fingers. Rather than sit in the chair she pointed at, I leaned over its back and clasped my hands together.

"Why? You're White Fang." I scrunched my nose and jutted my chin at her. I searched the room for some sort of toothpick or a cigarette, even a sheet of paper to tear and roll up. Going so many days without anything to chew on was driving me insane. I shifted uneasily on my feet.

"White Fang, Nightshade, Crimson Dagger... different clans, but we're all one and the same." Dr. Ivanov shrugged. "You don't want to sit?"

"I prefer standin'. What do ya want from me?" I asked with a scowl.

"I was looking into your history." She looked down at the papers with a small grin. "You somehow became a Nightshade after being Turned as a young adolescent."

"It don't take much to become one. Uriah takes in all kinds of fledglings, all ages." I turned over my palms with a shrug. "What's your point?"

"Indeed, but you were taken against your will as result of—" Dr. Ivanov shook her head, her mouth parting slightly as if the rest of her words escaped without a sound.

"Result of *what*?" I slowly rounded the chair, my claws digging into its fibers as I contemplated hurling it at her.

"That's... for a later date. Anyways, you're the first Turned Vampyre I've acquired for my experiments. I think you will make an excellent candidate for the serum I've been working on."

I laughed. "Listen, lady, I get the Nightshades gave me up, but that don't mean I wanna volunteer in your crazy science tests."

"Not even for a serum that could guarantee a diurnal life?" Dr. Ivanov's blood-red lips twitched into a smirk. "Don't you want the power of a Vampyre, but the freedom of a Sun Dweller?"

"Not if it means growing a third arm or fifty more teeth," I said.

"I have a theory that with the right blood type, you can have all the benefits without the side effects." Her vermillion eyes twinkled, as if she'd received yet another bright idea. "Additionally, there's some evidence that traits of one Vampyre transfer to whomever they Turn, which may be a factor in accelerating our evolution."

I sank into the seat, suddenly feeling sick.

"Good for you," I finally said, my voice tight.

"Do you remember who Turned you, Draven?"

"I was fourteen and I'd rather not talk about it," I said curtly. "Is this all you called me here for? To talk about science and how I'm not Vampyre-born?"

"That's not all." She gathered the papers, stacked them, then tapped their edges on the desk to straighten them. "The blood type you had as a human changed when you became a Vampyre. That... is an extremely rare anomaly that I've never seen in any fledgling."

"What's that gotta do with anything?" I grumbled.

"It means we have a lot to learn from you, Draven." She clasped her hands together and leaned forward. "That Vampyre we lost to the police's flamethrower was a purebred."

I laughed and said, "I ain't got nothin' for ya." I rose from the chair.

"Sure, you do. And if you want Briar in one piece... you'll co-operate. I'll even throw in your favorite meal or item to ease the dis-comfort." Her voice was laced with sweet venom.

I paused at the door. If Cyrus didn't know Briar and I knew each other, how did this woman know?

"I have eyes everywhere, Draven. While I detest your fondness of humans, I think it plays an important role in what we're trying to achieve here." The chair rolled against the floor. Shortly after, Dr. Ivanov's lithe hand rested on my shoulder.

"How?"

"Your contribution gives their kind value." She dropped her voice like there were Sun Dwellers crowding outside her office door. "A horse is useless until it provides transportation. Now what about that item?"

"A gun," I remarked snidely.

"Toothpicks it is." Dr. Ivanov smirked, then patted my shoulder and returned to her desk. I shook my head with a scoff, then opened the door without another word. The Keepers waiting outside escorted me to my cell.

I scoffed at the box of toothpicks lying on my bed. My pride stopped me from picking them up, but my desperation for something to chew on was stronger. It wasn't long before the sharp point of the toothpick was scraping against my teeth.

Briar's voice echoed softly down the hall while she spoke to whomever was near her. I wanted to listen to what she said, but was interrupted by a new face watching me in the formerly empty cell across from mine.

The boy had curly hair the color of wet sand and two-toned skin that mirrored the planet's geography, as if he already carried the whole world on his shoulders at such a young age. His black cherry eyes were devoid of feeling. He couldn't have been any older than eighteen, but he already had piercings all over one of his ears and—judging by the pale purple flower petals peeking out from the end of his sleeve—was a new Nightshade member. I wondered if he was a fledgling who'd joined out of desperation or a lost Vampyre who'd joined in search of a family.

I turned my back and crawled into bed.

"Wow, you look a lot different from the pictures back home." His voice was brighter than his demeanor. "You're Draven, right?"

"Who are you?" I sat up, tensing. I glared at him from across the hall, already suspecting that Uriah sent him to keep tabs on me.

"Oren Jacobs. I volunteered here 'cause they said they could make me stronger. I heard about you and the things you used to do for Uriah. Also the rumors." Oren ran his mouth while staring at an empty spot on the ceiling.

I narrowed my eyes. "What rumors?"

"That you're a Sun Dweller-lovin' traitor." Oren's voice dried out. I chuckled softly and leaned my head against the white cinder block wall.

"I ain't a traitor. Never was, but I've been considerin' it lately," I said.

"Well, I instantly became a fan of yours when I heard the stories. I just… don't understand how you'd wind up here."

"They told you I was a traitor but didn't tell you why I'm here?" I rolled my head in a lazy tilt toward him.

"Nah. I'm guessing you didn't volunteer?" Oren lowered his dead gaze. Even the highlights from the recessed sconces were consumed by his black-hole irises.

"No, but there's someone important to me here, and I intend on making this visit worthwhile for her sake." I balled the sheets in my fists with a hard swallow.

"Even if it kills me."

12
CASPIAN

I PUNCHED THE ADDRESS INTO THE GPS AND IT LED ME TO A gated Diurnal Zone named Amethyst Cove. Guaranteed to be populated by only Sun Dwellers, and teeming with security guards.

I cursed under my breath. Why didn't Uriah give me a heads up? I couldn't call him now, because he was the type to tell me to figure it out.

I parked across the street in a small shopping strip where half the stores were shut down, but didn't get out. The gate was plated in silver, so I couldn't climb over it. The longer I stared at the scene before me, the more I realized I had no choice but to go through the gate. I reached in the glove box for my contact lens case, then carefully put those irritating things in my eyes. I turned on the headlights again, took a deep breath, then drove out of the parking lot.

One could only hope they didn't ask too many questions. I certainly wouldn't volunteer any information.

The driver's window rolled down with a quiet hum. I forced a tight smile as the security guard approached, and winced at the beam of light he pointed at my face to check my eyes.

"I don't recognize you. State your business," he demanded with a squint. His suspicious demeanor reminded me of the security guard at the hospital. The paleness of my skin wasn't common among Sun Dwellers and was often attributed to Vampyrism. But I figured I'd look just like this in another life as a human.

"Just delivering this phone to someone who lives here." I raised it briefly. The security guard scratched a shadow on his chin, a bristly sound like walking through dry leaves.

"What's the address?" he asked. I chuckled softly, sliding my gaze to the gate for a moment. I checked my rearview mirror to see three cars pile up behind me.

"Fifty-four-fifty-four Iron Street," I said flatly. The security guard nodded slowly.

"Do you have an authorization? You're out here pretty late, man."

I sighed and reached for my wallet. I had an inkling this particular security guard had once dreamed of wearing blue instead of grey, but didn't make the cut. He put his hands on his hips and I instinctively followed the movement to make sure he wasn't pulling a weapon as I handed a fake authorization card over. He examined it closely, then shrugged and held a thumbs up at his partner by the gate. I gave him a nod of acknowledgment as the doors slid open.

I rolled my window back up and held my breath until I passed the gate.

The neighborhood was filled with square houses with vinyl siding, young trees that had barely sprouted their first leaves or flowers, and lawns that looked like green carpet. I followed the GPS to the back of the neighborhood, toward the largest house I'd ever seen. Its architecture was French Provincial, its driveway circular and wrapping around a large, narcissistic statue of Mr. Barnaby at the center. I frowned and pulled out my phone, taking a picture of the house. I sent it to Uriah, then called him.

"Uriah," he answered almost instantly.

"I sent you a picture," I replied by way of greeting.

"Were you followed?"

"No, sir," I said.

"Go around the backyard, there's a shed. Use the passcode from the phone. Text me photos after you've gone inside," Uriah calmly ordered.

"Yes, sir."

I pulled my phone from my ear and saw a text from an unknown number. I took a moment to look, and a subtle smile pulled on one corner of my lips.

Hi, this is Astoria. My brother said he has someplace to be next week on Saturday. I can meet with you then.

Next week? I frowned. That was too long. Who knew what could happen in a matter of hours, let alone seven days?

I tucked away my cellphone, deciding to deal with it later. I was sure Uriah was counting each second it took for me to show him whatever he needed to see.

I got out of the SUV and flashed to the backyard in seconds.

The shed was ordinary. It was made of beige plastic and aluminum siding with red shutters. I peered inside, my breath fogging up the window. There was nothing but woodworking tools. Regardless, I unlocked the door as Uriah instructed.

There was a work bench with a blueprint of a dresser rolled across it, tools hanging on pegs along the walls, and many other irrelevant items. My steps were so soft that I could've been floating over the wooden floor as I searched for whatever Uriah could possibly want.

Until my boot hit something with a hollow thump, and I nearly tripped. I glanced down to see a subtle, thin rectangular line cutting through the wooden slats with a keypad bolted to a trap door.

There.

Without question, I knelt down and punched in the code from Mr. Barnaby's phone. I coughed as a cloud of dust flew into my face when I lifted the door. Concrete steps descended into a deep black hole. I took a picture, but didn't send it just yet. I descended the stairs, waving cobwebs out of my way.

The lights cut on when I was halfway down the stairs. I hissed, fangs extending, my eyes darting back and forth for an enemy until I realized there wasn't one. Then my eyes widened at the sight before me.

A vast concrete room illuminated by horizontal lights that gilded endless rows of artillery ranging from pistols and rifles to grenades and cannons. Enough to arm the entire city. That unassuming shed... was a front to an armory.

I gulped and slowly pulled my phone from my pocket. I opened the camera, thumb freezing over the button. It didn't feel right to have this picture in my phone, let alone send it over text. Nonetheless, I had a part to play, and I couldn't raise suspicions now.

I sent the text and resurfaced in the shed, locking everything behind me. I moved swiftly to the SUV in a short burst of speed and hurried out of the neighborhood. Uriah sent a thumbs up text in response as I passed through the gate.

I couldn't help but feel some sort of heaviness, as if I was being pulled through a maggot-filled grave and was choking on the soil. Life was better when it was outrageous rumors, but now...

There was no denying the Nightshades would be going to war soon.

✳

I returned to my apartment at Crow's Nest. I didn't have the patience or mental capacity to face Wraith or Larkin, and I didn't have an appetite when I opened my fridge full of blood bags. Instead, I reached for the bottle of whiskey that I only touched perhaps twice a year. I poured two fingers worth and eased on the couch, kicking my feet up over the rounded coffee table. I unlocked my phone to respond to Astoria's message and hoped she was still awake to respond.

Your sister might not have a week.

I pressed send before I would overthink it. She needed the hard truth, not coddling. I stared at the screen as I took a sip of whiskey, and subtly winced at the burn in my throat. Then I waited.

And waited.

And waited.

Two hours later, I had finished my second glass. I was about to pour a third—assuming Astoria was asleep—when my phone buzzed.

Tonight, then?

I pinched the bridge of my nose and blinked three times to reread the message. If she'd messaged me thirty seconds later, I wouldn't have been able to smell or see, let alone drive. I responded immediately.

Where do you live? There was a ten-minute pause before she texted with her address, almost as if she was hesitant to give it. I understood, but I was already standing at my front door with keys in hand, waiting for the green light. I didn't want to show up at the house without her giving it to me, because then she'd ask questions on how I knew where she lived.

I almost walked out the door without putting my contacts back in.

✳

The road snaked into the country, lined by trees peppered with yellow leaves. Endless fields shadowed by minimal light pollution allowed the stars to freckle the sky. The only thing I could see for miles was the yellow house Draven had described. Its windows were grey, and the perimeter was devoid of sound aside from distant owls and crickets.

I pulled onto the shoulder of the road about half a mile away. There wasn't a single place for cover except one oak tree in the middle of the field behind the Shaws' house. With Astoria's brother being a police officer, he probably had cameras around the house. I couldn't risk driving any closer if I didn't want the license plates to be caught.

In one short burst, I flashed to the porch just in time for Astoria to creep out of the front door. She shut it carefully, then jumped out of her skin when she turned to see me already standing there. I flinched, my heart lodging into my throat.

Astoria's hand shot to her necklace with a stiff smile. The whites of her eyes almost glowed.

"Are you ready?" I kept my voice low.

"I don't know if I should do this. Sterling is upstairs sleeping, but... what if he wakes up to check on me?" She spoke in a breathy whisper, sliding her necklace charm back and forth.

"What's the worst that can happen?" I asked with a nonchalant shrug.

"He'll arrest me," she whispered harshly, hiking her shoulders up to her earlobes.

"You'll be back home in time for breakfast." I extended my hand, failing to remember how cold it would be if she touched it. Before she could take it, I used the same hand to point at my car down the street.

"I'm over there," I said, then walked swiftly off the front porch with my head low. If there were cameras... the most Sterling would see was my hair color and the generic all-black attire.

I glanced over my shoulder when I was at the edge of her property. She shuddered before finally stepping off the porch. I got in the SUV and waited, applying eye drops before she got in the back seat. I smirked, finding it adorable as she clutched her purse tightly across her stomach.

13
ASTORIA

I DIDN'T REALIZE HOW TIGHT I WAS CLUTCHING MY PURSE until I let go and every knuckle barked in protest. We were already entering Neoterra's metropolitan area when it dawned on me that Christian could've been Briar's captor and I was his next target. I reached in my purse and wrapped my hand around pepper spray laced with silver dust—a new addition my brother had given me since I refused to carry a gun. I watched Christian through the rear-view mirror, but it was angled to only show his forehead. The silence within the cabin only added to my discomfort.

Christian straightened in his seat, his dark eyes suddenly popping up in the mirror. I quickly veered my gaze to the window as if I'd been observing the buildings the whole time.

"There's no need to fear me, you know," he said. Of course he'd seen me.

I have every right to, I wanted to say. I opened my mouth to speak, but shut it and nodded instead. Christian switched his focus back on the road.

I surveyed the Vampyres living their lives as we did during the day. I squinted, trying to see the appeal that attracted Briar like a moth to a flame.

They walked with grace, confidence, energy. I hated to admit it, but they seemed more alive than the humans. Everyone in my classes was always rushing, stressed, or complaining. Worried about their grades, drama in their circles, or if their futures would be successful.

Yet here under the neon lights, it didn't seem like there was a care in the world. Vampyres ruled the night while the day ruled us.

We passed a café with outdoor seating beneath glowing string lights. Christian slowed to a stop at a traffic light and I took the moment to watch the patrons dine. I cracked the window and the aroma of garlic and spices wafted inside. Most of the glasses on the tables were filled with a dark liquid. My stomach turned, but I was fascinated by the other tables that still had different drinks. It had never crossed my mind that they'd crave anything beyond blood.

"Are you okay back there?" Christian called flatly.

"Yeah. I'm just... looking." I grinned at the sight of children running around the sidewalk with glowing sticks and bracelets, then stopping at a small ice cream booth already donning Halloween decor. My smile fell as I once again heard Sterling and Briar's voices war in my head.

*They're monsters, h*e would say.

Humans are worse, Briar would shoot back.

I always thought Sterling saw the ugly side of Vampyres while

Briar saw only the beauty, but in the end she was missing and Sterling wasn't. So far, my brother's views remained justified.

My eyes burned. I wanted to love the Vampyres as much as my own people, but it was so hard. As I sat in that back seat, my mouth went dry at the thought of betraying my brother's trust just by being here.

Christian's forehead was unreadable. No veins bulged in anger, no sweat beaded from anxiety. I couldn't tell if he lacked emotion in general or was comfortable with breaking curfew for the millionth time.

Christian kinda reminded me of some characters I read about in my books. A mysterious man with a guarded, cold shell encasing something else. If he wasn't a psychopath like I feared... perhaps his cold shell encased a diamond.

"Are there more people like you breaking curfew?" I asked, wondering how many humans Briar could've met during her adventures.

"Other than Briar, no." He spoke in short bursts, like specific text cut out of a magazine. It made me feel off-kilter and... I desperately wanted to go back home.

"C-can we go to Sundance?" I was already out here, and I might as well follow up on the one lead I had. I was sure Sterling had already gone there after searching her room... but I wanted to see what information they'd give me instead. I doubted he was nice when he asked for intel.

"Are you sure you can handle it?" Christian raised an eyebrow.

"What do you mean?" I challenged. He shrugged, switching his gaze from the rearview mirror to the road ahead. I was left seeing his forehead again.

"Nothing, you just seem anxious," he said with a gentle tone. Always so gentle, yet hollow. I balled the hem of my shirt in a fist and took a deep breath.

"You're not?" I laughed softly.

"Vampyres have a lot more self-control than you think. If they wanted to, someone would've killed your sister the first time she snuck out," he said. "Would've killed me too."

"You sound like Briar," I mumbled with a sigh.

Christian turned down another street. "She was right. She was probably just in the wrong place at the wrong time."

My cheeks heated. I didn't expect him to hear me. I wanted to believe he was human, but the more he spoke, the more I worried I was in the presence of a wolf in sheep's clothing.

He glanced at me with furrowed eyebrows after several seconds of silence.

"I got something to show you first." He made a U-turn at a stoplight. My heart jumped when he changed course, and I gripped the handle on the ceiling.

"Where?" My voice shook. Christian released a soft, alluring laugh that rattled my bones.

"Loosen up a bit, Astoria," he crooned, then drove further north toward the Nocturne District.

※

I was one number away from calling the police in Christian's back seat when we pulled up to the boardwalk. The black water of the sea swelled as distant lightning cracked ten lashes across the horizon. I

115

put my phone away for two reasons: he hadn't led me to a dungeon and the police wouldn't help me after breaking curfew anyway.

Christian got out of the car and opened my door. He tilted his head expectantly. I was still sitting, clutching my purse tightly in one hand and my necklace charm in the other. I stared at him with lips slightly parted, searching for words that had escaped long ago.

"Do you like the beach?" He frowned, his eyes scanning my face for answers.

"Y-yeah," I croaked.

"Then come on." He nodded toward the boardwalk behind him and started walking, leaving the door open. I released a shaky breath and got out. My heart raced so fast I thought I'd have a heart attack. I placed my clammy palms on my cheeks and looked up at the sky, wondering what had gotten into me. What was I thinking?

Christian was halfway across the grass dividing the parking lot from the boardwalk when he caught me still standing by the SUV. He pursed his lips as he ambled back.

"What's wrong?" Christian whispered. For a moment, his cold, barren face was soft and welcoming. Enough for me to want to tell him everything that bothered me. He seemed like the type that anyone could confide in without worry of it being repeated or judged, like a confession to a priest. Yet, every time I was near Christian, I felt like I was about to fall from the top of a skyscraper and splatter all over the ground.

"You took me to the most dangerous district in Neoterra for the *beach*?" I narrowed my eyes. "We're wasting time and we already have targets on our backs."

"If you're anxious to talk to Vampyres anywhere, you might as well survive the worst area in the city." Christian shrugged nonchalantly. "Besides, you've got nothing to worry about around me."

I gritted my teeth.

"Why, because you're a Vampyre too?" I folded my arms. Christian blinked, then smirked as he slid his hands in his pockets. He strode forward, and I took several steps back until I bumped into his vehicle. He inched closer, placing his hand against the roof of the SUV over my shoulder, boxing me in. I stared at his parted lips, expecting fangs to emerge.

"If I was, would you be opposed to finding your sister just because of that?" Christian spoke low, but I swear a growl reverberated in his throat.

"N-no..." I shrunk, lowering my gaze.

"Would you go running to your brother?" Christian touched my chin, forcing my eyes to meet his again. Chills ran down my spine from his icy fingertips and my breath hitched. I squinted, searching his eyes for the telltale edge of contacts.

"Do I need to?" I replied quietly. Christian stared, his face unreadable. He finally backed away, his shoes softly padding against the grass as he resumed his trail to the beach.

I loosed a shaky breath and leaned against his car, fighting to keep my knees from collapsing. I legitimately thought he'd attack me if I said the wrong thing. He reached the sand dunes past the tall grass, and didn't look back this time.

Loosen up a bit, Astoria.

He was probably right. Briar never hesitated to call me out for being Type A growing up. My friends used to say I never knew how to have fun. But why was it that everyone else's fun involved break-ing the law?

I pushed myself off the door and jogged after him. Whether or not I wanted to follow, I didn't want to be left alone at the heart of the Vampyre underworld.

I stopped at the edge of the pathway and removed my shoes, then ran through the sand to catch up to Christian. He was star-ing at the ocean with a sullen face, almost with longing. I zipped my charm along my necklace as I looked around the shoreline for Vampyres. Only a few were hanging out, but they were far from us. Most were perusing the vendors on the boardwalk.

"Why here?" I asked breathlessly as I took my place beside Christian.

"I always wanted to learn to swim," he said, staring at nothing in particular. He inhaled deeply, taking in the sea salt.

"What's stopped you?" I hugged myself as a cool breeze swept over the sea and passed the beach. I dug my toes into the cool, stiff sand.

"Fear," Christian replied. I blinked. For a guy who constantly broke curfew, I didn't think he'd fear anything.

"Oh..." was all I could reply.

"We all have one," he said as if he'd read my mind. "You have Vampyres, I have water."

"I don't *fear*—"

"We fear what we don't know. I don't know how to swim, and every experience I've had with water was negative." Christian kicked up a cloud of sand. He gave me a sidelong glance before returning his eyes to his dusty Oxford shoes. "You don't know any Vampyres. To you, they're bloodsucking monsters, drooling over their next meal."

"Why haven't you learned how to swim?"

I watched the dim light in his eyes die out in a void. "My father once tried to drown me in a bathtub when I was a child," he said flatly.

I pursed my lips and fell silent. My mother did a lot of horrible things in my childhood, but she never tried to murder any of us. I turned my focus to the waves gently rolling up the shore, then receding, over and over. Seashell shards would appear, then disappear. Like everything else, what once was... was no longer. Just like my grades. My friends.

My father.

My sister.

You said life is too short, so I wanted to live for a night.

None of this would've happened if I hadn't said life was too short. Briar wouldn't have twisted my words and broken curfew, and she'd still be safe at home.

I flinched at a cold sensation against my cheek, wiping away my tears. Christian snatched his hand back, then let it fall slack at his side.

"Are you still afraid?" he muttered. I looked around, and even with the wind blowing our human scents toward them, the Vampyres on the boardwalk were minding their business. In the Nocturne District, of all places.

The only time I braved coming out here was during the day, heading to the ferry slip for Helios.

But... Christian was right. There was no horde of Vampyres sweeping through the beach to fight over a piece of meat.

"Do you think you can handle Sundance?" he asked, crinkling his forehead with a raised brows.

I nodded quickly, then fell into stride next to him. The queasiness in my stomach had vanished.

✳

Christian circled the block three times before he was able to parallel park near Chen's Den food truck. The salon was across the street, with a sign saying "Bethany's Corner" instead of "Sundance." There was a truck and trailer parked across six parallel spaces with four women going in and out of the shop with boxes, heads all hung low.

"What's going on here?" He asked. One of the women froze. Her gold choker glinted and reflected every color from the storefronts' neon lights, bronzed skin flecked with glitter across her high cheekbones. Almost every finger was adorned by gold rings to match the long dangling tassel earrings that swept over her shoulders. The woman stared at Christian, her blank face hardening.

"What are you doing here?" she hissed.

"You're Samara, right?" he asked. "You worked with Briar Shaw?"

Samara's eyes flicked back and forth between us.

"The Sun Dweller." She pushed past Christian with a laugh. "We never should've hired her. Sweet girl, I loved that she didn't hate us, but this world wasn't for her." Samara slid the box across the truck's tailgate. She dusted off her hands and stepped on the curb, watching Christian warily all the while.

"Why do you want to know about Briar?" Samara asked.

"I-I'm her sister," I cut in, moving closer. "She's missing... Christian is her friend and he's helping me find her."

"Christian?" Samara used her thumb to rotate the ring on her middle finger pensively. "The last time I tried to help someone find Briar, I got the shop shut down for good."

"Who would ask about her?" I asked tightly, my brows pulling taut.

"Some red-headed Sun Dweller." She shrugged. "I can't remember if he told me his name or not. He was a detective."

Sterling. Why would he get this place shut down if she helped?

"Well... not much to lose now, right?" Christian tilted his head and Samara's lip curled back. Her fangs glinted.

"It's not the first time. We'll be back. We always come back," she snapped as she raised her chin proudly.

"Hm." Christian rocked on his heels. "So what did you tell him?"

Samara shrugged, filling her cheeks with air before blowing it out. "The truth."

"Which was?"

"The Nightshades probably took her," Samara said with a pointed glance in Christian's direction, then she turned to me. "Be careful of the company you keep, girl."

I frowned and took a microscopic step back.

"Who are they?" I asked.

"He can tell you. If I do, I might actually disappear this time." Samara vanished into the salon. I bit my lip, fighting the urge to clutch my necklace.

"What is she talking about, Christian?" I whispered.

"I don't know, but we can check out the club across the street. It's called The Nightshade, maybe they can tell us something." He grabbed my hand and marched us across the street before I could protest.

14
DRAVEN

I HAD TWO CHOICES. I COULD EITHER BIDE MY TIME BY LEARNing the routines of the guards and find a small window of opportunity to break Briar out, or betray her trust and Turn her despite her protest at the Nightshades. Whether or not her blood type remained the same, her DNA would still change as a Vampyre, and she would be useless to Dr. Ivanov. They would probably try to kill her, but she'd have a fair chance of fighting back.

They'd definitely kill me, but at least I would die knowing I'd done one good thing in this life.

Ideally, I'd choose the first option, but time wasn't promised to any of us at White Fang.

Oren was taken away for testing, and I assumed he'd never return again. I spent a couple hours staring at the ceiling, listening to

Briar's conversation with two humans I learned were named Azha and Malachi.

More importantly, I learned more about the facility.

"I need to get to him," Briar said. "They're going to kill him."

"You got in trouble the first time, they're definitely going to keep an eye on you. I wouldn't go near him so soon," Azha warned.

"Well..." Malachi started. "The shift change starts today."

"Shift change?" Briar's voice perked up.

"Yeah, once a week, the guards switch rotations. They work one week on, then one off. The rotation this week doesn't know about you trying to get close to any Vampyres. You could try again until Cyrus returns," Malachi suggested.

"Does that mean I get a new Keeper for this week?" Briar's tone brightened with hope.

"No, you might have lower-level ones, but he'll be your main one no matter what. He's on call while he's gone. So keep in mind that he might come back if you get caught." Azha spoke flatly, as if she read from a textbook.

I guess Fate will choose for me.

I swung my legs over the edge of the bed. The cold floor bit into the soles of my feet, but they adjusted after three steps to the barred door. I peered between the bars in both directions of the hallway. To my surprise, there weren't guards posted on either side.

Thankfully, since Briar and her new friends were carelessly discussing plans.

"Briar?" I called. It wasn't quite a whisper, considering she was roughly four or five cells away. I was confident no one relevant would be listening. "It's Draven."

"Yeah?" she responded in a quiet rasp, but her voice was amplified to my Vampyric ears.

"You know where to find me," I said. "I'll be waiting."

My voice was shut off by the doors being kicked open at the end of the hallway.

"Chow time, rats!" one of the Keepers bellowed as ten of them flooded through the corridor. Each one posted at a cell to unlock. The petite woman who stopped in front of mine had makeup caked into pitted pores, a septum piercing, and ruddy hair pulled back in low space buns. I gave her a hollow smile and she returned a subtle grin. I hoped that if I cooperated as much as possible, she wouldn't feel the need to closely monitor me.

"Morning, Mr. Hawthorne." Her mumbling was nearly drowned out by the grating of metal as she slid the bars open. I held out my wrists to be cuffed, just for her to shake her head and turn away dismissively. She stepped to the side and held her hand out, gesturing for me to fall into step ahead of her with my arms free to hang at my sides. I didn't swing my fists at the woman or glance over my shoulder to see if Briar was being led behind me—no matter how much I wanted to.

"Are you my Keeper?" I asked.

"For this week. I'm Rowena." And that was that.

Rowena led me to the cafeteria and I played along, catching an early spot in the line. I received food that I knew I wouldn't eat, and went to the courtyard to sit under the willow tree.

The grass was damp and the air was sweet with rain. The overcast sky encrusted everything in the courtyard in silver like moonlight. It was days like these that Vampyres could feel most human, when the sun didn't blister our skin. Still, I let the frigid shadows under the slack tassels of the weeping willow cloak me. I kept glancing at the door, waiting for Briar to appear.

It felt like I waited a lifetime. Realistically, five minutes passed before I saw those stormy eyes meet mine. Briar paused at the edge of the tree's tendrils before she ducked underneath with her tray of food. I jumped to my feet, wiping off the water and grass from my pants. The grass sighed beneath her slippers as she approached.

"I'm gonna ask you this one more time," I whispered, closing the space between us. "Do you want to Turn?" Briar paused, pressing her tongue against her lip piercing as she always did when deep in thought. She shut her eyes tightly with a sigh.

"I don't want to be dependent on blood or to have to hide away from the sun," she muttered. "Vampyres are always getting the short end of the stick. Worst of all, my sister would fear me and my brother would *hate* me." Tears pearled among her lashes.

My shoulders sank as I realized I'd have to do it without her consent —for her sake. I'd have to come to terms with her loathing me for eternity. I looked away with a heavy sigh, my fangs lengthening at will.

"But I should've let you do it when I was at the Nightshades."

I snapped my head forward. I didn't expect her to change her mind, but I guess... this place was far worse than whatever Uriah did to her. The dam holding back her tears was building higher at her waterline. I raised my hand to caress her cheek, preparing to catch the flood whenever she blinked.

"Do it." Her voice cracked. "I can't let them kill you with my blood like they did Frankie."

"They're gonna kill me either way."

Briar craned her neck to the side. She closed her eyes, the tears finally falling. I leaned forward, placing one hand at the small of her back for comfort. I felt a hot droplet land on my cheek as I planted a soft kiss on her neck. Her body was rigid against mine, trembling.

"It's going to be okay," I mumbled against her skin, then stretched my jaw wide to sink my fangs into her neck—

More lightning.

More fire.

More *Hell.*

The air was knocked out of me when I hit the grass. My eyes rolled to the back of my head as my entire body locked in place until Rowena finally let up on the taser. Every breath came out as a strained wheeze. Another Keeper was dragging Briar away by what little hair she had left.

"Dr. Ivanov's gonna hear about this," Rowena hissed through tight fangs.

"I don't care," I growled weakly.

The last thing I remembered was her fist cracking against my nose.

✳

"Hey, wake up." A splintered stick poked my cheek, and I woke up with a boy hovering over me. He still had baby fat on his cheeks, his small body tucked under himself as he squatted in front of me. His hair was cut in a mushroom style around his small, eleven-year-old head.

I groaned, sitting up with my temples pounding. His blurred silhouette came into focus after a few blinks. We were somewhere dimly lit and without a window. For some reason, I was sleeping on the concrete floor instead of the bed behind me.

"Who are ya?" I rubbed my eyes, smacking my mouth like cotton was stuffed inside it.

"My name is Caspian. Boss says you're a new kid." He tilted his head slightly, sizing me up.

"Where am I?" All I could remember was an officer telling me that my parents had died, a social worker forcing me to go to school the following week, and a windowless van pulling up next to me as I walked down the sidewalk when I skipped class.

"I'm not allowed to tell you that. How old are you?" He tilted his head in the other direction, like an animal.

I finally looked up at him, then gasped and scrambled to my feet. I don't know why it took me so long to recognize the scarlet irises staring back at me. I ran toward the heavy metal door, yanking on its handle.

Caspian slowly straightened to a full stance.

"Get back!" I shouted, and snatched the empty bucket from the floor and held it over my head, preparing to launch it. Caspian laughed quietly, shaking his head.

"A bucket?" He folded his arms. "Aren't you a little old to have never seen us before?"

"I'm fourteen," I barked, lowering the bucket. I was more offended than afraid... who did this kid think he was?

"Where am I?" I demanded once more.

"Your new home, I guess." Caspian shrugged. He swung his stick around, tracing random invisible shapes on the floor. I gritted my teeth, clenching my fists at my sides.

"No, it's not," I said, assuming he was messing with me. I didn't even know kids could be Vampyres. The only ones I ever saw were adults, and that was when I broke my ankle falling down the stairs and went to the hospital in the middle of the night.

"Yeah, it is." Caspian rolled his eyes and sat on the floor. He crossed his legs and propped an elbow on his knee, leaning into his hand. "Wraith is coming to make you one of us."

"W-who's—"

All the color drained out of my skin and before my stomach could jump out of my throat, the door swung open. A dark haired teen with tattooed sclerae probably three or four years older than me came sauntering through the chamber.

"Which arm hurts the most?" Wraith asked, his lips stretching into a reptilian grin, every tooth sharpened to razors.

"Sorry," Caspian mumbled as he disappeared beyond the door. Wraith prowled toward me until I was cornered. My screams filled the small cell.

✳

I lurched forward, heaving at the precipice of empty vomiting, but a belt strapped across my chest held me against a leather seat. I dug my claws into the armrests and gnashed my teeth at the feel of metal cuffs around my wrists. I fought against them, scratching at the chair, but my body felt as weak as a Sun Dweller's. I switched my attention to the saline bag hovering over me and suspected whatever was in it was responsible for my weakness.

Briar was in a chair on the other side of the room, strapped down in all the same places I was. Her head hung limply forward, and her skin was so pale it looked grey.

129

"Briar?" I called. A steady stream of her blood fed through an IV and into a bag hanging on the drip pole next to her. My body somewhat eased at the indication she was still alive, but they were draining too much at once. They didn't feed the humans well enough to keep up with the taxing blood donations they forced upon them.

Briar groaned and flopped her head back against the headrest. Her eyes slowly cracked open. It only took her a few seconds to realize where she was before she began to whimper and tug at the binds.

"No... no, no, no, no!" she cried shakily.

"I think we really messed up this time, Sunny," I said with a weak chuckle.

"No, you don't understand!" Briar shouted raspily. "*They blew him up!*"

I gripped the armrests tighter to keep the fear from trickling through the cracks. She tried to break free until her body crumpled with defeat.

"I can't watch you die." Briar's voice was coated in breathless despair. "I can handle the others but th-this... *not* this."

"Maybe I won't," I said quietly, although I debated whether or not it would be for the best. "If I do, sounds like it'll be quick."

"Shut up," Briar whispered despondently, shaking her head with disgust. "You just don't get it."

"I don't think *you* do," I said. "I deserve everything that's comin' to me. If this is the kind of experiments you've been enduring and its us Vampyres they're killin'... then maybe I ain't got nothin' to worry about."

"You don't deserve it, Draven. You never deserved any of this." Briar sighed and lifted her eyes to the ceiling with thick sniffles, her upper lip glistening with snot.

It had been a long time since I'd felt fear swell in my chest. Probably not since I was forcefully Turned.

The white fluorescent lights flickered briefly. The mirrors wrapping around the room trembled when the metal door opened and shut heavily. Briar's cheeks were damp and ruddy from crying, but her face hardened at the sight of Dr. Ivanov.

"Good morning, children." She grinned as she began covering everything in the room with plastic. With quiet steps, she moved to Briar's IV. With her eyes fixed on mine, I watched them redden deeper as more tears glazed over them. I wondered how many of us she'd watched die. I thought it'd be satisfying to see my kind go down one by one after what she went through at the Nightshades, that perhaps she'd become more like Sterling through her traumas.

I assumed too much. Her grief made my heart wrench.

I wished I could've bitten her sooner. How many more of my choices would continue to haunt me?

Dr. Ivanov switched to my side of the lab room, carrying Briar's blood bag. I stared at it, my mouth instantly watering. I'd lost track of how many days I'd gone without... but judging by how much my stomach roiled, perhaps it was best I didn't get a chance to bite her.

Dr. Ivanov replaced the saline hanging from the hooks above me with Briar's blood. I looked steadily at Briar, admiring every curve and plane of her face, even in her sickly state.

I'd apologized to her a million times, yet with death knocking at my door... it still didn't feel like enough. I never got a chance to tell her how she made me feel, how she became the lifeline I needed—

My back locked straight as I threw my head against the chair and released a bellowing roar that shredded my throat. Agony so torturous crawled up my arm, snaked across my chest, and spread through my body until my thoughts were no more.

15
BRIAR

I GAWKED AT THE BLACK VEINS BRANCHING UP DRAVEN'S forearms, neck, and face. His fangs were sharpened. His jaw couldn't stretch wide enough for the agonized roars and screeches to fit through. Draven's bronze skin brightened to an angry copper as he thrashed. Red foam bubbled at the corner of his lips, then poured down his chin.

This was so much worse than Frankie.

Smoke whirled past Draven's lips and nostrils like a brazen bull.

"What are you doing?! *Help him!*" I screamed as I watched in terror. Dr. Ivanov's heels clicked across the tile nonchalantly. She lifted the plastic covering her desk and sat underneath the sheet, her nails clacking across the keyboard.

"Help him!" I cried desperately.

Draven's uncontrollable shaking stilled.

Time stopped.

I couldn't move. I couldn't blink. I couldn't *breathe*.

But then... I noticed the subtle rise and fall of his chest against the belt strap on the chair. Steam continued to waft from his skin as if he'd just gotten out of a scalding bath.

"Well, that was new," Dr. Ivanov mused, and pushed her glasses up her nose before typing additional notes on the computer. She slid from beneath the plastic and left the room, just as she had moments before Frankie died.

My choked breaths rattled in my chest.

"No, no, please! *Please!*" I tried to twist out of the seat despite my million failed attempts. I kept begging, screaming until my throat was raw and burning—

The UV lamp cut on. The burst of light, like lightning, chased every possible shadow away. The backs of my eyes stung and I braced for the viscous impact of Draven's remains raining in all directions.

As my vision adjusted, I noticed I was dry. My white scrubs still retained their purity. I quaked so violently that I could barely control my head to look at Draven's seat.

Only a quiet gasp escaped.

He was there. Unconscious, but still in one piece.

First and second degree burns plagued all over his face and arms. Dr. Ivanov and roughly ten other scientists came pouring inside the lab room to marvel at the fact that Draven wasn't mush.

I melted into the seat, relieved to see Draven in one piece. Without a doubt, he'd heal. His life was intact, and maybe we'd have a second chance at sabotaging the White Fangs' experiments.

A Keeper entered and released me from the straps while another

Keeper handled Draven. I staggered out of the chair, my head swimming. I paused in the doorway, double-checking that his body was whole before the Keeper shoved me forward.

"Hey! Unnecessary," I snapped, then rolled my shoulders to crack my back. I scanned the corridor, my eyes landing on a fire extinguisher.

I snatched the fire extinguisher off the hook and swung with a loud grunt, the red metal cracking against the Keeper's cheekbone. I dropped it with a loud clang as he staggered to the side, hitting the wall. I took off, blindly turning down a new corridor in the short seconds he was stunned. I didn't look back as I burst through the door at the end of the hallway that led to a stairwell, then hopped the railing to slide down each flight. My gut flailed when I nearly fell.

I paused a couple flights down. This seemed too easy. They could track my scent and catch up with me in half a second. Yet the stairwell remained silent.

Are they waiting for me on the first floor? I cursed under my breath, peering up and down the stairwell as I decided my next move. I shut my eyes tightly and took a deep breath, counting down from five to force myself to calm down.

Think, Briar. This isn't you. Calm down and think. I took a slow step down, then slid on the railing the rest of the way.

I quietly opened the double doors and stepped onto the first floor, then froze in place when I saw Cyrus. His snowy eyebrows pressed tightly together, but his lips curled into a sinister smirk.

"You've been busy while I was gone." He snatched a fistful of my short hair, and my knees buckled as my hands shot up to his. "I don't like my days off getting interrupted, girl."

"Let me go!"

Cyrus dragged me across the tile to the elevator, then threw me against the metallic wall. The relief of release diminished beside the impact that ripped air from my lungs. I crumpled to the floor, gasping and coughing.

"I've been waiting for this," Cyrus said as he pressed the sixth floor button. My blood ran cold.

"I'm sorry," I pleaded through sobs, but Cyrus yoked me by the neck. My skin went taut as my breath caught in my throat.

"Too late for that, girl," Cyrus growled. He dragged me down the halls. All my screaming, thrashing, and bucking was always futile. I didn't know why I kept doing it.

Cyrus threw me in a room similar to the one I woke up in when I first arrived at White Fang. It was roughly ten feet wide with only a single door and a wooden post at the center. Two metal cuffs were attached to the top of it. I screamed as Cyrus forced my wrists into the handcuffs. He inhaled sharply and pushed his hair back as he stepped away. I sank to my knees when the metal cut into my wrists.

"What are you going to do to me?" I whispered, partially hesitant to hear the answer.

"Twenty lashes, then you're good to go back to your cell." Cyrus pulled a small black tube from his belt, then extended it into a skinny black whip with short, bladed thorns along its leather.

I shut my eyes tight and sucked in a breath as I braced for the first strike.

"Welcome to the Box, doll."

16
DRAVEN

WRAITH WIPED THE BLOOD FROM HIS GRINNING LIPS AS I writhed against the stone floor. I held my wrist, watching blood drip from the gash he'd created as fire coursed through my veins. I cried, arching my back and gnashing my teeth as my mind scrambled to slush.

"Welcome to the family, buddy." Wraith turned on his heel and strolled out of the chamber. Caspian peeked around the corner of the cell door. I could barely make out who he was through my tears.

My mouth filled with a metallic, coppery taste, and my gums felt like they were splitting apart.

My nail beds stung. I bent my fingers sharply at the joints as my nails extended to claws.

"What... did he do... to me?!" I shrieked.

"You're one of us now," Caspian said coolly. Slowly, he approached. His face became clearer, but it was still devoid of emotion. I rolled back and forth on the floor, holding my wrist and weeping. Between this and my parents dying, I realized my life as I knew it was over.

✳

I choked in short, rapid breaths with sweat rolling down my face. The acrid air smelled of burnt hair. I was now in a long, narrow room with my back against a padded wall. My shirt was gone, exposing the Nightshade crest on my left pectoral, the dragons along my arms, and heart monitor electrodes stuck all over my torso. Steam rolled off my skin like fog over a lake.

There was a line of five Keepers pointing rifles in my direction. They wore masks, but unlike the cops, their entire faces were concealed.

I opened my mouth to speak, but it was dry as if coated in sand.

"Fire," Dr. Ivanov's voice emitted from the speakers behind the Keepers. Before I could process what she meant, they rained their bullets on me. I expected excruciating pain, but I felt nothing but pressure and repeated force knocking me against the padded wall. Silver bullet casings littered the floor.

"Stop!" Dr. Ivanov shouted through the speakers once again, and the Keepers instantly ceased. They snapped into position with their feet shoulder-width, holding their weapons with two firm hands.

Blood flowed until the wounds sealed. I reached behind myself with quivering hands and grabbed one of the bullets that had gone right through me like butter, staring at the blood that coated it. It took me a second to realize I had just faced Death and survived.

Impossible...

I slowly rose to my feet, vapor swirling past my lips like cigarette smoke. Wrath took hold, each heaving breath ticking down to an explosion. I clenched my burning fists, tightening my jaw so hard I thought my teeth would crack.

"Ya tried to kill me?" I shouted, my voice bellowing against the four walls. I took a step toward the Keepers and they quickly pointed their barrels back at me. I paused, then chuckled.

"Ya think those guns will scare me now, after I just survived them?" I asked with a low growl. "I ain't got nothin' stopping me from snappin' your necks now."

Everything was tinted red. I snatched a gun from one of the Keepers and threw it across the room, then seized his neck, all in the blink of an eye. I kept squeezing and squeezing and—

"If you want your little girlfriend alive, you'll stand down!" one of the Keepers threatened wildly.

"You expect me to believe you'd do anything to Briar with her blood type? She's too valuable to all of y'all." I watched the Keeper in my grip's skin go from red to purple, and the will to fight slowly leave his bulging eyes.

"She's not the only one with AB negative blood," another Keeper cut in. "She's not special, Mr. Hawthorne."

I considered, then growled as I threw the Keeper. A couple of his colleagues dropped their guns to catch him. He gasped for air. I stepped back, freezing when I saw the scorched footprint I'd left in the tile.

She had a point... Briar wasn't the only one in the world with that blood type. It was rare, but not extinct, and I couldn't say for sure whether or not they'd finally found someone else.

I swallowed my fury, taking deep breaths.

Bide your time. Be patient, for Briar's sake.

Two Keepers approached and cuffed me—the usual routine. I wanted to snap out of these thin, weak things. I wanted to snap their *necks.*

Something swelled within my chest. Something that made me feel like I could tear down mountains.

Destroy cities.

Consume souls.

It was getting harder to breathe.

I left a trail of black footprints on the white tile. The edges of them glowed like embers waiting to ignite. Surely, the Keepers had noticed and just decided to keep their mouths shut. I suspected they'd report the strange anomaly to Dr. Ivanov.

I craved jumping into a pool of ice. My ears pounded while my head throbbed. Sweat rolled and cascaded down my face, back, and chest.

I paused when I heard a distant scream.

"Keep it moving, Mr. Hawthorne," one of the Keepers demanded.

It was a desperate cry I knew all too well in this hellish place.

My palms glowed like heated glass. I pulled my wrists to my sides, snapping the handcuffs in two as if they were made of toothpicks. Before the Keepers could react, I snatched one by the neck— his skin melting down to the bone—and ripped the throat out of the other with a feral snarl. His blood... wasn't bitter.

I didn't allow myself to dwell on it.

I flashed to the stairwell, following the screams to the sixth floor. I stopped in front of a heavy metal door with no sign or window.

After every cry of agony, a hitched hiccup and heavy breath followed. I placed my palms on the door and watched the metal glow bright orange, warping and melting until a hole formed and I could step through.

The floors were stained scarlet, blood flowing from the lashes splitting Briar's back. Her scrubs hung in ribbons. She was crumpled against the wooden post as Cyrus stood above her, gripping a whip tightly in his blanched, blue-veined hand. He stood frozen, gaping at me.

"Stay right there!" Cyrus pointed the whip at me, quickly reaching for his radio on his belt with his other hand. "All units, go to—!"

I lunged across the room in one leap, and Cyrus flashed back to the door, disappearing into the corridor. I heard him shouting, but I turned my focus back to Briar. I snapped the cuffs and pulled her away from the post. She winced and I reeled back, gasping at the burns I left on her arms.

"Draven?" Briar croaked, looking up at me with a hard blink.

"I-I'm sorry, I ain't got no idea know how to stop it," I rambled. "I'm gettin' ya outta here regardless, you just gotta fight it."

I snatched her up in my arms and she cried out. I couldn't tell if my scorching arms or the gashes on her back hurt worse, but I sped as fast as my legs would carry me to the stairwell. Marching footsteps thundered through the corridors all around us. None of the doors were safe to exit through, but I took us to the first floor anyway.

Briar bit her lip as she stifled her cries. I knew I couldn't carry her for long. Not with the uncontrollable, fiery heat seeping out of my pores. We were running out of time.

White Fang didn't have signs leading to the outside, but it became easier to figure it out as I relied on my senses. I wove through the corridors, following the scent of rain that grew ever stronger as I drew near an exit door.

Briar's teeth dug in her bottom lip as she whimpered.

The second we burst outside, I set her down.

Cold rain pelted my skin, and even though a chaotic alarm blared thirty feet behind us, I paused for a moment to savor its relief.

Briar sat on her calves, staring at the tree canopy as the rain filtered through the leaves and hit her face.

"We... we're outside... How—" Her eyes widened.

"Is that smoke coming from your skin?" She touched my forearm and flinched with a wince.

"I don't know what's happenin', but listen." I knelt in front of her, allowing my fangs to grow. "They're comin' for me. They're definitely gonna come for you."

The distant shouts were getting clearer. Groups of Keepers were already splitting up to hunt for us through the surrounding trees. The rain masked our scents to a small degree, but it wouldn't be long before one of them got close enough to detect us in the brush.

"I hear talking!" someone shouted.

"You were the sun I always wanted," I whispered as I caressed Briar's cheek. I hooked my hand behind her neck, pulling her close enough to press my lips against hers before she could say anything else. I pulled away quickly, and she gasped as I sank my teeth into her shoulder without warning. Briar's blood was as sweet as honeysuckle and for a split moment, I wanted to drain her. I pushed her away before I could lose my mind.

"Run," I demanded in a low growl. Her face began to shift into a stranger's. My stomach ached for more, and I was seconds away from turning feral if she didn't get as far away from me as possible.

Briar hesitated, glancing between the endless trees behind her and me. The angry scalds on her arms already began to lighten.

"Come with me!" Briar pleaded.

"Run or I'll kill you myself!" I roared.

Her eyes instantly glazed over. She gave a short nod and took off, running deeper into the trees. I turned on my heel to buy her some time. My outburst would lead them right to me.

None of this would've happened if I hadn't stepped into her life. Perhaps if I'd killed her as a witness instead of succumbing to my curiosity, she wouldn't have endured so much suffering.

I wouldn't have had to rip her humanity away just so she could survive a narrow escape.

I wouldn't have developed these feelings for her, only to never be able to tell her directly.

As I ran toward my death, my list of regrets kept growing.

PART 2

Chrysalis

17
BRIAR

My lips still burned from Draven's kiss. My heart still raced, still ached.

Why couldn't he come with me?

The rain weighed my clothes down against my skin and froze my scalp. The ground was slick with early fallen leaves and pine needles. I tried to ignore the pain in my legs and the venom creeping through my body like wild wisteria.

Why would he tell me that if he was just going to get himself killed?

I staggered through the foliage, rocks and branches pressing through the thin soles of my slippers. My tears mixed with the rain as the butterflies torpedoed my stomach while every step was like walking on hot coals.

Every time I blinked, I grew closer to collapsing

I have to keep going.

Draven's roars of pain echoed through the woods, sending flocks of birds retreating to the skies.

You were the sun I always wanted.

The thought fell out of my mind when invisible hands clamped my head in a vise. I paused, leaning against a tree and gasping for breath. One scream, and White Fang would find me in seconds— with or without the rain masking my scent. One scream, and Draven's sacrifice would be for nothing.

When the invisible hands let up, I caught a winding road that cut through the trees. Every breath sliced my throat as I trudged forward, every step brought me closer to collapse.

I threw myself onto the road with no regard for oncoming vehicles. Once I hit the concrete, it was impossible to stand again. I weakly raised one of my arms, waving in hopes of a passing car noticing I wasn't roadkill.

The rain was so cold, I thought it was sleet. For the middle of August, it was definitely strange, but everything felt frigid.

There was no telling how long it would take for a car to see me, or if Keepers would find me first.

I may never see my family again.

Threads of hope unraveled. An invisible rope wrapped itself around my neck and squeezed. I thought about how my disappearance would inevitably shake Astoria to the core— possibly to the point she'd drop out of college. How Sterling probably assumed I ran away and resented me for it.

I whimpered under my breath, resisting the urge to scream. My bones twisted, and the vise grips returned.

Two bright stars rounded the corner, then raced in my direction. A dark green SUV screeched to a stop in front of me and I hoped it was a human rushing to get home. It was hard to tell the time beyond the thunderclouds.

"Oh my God, girl, what happened to you?!" An older, white-haired man with rich maple skin seasoned by the sun slammed his door shut. He took off a straw hat and rolled up his sleeves, revealing large veins cording hairy arms with faint sunspots. He knelt at my side in his ripped jeans. "You poor thing! Let me get you to a hospital—"

"N-no! No hospitals, please," I pleaded, fumbling his arm with a quivering hand. He raised his eyebrows.

"You look like you've been bitten! If you're Turning, you'll have to get registered—"

"I'll do that later, I just can't go to a hospital right... now..." I fell into a fit of suffocating coughs and wheezes. The old man nodded quickly and picked me up with a labored grunt, then rushed to lay me in his back seat. He jumped in the driver's seat just as another car headed our way.

I tried to count the raindrops against the windows, even focus on a pair streaking toward the bottom to see which one would win the race.

"What happened to you, girl? What's your name? You can call me Moses." He glanced at me through his rearview mirror, turning his country music down to hear my response.

"Briar," I strained, then gasped as sharp pains splintered across my body. I screamed, writhing on the seat and arching my back. The SUV's engine hummed louder as Moses accelerated.

The taste of pennies invaded my mouth. The same pain I'd once had as a teen when my wisdom teeth pressed against my other teeth was amplified across my entire mouth. My hands—no, my *nails*—throbbed as if someone was chopping each fingertip off with a dull blade.

Then finally, the world was shut off.

❊

I grew up hearing the crickets whisper, the owls murmur, and the trees singing against wind.

Now... all of it bellowed.

I woke up tightly tucked in a thick quilt among three fluffy pillows cradling my head. It smelled like a mix of mildew and laundry detergent, as if the blankets were once cooped up in an attic and the smell could never fully leave. I surveyed my surroundings, noticing I was in a small bedroom with one window, a vaulted ceiling, *tons* of paneling, and walls dressed in brown leaf-patterned wallpaper.

I lurched upright with a low growl, shifting the entire bed forward, and zeroed in on a sound in a dark corner. It was the discreet tap of a spider's legs as it crawled toward the ceiling.

I smacked my lips, noticing the coppery taste was still there. My gums ached and I ran my tongue over my teeth until it pricked over something sharp. I jumped out of the bed with a loud *thud*, approaching the full-body mirror made of oak beside the rocking chair and knee-high bookcase.

Before I took a closer look, I instantly noticed whatever little pigmentation I had in my skin was completely sopped out. I looked like Caspian's sister more than Sterling's. My eyes of steel were now the color of rose quartz. I leaned into the mirror, baring my teeth. I reeled back with a gasp at the four fangs filling my mouth. I reached up to touch them, noticing my nails were longer, sharpened to claws like the *one* time I got acrylics from the nail salon and regretted it because they were too long. Except... these were *mine*.

I didn't know how to feel about that.

I pulled my t-shirt sleeve down to examine my shoulder, then noticed the shirt was completely different. It had faded graphics of superheroes on it. My pants were loose, matching pajama bottoms. I loosed an unsteady sigh as I stretched out the collar to look at the crook between my neck and shoulder.

No bite mark.

No scar.

I was about to remove my clothes to further examine the rest of my scars and see if they were still there when I heard stairs creak. I ran to the bed, stumbling into the wall from the unexpected flash of speed. The small sting in my arm from the impact faded before I could even rub it. I quickly climbed back under the covers as the door opened and Moses came in with a tray of food.

My mouth watered. Not at the sight or smell of the food, but at the sight and smell of *him*.

"How are you feeling, Briar?" Moses set a tray down of pancakes, bacon, and eggs along with a glass of orange juice and a mug of coffee on the nightstand. I glanced at it, but locked my gaze on him and his neck again. I wondered if his age would have had any affect on his taste. I imagined it would taste like either aged wine or old bread.

"Hungry," I whispered. Moses returned to the doorway, and I

noticed a holstered gun at the small of his back. I tensed, leaning against the headboard warily.

"I reckon it ain't for that food I just sat there, right?" he asked.

I looked down at my hands in my lap, lacing my fingers together in shame.

"Try it. The food might help some of the cravings for the time being."

I slowly reached for a piece of bacon. Its saltiness masked some of the copper. I grabbed the tray and set it on my lap, devouring every bit of it.

"Now, are you gonna tell me what happened? Somethin' tells me you ain't get bit with your consent." Moses stepped away from the door and sat in the rocking chair. It creaked quietly as he rocked.

"Where am I?" I couldn't answer his questions. I still didn't know where White Fang really was, and thinking about Draven, the words he said, how we parted ways—

I lowered my gaze again, fighting off tears.

"A small town called Eclipsis," Moses replied. "Ain't much 'round here, ain't many Vampyres 'round here neither."

"Eclipsis?" I repeated with a small frown. I vaguely remembered Draven saying this was his hometown. "How small are we talking?"

"Almost five hundred people live here," Moses explained. "We got two restaurants, one for breakfast and the other for dinner. A gas station with two pumps, a hardware store, and a grocer connected to the hardware store. That about covers it. The Red Plague ain't touch this place much either."

Every time his Adam's apple moved, I had to fight the urge to rip it out. I avoided looking at him so I wouldn't think about it, because so far Moses had been nothing but nice to me.

"That's... good..." I spoke through tight lips.

"Now, are you gonna answer any of my questions, Miss Briar?" He raised his eyebrows expectantly, like how my father used to when he asked if I'd stolen from the cookie jar before dinner. As if he already knew the answer, but was testing me to see if I would be honest or not. I twisted the sheets in my fists.

"I gave consent, but only so I could get to safety. I just... need to warn my family and save my friend too."

Draven had been oozing heat. Whatever my blood did to him had turned him into a volcano waiting to blow... and I only hoped that gave him enough strength to get out of there rather than melt from the inside out.

"Where did you come from?" Moses pressed.

"I think the less you know, the better." There was an edge to my voice that I failed to smooth out, but hopefully it would be enough to get him to stop asking questions.

"You know..." Moses stood up with a grunt as his knee popped. "I had a son that was Turned. He had to move away 'cause of it. Then there was a young man that I considered family, and he was taken by some very bad people. Are ya involved in something like that?"

I curled my legs against my chest, wrapping my arms around them.

"Please... I don't want any more people to die because of me," I mumbled. *Please don't make me say it.*

"My son's name was Booker," Moses said. "And the one that filled the void after Booker left, well…"

"What?" I rested my chin on my knees expectantly.

"He came from a family that owned half the farms here, but it didn't end well for the poor boy. He was too young when his parents were killed. I wish I could've helped him… I'm sure he's like you by now."

"What was his name?"

Moses leaned back in the rocking chair, watching the ceiling as if his memories projected on it. His chest ballooned, then deflated with a thick sigh through his wide nostrils.

"Draven Hawthorne."

18
CASPIAN

The second I dragged Astoria to The Nightshade club and she yelped at a Vampyre bumping into her, I regretted it. The bouncer, Damien, cut his growl off when he saw me holding Astoria's hand as I guided her to the front of the line.

"Enjoy your night, Mr. Bishop." Damien extended his hand toward the doorway. I gave him a short nod, hoping Astoria hadn't notice his salutation. I pulled her through the entryway, the music now deafening. I glanced over my shoulder, and her head was turning to observe every passing Vampyre.

"Christian, I don't think I can—" Astoria's voice cut off and I paused at the threshold between the hall and the clubroom. I turned to face her, waiting for her to speak again.

"Why are we here?" She pressed against the wall as if it'd render her invisible. I chewed my bottom lip pensively, hooking my thumbs onto my pockets.

"Samara said your sister was taken here. But, um... you know what? Why don't you wait for me outside. I'm better versed at handling... Vampyres," I shouted.

"You're going to leave me alone after bringing me here?" Astoria peered at the exit, then back at me, clutching her necklace so tight I thought she'd break the chain.

I tilted my head. "What did we say about fear?"

She pouted and let her hand drop at her side. "I feel like they're all looking at me!"

"They're not. Nobody is going to hurt you. Why don't you get a drink while I go ask questions?" If I could vanish for a few moments and act like I discovered more information, then working with Astoria could end tonight, and all the dominoes would fall into place.

"I'm not old enough! I don't drink anyway!" She cupped her hands around her mouth, her voice growing hoarse from screaming over the music. I shook my head with a groan and leaned close to whisper in her ear.

"Wait outside for me in the alley. I'll be quick," I said. In the grand scheme of things, it was a huge risk to bring her here anyway. On a weekend, there was a chance Wraith and Larkin could be hanging around, cutting up in the VIP lounge. The first place I'd check was the bar, where Wraith would torment Stella for the hundredth time.

"Please hurry," Astoria said, then nearly jogged toward the exit door that led to another alley on the other side of the building.

I went through the clubroom, squeezing past dancing bodies

and weaving through the crowd to get to the men's room. My eyes burned from these horrific contacts. I reached for the eye drops in my pocket the minute I stepped inside.

"What are you up to with those things in your eyes, son?"

My heart leaped out of my chest at the sound of Uriah's voice behind me, but my face remained blank as I calmly looked at him through the mirror.

"You're back," I said in a flat tone.

"No need to get too excited," Uriah snarked, then pulled me into a hug. He instantly adjusted his tie once he pulled back. As always, his suit and gelled hair were immaculate, although I couldn't pinpoint why he'd use this restroom instead of the VIP one.

"I'm glad to see you, I didn't mean—"

"Calm down, now. I'm only messing with you. So, any news?" Uriah examined himself in the mirror as he washed his hands.

"No, sir. Everything looked fine. I made sure no one followed me." I observed him carefully. He was just as volatile as Briar was reckless.

"What else?" Uriah grabbed a couple of paper towels folded neatly on the counter and dried his hands.

"Nothing, sir."

"You smell like a Sun Dweller, son. Don't tell me you haven't learned from Draven's mistakes, have you?" Uriah slowly turned from the mirror to face me directly, the light in his eyes darkening. I glanced at his hands, mainly at the golden ruby ring that often crushed the skulls of Nightshades who wronged him.

"I have, and I was doing some Diurnal patrols today for potential subjects. I found a couple." The lies rolled off my tongue. Every lie I said, whether it was to Uriah or Astoria, necrotized my insides.

But it was a mask I needed to keep on for the lives of Draven and the woman he loved.

"Is that why you're wearing contacts, Cass?" Uriah tossed the ball of paper towels in the small trash cutout in the granite countertop.

"Yes, sir. I just forgot to take them out." I pulled my contacts case out of my pocket, leaned over the counter, and started to remove them. I blinked rapidly.

Uriah folded his arms with a soft chuckle.

"You wouldn't lie to me, would you?" He dropped his volume. I looked him right in the eye, keeping every muscle in my face relaxed.

"No, sir."

"Good. I have a little project for you." Uriah shuffled to the bathroom door and locked it, then checked under the stalls to ensure no one was around. "The final recruit White Fang needs before we move on to Phase Two."

"Who?" I leaned against the tiled wall, folding my arms expectantly.

"We did a little digging and found out that Briar has a brother, and guess what?" Uriah's lips stretched into a wide grin, the kind he always had when he discovered a gold mine.

"What?" I lifted my chin slightly.

"White Fang was demanding a replacement after Briar's escape and it turns out he has the same blood type. You're my best man to retrieve him. Yes, he's a cop, but the department is already thinking about letting him go. He was getting too close to their operations with us." Uriah paced back and forth in front of the stalls, clasping his hands behind his back. "Oh, and have you heard?"

"Heard what?"

"Your friend's experiment was a success." Uriah beamed, extending his palms to his sides.

Draven being experimented on and it being a success could've meant anything. The deformed Vampyre who'd killed an officer was technically considered a success since the silver bullets didn't affect him.

I narrowed my eyes. "How so?"

"Draven underwent both the lamp test and the firing squad *and* survived without any defects. They think he could lead our armies." Uriah dropped his voice a little lower. If it weren't for our supernatural hearing, the muffled bass through the walls would've drowned his words.

For a moment, my mind left the bathroom and flew beyond White Fang's gates. What was the lamp test? What did the firing squad entail? Were those tests the reasons why our Nightshade members had been dwindling? Armies? Just how many Vampyres did Uriah plan to have fight? Was this fight going beyond Neoterra's borders?

"Did you hear me, boy?" Uriah chided. I snatched my head up and forced a tight grin.

"Yeah, that's great news." The only good news I heard was that Briar escaped and Draven was alive. Her escape made it easier to tell Astoria the truth without implicating myself... but Draven still needed help.

"You don't sound too eager."

"Well." I pushed off the wall and ran a hand through my hair. "What makes you think Draven would want to help you after you kicked him out of the Nightshades and handed him over to the White Fangs? If he becomes the first immune Vampyre, don't you think he'd rather use that strength against you?"

Uriah's toothy grin closed to an arrogant smirk.

"I'm sure that girl is still his weakness, and if he knows we'll kill her without his cooperation, everything will be fine." Uriah shrugged.

You'd have to find her first, I thought as I gave him an agreeable nod. Uriah laid a heavy hand on my shoulder, then patted it a couple more times.

"Enjoy your night, son. But get started on that hunt for Sterling Shaw as soon as possible, because time is of the essence." Uriah unlocked the bathroom door.

"Yes, sir," I called, then stood a few more moments in the men's room after he left to reprocess the heavy load he'd dropped on me.

✳

I might've been in the men's room for a total of ten minutes, including my conversation with Uriah. Ten minutes too long, because when I stepped outside the club, Astoria was crying and screaming and spraying clouds of peppered silver dust at a group of three Vampyres. One of them blindly shoved her into a bunch of metal trash cans and they scattered with a loud clamor.

Blood ran down Astoria's arm and my nose was greeted by the scent of sandalwood and jasmine. The three Vampyres wiped wildly at their faces, snarling maliciously. With the speed of light, I ripped one's head off his shoulders, gutted another's torso, and

160

tore through the last one's chest. My hands and mouth were slick, a feeling I had grown numb to a long time ago.

At least... I *thought* I did. The fear exuding from Astoria's face felt like a knife twisting in my ribs. She still sat among garbage bags and toppled trash bins, gaping at me with the silver pepper spray in her hand.

"Are you okay?" I stepped toward her. "Are you bitten?"

"*Get away from me!*" Astoria shrieked, then scrambled through the trash to find her footing. I could've easily killed her. If I wanted to, I could've killed her in the middle of St. Brine's Bibliotheca. I'd just saved her life, yet she still cowered.

But that's fear. Logic and reason cannot exist in the same room as fear. It was the very thing I predicted coming from her, despite my attempt to desensitize her at the beach. Bottom line, she was nothing like Briar, who lived her life among us no matter what we were or what we could do.

So why did I still feel surprised at Astoria's reaction? Maybe even... hurt?

I took a step forward and she tripped over a bag when she tried to leap out of my extended hand's reach.

"*Don't touch me!*" she cried, and took off running down the alley. It only took one vault to land in front of her and block her from stepping off the sidewalk. I gripped her arms tightly before launching us onto a nearby building's roof. She thrashed against me, nearly stumbling to her knees when I let go.

Astoria hyperventilated as she pointed the spray at me.

"Don't come any closer!" she warned in a warbling tone.

"Astoria." I kept my voice low and gentle, slowly raising my hands as if she were pointing a gun loaded with silver bullets. That spray could blind me for days if I didn't play my cards right.

"Whatever you say, I won't believe you because you're a freaking *liar*!" she shouted breathlessly.

"I'm a Vampyre, I know, but it's true I knew your sister." I tried not to focus on the spray and instead held her gaze. Astoria's wet cheeks reflected the neon lights surrounding us, her cold, brown eyes violent earthquakes.

"If you really weren't trying to hurt me, why would you lie?" she whimpered.

"Because I've done some things, and Briar got involved in some things she shouldn't have. I couldn't just tell you without risking you reporting me to your brother." I spoke quickly, silently praying my words would convince her to lower the spray. Astoria took several steps back. I gasped and held my hands out in front of me when the back of her heel hit the edge of the roof.

"Watch—"

Astoria looked down and wobbled. I sped toward her, snatching the spray out of her hand and wrapping an arm around her waist to pull her close. She strained against my arm with the strength of a mouse.

"I'm not your enemy." I sounded out every syllable. "Take a deep breath."

"What have you done with my sister?" she rasped.

"Nothing. Some bad people took her and sent her off to a mob known as White Fang for experiments. I just found out she recently escaped. She could be anywhere, but right now..." I released Astoria when I felt like she could finally act civil, far from the edge. "You and your brother need to get out of Neoterra."

At the very least, it didn't seem like Uriah knew Astoria existed, but that couldn't last for long.

"Why?" she croaked.

"Because they want your brother's blood," I said plainly.

Astoria paced across the dusty roof, twisting her hair in her fists.

"I should've known," she mumbled. "I should've known, I should've known!"

I frowned. "Hey, do I need to repeat myself?"

"Is your name even Christian?" she barked.

"No," I said blandly. "It's Caspian."

Astoria scoffed, slapped her forehead, then resumed pacing and grumbling under her breath.

"How do you know my sister escaped if you weren't behind her abduction?" She paused, placing her hands on her hips.

I flipped the spray in my hands, turning it over in my palms idly. "Believe what you want, but that's information I learned from my boss."

"Who's your boss?" Astoria pressed.

"I'd actually have to kill you if I told you that, and I've grown fond of you and your sister. I'd hate to do that to either of you." I tossed the spray back to her. "Right now, your biggest problem is relaying this information to your brother and getting him to listen—without getting me involved."

19

STERLING

I HAD TO RETURN TO WORK SHORTLY AFTER LYRA AND I CAP-
tured the drug dealer at the abandoned warehouse. We were supposed to meet up tomorrow night in the same spot and watch him
do a drug exchange, then capture the Nightshade he was dealing
with. It didn't really settle with me that the Nightshades would be
willing to meet in the same spot after getting busted the first time,
but it was too late to address that.

I obsessed about the exchange through the week.

The first night back at Neoterra Police Department felt so...
strange. My locker was filled with cards of condolences for my loss,
a few "Get Well Soon!" cards for my concussion and mental health,
and some of my favorite snacks. A few of them said I was a hero,
even though I wasn't the one that deployed the flamethrower that

finally killed the rogue Vampyre. Rather, I was the one that couldn't get to Cyrene in time.

Cyrene's desk was empty, and while I imagined myself sprinting to the restroom to throw up, I experienced a dull ache in my chest instead. My desk was diagonal to hers, and had been kept exactly the way I left it—my name plaque at the edge, next to a cup of pens and paperclips, and my file cabinet full of manila folders locked. I stared at the empty space and I could see her diamond smile beam every time I arrived in the morning. She'd release a witty quip, and I'd shoot one back, then we'd get to work. I felt my eyes burn and quickly averted my gaze. I sifted through drawers to find the keys to my cabinet. Once I did, I opened the drawer to see most of the files gone except the cases I'd already closed.

I blinked once, twice, even rubbed my eyes. I skimmed through the layers in every drawer three times and there wasn't a single file addressing the missing persons or Cyrene's death. I jumped to my feet as heat rose up my nape. I stormed toward Chief Duncan's office, ignoring the bright greetings from colleagues who hadn't seen me since before I went on leave.

I paused at his door and took a deep breath.

Don't be unstable. Calm... down.

I knocked and waited patiently for his answer.

"Come on in!" he shouted. He was muffled behind the thick wooden door, but I could sense his tone was bright. Despite being in a serious position and rank, he was always pleasant when he didn't have to be. I sighed before I opened the door, reworking my attitude.

"Oh, Sterling! Welcome back." Chief Duncan wore a pair of

plain wire-framed reading glasses at the tip of his nose. He was reading paperwork—which from a brief glance as I took a seat in front of his desk, looked like another officer's file.

"Good evening, sir," I said as I leaned forward, bracing my elbows on my knees.

"Everyone treating you well tonight?" Chief Duncan removed his glasses and set them next to his keyboard.

"Yeah, everything is fine..." I observed some of his framed family photos on the wall behind him and across his desk. I chewed my cheek as I tried to muster up my courage.

"I hear a 'but' somewhere in there." Chief Duncan clasped his hands together patiently. *Just get it over with..*

"I was just wondering where my files in my desk went. Everything is gone except the cases I've already solved," I said. I was hoping to view them with a fresh set of eyes, looking for clues I previously ignored when Briar was still safe. With more information about the Nightshades, I figured there could be a breakthrough.

Chief Duncan rubbed his shadowed chin, the bristles scraping loudly in the silence. "Ah, of course. Yeah, I'm sorry about that, son. You've been taken off those cases. I didn't want to tell you about that while you were on leave."

"I'd like to be put back on them, please." It was an effort not to demand it.

"That won't be happening." Chief Duncan put his glasses back on and picked up the manila folder again.

"Why not? Sir, I'm telling you, I'm close to finding where they were all taken from. If you would just let me—"

"Officer Shaw." Chief Duncan's voice sharpened as he slapped the folder shut and tossed it on his desk. He snatched his glasses from his nose. I sat upright, my spine locking in place at the tone.

"Those cases are already closed. They were all on drugs, trashed their homes and ran off somewhere. Let. It. Go," he growled.

I turned to a family portrait of him, his wife, and their daughter in a black cap and gown. It looked like she'd graduated university, and for a moment, I imagined Astoria in that position—a brief reprieve as I recovered from the blows of this conversation.

"Yes, sir." I sighed dejectedly, then stood. "What would you rather have me do?"

"Until I know you're mentally stable to go back to detective work, you'll be issuing parking tickets downtown." Chief Duncan returned his focus to the folder, indicating the end of the conversation. I scoffed as I stormed out of the office before I'd say something I'd regret.

Lyra must've told him something.

Steam could've been rolling out of my ears for all I knew because all the smiles everyone gave me earlier switched to worry and concern. Rather than approaching me, they cleared a path like I was a runaway eighteen-wheeler.

I snatched my keys from my desk and stormed to my new car. Parking tickets? At the very least, he could've put me on a simple robbery case. I hadn't issued a parking ticket since I was fresh out of the Academy.

After everything I had done for this department? For this cursed city?

With thundering footsteps, I crossed the parking lot and yanked my car door open, then slammed it shut. I gripped the steering wheel and released a furious roar, punching the wheel repeatedly until I lost my breath.

I huffed loudly, leaning back in the seat and catching two officers staring at me from across the parking lot. I groaned, then started up the car and rushed away from the station.

I drove downtown, contemplating giving everyone a freebie out of spite. Even if the parking was blatantly wrong, I didn't want to allow Chief Duncan to walk all over me.

I doubted Lyra sincerely wanted to help find Briar. Matter of fact, I suspected she could've had a hand in the Nightshades' dealings, and that was why she was so guarded.

Lyra might sabotage tomorrow's plans.

I flinched when my phone buzzed against the passenger seat, and slammed on my brakes when the yellow light quickly changed to red. I let my cellphone continue to ring, unsure if I should answer.

I didn't decide until the last ring.

"What?" I snapped by way of greeting.

"*That's* how you answer your phone? Wow." I could imagine Lyra rolling her eyes, or scrunching her nose.

"When *you're* calling, yeah. What do you want?" I grumbled.

"I was calling to see if you were working tonight and wanted to meet up," she said with annoyance in her voice. "Now I don't think I want to."

"Yeah, probably for the best, since you'd just run off to Chief Duncan and tell him everything," I snapped. Lyra scoffed.

"There you go again, assuming you know everything. Crack a few cases and the man thinks he's a mind-reading genius!" she jeered.

At this point, I was so angry and engrossed in the conversation that I didn't know where I was driving.

"Well, why else would he have taken me off of all my cases? Let's face the facts! You never completely opened up about the Nightshades and you're still mad at me for leaving you at the club that night. That's two different motives—"

"You want to know why I haven't opened up to you? It's because I know you couldn't care less about learning that my husband was killed at their hands!" she yelled so loud I had to pull the phone from my ear.

"When you told me I couldn't possibly understand how you felt when you lost Cyrene, I wanted to throw you out of the car right then and there." Her voice shook with broken, breathless rage. "I've spent every day of my career hunting those Nightshades down and trying to find my husband's killer. They took everything from me!"

"Lyra, I had no idea—"

"After the drop tomorrow night, don't ever speak to me again," she growled, then the line cut off.

20
STERLING

I set aside my rebellion for the night, pondering Lyra's revelations and the attitude I'd had toward her since the day I met her. I idly wrote tickets and slapped them on windshields whenever a vehicle blocked a fire hydrant, parked in a handicap spot without the right sticker, or needed to be towed.

Lyra's pain weighed heavily on me. I had done nothing but kick her while she was already down without knowing her history. I couldn't even be angry at her for not wanting to help anymore. I was the dog biting the hand.

Ordinarily, I would've been cooped up in the police station well into the afternoon, working overtime. But the sunrise possessed an opalescent glimmer as I headed home that morning. When the roads cleared and shrunk to the narrow passage winding into the edges of Neoterra, I basked in the sky's beauty. I couldn't remember the last time I'd reveled in the daylight without darkness looming over my shoulders.

I pulled into the gravel driveway and got out of my car, leaning against its hood to admire the gold-trimmed clouds when the sun hit them just right.

There was nothing like being human. I loved every minute of it, despite the pain that still gnawed at me and the nightmares that spilled into my sleep like ichor. At least I didn't have to drink blood or spend an eternity mourning the loss of someone I loved.

Once I brought Briar home... I knew I'd start feeling whole again. Cyrene would always be in my heart, but that would heal with time too.

I knew Briar was alive. She had to be. I could *feel* it.

Just like how I could feel an unease around Neoterra Police Department. Something didn't sit right with me, especially after finding out they'd cleaned out my files and reassigned me. The assumption that the department crawled with corrupt officers crept back into my mind, but this time, my suspicions circled Chief Duncan. Especially with the Governor's election coming up next year.

I supposed the tranquil morning sky couldn't completely pull me out of my mental disturbances.

Astoria sprang out of her skin when I opened the front door. Her skin was a sickly blue-green, with sagging grey circles under her eyes.

I frowned, shutting the door. "You okay? Why are you so jumpy?" Astoria flipped her hair forward, then quickly tied it into a long, high ponytail.

"I, um, I've done some digging to try to help you with Briar this past week." She reached for a tissue, and instead of blowing her nose, twisted it in her hands.

"What do you mean?" I leaned against the staircase railing and crossed my arms. Astoria was too innocent, too fearful to do the things Briar did. I couldn't imagine her breaking curfew.

"I found out Bri had a friend named Draven Hawthorne, and they were both taken to a place called White Fang, who are supposedly doing experiments. But I also heard she escaped s-so hopefully she's safe somewhere." Astoria spoke so fast her words almost ran together.

"Wait, wait, wait, hold on." I crossed the foyer to brace myself against the couch. I paused, staring at the rug beneath the coffee table and rerunning her words through my mind. "White Fang? Bri escaped? Who told you all this?"

"A, um..." Astoria raised her hand to her mouth and bit her thumbnail. "An anonymous whistleblower."

"No such thing." I narrowed my eyes. "*Who* told you all this?"

"Sterling, that's not important!" Astoria yelled and stamped her foot. My eyes widened at her outburst. She paced again, placing her hands on the sides of her face as she shook her head with a frustrated groan.

"Ria... I only ask because whoever had that information could potentially be a suspect. It *is* important." I lowered my tone.

"Just do research on White Fang, okay? Unless you have other leads better than that?" Astoria put her hands on her hips. "From what it looks like on my end, you've been wasting time and going in circles since you refused to get Vampyre help."

I exhaled wryly.

"Actually, I've been getting help from Officer Hart. She's a Vampyre," I said. It wasn't something I was proud of—ignoring my own reservations about her kind—but I was tired of Astoria making me feel like I wasn't doing enough.

"Oh yeah? Did you hear about White Fang during your investigation?" She cocked her head, her ponytail whipping with the spastic motion.

"Alright!" I threw my hands up. "Since you know everything, who are they?"

"I don't know, maybe some rivals of the Nightshades! You're the detective, figure it out!" Astoria stomped into her bedroom and slammed her door shut. I followed behind and banged my fists against her door.

"Hey! What's gotten into you?" I shouted. I closed my eyes with a sigh, then lowered my tone again. I rubbed my temples.

I couldn't argue with her like Briar. Astoria was gentle, and I didn't want to make her clam up. Perhaps that was partly why Briar did the things she did. We never talked like adults.

"Did you break curfew to get that information?" I asked quietly.

"No," Astoria called through the door. It had to be a lie, but I couldn't fathom Astoria braving the streets alone at night. She was not only timid, but she also respected laws as if they were gospel. We were similar in that respect.

"Okay, then. I'll look into White Fang like you said, and I'll try to have a search party set up since she's escaped," I said, then slipped from her door. I didn't know how to set up a search party when I never reported Briar missing in the first place, or with the department keeping me under their thumbs. It wouldn't hurt to try.

It was finally time. A low-level gangster belonging to the Crimson Daggers was going to help us capture a Nightshade. If they were buying sedatives, then perhaps Astoria's information was plausible. Sedatives on the streets were strong enough to put a Vampyre down, so concentrated that it was near fatal for humans if they weren't careful. The sedatives were banned from hospitals when medical malpractice caused a rise in deaths.

With Crimson Daggers being the supplier, my sister getting abducted by the Nightshades and then sent off to White Fang... it was safe to say there was a more complex operation at play.

The notion that former rivals were working together for a bigger cause was concerning. I needed to know what kind of experiments were happening—and for *what* purpose—if it was true.

I requested a night off with Chief Duncan, saying I needed a little more time to readjust after Cyrene's death. I was a disgrace for using her as a crutch, but if I went to work, I would be put back on parking duty. I was sure White Fang or whoever else would be looking for Briar. Whatever operation was underway, I needed to make sure I shut it down before they got to her again.

I also needed to look more into this "friend" of hers—Draven Hawthorne. I wondered if it was the man I thought was her Vampyre boyfriend, and who I was later told she was trying to get away from at The Nightshade bar. I would know for sure if I was able to lay eyes on him.

I waited at Aurora's Diner around twilight. The doors to the restaurant were still locked as Vampyre staff rushed to prepare for the night.

I scratched my stubbled chin pensively, analyzing Lyra's grudge against me for leaving her at the club. I couldn't help it, every time I saw a pair of red eyes I felt like I was looking into the face of a murderer. Murderers that I had to accept and could never arrest.

Leaning over the center console, I searched Draven on my company laptop. The only records of his I saw were sealed as a juvenile. His status was a Turned Vampyre, and he had to register his newfound species at fourteen. I assumed whatever crimes he was arrested for as a child were fledgling related. For whatever organized crime he was involved in, his record was immaculate.

Draven was either really good at covering up whatever he did, or the police department were in the Nightshades' palm.

Lyra's black SUV arrived at the dilapidated lot and parked next to my car. I shut the laptop. For once, my face didn't heat with rage at the sight of her. I supposed she was getting a little more bearable to look at, but that could easily change if she said something untoward.

Lyra stepped out of her vehicle and went straight into the passenger seat of mine.

"Evening," I said stiffly.

"The friendly ship has sailed a long time ago." Lyra propped her elbow on the windowsill, gluing her gaze to the back of the building. Meeting with the Nightshade wasn't supposed to happen for another five hours at midnight, but we agreed to arrive early in case our Crimson Dagger, Jared, rescheduled to avoid us.

"I'm sorry you lost your husband to them, Lyra." She released a wry chuckle.

"I don't need your sympathy." Lyra leaned back against the

headrest. "You shouldn't need to know someone's backstory to treat them with respect."

I chewed on my bottom lip and turned away.

We sat in silence. I rolled my window down so I wouldn't choke on my own thoughts, trying to focus on anything but the clock.

Luckily, just as we predicted, the two fiends showed up three hours earlier. I wanted to arrest Jared for possession and distribution right then and there.

But... he wasn't priority. Not by far.

The Nightshade wore a black hood over his head, his nose and mouth barely visible. He wore a gold chain that hung outside of his hoodie, baggy ripped jeans, and black boots that had turned brown from dried mud.

Lyra carefully opened the door, easing out of the seat like stepping on ice. I followed suit, slipping my gun out of its holster before I opened the door. We crept along the brick wall of Aurora's Diner and stopped at the corner.

"I asked for four boxes, where's the rest?" the Nightshade demanded in a low growl.

"I-I'm sorry, man, we're just running low on supply between you and the White Fangs." Jared's voice was forced and rushed. "I'll give you the rest for free when we get more in."

"This ain't gonna fly, dude. This stuff ain't being used to get high, it's for something bigger. You *know* that!" The Nightshade shoved the box into Jared's chest and bared his sharp fangs. "You must think I'm a fool. You're holdin' out on us!"

Lyra lunged from the corner and crashed into the Nightshade. They tumbled in the dirt, a cloud of dust, gravel, and obscene words swirling around them. I charged forward, pulling out the silvered pepper spray and shoving Lyra out of the way before deploying it. The Nightshade screamed and writhed as we put silver handcuffs on him. The skin on his wrists instantly became inflamed. Lyra coughed violently, but dragged him to her car and threw him in the back seat.

She slammed the door shut, looked at me with a dry grin and watery eyes, and said, "Thanks."

*

We returned to the secret warehouse, the Nightshade Vampyre wincing and groaning in pain the entire time. Whether or not he got his sight back depended on how soon he drank blood to boost his healing. Lyra had already fixed her blurred vision with a vial she kept in her coat pocket for emergencies. If we were doing this by the book, we would've given him some blood on the way back to the station.

But after the first interrogation with Jared, I supposed I was henceforth a dirty cop, because I hadn't done anything by the book since.

I glanced at Lyra as she drove, her eyes fixed on the road ahead. I couldn't help but wonder how long she'd strayed from the law's path too, and if her husband's death had triggered it. At first I'd viewed her as a shallow pond, but after throwing countless rocks at her, I learned she was an ocean full of endless depth.

For once, I was curious to know more.

The abandoned warehouse's weathered brick and aged cobwebs were virtually invisible in the dark. The crescent moon provided little light compared to the lilac dawn we'd operated under last time.

I helped Lyra drag the Vampyre inside, although I knew she

could've hoisted him over her shoulder like a featherweight. Every time I tried to help, she gave me a wary sidelong glance—but allowed it nonetheless.

We threw the Nightshade in the middle of the dusty floor of what was once surrounded by functioning machines with conveyor belts. I snatched the hood from his head.

"You blinded me!" he growled. He sniffed the air, the grimace of his face slowly softening to a sickly grin. Every single tooth was sharpened. The tattoos on his bald head were primarily skulls and flowers with profanity and gory images. He also had the Nightshade crest in more than one place around his neck. The Nightshades' culture was only having one crest tattooed, but he appeared a lot more die-hard than the average clan member.

The Vampyre began to chuckle, rising to a full-on cackle.

"What's so funny?" Lyra kicked his chest, knocking him back. Even with the air forced out of him, his wheezes were laced with strained snickers.

"Nothing, just everything happens for a reason," he shrugged. "I ain't even mad about being blind anymore."

"And why is that?" I frowned, tilting my head.

"You'll see," he smiled. "Ask me anything while we wait."

"Wait for *what*?" I turned in a small circle as I examined every inky abyss with a flashlight.

"He's just messing with you," Lyra said. "I don't smell anyone in here other than us."

I turned toward them, but spiders continued to crawl up my spine, as if someone were watching our backs.

"What do you know about the White Fangs?" I asked. The sooner we got our information, the sooner we could leave.

"Frenemies," the man said with a nonchalant shrug. "With common enemies, there come great allies."

"And who are you? I see you have Nightshade tattoos all over, but have you pledged loyalty to other clans too? What are you doing for the White Fangs? Is that where all those missing humans went?" I crouched in front of him.

I wanted to ask about Briar, but it was too soon and I didn't want him to connect me to her.

"My, my, you're asking all the wrong questions," the Nightshade intoned. He knocked his boots together casually, then lay back on the floor. The skin around his tattooed-sclerae was an angry red, shining like blisters.

"Stop playing games." I removed my gun from its holster and rose to my feet. The cool steel bit into my palm.

"Stop playing?" He sat upright and sneered at me. We held eye contact, as if he could see me in his blinded state. He grinned with malice, drilling chills down to my bone marrow. "The game just started, *Officer Shaw.*"

I had just enough time to exchange a wary glance with Lyra before eight Vampyres burst through the glass ceiling.

21
BRIAR

"You knew Draven?" I gasped at Moses, failing to consider that this stranger was fishing for information. I forgot I had fangs when I bit my lip and punctured it. I grimaced at its bitterness, then I reached for the orange juice to erase it.

"Yes, ma'am. He was such a happy little boy. He often helped me around my house for money in the summer, and I taught him some guitar." Moses stood from the rocking chair and grabbed a tissue from the dresser, then handed it to me. "I'd offer ya some bags of blood but while you're in this phase, it'll put ya in a frenzy sooner than I can handle."

"Thanks." I took the tissue and pressed it against my lip until it healed completely. I smiled softly, imagining Draven singing a gentle melody as I swung lazily in a hammock on the beach under the white-silver moonlight.

Maybe there could be a bonfire, where Astoria and I could finally spend more time together, and she'd enjoy his singing, and everything would be perfect.

"What... what happened?" I crumpled the tissue in my hand, snapping back to reality.

"Word on the street is Draven's daddy was involved in some drug dealing. He hid it in his crops, provided the supply to some secret mob up in Neoterra. When the crop's yield went bad one year, and he didn't meet his quota, that was when Draven's parents died in a fender bender." Moses shrugged. "People talk up all kinda crazy stories when reality don't make sense."

"It makes sense to me." I tightened my fist, then threw the blankets off and rushed for the door. Moses quickly stepped in front of the doorway, and a sweet and savory scent emitted from his skin. I sucked my teeth and threw my hands up, backing away before the smell became too unbearable.

"Please move out of my way. I need to get to my family, and save him" I said, voice crumbling.

"Is *he* that friend ya mentioned earlier?" Moses folded his arms. I paused, then nodded.

"You're in too much of a fragile state to be a hero, girl." He held out his hands, as if they had the power to block me. "You need to focus on yourself for now."

"You can't keep me here," I warned.

"Oh, I know, believe me." Moses laughed, stepping aside and gesturing toward the door. Beyond its threshold, shining maple floors paved the way to a polished staircase. "I just don't want a young'un such as yourself makin' any bad decisions."

"You don't know me." I really wanted to sound gentle, but every word that slipped past my lips had a sharp edge. I hated that, especially when the man had helped me so much already. He could've left me in the street, either pummeled by a truck or dragged back to White Fang.

"I know you probably love that boy more than yourself and you're willing to throw your life away at the drop of a hat." Moses narrowed his eyes. I paused, pressing my tongue against my lip piercing.

"Come on, Miss Briar," Moses pressed. He placed his hands on my shoulders and gently guided me to the bed again. I peered back at the door beyond him, and could've sworn I heard Draven's screams right outside the house.

✳

When Moses finally left me alone, I spent the time pacing across the bedroom. I chewed my thumbnail—thumbclaw?—down to a normal human's length as I worried about my family. If the Nightshades were able to track down and murder Draven's parents, how easy was it for them to find Sterling and Astoria?

Then there was Draven. What if he met the same fate as Frankie, just delayed?

I pressed my fingertips against my lips, remembering how scorching Draven's were when he kissed me. What if... he truly became an explosion?

Stop it. Stop thinking about it. They only found them because Draven's dad was involved.

I took a quiet step outside the room.

I need to get to a phone. I figured if I could call Sterling or Astoria, then I could let them know I was safe.

At least... before I threw myself into the viper pit again.

I traced my finger along the banister, collecting dust at my fingertip. I followed the stairs to the foyer. Warm light emitted from the antique brass sconces hanging next to each narrow, textured window on either side of the front door. I could see Moses' distorted silhouette in the front yard, tending to plants around his mailbox.

Every room was squared off—from the formal antechamber by the front door to the dining room leading into the kitchen.

My eyes widened at the teal phone attached to the pin-striped wallpaper in the kitchen, glaring against the knotty-pine cabinets and iron handles. It was the first time I'd seen a landline phone outside of a museum on a middle-school field trip.

Even though the phones were made in the twentieth century, I still held hope that they still operated. I crept into the kitchen and pulled the phone from its base. My ear stung from the dial tone buzzing on the other end. I fidgeted with the spiral cord as I dialed Astoria's cellphone number.

"Hi, this is Astoria. Sorry I missed your call, but—" I hung up and redialed. Maybe she thought it was spam.

Another voicemail.

I dialed one more time, pressing the buttons harder and shifting the whole phone on the wall. I inhaled slowly through my nostrils to calm my growing frustration.

"Hello?" Her sweet voice finally broke through. My knees went slack and I slid against the wall as I fell to the jaundiced tile floor.

"Ria!" I smiled, placing a hand over my heart with a sigh. "Thank God I could reach you."

I never thought I'd hear her voice again.

"*Briar?!*" Astoria exclaimed. "This better not be some sort of sick—"

"It's me! It's me, I promise." I could hear the grass rustle beneath Moses' boots as he crossed the front yard. "Look, I don't have much time. I just want to let you know I'm safe. Tell Sterling I'm okay. I love you, and I'll be home soon, okay?" I reached to hang the phone back up, but paused when Astoria's voice shouted through the microphone.

"Wait!"

I gripped the handle tighter as I pulled the phone back to my ear.

"What?" I whispered, glancing back at the kitchen archway.

"Are you in trouble or did you run away?" Astoria's voice was hushed but forced, as if she were trying to fit in as many words as possible before time ran out.

"Don't worry about that. I got away," I said. "But I have something to take care of."

"Wait, wait, we can help!" Astoria pleaded, but this time I hung up.

"I'm sorry," I muttered with a whimper, then slipped away from the phone and rushed to the refrigerator when I heard Moses' steps climb the front porch stairs. I didn't completely trust him, and I wasn't sure how he'd react if he knew I'd reached out to someone.

"Ya hungry?" Moses shuffled into the kitchen, tracking dirt and grass on the floor. He removed his work gloves and stuffed them into one of his overalls pockets.

"Yeah, but not for any of this,. I scanned all the ingredients and snacks he had piled on each shelf. My mouth didn't water until he came around the corner. I tightened my grip on the door handles, fighting the urge to attack him.

"I'm sure. It's bound to get worse. Are ya ready to go to the hospital today?" Moses leaned over the counter and laced his fingers together. I shut the fridge and spun around.

"No, I'm never going to the hospital. I already told you... no hospitals." I folded my arms.

"It's law, Miss Briar." He straightened, inching in my direction. "You gotta notify them and register as a Vampyre now. You could get in serious trouble if ya show up in the system as a human and ya ain't."

I slid my back across the fridge and the adjacent wall, backing away as Moses crept closer. He reached for my arm.

"I don't have time to be trapped in a hospital for six weeks!" I shouted, and shoved him away when he got too close. Moses staggered and hit his head on the corner of the counter as he tumbled to the floor. I gasped, quickly covering my nose and mouth as a pool of blood formed around his head. It was as dark as wine, catching the reflection of the stained-glass pendant light. My eyes widened at the sight. The horror, the beauty.

My knees buckled and I collapsed on the floor. I buried my head against my chest, pulling tightly at my short hair and gnashing my teeth.

Don't do that to Draven. Moses was good to him. Good to me.

Not him. Moses doesn't deserve it. Not... him.

Moses' face grew ashen. I wanted to crawl to him and check his breathing, but I feared I'd reach for that puddle instead. I stared at it, hugging myself as I sat on my calves and rocked.

Don't do it.

Eat.

He could've kept driving and left me for dead!

Eat.

He was like a father to Draven!

EAT!

"I'm s-sorry."

I pounced on Moses and sank my teeth in his neck.

A small, weak groan escaped his lips. My mind screamed at me, saying I was killing him. The thoughts kept trying to pull me away until they finally went empty.

And my fangs sank deeper until there was nothing left to drink.

22
DRAVEN

I LEFT WILTED GRASS AND BURNT LEAVES IN MY WAKE AS I pushed through the thickets surrounding White Fang's compound. Rain pelted at me, sizzling at every touch.

"Come and get me!" I roared, sparks igniting at my fingertips. A drove of Keepers spun in my direction and rounded the side of the building with their guns raised. I slammed my palm against a tall, mature tree, and pushed until it came tumbling down. They shouted warnings among each other as they scattered to avoid the falling branches.

Bullets flew and I jumped into one of the trees, running across a thick branch to dodge. Bark flung in all directions as I leapt between the trees and narrowly evaded their shots, until one sliced through my Achilles tendon. I slipped and held onto the branch until it turned to ash under my palm. The Keepers were already surrounding me as I plummeted into a bush. I let one of them get close enough to grab his leg, then flung him deeper into the forest. I leapt to my feet and roared, turning in a small circle to lay eyes on each of them. Gun barrels pointed at me from every angle.

"Don't make this any harder than it needs to be, Mr. Hawthorne," one of them growled.

I swung a clawed hand at a Keeper who stepped too close. I would've shredded her face if she'd dodged a second too late.

"I'd listen to the gal. We have your best interests at heart, after all." A cool voice came from behind the circle of Keepers, and I winced at a familiar pinch in my neck. I pulled a tiny needle with a green vial the size of my fingernail attached at the end.

Not this again.

I staggered to the left as the ground shifted. Cyrus broke through the circle of Keepers, standing beside Larkin, who did nothing but grin while I gradually lost feeling in my legs.

"Give my son my regards," Cyrus said to him before sauntering back into the building.

✳

They bound me to chains in a room coated in ice, like a giant freezer. There was a large picture window, putting me on display like a caged animal in a zoo. Scientists and Keepers alike often stopped at the window to gawk at me. Luckily, they'd given me an antidote to Larkin's poison and I was already gaining feeling back in my extremities. I supposed they thought the subzero temperatures would keep whatever I had going on under control.

I didn't really care about what would happen to me. All I hoped was that I'd distracted the Keepers long enough for Briar to get away, and she was in a safe place to handle the fledgling phase. Ideally she would go to a hospital... but knowing her, I doubted it.

The cold burned. It wasn't the pain of frostbite. It was like pelting rain on a forest fire, a candle flame fighting against a breath, a campfire starving among charred wood. Clouds of frost puffed past my lips as I suffered tremors and aches throughout my body. I tried to distract myself from my discomfort with my thoughts.

There was no shortage of them.

It didn't sit right with me that Larkin was at White Fang. Of course, the Kline brothers had always had a bad vibe. But there was something about how comfortable Larkin appeared among them that made the hairs stand on my neck.

On top of that, Cyrus appeared to have a son at the Nightshades, and if it was who I thought it was...

I swallowed the bitter taste in my mouth.

I lifted my weak head to the window, peering out into the hallway. I bared my teeth at the scientists and studied their faces for when I'd have the opportunity to kill them. Dr. Ivanov was among them, grinning like a cat that had finally caught its mouse.

"Mr. Hawthorne, do you have any idea what this means?" She pressed a button on the wall and her voice emitted through a speaker inside the room. I merely rolled my eyes.

"Miss Briar's AB negative plasma is a universal donor. It eliminates the need for compatibility. You, on the other hand... I'm still working on a theory as to why you're emitting heat and fire. Why it worked so perfectly with *you* and not the others."

It doesn't feel like anything worked, you just turned me into a bigger freak than I already was.

Dr. Ivanov didn't lift her eyes from the clipboard. "I have yet to see if it has anything to do with your blood type changing after you were Turned, or your temper."

I didn't care about the science behind it, I just wanted to kill her. Nevertheless, I let her ramble because I was too busy trying to ignore the cold.

"What if Briar's blood somehow improved your immune system so much that it's reshaping the virus? What if it triggered your evolution?" She finally lifted her gaze, and I flashed my fangs in response. She smirked and whistled as she retreated in the corridor.

"Maybe I'll use it to destroy all of you," I whispered to myself.

About an hour later, a Keeper shoved a blindfolded man and woman down the hall. The crowd of scientists blocked most of my view, but I could tell they both tried to defy him. Still, the man had little strength against the Keeper. He was almost thrown across the corridor, so he must've been a Sun Dweller that refused to go down without a fight. The woman carried more resistance, so I assumed she was a Vampyre. I sucked in a sharp, icy breath that stabbed the back of my throat when my view of the newcomers was no longer unobstructed by the scientists ogling me.

That's when I saw it.

The loosely curled, rust-colored hair and the freckles across a face full of hate. He had a muscular build and height similar to mine.

I was certain it was Briar's brother, Sterling.

The woman with him must've been an unfortunate bystander. She certainly wasn't a Nightshade, and she didn't have the frailty of a fledgling.

She perked her shoulder up and rubbed her face against the

blindfold until it slipped around her neck. Her eyes darted around the corridor before she threw her head backward into the Keeper's face. She snapped her handcuffs and snatched Sterling's blindfold down. My eyes widened. I vaguely remembered her from the night Wraith, Larkin, and Delilah tried to force me to hunt them. She must've been an officer too. There was no other scenario where Sterling could've tolerated her.

The scientists reeled from the chaos, huddling in a corner and holding their clipboards tightly against their chests. Sterling bent his knees and swiftly swung his handcuffed arms from behind his back to the front, jumping over his forearms like a jump rope. I raised my eyebrows, slightly impressed.

Sterling and the woman charged at the Keeper before he got his footing. She held him down while Sterling yanked the gun and his watch from his wrist. A few of the scientists flashed toward them, and a couple others shouted on their radios, and—

BANG!

A flash of white lightning, and deep carmine spreading across a white lab coat seconds before the scientist's body dropped.

I mustered up enough strength to roar, yanking against the frostbitten chains to get their attention. Sterling whirled in my direction as more Keepers flooded the corridor. He paused for a moment—a glimmer of familiarity in his eyes—before diving to the ground when the Keepers rained darts at them. The woman dodged every dart, running toward the wall and backflipping off it. A Keeper sped toward her to catch her mid-air, but she snapped his neck in a heartbeat. The other Keepers bounded down the hallway, and she fought like hell to keep them at bay while Sterling scanned the Keeper's watch on a panel outside my room. He reached behind him to shoot into the crowd of Keepers before bursting inside.

My heart pounded violently against the cold. I tried to pull the chains when he started running through the keys on the ring. Despite the burning and partial paralysis , I felt energy shooting through my veins and rage boring into my bones, like a wild dog foaming at the mouth, pulling on its leash to get to the postman.

The woman was almost impossible to see in the crowd of Keepers. Sterling kept checking over his shoulder for her status, and attempted every key until the last one. He paused with it just centimeters away from the hole.

"What are you doing? Let me out!" I growled.

Sterling shot a sharp look at me. "You need to tell me where my sister is."

"She ain't here, I helped her escape. But I can track her down, just hurry up!" I shouted. Sterling unlocked the shackles. I rubbed my wrists, the pain taking longer to fade than I anticipated. My legs wobbled as I stood and stumbled out of the frozen chamber.

Once I entered the corridor, the Keepers froze around the woman. She held her bleeding arm—she must have caught a stray silver bullet—with labored breaths. For a moment, time stopped, and for the first time...

There was fear in the White Fangs' eyes.

I inhaled the warmth of the corridor. With the summer dying out and autumn drawing near, the smoky heat indicated they'd turned on the heater. Just the smell of it removed the pain from my wrists and rejuvenated me. My knuckles cracked as I balled my fists.

I rolled my neck, popping it. The red irritation around my wrists faded back to tawny.

"I'm sick and tired of y'all gettin' away with everything," I growled. The more I thought about being at Uriah's mercy since I was fourteen, the countless beatings and assassinations, Briar's capture, and my own, the more fury seared through. Steam began to roll off my skin, intensifying with each heaving breath of wrath.

I fixed my gaze on the Keepers from under my brow, my fingers sharply bent at the joints. I dared any of them to make the first move.

"Listen, Mr. Hawthorne..." Rowena's small frame appeared from among her brothers and sisters. She raised her hands. "You're here for the greater good of our kind. Please... calm down... take a deep—"

"I never asked for any of this. I never even asked to be *your kind*." My body swelled with so much rage that black spots dotted my vision.

Sterling pulled the woman closer to him and dragged her down the corridor back to where they came from. They'd been blindfolded when they were brought here, but if Sterling was as sharp as his reputation claimed, he'd counted his steps and kept track of every corner they turned.

Embers sparked from my fingertips, down to my palms like a live wire.

"Get control of your patient, Keeper Rowena!" one Keeper demanded. She pulled the trigger until it clicked. The bullets went right through me just as they did with the firing squad. I laughed, shaking my head at their useless attempts to put me down.

"Someone get the flamethrower!" a Keeper shrieked into the radio. My fists tingled, the white smoke darkening to black as I drew closer to the edge.

Dr. Ivanov stood near the double doors at the end of the hallway with wild eyes and a wide grin. Cyrus, appearing next to her from the elevator, raised a flamethrower without another word.

Before I could blink, I was covered in flames.

23
CASPIAN

I was destined to be a killer. I was raised to embrace the innate desire to hunt, the insatiable cravings, the need for survival.

My mother didn't survive my emergence from her womb. My father hated her. He suspected she'd had an affair and assumed I was a bastard son until my appearance mirrored his own down to the minute details.

A Sun Dweller's agony was the only thing that brought a smile to my father's face. I didn't feel anything about it—happy or sad, excited or unenthused. I never crossed a Sun Dweller's path unless I needed to hunt when we were too poor to afford blood bags from the grocery store or it was business related. I never took the time out to get to know one. They were cattle, and I was the wolf.

Until I met Briar. I heard her hopes and dreams, her anguish, and I watched those hopes slowly die out like withering flora. She reminded me of other Vampyres like Stella from the club, Samara from Sundance, and even Arlo when he was in his prime with a wife and children. Briar had a heart half full rather than half empty, and she left me wondering if I was the one with the problem.

Then I met Astoria. As drastically different from her sister as the ocean is to the mountains, yet I could imagine that they complimented each other. Her innocence and quiet observations, and her efforts to find her sister despite being terrified… it moved something within me. Her terror with those Vampyres in the alley enraged me. Watching her nearly fall off the roof *frightened* me. I couldn't help but wonder if these were the emotions that tormented Draven and clouded his judgment.

Then there was Uriah's assignment to capture Astoria's brother and bring him to White Fang. Ordinarily, it would've been an easy task. I was already close enough to Astoria and knew where she lived. Yet… it didn't settle right, even though Sterling was a police officer whose sole duty was to keep Vampyres under control, and his heart remained blackened with unfiltered hate.

I stood in the middle of Astoria's living room, watching her pace across the worn runner rug from the front door to the kitchen's archway. I occasionally peered through the sheer white curtains and winced at the dawn leaking through as I waited for Sterling to arrive in the gravel driveway.

"You can't mention my name, what I do, or what Draven does," I said calmly, leaning against the fireplace with arms crossed.

"How am I supposed to tell Sterling what's happening without any of that? He's going to ask where I found out this information!" Astoria spoke in a harsh whisper, like she wanted to scream at the top of her lungs but her brother was listening through the front door. I pushed from the fireplace and approached her carefully.

"Hey, hey." I grabbed her arms to hold her in place. "*Breathe.*"

"I don't know what to do, Caspian," Astoria said breathlessly, fighting off a wave of sobs. She looked up at me with eyes of glass. I could see my own reflection in them, the ghost that everyone else always avoided.

"I need you to be strong. Draven and Briar need you." I sucked in a breath before adding, "*I* need you." I slid my hands down her arms until they reached her palms. I squeezed her slender fingers gently, careful not to break them.

"The next thing I'm about to tell you won't be easy to take," I warned.

"W-what do you mean?" she whimpered.

"The Nightshades and White Fang want Sterling to replace Briar because they have the same blood type. I—" I swallowed and looked down at our hands intertwined. I pursed my lips in a tight, thin line and took a step back, letting go. The mild warmth from her hands dissipated instantly. I clenched and unclenched my fists to rid myself of the phantom of her palms.

"What?" Astoria pressed, her hands retreating to her necklace.

"I'm supposed to take him to them." I stared at the lamp on the end table, unable to look her in the eye. She gasped, her hand shooting up to her mouth.

"N-no, Caspian, p-please, he's all I have—" Astoria's voice choked, every word stampeding through a bottleneck of panic.

"He will be taken tonight. He and his partner are planning to capture one of my men. They will be ambushed. Once they're at

White Fang, he will find Draven and hopefully help him get out of there. Draven should be able to track Briar once he's free." I lifted my gaze from the lamp, to Astoria. She had sunk to her knees, gripping the back of the couch with eyes shut so tightly she forced the tears to escape. Her shoulders trembled, her chest heaving as she fought against hyperventilation. I moved around the back of the couch and crouched next to her.

"I need you to be strong," I murmured again. "And I need you to trust me."

I couldn't tell her the full plan. She'd tell Sterling, and his reaction would drastically change how everything could play out.

The gravel outside crunched, shortly cut off by the slamming of a car door. I gave her a reassuring pat on the shoulder before bolting upstairs. I hid in what I assumed was Briar's room, judging by the rock band posters and vinyl. I stood near the window in case I needed a quick escape, but stuck around to listen in on their conversation. I hoped Astoria was able to pull herself together.

To my surprise, Astoria held her own. Sterling tried to pressure her about where she got the information, but in the end he was dragging his feet up the stairs.

At that point, I disappeared through the window and rushed home before the sun's rays became too strong and turned me to dust.

✳

Later that night, I hunted Wraith down at the King Estate. He was in charge of obtaining the sedatives White Fang needed, and what his brother used to mix in his toxins.

Word had gotten around about the last exchange's bust and the

Crimson Dagger's capture. It was fortunate the guy communicated with us about his incident and how the police planned to stake out tonight's exchange, otherwise my plan would've been impossible.

It didn't feel right to warn Wraith. I wished he could be taken away for good, but I needed Sterling to get into White Fang and find Draven.

I would feel even more guilty if Astoria didn't already expect it to happen. After all this was said and done, though… I knew she'd never want to face me again. Perhaps it would be for the best, considering what happened to Briar after walking into Draven's life.

I told Wraith about my mission to capture Sterling, after which he eagerly accepted wearing a tracker before going to the rescheduled exchange in the same location. I followed the GPS to an abandoned warehouse an hour and a half away. Neoterra was huge, but this was a place in the outskirts.

Eight of us drove out there just in case they proved to be extremely elusive. I wore a gaiter mask and black beanie with a long trench coat, turtleneck, and slacks as I waited. I blended into the van's chipped ebony paint, watching my colleagues scale the building and carefully prowl across the skylights. Soon after, I listened to the glass shatter when they dropped inside. Gunshots ensued, and out of the eight Nightshades that entered, only three came out with Sterling and the woman.

I loosed a relieved sigh. That alone proved they had a fair chance to escape White Fang with Draven.

"I'll take it from here." I snatched both of them and chained them to the bench across from me in the back of the van.

"Where are you taking us?" the woman raised her chin with defiance.

I remained silent, raising my finger over my covered lips. I held up my phone with a typed message explaining the situation. How they would be sent to White Fang, but Draven would be there held captive, and he was the only one that could track Briar down after her escape. Sterling and the woman glanced at each other with knowing expressions, as if they'd developed a silent language of their own.

I didn't have enough time to explain everything. I could only hope that it all worked out as I calculated.

※

Uriah sent a mass text ordering everyone to meet at The Nightshade bar downtown. The sun was high and our curfew was in place, but we all had our fair share of breaking the law. Especially for his sake.

However, a meeting of this scale had never happened before—at least not in my lifetime in the clan—and Uriah insisted in his message that it needed to be when the bar was closed to the Vampyre public.

Uriah stood on the stage where bands would ordinarily perform, surveying the crowd. I forgot how many of us there were—how many of us didn't live at the King Estate. The entire club was filled wall to wall at nearly two hundred. This was only the tip of the iceberg, as the Nightshades clan stretched across the entire country.

I stood at the edge of the crowd near the bathrooms.

"Ladies and gentlemen," Uriah's voice clipped through the microphone. "Today has marked a new phase for us. Not as Nightshades, but as Vampyres."

I tugged at my turtleneck collar with a quiet sigh as the air became tangible with dense humidity.

"With White Fang's new success, we will move forward with purging the NPD. I have a list." Uriah reached in his breast pocket for a sheet of paper. He unfolded it, then held it up. There were three columns worth of names, and I surmised it was—

"A list of the entire NPD personnel." Uriah scanned the crowd and looked toward the back. I went rigid as his eyes fixed on me. Even among hundreds, I knew I stuck out like a sore thumb. His shoulders relaxed once he saw me, probably relieved that I was still loyal to the clan.

"Once the city's protectors are gone, we can take Neoterra by storm!" Uriah extended his arms out to his sides with a bone-white smile.

The entire club erupted in applause, throwing their fists up and punching the air. They began to chant the Nightshade manifesto.

"We will crush the bones of our enemies! We will bathe in the blood of their descendants! We will poison the weak, and nurture the strong!"

For once in my life, I didn't utter the manifesto. Instead I shrank deeper into the hallway, allowing its shadows pull me in as their battle cries galloped against the walls of my chest.

"We will rise and conquer, for the world is ours!" They restarted their chant, and by the time they were on the third cycle, I was already outside.

This was bad... and the sooner Briar and Draven got back to safety, the sooner they could leave Neoterra before it was bathed in blood.

24
DRAVEN

I was blinded by whips of orange, red, and yellow. I shut my eyes, anticipating agony.

But instead there was comfort.

I opened my eyes slowly when I felt nothing but a warmth similar to that of my late Ma's hugs, seeping through my pores and into my soul. Then the heat intensified, and all I saw was red as I barreled out of the flames and extended my palms, releasing columns of fire right back at Dr. Ivanov and the Keepers.

The fire caught on the walls. Some of the Keepers shrieked in anguish as they ran to douse the flames eating through their sleeves and lapping up their skin. Sprinklers sprayed as flashes of red light and shrill alarms blared throughout the building. I released a vicious roar while everyone dispersed.

The inferno grew and whipped from my body with a rebellious

strength against the sprinklers. The flames spread across the ceiling in sheets as I stormed down the hallway toward the stairwell.

I stopped at every floor and searched for holding cells. I ran my hands across the bars, watching them glow like the sun as they melted with my magmatic touch. I didn't care if they were empty or not, I wasn't going to let the victims die on account of my lack of control.

Dry, violent coughs echoed through the corridor from the smoke. As soon as the bars melted, Sun Dwellers and Vampyres alike took to the stairwell. I didn't stop until I reached the people across from Briar's old cell. Azha and Malachi were both backed in the furthest corners of their cells, gaping at me with wide mouths. It was a new form of fear I had never seen before as a Vampyre, not even as a fledgling.

I looked down at my arms—

My skin was gone, replaced by flames themselves. Lava ran through my veins.

"Get out." My voice was a low, rumbling growl, like the reverberation of a churning volcano waiting to erupt. I didn't have to ask twice for them to bolt and disappear into the stairwell.

Everything was tinted red, and despite the loud alarms, all I could hear was my pulse pounding in my ears like the beat of a drum in an ancient ritual.

Ceiling panels dropped to the floor as more of the White Fangs' laboratory fell apart. The air vibrated with heat waves and I stood among the flames, hypnotized by them. The walls groaned and whined, and the more the fire spread, the stronger I felt... as if I was also feeding on everything it devoured.

I slumped to the ground. I couldn't remember what floor I was on or how long it had been since I'd escaped. I had no idea how to turn it off.

I watched the window set in a metal door gradually crack, then implode moments before the whole ceiling caved in.

***

A cool breeze wafted over my skin, sending mountainous goosebumps prickling along my arms and neck. I lifted my face from of a pile of charred wood and fell into a fit of dry coughs. Blackened metal and debris slid off my back as I sat up on my knees. My scrub pants were tattered and turned into shorts, nearly burned into non-existence like my shirt.

I looked around with a squint. The sun was a weak star beyond the thick blankets of fog and smoke. Yet... rather than a mild burn across my skin, I felt an energy—a desperate craving for more of its light as if I was starved. Soot covered the ground, and as I lifted my face at the sky, ashes floated like snow. I climbed to my feet with more coughs and stumbled over debris. Silhouettes of trees resided beyond the smoke line like sickly, twisted arms and hands reaching for me.

I was surrounded by what was once White Fang's headquarters. The wooded area was barren, the trees' leaves dissolved to ash. I kicked some of the rubble around until I found a box of cigarettes underneath a skull.

I released a quiet, incredulous laugh and reached for them, the skull's brittle jaw snapping off. I dusted my shredded shorts and dug through the box. It was half empty. I grabbed a cigarette with hands covered in sediment. It was my first one in a while, and I contemplated leaving it since I didn't crave it like I used to.

But out of curiosity, I snapped my fingers. Nothing.

I inhaled deeply, reaching into the depths of my mind for a small speck of rage. I snapped again and a spark flashed. I raised my eyebrows, then kept snapping my fingers until a soft flame grew on my thumb. I kissed the end of the cigarette to it, inhaled a long draw, then stepped over the rubble into the barren forest.

The fog stretched for miles. I couldn't tell if it was from the fire or the earlier rain, but I moved forward blindly. Among the scent of smoky earth, I could smell cedar laced with sweat and terror. I followed it, hoping it was Briar.

I looked down at my feet, relieved to see they weren't scorching the ground with each step. I let the cigarette rest on my lips as I hugged my arms, finally feeling cool, damp skin once again.

The further I walked, the more bountiful the trees became. I roamed through the woods until I ran into a road and paused at the white line snaking along the shoulders.

Did everyone get away?

I didn't want to risk going in the same direction as the surviving Keepers or White Fang scientists. I was certain they had another base somewhere around Neoterra or the nearest town to retreat to like the Nightshades did. For now, I needed to get as far away from this area as possible.

"Hey!" I whirled around at the harsh whisper cutting through the trees behind me. Sterling and the woman he left with crouched in a thick bush. I stiffened, hesitantly dropping the cigarette and smashing it beneath my bare foot. The heat didn't even sting.

"Yo." I looked around warily, anticipating other officers. I didn't leave the edge of the road. Sterling waved his hand, beckoning me to come closer. I chuckled softly, shaking my head. "Nah, I'm good. Whatever ya got to say, you can do it from there."

The woman scoffed and rolled her eyes, then whispered, "Do we really need his help?"

"Yes." Sterling's response was clipped. They emerged from the bush and moved toward me instead with soot smudged all over their faces and clothes.

"I don't know how or what just happened," Sterling said in a subtly louder tone. "But we really need your help to track Briar. Lyra here can't do it since she doesn't know what she smells like to begin with."

"What makes you think she wants to be found?" I tilted my head slightly. I wanted to track her down by myself. If Sterling saw what she was now... I couldn't imagine how he'd react.

"I doubt she'd want to be by herself after what she's been through." Lyra folded her arms. I shrugged.

"Maybe y'all don't know her as much as ya think," I said.

"Maybe you're the reason she got in this mess and that's why you don't want to help." Sterling's jaw feathered as he balled his fists. "Maybe I should've left you in there to freeze to death."

I chuckled wryly and looked along the slinking road in both directions. I rolled my neck, cracking it with a grunt.

"Alright. We'll find her." I narrowed my eyes and added, "But I want immunity."

"I can't promise—"

"Deal," Lyra interjected, and extended her hand. I looked down at her wan, cold palm before I finally shook it. I returned my focus to the road and closed my eyes, inhaling deeply.

Faint cedar and roses lingered on the center of the road, right over the double yellow lines. I crept along the trail until it became clear she went south.

I could only hope she wasn't dumb enough to go back to her house.

25

BRIAR

I wasn't sure how long I stared at Moses' rigid body after I finally tore myself from his neck. My hands, clothes, and face were saturated with red. His blood provided the splash of color his dingy, yellowed kitchen needed, and for a brief moment I laughed at the idea of being an interior designer.

I blinked, my feral thoughts replaced by a new clarity and gasped at his body as if seeing it for the first time. I crawled backwards until my back hit the corner of the cabinets. My hand shot up to my mouth, tears instantly streaking down my face when it finally hit me.

What have I done?

This man went out of his way to help me. He offered his hand, and I robbed him of any chance of coming back as a Vampyre because I was too greedy to stop drinking.

Moses was a father, son, and friend, and just as quickly as he entered the world, I snuffed him out.

My breaths became deeper, harder, thicker—

I covered my ears and screamed.

✳

I flinched at the sun while I closed as many curtains and blinds as possible. I searched through Moses' house until I found a plastic shower curtain in a spare bathroom. I wrapped his body in the curtain first, then rolled him in the rug from his living room. I left him by the backdoor while I scrubbed the floors until Gloaming returned, when I'd dispose his body.

I guess it had never occurred to me how unnatural I now was until I slung his two-hundred-something-pound body over my shoulder like a flimsy jacket, and the darkness outside was just as clear as daylight. The anvil I dug out his shed was also nothing but a paperweight.

I trudged across the open fields where dry, brittle stalks of harvested corn had been cut down and puddles had settled between harrowed rows. I headed for the tree line, following the smell of damp dirt and fish until I ran into a lake. I crouched at the edge to observe the pebbles and guppies just beneath the surface. With a heavy sigh, I began to unroll Moses' body from the rug. I tied rope around his ankles, and let my hands do all the work while I kept my mind elsewhere.

I didn't kill him, my shadow did. I didn't kill him. I didn't—

Ravens circled the wooded canopy when I hurled the body across the water. I wanted my secret to sink into the depths of the lake with him, but the ravens knew. They were watching the whole time.

I pulled my hood over my head and burrowed my hands in my pockets, then navigated deeper into the woods.

I returned to Moses' old brick house, where the windows were still glowing like floating lanterns against the starless sky. I searched through the house one last time for his truck keys, then took to the road back to Neoterra. He had an old map on his passenger seat, which to my frustration was my only source of navigation.

Eclipsis was an hour away from Neoterra. It was a shame how Moses fatally crossed my path on his way home.

I told Draven he didn't deserve any of his suffering.

But I did.

✳

Autumn was looming and the fallowed fields were destitute. The farmlands in Neoterra's countryside were identical to the ones surrounding Moses' homestead. I thought I would be excited to return home, but instead a heavy rock sat in my gut.

I had to accept that I couldn't live there again. I had become the very thing that justified Sterling's hatred of Vampyres. A *real* monster.

I straightened in the seat and tightened my grip around the steering wheel, making the final decision to drive past the house and focus on freeing Draven from the White Fangs. Somehow.

The horizon glowed like the sun was returning early. The truck rattled as it worked hard to trudge up a hill. I knew my house would be on the other side and my core twisted with trepidation.

I gasped when the siding was no longer yellow, but burning beneath flames.

"Oh my God—" I slammed my foot against the gas and accelerated, cutting through the field and swerving into the gravel. Astoria's car was the only one in the driveway.

"*Ria!*" I blew the truck door off its hinges and bolted, leaping over the porch steps and barreling inside. Fire lashed every inch of the walls, and thick smoke already filled the space. I tried to scream Astoria's name again, but the smoke singed the back of my throat and I suffered a fit of coughs. I staggered to her room, hoping she wasn't in there.

Then I froze in place at the sight of a curvy silhouette standing in the kitchen near the back door. She slowly turned to face me and my blood went white hot.

Delilah smirked with those flawless, pearly white fangs glinting against the blaze. She gripped the straps of her backpack with a wink, then dashed outside in the blink of an eye.

"You *witch!*" I screamed my throat to shreds, taking a step forward to chase her. The fire began to swallow up the archway between the living room and kitchen, blocking the path to her. I faltered, refocusing on the possibility my sister was somewhere in here—dead or alive.

I burst through Astoria's bedroom door and held my arms up to cover my face when embers sprayed back at me. I gasped at the sight of Astoria sitting on the floor with her hands tied behind her back around her desk's leg. Her head hung limply and her body was smudged in ash.

"Ria!" I dropped to my knees and snapped the zip ties in half, pulled her over my shoulder, then froze for a heartbeat when I remembered my brother's gun safe filled with ammo upstairs, turning the house into a ticking time bomb.

A flurry of panic entered my chest. I caught a glimmer in the corner of my eye and saw Astoria's opal teardrop necklace on the floor just barely under the bed. I squatted with a grunt and snatched it, then launched from her bed through the window.

I landed on damp, cool grass with a thud and wheezed from the air jumping out of my lungs. I bounced back within seconds, clambering to carry Astoria as far from the house as possible. I didn't want to worry about Delilah just yet, I had to—

A hollow *BOOM*.

Vibrating heat waves sent us flying through the air across the front yard. We slammed into a ditch, and Astoria was flung from my grip.

For a breath, everything was muted and moved in slow-motion. I coughed and spat dirt from my mouth as I rolled onto my back and poked my head up from the ditch. I watched our house burn like the arson I'd witnessed when I first broke curfew.

Our home was the perfect target. There was no one around to call for help. And all I could do was lay there in the prickly grass and stare at the house, wondering... *how did we get here?*

I wanted to break down and sob, but I looked to the sky and wiped my eyes before the tears fell. I had to focus on getting Astoria somewhere safe. With her necklace chain wrapped tightly around my fingers, I hoisted her over my shoulder and carried her to the truck. At least I'd parked far enough away that the explosion didn't hit it.

❋

Cold air slashed through the truck from the missing door. In the rearview mirror, I could see the blaze dying out with little embers sparking among the rubble like fireflies.

Deep in the city, the streets flared with the usual vibrant neon energy. Vampyres ebbed and flowed along the sidewalks. I sighed quietly, remembering just a few weeks ago when life was so much simpler.

When I was just a curious human seeking some excitement, some kind of purpose.

Then I became a prisoner, a lab rat.

A Vampyre.

And now... a murderer.

The hospital loomed on the hill at the edge of downtown, the epicenter of the medical district. As always, the parking lot was full. I drove under the canopy and hopped out of the truck, then jogged to Astoria's side and carried her inside.

I wished I had the medical knowledge to take care of her myself, because I knew the second I set foot in that lobby, they were going to question me. I tightened my grip around her like a security blanket, careful not to break her.

I guess I couldn't hide my new species status forever. I wasn't going to risk Astoria's life for it either.

I lifted my chin and straightened my shoulders as I carried Astoria's dead weight into the hospital. I finally noticed a crusted bloody gash on her forehead. Judging by its dryness, it must've been Delilah's doing rather than from the explosion.

I stepped in the lobby and the security guards instantly crowded me.

"Hold right there!" they demanded.

One of them shouted for a nurse while the others closed in on me. I shrunk near the front door, debating on making a run for it. It was a bad look with my human sister lying lifelessly in my arms while I possessed fangs.

A couple nurses rushed to the front doors, taking Astoria and placing her on a gurney. I almost didn't let go of her.

"We need to search you before reception asks you some questions." One lanky security guard sniffled something so thick it sounded like he'd sucked up the brassy mustache over his lip.

"Go over there." I followed his pointed finger to a metal detector.

Another security guard stood behind the counter with a grey bin, waiting for me to fill it with whatever was in my pockets. I pulled out lint-covered fabric with an exaggerated shrug. The guard rolled his eyes and waved his hand for me to walk through. My stomach twisted even though I knew my piercings wouldn't set it off. I glanced at them before creeping hesitantly to the front desk.

I held in a laugh when I recognized the gum-chewing, gaudy-red-glasses-wearing woman clacking away at the keyboard. The last time I'd set foot in this place was to check on my brother's well-being when I thought he'd run inside that house fire. I managed to slip by the jaded receptionist with a visitor pass and she was none the wiser.

"Before we get that young lady's information, I need to know your first and last name to check your registration status." The woman spoke around the shriveled white gum that occasionally poked past her glossy pink lips. I clasped my hands together on the laminate countertop.

"Actually, I was hoping to remain anonymous," I said with a forced saccharine smile.

"That's not how it works around here, baby girl," she said, glancing at me over those thick frames. "If *she* was a Vampyre, maybe."

"Well..." I pressed my tongue against my lip ring and tapped my nail pensively. No matter how many ways I looked at it, I couldn't con my way out of this one.

"Briar Shaw." As much as I wanted to say a different name, everyone's picture was in the database and I didn't want to risk someone entirely different showing up on her screen. I'd just be digging a deeper grave for myself.

I watched the woman click her nails loudly against the keyboard and stood on my toes to sneak a glance at her name tag. Charlene's chewing jaw froze in place. I smiled dryly with a short nod, bracing for what would come next.

"When were you Turned?" Charlene dropped her voice lower. I swallowed, running quick math in my mind to calculate *at least* six weeks ago.

"Some time in June, I think," I said with a nonchalant shrug.

"How come you never reported it?" She narrowed her eyes, cocking her head with a sass that reminded me of Vivian.

"I... I wasn't comfortable with it..." My voice faded like a piano key. I pulled my hands back and tucked them in my pockets. I didn't want to implicate Draven.

"If you were bitten without consent, we can write up a report for you to speak with an officer—"

"No," I spoke firmly. I didn't want to be anywhere near the police. Not with Sterling being a cop, and especially not after what I did to Moses. "I just want to move on from it. I'm fine, seriously. Can we get my sister's stuff done please?"

"Oh, that was your sister, huh?" Charlene pushed her glasses up and stood from her seat with a grunt. "This ain't gonna be your night."

"What do you mean by that?" I called after her as she went into an office behind the desk. "Hey!"

I looked around the lobby frantically with blood pounding in my ears. I already gave her my name, so I couldn't necessarily run away. I was observing the exit and the Vampyre security guards when Charlene returned with a sheet of paper.

"Here's a form you need to take to City Hall." She plopped back in her roller chair and pulled herself closer to the counter. "That is a registration form pre-filled with your information. Once you give it to them, they'll screen you for restraint to determine if you're officially out of the fledgling phase. They'll also give you a thirty-day notice to vacate your home and move to a Nocturnal Zone."

I stared at the paper filled with rows and columns with my personal information typed in a bland font. Her words echoed through my mind several seconds after she said them, and that's when it clicked.

"What about my sister?" I frowned.

"Unless she's Turned, you won't be allowed to see her or any other human relatives again, honey. Sorry." The phone rang and

Charlene didn't skip a beat to answer it, leaving me with more bad news to swallow.

I took the paper from the counter with a scoff. I glanced down the corridor and at the stack of visitor passes, tempted to steal one again. Only this time, I exited the building and hoped the best for Astoria while resisting the urge to trash the place.

They could put a mountain between me and my family and I'd still find a way around, beneath, or over it to get to them. I just needed time to regroup.

Once I stepped outside, I ripped the paper to shreds and tossed it into a nearby trashcan. I headed downtown, to the Sundance hair salon that had once made me feel welcome in their foreign world of night. A place that could've been a refuge for anyone if this society wasn't so disgustingly divided. I hoped either Jocelyn or Samara would be there... because at this point, I felt so lost that I feared I wouldn't be able to recognize myself in the mirror.

26
BRIAR

I kept my head low under my hood, trying to shove thoughts of killing Moses and never seeing my family again out of my head. Of all my years living in Neoterra, it never occurred to me that people who were Turned were then separated from their own families. I thought the government at least trusted Vampyres enough to preserve their own blood, even if their species status changed.

I wished they could've let me know if she was okay. That was a privilege only humans had, I guessed. A privilege that was instantly wiped away once I switched sides, and one I took for granted.

And one that I didn't deserve to have anyway.

I kicked an empty can out of my path. It clattered across the pavement and into the street. A car crushed it instantly.

I gazed up at the sky, the stars finally breaking free from the clouds' chokehold. I couldn't stop asking myself if I'd stayed home and didn't follow Sterling's GPS that night, would this still be the outcome? Would I still have turned into a murderous monster?

A cool breeze passed through, curling around the back of my neck under my hood. It didn't send shivers down my spine as it normally would've when I was human. I hugged myself, wishing Draven was holding me the way he did when we danced together at The Hole.

I hoped he was in one piece, pushing through the day-to-day horrors we endured at White Fang. At least until I came back.

The medical district shrunk behind me as I approached downtown. The bright neon lights became blurs, the scents of cologne, restaurants, and rain all at once—I had to stop walking and press my back against a brick wall to hold my head in my hands.

Calm down.

Act like you know what you're doing.

I tried to separate every sight and smell into individual pieces. Perfume... liquor... cigarette smoke... exhaust... smoked meat...

I lifted my head and looked across the street at Chen's Den food truck. I tilted my head slightly, wondering if Chen—or whatever that man's name was—remembered me from the first night I broke curfew and he denied me service. I didn't want to try his food out of sheer principle... but I was still curious.

I swept across the street in a rapid streak and approached the window. The line wasn't long, but there were still two cooks sweating relentlessly over the stove behind the scrawny owner in the window.

"What can I get for you?" he droned. His nose was a lot more crooked than I remembered, as if it was broken at some point and had healed the wrong way.

"Cotton candy," I said, narrowing my eyes.

"That'll be a buck-fifty." He reached up to a rack hanging in the window and grabbed a stick of the sugary cloud. I sighed, remembering I had no money or a phone to pay digitally.

"Do you offer samples?" I asked. Chen groaned and rolled his eyes, scratched his head and shuffled across his truck. He returned with a small plastic cup of pink fluff.

"Thanks." I took a step to leave, then turned back around. "You don't remember me, do you?"

"Oh, I do. You were that Sun Dweller that almost got me put out of business," he sneered.

I gave him an incredulous look. It sounded like a royal exaggeration. He had shooed me away before any police officer could see.

"Well, lucky for you I'm not a Sun Dweller anymore," I said.

"Congratulations, you're now on the losing side, kid," Chen droned, then wrote something on a small pad and counted sleeves of plastic cups next to him. I took the small piece of fluff and tasted it, then grimaced at the sensation of sand on my tongue.

"Wow, your food really does suck. You got a real talent if you can make cotton candy gross," I said, then tossed the cup in the trash and strolled back across the street to Sundance. Chen shouted obscenities at me, but I didn't look back or entertain him further.

My gloating grin turned into one of hope as I approached the salon. Then it faded when I saw that the usual warm amber glow that poured from inside was nothing but darkness. I frowned and broke into a quick jog, then pressed my face against the glass to peer inside.

There were no more black walls adorned by a collage of paintings and drawings. There weren't industrial motifs like exposed brick, piping, or polished cement floors. Instead, it looked like Easter and the eighteen hundreds had vomited all over the place. The vanities were in a regency aesthetic, the walls alternating between baby blue and pink with ruffles and gold accents everywhere.

My heart sunk as I pulled away from the window and noticed "Humans Only" in giant letters on the front door. I took more steps back until I was able to see the salon's sign. It was no longer Sundance, but Bethany's Corner.

My mouth gaped open and my eyes burned. I wondered if Delilah had anything to do with it personally or if it was the Nightshades as a whole, or maybe I'd caused it as word got around about a human apprentice. Either way, the list of things that had been taken from me kept growing.

I released a furious roar and kicked a nearby light pole, causing the light to flicker. My mouth watered at a sudden smell of sweetness and I jerked my head in its direction. There was a patrol car posted in one of the parallel parking spots, a human officer devouring a burger inside. Lucky for me, he didn't see me nearly vandalize a light pole. Unlucky for me... it was taking every fiber of my being not to break that window and devour *him*.

I wiped the drool from my chin on my hoodie sleeve.

"Whoa, what's up with you? Can't get your hair done tonight?" I whirled around to see a man in joggers and a baggy t-shirt and an untamed beard mocking me. I glared at him, baring my fangs.

He sniffed the air. I took a step closer, listening to the calm beat of his heart.

"You ain't no Vampyre." He laughed. "That's some silly fake contacts and fangs."

I blinked for a moment, confused. Vampyres could easily differentiate between humans and themselves. At least... they were supposed to. Whiskey clung to his breath, so maybe that made a difference.

I straightened and gave him a flirtatious grin, lowering my hood. "Why don't you make me one then?"

The man raised his eyebrows and smirked, allowing me to take his hands and lead him to an alley behind a group of silver dumpsters. He held me by the waist and leaned in. I closed my eyes, still listening to the sound of blood rushing through his veins. I never understood why we needed mandatory donations when Vampyres had blood too.

I rammed the man's head into the brick wall and sank my teeth in his neck. Bitter liquid, like the taste of fish with a burst gall bladder, flooded my mouth. I recoiled and snapped his neck before he could react, then spat as much blood out as I could. It was nothing like Moses' blood, which gave me the same comfort as drinking hot chocolate or eating potato chips as a human.

I guess I understood now.

I crumpled to the ground in the fetal position, holding my head as a pounding migraine crept up my neck. I shut my eyes tightly, hearing my own mind scream at me about how hungry I was.

How long is this supposed to last?!

There weren't any humans roaming around breaking curfew

and I didn't have money to go to the grocery store and buy blood pouches. I curled into a tighter ball, wishing I could turned in a grain of dirt without any wants or needs... or feeling.

"Briar?" A calm but empty voice. I opened my eyes to see champagne hair, ivory marbled skin, and piercing scarlet eyes. Cyrus had found me.

I quickly crawled away, my claws digging in the dirt. I inhaled sharply, poised to cry out for help, until a hand pressed tightly against my mouth and the weight of his body pushed into my back.

"Wait, wait, shhh!" he hissed. "Don't you remember me? Caspian?"

My eyes widened, but my tense body relaxed as Caspian moved his hand and stood. I looked at him again, rubbing my eyes. I surveyed the alley for more Nightshades nearby, but there was nothing but trash and bricks filling the space around us.

"It's just me here," he said lowly. All the memories came flooding back at once, being in the cellar, being cut over and over so those creeps could sample my blood, being so angry at Draven...

Then there was Caspian, the one Vampyre without a heart—so stoic and guarded—becoming the only one I trusted in those dark times. Now, I wished I could be that for Draven as Caspian was for me. I wished Draven had trusted me enough to warn me about the dangerous clan he belonged to.

I threw my arms around Caspian's neck, buried my face in his chest and sobbed into his shirt. Caspian froze in place for a moment, but then I felt his hand lightly pat my back.

"I'm glad you're okay..." He squeezed out of my grasp and gripped my shoulder, keeping me at arms length. I wiped my drenched cheeks. Caspian's lips parted slightly, but it was hard to read if it was shock or if he was simply about to speak.

"You... you're one of us, now..." Caspian raised his frosted eyebrows—a reminder that he wasn't emotionless artificial intelligence. "Was this your choice or...?"

"Draven had to Turn me so I could get out." I rubbed the goosebumps out of my arm.

"How is he?"

"I don't know." My hand shot up to my mouth as I stifled another wave of sobs. "H-he told me to run and then went toward the Keepers..." My voice trailed off as I remembered Draven's last words.

Run or I'll kill you myself!

Another empty threat, but in Draven's heightened state, I wasn't going to take any chances. I'd known I needed to leave before his venom rendered me useless.

Regardless, I hated myself for being out here and him being in there, especially when all I'd managed to do was murder an innocent soul in cold blood.

"I'm so hungry," I whispered, crossing my arms over my stomach. I folded over, staring at my feet with a grimace as a wave of knots clenched inside me.

Caspian jerked his chin toward the end of the alley and said, "I figured you must be. I can help." He started to walk away. I followed because, frankly, I didn't think I had any other options.

27
CASPIAN

B RIAR SAT IN THE FRONT SEAT WITH HER ELBOW PROPPED ON the edge of the window, staring blankly at the passing buildings and trees. I drove further north in silence, waiting for the moment she'd realize and possibly suspect I was taking her back to the Nightshades. Despite the tension in my shoulders, there was a tingling in the pit of my stomach as I anticipated the smile on Astoria's face when I had the chance to tell her I'd found Briar.

"Have you seen your sister yet?" I asked to break the stillness. Briar's rose-colored eyes were laced with venom.

"Who told you I have a sister?" she asked, a sharp bite in her tone.

"Draven. When he made me swear to protect your family and find you before they took him away." No games, just transparency.

Especially while she was in the fledgling phase. She was already unpredictable as a human. Now...

Briar slowly turned her head toward the window before she moved her eyes with it.

"Well, you did a great job doing that," she grumbled.

I frowned slightly. "What do you mean? I couldn't just go breaking down White Fang's doors and get you both out. I did the best I could."

"Yeah? Well, *Draven* helped me get out and Delilah burned my house down and nearly killed Astoria." Briar's spitfire words were merciless.

I slammed the breaks, the tires screeching to a stop in the middle of the street. The car behind us did the same, and I could hear them shouting obscenities as they threw a vulgar gesture out the window. They swerved around us, a small trail of traffic following suit.

"Is Astoria okay?" I gripped the steering wheel. Briar shrugged.

"The hospital took her away and told me I'd never be able to see her again." She dropped her gaze to her lap, interlocking her fingers and flicking her thumbnails together.

"Why not?"

Briar scoffed. "She's human. I can't see my brother either. Doesn't matter, though... the house is gone so I guess I don't have a choice but to go somewhere else." She leaned her head against the window with a sardonic chuckle.

"You don't have to abide by that," I murmured.

"Don't worry, I didn't plan on it. It'll just be another crime to add to the list." She forced a smile, then closed her eyes. I hoped she would keep them closed long enough until I reached the Crow's

Nest. Of course, she couldn't possibly have been sleeping, not with the loudness of her stomach and the tremors she suffered from.

※

Briar kept her hand on the door handle like she was ready to bolt out of the moving vehicle any moment. I reassured her countless times that she could trust me, despite everything that had happened and what I stood for. She didn't say anything, just stared at me as if I were a human waiting to be killed.

We reached my apartment complex, where Briar's shoulders subtly rounded forward as she slumped in the passenger seat and pulled her hood over her head. Like always, the complex was teeming with Vampyres driving in and out of the parking lot, or hanging around the pool and hot tub.

Once we reached my building, I crept up the stairs with a grace that she quickly caught onto and mirrored. I flinched and hissed under my breath when the door across from my apartment swung open.

"Nadia," I gasped, quickly jumping in front of Briar. Nadia's merlot eyes flicked between me and her.

"Hey, Cass." She held a teal box with a plastic window, revealing a dozen mini cupcakes. She hooked a lock of her golden blonde hair behind her ear with a sheepish, yet sullen smile. "I heard it was your birthday today."

"From whom?" I snapped, then cringed and held my hand up apologetically. "I'm sorry, I just... I don't celebrate it." I tried to soften my tone. Nadia may have been nosy, but she was always sweet.

"The front office... and you don't? Is it because you don't have anyone to spend it with?" She extended the box further while trying to crane her neck to inspect Briar behind me. I shook my head.

"No, I'm fine." I started to step back, pushing Briar toward my door. "I'll pay you for the cupcakes." I quickly turned around and undid the lock, shoving Briar inside and slamming the door shut.

"Wow, man. I knew you were a little weird and cold but... I didn't know you were like *that*," Briar said, turning in small circles as she scanned my apartment. I scoffed and stalked into my kitchen, snatching the refrigerator door open and tossing her a blood bag.

"She's always in my face," I grumbled.

"Looked like she was clearly into you, Cass." Briar swiftly caught the bag and bit right through the plastic. I watched her until she finished, then pulled the bag from her fangs and examined the holes she'd made.

"Do you have more?" Her pale cheeks began to look pinched and her fangs appeared sharper when she smiled.

"Yeah, but let's drink it from the actual cap, shall we? Like a normal Vampyre?" I laughed softly as I tossed her another one. "Help yourself. I planned on going to the store soon anyway."

I grabbed one for myself and leaned against the counter with a sigh. Astoria had weaseled herself back into my mind for the hundredth time.

"So..." Briar began, wiping excess blood from the corner of her lips. She roamed around my living room until she found a chair worthy of sitting in. "Have you actually met Astoria or did you protect her from the shadows? Did you know I have a brother on the force that absolutely hates your kind?"

"You mean *our* kind?" I tilted my head slightly. Briar laughed, but there was a pang of grief in her face that was quickly masked. I always wore a mask, so I knew the thought of becoming the very thing her brother despised was her biggest thorn. Not telling her about Sterling's capture would be mine.

She rolled her eyes. "It's gonna take me a second to get used to the language."

"I wouldn't know," I said, but imagined it had been a struggle for Draven too. He was the best person on this planet to help Briar with this fledgling phase, both physically and mentally. I couldn't relate to whatever was going on in her head.

"But to answer your question… yes. I met her and I know about Sterling." I moved around the counter to sit on one of the barstools on the other side. Briar raised her eyebrows.

She laughed. "How did she take you as a Vampyre?"

"She didn't. Not at first. I had an alias… inspired by you, actually." I swiveled on the stool and propped my elbows on the counter behind me with a small smirk. "I was Christian, the human that broke curfew like her missing sister, and was trying to find her and her Vampyre boyfriend."

Briar nodded, scratching the side of her face with a pensive look. "She fell for that crap?"

"For a while, although I think she suspected the opposite. I got her to break curfew." I shrugged.

"Shut up, no you didn't!" Briar burst into laughter, slapping her knee. It was the brightest I'd ever seen her face. I nodded insistently with a small chuckle.

"I did," I said, staring up at a blank spot on my wall as I reminisced. "She was terrified the whole time, but there was a moment

I took her to the beach to help her with her fear and, just for a second..."

My voice trailed off as I remembered the tears she'd borne in the sand, and then imagined the tears she must've wept as Delilah tried to burn her alive when I wasn't there to protect her. I wondered if she'd called for me.

I wasn't quite sure what the Nightshades stood for anymore, or whether I truly wanted to be on their side. Not after this.

No matter if that arson was sanctioned by Uriah *or* a result of Delilah's personal spite.

"It's Astoria you're interested in, isn't it?" Briar's voice was a hot rod searing through my thoughts.

"I feel nothing for no one." I stood from the barstool and went into my bedroom to prepare for Briar's stay. She followed me and stayed in the doorway, leaning against the frame with her arms crossed.

"I don't mind it if you do. Whether you like it or not, you *do* have feelings, and they're kind," she said.

I almost laughed, but suppressed it as I fluffed the pillows and put a new set of sheets on the bed. I hardly ever set foot in here unless I had a long, rare night in the VIP lounge at the Nightshade bar. But fledglings would have sporadic sleeping spells until they matured into a full Vampyre.

"If you felt nothing, you wouldn't have made that promise to Draven or made your presence known to my sister. You wouldn't even be making the bed for me right now." Briar pointed at me and my jaw tightened.

"Not true, I'm just doing all of this to clean up Draven's mess,"

I droned. I straightened from the bed and put my hands on my hips with a sigh. "You're still a fledgling, so you might have some sleeping spells before they go away. Use this however much you want. I have other obligations. I'd give you a copy of my key, but the less you're seen out there the better."

Briar nodded and scratched the inner crook of her arm with a sniff. "Do you ever have visitors?" she asked.

"No. Nobody knows about this place and I'd like to keep it that way." I brushed past her in the doorway and grabbed my keys from the counter. "I'm going to restock the fridge, and then I need to get back to the Nightshades."

"Where would that be?" Briar's eyes darkened.

"None of your concern," I replied curtly. I clutched the front doorknob, ready to swing it open.

"Then take me to the White Fangs," she demanded.

"Are you insane? You just left there. You don't think they're already looking for you?"

"I don't know where they are, but I need to get Draven out somehow." Briar balled her fists at her sides, her eyes glazing over and shimmering under the recessed lighting.

"Like I said... you're a fledgling. It would be a suicide mission. I'd rather tell Draven that you're alive," I said, then rushed down the stairwell before she could protest further.

28
DRAVEN

The silence between me, Sterling, and Lyra was palpable. We walked along the shoulder of the road as I tracked Briar's mild scent. They trailed behind me, keeping a fair distance from each other as well as from me.

Two hours passed and I wondered if Briar was taken to Eclipsis, my old hometown. My throat tightened. I hadn't been there in years, not since the Nightshades came and took me away after my parents died.

"Are you okay, Draven?" Lyra asked, holding a jacket over her head. Burns littered across her forearms.

"Yeah, why?" I glanced at the both of them over my shoulder, squinting at the sun beaming down on us.

"Well, you're walking slower and you look like you're sweating even though it's like sixty degrees out here," Lyra responded.

"I've been pretty hot lately," I mumbled. I paused in front of a bus stop. If Briar was where I suspected, then there was no way we could make the trip to Eclipsis on foot. Not with a human dragging us down, anyway.

Sterling still hadn't said anything since the deal we made, but I could feel his eyes boring through my back the entire time. I sat down on the cold, metal bench. "You got somethin' you wanna say, Freckles?"

"That's Detective Shaw to you," Sterling remarked in a low growl. "I want to know why you chose my sister's life to ruin."

I scowled at him. "Actually, I was supposed to kill her."

Sterling sucked in a sharp breath, his chest puffing out as if readying to breathe fire—

"Why didn't you?" Lyra cut in, dousing his bellowing roar.

I think... I might love her.

"She was breaking curfew and I ain't never seen a Sun Dweller do that before." My voice was a breathy whisper. I peered down the road, watching the memories unfurl in my head like film.

"What does that have to do with anything?" Sterling grumbled.

"She was the first human I've seen to *want* to be around my species, and what can I say? She's pretty too." I smirked, snapping out of my daydream just as Sterling reared his fist back, but Lyra held him back by his shoulder.

"I bet you have a whole string of victims in the ground." Sterling's voice was saturated with the venom of an asp. "Briar was next in line."

"No, she wasn't. She's *alive* and free." I rolled my eyes and looked in the other direction. He wasn't totally wrong about the victims. They were either self defense or sanctioned by Uriah. Briar was a problem I tried to handle before Uriah knew about her, and I hadn't had the heart to do it.

The bus finally approached. "I think you're just tryin' to argue to pass the time."

❇

Eclipsis was just as I remembered when I was a child—quaint. There was one main road that cut straight through, between the only two restaurants, a gas station, and a local grocery store where half the food was expired. Flocks of ducks sang above us in their chevron formations—the only sound standing between me and Sterling falling into another argument.

For a moment, I felt human again, ready to approach some familiar faces going in and out of the gas station… until I looked down at the tattoos on my arms and the tattered clothing, and remembered I'd destroyed a whole building hours ago.

Worst of all, I had the eyes every Sun Dweller feared.

"Follow me," I said quietly, and took longer strides toward the surrounding corn fields ready to be harvested. Sterling and Lyra remained silent, following closely behind. I disappeared in the stalks, still following Briar's faint trail from the street. I wondered if she remembered this was the place where I'd grown up.

Eclipsis had a very human population—a buffet for a fledgling.

My temples throbbed at the thought of it.

"How far did she go?" Sterling mused, fighting against the stalks and leaves slapping him in the face.

Briar's scent was gradually getting stronger, and my heart clanged against my chest with every step in the soft earth. I led us to a narrow clearing that acted as a demarcation line between the corn fields and the swamp.

Lyra and Sterling were swatting at bees and mosquitoes behind me, but soon it all became silent as I zeroed in on Briar's scent among the manure and corn. Beyond the fields was a large white farmhouse with a wraparound porch. There were once horses and cattle that grazed in the yellowing pastures.

"What are you staring at? Is Briar over there?" Sterling stepped next to me and held a hand over his brow to shield his narrowed eyes.

"Nah... it's..." I tore my gaze away from the house I used to live in, where I'd once had a perfect life on a farm with my parents... before it was all taken from me. "Nothin'."

I pressed forward, fighting the burning in my eyes, the knot in my throat, and the memories that churned through my mind like blood in water.

※

We reached a small homestead that I'd once revered as a second home. It was the place I went after school until my parents were home from work, until I was old enough to go home and start on the farm chores. Mr. Moses was the one who always smiled and told me he was proud of how quickly I was learning the guitar. He encouraged my passion for singing when my father condemned it. He snuck my favorite desserts to me, like a grandfather who always carried hard candies in his pockets. I remembered the smell of honeysuckles and freshly cut grass as I rode my bike to Mr. Moses' house to help with his landscaping for extra money during summer breaks.

I knew if he saw me now, those wrinkles wouldn't deepen with a smile. He'd see the gang tattoos, the fangs and eyes. He'd see how black my soul was and how far I'd strayed from the principles he taught me.

I stopped at his mailbox when the lingering scent of cedar and roses was at its strongest. Fresh tire tracks had left their mark in his driveway.

I sniffed again, catching the coppery tang of blood and an acrid stench of death mixed with bleach coming from the house.

The birds didn't sing and the wind didn't blow. It was like I'd fallen backwards from the roof of a skyscraper. I was weightless, waiting for the moment I'd hit the bottom with a splatter.

"Mr. Moses?" I cried out, my voice higher than I ever intended, and darted across the yard. "Briar?" I banged on his door rapidly, shaking the stained glass that adorned it. I snatched the door off its hinges and stormed inside. Lyra yanked Sterling by the hand and flashed inside behind me.

"What—" Sterling was ready to demand information until his hand shot up to his nose, his eyes instantly watering.

Then I saw the rust-stained grout in the antique tiled floor.

"No..." I croaked, walking up to the kitchen archway. My hands began to shake, thin swirls of smoke rising from my skin. "This... can't be..."

A million different scenarios formed in my mind, all in attempt to explain Moses' death without Briar in the picture. Yet, deep down, I knew she'd lost control. Her aroma mixing with the smell of bleach was too strong on his property, and the tire tracks too fresh. With the low Vampyre population in Eclipsis, it was next to impossible that any other Vampyre had killed him.

And with Sterling here…

I couldn't let it slip that Briar had changed. Not before he saw her himself.

"You know who lives here?" Sterling appeared behind me, having already scoped the rest of the house with Lyra while I was grasping at threads to pull myself together.

"Yeah…" I ran a hand over my face grimly. "He was like a pops to me."

"What happened?" Lyra's nostrils flared.

"Someone killed him… maybe they took Briar with them." My voice was vacant as I tried to separate myself from the present moment. Just when I thought I was at my lowest, I was somehow buried below it. How much more did I still have to lose?

"They had to. There's no sign of her here," Sterling said as he passed a pistol to Lyra. "I found these in the owner's room."

Maybe if I played along, Sterling could blame someone else for her transformation. I shook my head.

"Mr. Moses probably saw her on the side of the road and offered to help," I mumbled as I rubbed the back of my neck. I crouched to the floor and swiped my fingertips over the floor, then brought them to my nose for a closer inspection.

"Whoa, whoa, whoa." Sterling held his hand out and frowned deeply. "You shouldn't touch anything in here! This is a crime scene!"

"Oh, like how ya went gun shopping in the last five minutes?" I released a dry laugh. "Besides, who's dustin' the *floor* for smudged fingerprints?"

"We can't guarantee you immunity if you get caught being stupid." Sterling tucked his hand behind his back, holstering the pistol.

"Trust me, Freckles, I ain't worried about you cops." I stood straight and went back through the front door, my shoes crunching over the shattered glass. I examined the skid marks leading to the road.

Maybe she went back to Neoterra. If not for her family, maybe to Sundance for guidance.

I strode to the wooden garage at the back of the property for Moses' most prized possession. I pulled the dust cover off his Corvette, an old model predating the Crimson War that he kept in mint condition. He hid the keys under the floorboard directly beneath it, and just as I promised him, I'd never told a soul. Not even the friends I wanted to impress in middle school.

I could feel the memories radiating from the car. I still felt the summer wind blowing against my skin as I sat in the passenger seat when Mr. Moses took it for quick drives.

"Well... what now?" Lyra asked, hooking her thumbs in her belt loops. Sterling whistled and traced his fingers along the car's curves as he examined the chrome finish. I slapped his hand away and jumped in the driver's seat. The engine purred as if she'd just come off the lot yesterday.

"We go home."

29
CASPIAN

My calculations seldom failed me.

I mulled over Briar's concerns as I rushed down the stairwell to avoid Nadia and swiftly hopped in the driver's seat of my car.

If my calculations *were* correct, Draven would escape with Sterling and his partner. Then, Briar wouldn't need to put herself in further danger. However, if my calculations were wrong...

With Briar being in the home I worked so hard to keep hidden and Astoria being hurt and my best friend possibly still under White Fang's control...

I closed my eyes and squeezed the steering wheel when I felt my mask begin to crack. My breaths became ragged as I hissed through clenched fangs. I charged up to a roar, beating the steering wheel to the point of bending it.

Ten seconds. No more, no less.

I ran my hand through my hair and looked around to see if anyone had witnessed my breakdown. I sighed with relief and sped out of the lot to get to the hospital. If I had the ability to teleport, I would've.

✳

The security guards instantly recognized me. Uriah kept most of the hospital staff in his pockets—Sun Dwellers and Vampyres alike—to prevent them from reporting suspicious injuries that couldn't heal fast enough.

I walked through the metal detector without alarms and trekked down the main corridor without paying reception a visit. I wanted to run, but I didn't want to appear worried or draw attention to myself. I didn't exactly trust how deep Uriah's pockets were.

I followed Astoria's scent down the hall—charred, but still earthy and sweet—until it led me to her room. I cracked the door and peeked inside before entering and shutting the door behind me.

An oxygen mask pressed against Astoria's solemn, inert face. Her long, black hair was splayed across the white pillows, like dark branches in front of a full moon. I inched to her bedside and eased into a chair, then scooted closer. I closed my eyes, clinging to the steady beeps that served as a lifeline to my sanity.

"I'm so glad you're okay," I whispered, reaching for her hand. I stopped my fingertips centimeters away from hers and curled them into a fist.

Why am I so bothered hearing about you getting hurt? You've just been a pawn.

I leaned back in the chair, gripping the armrests and inspecting her vitals. Everything was stable. I could tell Briar the news and

240

move on to Uriah's for work. Despite wanting to make Delilah pay for everything she'd done to Draven, Briar, and now Astoria... I had to keep appearances.

At least... until I learned more information about Uriah's next moves.

I nodded with resolve and stood from the chair, already turning on my heel and reaching for the door handle when I heard Astoria weakly rasp, "Caspian?"

I went rigid. My heart cracked. She sounded so small and fragile, like a flower made of glass.

"You're awake." I returned to her bedside, but remained standing. "How are you feeling?"

She reached up to pull the oxygen mask away. "Fine, I guess." Astoria raised her fist to her lips as she coughed dryly.

"What happened?" I already knew from Briar, but I wanted Astoria to know I had no part in it.

"A woman came by claiming she knew where Briar was—" She coughed again and glanced at her empty tray with a deep wheeze.

"Do you need some water?" I interjected. Astoria shook her head and cleared her throat.

"I let her inside, hoping she'd offer some information. But then sh-she pulled out a gun and hit me with it." Astoria reached to touch the gauze wrapped around her head with a wince. She lifted her chin and look at me with glazed eyes.

I sank into the chair. "Then what?"

"She dragged me to my room and said she was sick of my sister destroying everything between her and Draven and her family. Sh-She said since Briar ruined her family, she was gonna ruin hers, starting with me. Then she poured the gasoline..." Astoria's whimpers escalated to sobs. She reached for her necklace and sat up when she felt her bare collarbone.

"Where's my necklace?" she exclaimed. "My dad gave that to me!"

"I don't know... I'll find it, alright? What did this woman look like?" I knew Briar hated Delilah. I understood that... but I needed to know for sure she wasn't trying to turn me against my own people.

"She was a Vampyre with black and white locs. Uh... she...wore an all-black sweatsuit. That's all I remember." Astoria stared at a blank spot on the sheets as she spoke. I pursed my lips with a nod, squeezing my clasped hands together to stifle the rage that simmered beneath the surface.

"I'm sorry you had to *endure* that..." I spoke quietly to conceal the quivering, icy wrath in my voice. I could feel the tightness around my eyes, and no matter how hard I tried, I couldn't soften them.

"I don't know how I got out." Astoria's hand rested on her collarbone as if she could still feel the ghost of her necklace.

"Your sister found you," I blurted.

Oh no.

"What?" Astoria's eyes lit up and she leaned forward with a wince. "Why didn't you tell me?"

"I wanted to make sure you were okay first," I insisted.

"I want to see her! Why isn't she here?" She looked around the room and then craned her neck to peek through the slender crack I'd left in the door to the hallway.

"They wouldn't let her see you. She's at my apartment right now. Once you're discharged—you can see her."

"When do they let me go?" she asked. I shrugged. Right now, Delilah should think she was dead. However... if Briar saw her, odds were she'd make her presence known and Delilah could assume they'd both made it out of the fire with Briar's newfound Vampyric abilities.

Astoria wouldn't be safe in the hospital, or at my apartment since Briar was in such an unpredictable state. But she also didn't have a home to go to.

I leaned back in the seat, running both of my hands through my hair with a loud sigh.

"Caspian... what's going on?" Astoria squeaked.

"You're in danger," I said plainly. "Delilah will surely come back here to check on your status during the day and try to kill you again."

Astoria's face became so wan it looked green. "Can't you protect me? Can't you get me out of here?"

Such a request made my heart wrench.

"I can, but your sister isn't safe to be around either." I slowly rose from the chair.

"Why not?" Astoria frowned. I tilted my head slightly. She was a smart girl. I didn't understand why she was making me say it.

"The only reason she was able to save you is because she's a Vampyre now." I spoke matter-of-factly, failing to consider how much it could impact her.

But then I saw Astoria flop back onto the pillow as if my words had taken the life out of her. I watched her face slowly crumple with anguish as she stared at the paneled ceiling. Her mouth opened and

I expected a shrill cry, but instead the tears streamed down her face in grim, wheezing silence.

A flower made of glass right in the palm of my hand, and I shattered her.

※

I left the hospital to buy more blood for Briar and more clothes for Astoria since hers were destroyed, then swiftly returned. After speaking with the nurse and promising to take care of Astoria's wounds, they released her into my care. The staff looked the other way while we walked together through the corridors, knowing full well that we were breaking federal laws and if word got out, it wouldn't be the police force marching this place. It would've been Mundus Novus' Onyx Sentries.

I wanted to keep the privileges the Nightshades provided regarding power and protection from the authorities. However, as we traded the fluorescent lighting of the lobby for the starlit darkness outside, I began to question everything I stood for.

Astoria hugged herself and trailed closely behind me from the emergency entrance. Any other day I would've been breaking into someone's home to do Uriah's dirty work, perching on a roof looking through a scope, or collecting the debts Draven would've done as a former Nightshade.

What I was doing—with Astoria walking so close behind me I could feel her breath against my arm—wasn't based on the principles Uriah wanted me to stand on. This was closer to what Draven believed in. For the past few weeks, since he was taken, I'd been acting like a Turned Vampyre rather than a purebred Nightshade.

Astoria gripped my elbow tightly as I guided her through the parking lot to my car. She wobbled when we crossed over the beds of mulch and bushes dividing the parking lot in rows. I helped her into the car and drove five miles under the speed limit to my apartment, dreading the moments to come.

245

30
BRIAR

I chewed on my bottom lip as I paced in Caspian's living room, nearly burning holes in his rug. The twenty bags of blood in his refrigerator were already gone and I was pulling my hair out for more.

How long was he going to be gone? How long was he going to be handling his "Nightshade obligations"?

I went to the bathroom and stared at the mirror. My eyes started out as a pale rose quartz, but now they were a little more saturated, closer to a blush pink. I supposed the blood brought more life to them. They still weren't red, but I assumed that was because I had light grey eyes as a human. Wraith's eyes were lighter too, and I doubted he'd ever let himself starve. Let White Fang or the Nightshades explain it, and it was probably my blood type.

I pressed my palms against my cheeks and pulled down, stretching my face. Then I dragged my claws along my cheeks and watched tiny beads of blood rise until the cuts sealed back up as if nothing had happened. I leaned against the bathroom door with a sigh. I wondered how much time I had before the police came searching for my blood donation quota. If Sterling reported me missing, then I shouldn't need to worry—

I heard the door open and ducked like the bathroom door was transparent. I shut the light off, then crouched in the corner near the bathtub.

"Here it is." I heard Caspian's voice and the light crinkling of plastic grocery bags. I sniffed quietly, recognizing his aroma and...

Oh my God, he brought Astoria here.

"This is a nice place you have here," she said. I took a deep breath as I slowly straightened and emerged from the bathroom. I killed Moses... but surely I had enough control to never lay a hand on my own family.

Right?

Could I trust myself to have that control?

"Ria?" I raised my eyebrows as I stepped into the light. I curled my toes over the shag carpet to focus my senses on it rather than the blood beneath Astoria's skin. How Draven had so much willpower when I bled from those Vampyres circling my motorcycle, I wasn't sure... but I needed him to teach me.

If I could face him.

"Briar!" Astoria's smile was bright and she took a step to run toward me with extended arms, but Caspian held his hand in front of her. The light died in her eyes, her arms sank to her sides, and the corners of her lips shrunk back.

"Cass, what are you doing?" I frowned. "You really just killed the hugging vibe, you know?"

"Sorry to mess up your *vibe*, but for Astoria's safety, you need to keep your distance. She shouldn't even be here right now." Caspian reached in the white grocery bag and tossed me a pouch. I only took in its ruby glimmer for a second before I opened the cap and drained it.

"What happened to you?" Astoria asked, reaching up to her bare neck. I remembered the necklace and reached in my pocket, letting it dangle from my fingers. The opal shimmered under the recessed lights like the sunrise I was once able to admire. Astoria gasped and took another step closer, but I shook my head and tossed it to her.

"I found it in the house," I said.

"Thank you! Hey—don't change the subject," Astoria frowned as she flipped her hair over her shoulder and worked to clasp the gold chain. Caspian quickly came to her aid.

"It's a long story." I went up to the granite counter and sat on a barstool as Caspian resumed restocking his refrigerator.

"I don't have anywhere to be." Astoria warily moved to his couch, the distance between us shrinking for only a moment.

"I was taken. I got Turned, and then I got away." I swiveled on the barstool side to side, eyeballing the vibrant cherries in Caspian's fridge. Astoria nodded, back to fidgeting with the opal stone.

"That wasn't long," she said.

"I summed it up enough," I insisted. I couldn't put into words how I was snatched from Sundance and taken to a mansion just to be put in a chamber without windows, how Nightshades cut me and sampled my blood repeatedly, or how the White Fangs poked and prodded at me. I couldn't explain watching a man be vaporized, getting whipped, Draven's smoldering, or killing Moses. I didn't know how much time had passed. It could've been a week or several months, yet it felt like centuries.

I was still trying to find myself again.

"Well... when you rescued me, did you see the girl?" Astoria asked, tucking her knees beneath her on the couch cushions. She leaned against the arm.

"Yeah, and I think I'm gonna kill her tonight," I said. The refrigerator door slammed shut.

"You won't be setting foot out of this apartment until you're not a fledgling anymore. I'll handle Delilah," Caspian said in a cold, firm tone.

"No." I dropped from the barstool and slammed my palm against the icy stone. "After what she's done to me and now my sister? She is *mine*," I growled.

Caspian stared at me, considering.

"You're not ready to face her. Especially with Wraith and Larkin on her side. I'm sure you remember those two, right?" Caspian tilted his head at me. Their names sounded familiar, but I was always better with faces.

"What about them? They're all Vampyres regardless. Except this time, *I'm* not a human they can push around." I jabbed my thumb into my chest.

"They're the ones that paid you multiple visits with knives." His eyes glanced at my arms, no longer covered in scars. I looked away with a wince, as if the memories had physically slapped me.

"You still need combat skills and resistance. Your brain is too fogged up because all you can think about is blood," Caspian continued. "I told you that it's a suicide mission. Besides, the Nightshades are busy right now and I need to find out when and where certain things will happen."

"What *things*?" Astoria cut in.

"Something serious enough to affect the whole city. Maybe even the country." Caspian grabbed his keys again and stopped at the door.

"If anyone knocks, don't answer," he ordered.

"Duh." I rolled my eyes and rested my head on the counter to savor its chill against my hot face.

✳

As soon as Caspian left, there was a heavy silence between Astoria and me. I hadn't felt anything like it since our trip to Helios when she was angry with me for breaking curfew. Except this one was heavier.

I hovered in the kitchen, hanging around the refrigerator as I anticipated a blood frenzy to cloud my senses while she lounged on Caspian's couch. Astoria hugged a decorative pillow and I could hear her inhale its fibers. I smiled with melancholy, wishing I had something of Draven's to bring me comfort as she had Caspian's.

Of course, that'd never happen. Especially when he found out about Moses. He'd loathe me more than I did him while imprisoned at the Nightshades.

But he could never hate me more than I hated myself.

The worst part? I was already impulsive and temperamental before I turned into a Vampyre, so was it really because I was a fledgling, or did Turning just bring out the darkness I was already harboring?

"How does it feel?" Astoria asked suddenly, turning her head to face me. She briefly pulled me out of my rabbit hole of despair.

"Well... I'm always hungry. It's supposed to go away after awhile, though." I reached in the fridge to grab a bag. I set it on the counter and stared at it. Maybe if I made a mindful effort to wait before drinking, I could develop the same strength Draven had.

"Are you excited?" Astoria angled her opal pendant with her fingertips to examine the different colors in the light.

"What do you mean?" I paused and scrunched my face before tearing my attention from the counter to focus on her.

"Well, I mean... you finally seemed happier when you were hanging out at night. Now that you're one of them, do you feel like you found your real home?" Astoria wiggled her toes in her socks before burrowing them into the cushion.

"Ria, you're still my family and right now I want to claw my stomach out. I can't exactly feel any excitement right now." I rocked on my heels as I went back to staring at the bag. I clenched and unclenched my fists, twitched my fingers, and swayed my hips.

"Well... you don't have to break the rules anymore. Neither do I, although I think this apartment complex is supposed to be for Vampyres only, so I'm kinda scared..." She buried the bottom half of her face in the pillow again.

You say that, but I'm still breaking the rules just by standing in the same room as you. I rolled my eyes at the thought.

"I don't think Caspian would leave you here if he didn't think you'd be okay," I said, then started rummaging through his cabinets as a distraction. There was one of everything—a plate, glass, bowl, pot, pan, and wine glass.

My eyes sparked and I immediately took the wine glass, then proceeded to hunt for the wine. I climbed the counter to examine the highest shelves and smiled when I found an unopened bottle laying on its side at the top. I carefully read the label to make sure it wasn't an expensive brand or something irreplaceable.

"What are you doing?" Astoria crinkled her nose.

"Finding a distraction," I said with a shrug. "Hey, can you look around here for a speaker or something?"

She curled her knees against her chest. "I don't think we should go digging through Caspian's things."

I rolled my eyes with a sigh and searched through his drawers for a corkscrew. Astoria flinched at the loud pop of the cork. I laughed at her reaction and she chuckled. I set the opened bottle on the counter and searched through Caspian's living room until I found a voice assistant device, then requested it to play rock music on shuffle.

"Ah, it's been so long since I heard any of my faves." I closed my eyes, bobbing my head and swaying as I made my way back to the kitchen. The music reminded me of The Hole, where I saw Draven's guitar skills and heard his singing voice for the first time.

A time when my hands weren't stained with blood, my soul wasn't black, and I felt at home.

I poured myself a glass, still glancing at the blood bag sitting on the counter.

I threw the pouch back in the refrigerator and drowned my cravings in wine until Astoria faded into the background, and I became nothing.

31
STERLING

Draven sped down the country roads like a madman. In my rookie days, I would've had to chase him down for a ticket, and he definitely would've been the one that got away at that speed. I told him to slow down, but out of spite, the fiend floored the gas.

I sat in the back seat. There wasn't much I could say to change Lyra's mind as of late. We were a better team when it was just the two of us, but as I expected—Vampyres sided with each other, whether they were on the same side of the law or not.

Draven kept the top down. Lyra's hair slapped me in the face as the wind whipped around. I scooted to the seat behind Draven, griping under my breath. Our hair would've been buzzed like Draven's if we hadn't escaped White Fang when we did. If Briar had been there, I would've had to do a double take to recognize her.

I wondered how much more of her had changed.

The drive from Eclipsis was endless fields with scattered hay bales. Occasionally, we'd pass a ranch with horses, Angus cows, or pigs. Draven's speeding cut the three hour trip in half, but he finally decelerated as we drew near my house. We rounded the hill and I gasped at the blackened rubble where the ugly farmhouse with chipped yellow paint once stood.

The place my sisters and I grew up.

The place my mother and father once lived.

The house haunted by memories of horror and delight.

Gone.

Draven swerved into the driveway, the tires kicking up dust like smoke. I was out before he even stopped, sprinting to survey the damage. Only part of the chimney and some wooden framing still stood, rotten and covered in soot. I didn't think about all the possessions we lost, but searched the debris for bones and teeth.

"How could this happen?" I asked, clipped, as Lyra and Draven approached.

"The Nightshades probably did this," Draven said.

Everything flashed red as I yanked the pistol from the small of my back and swung it toward him.

"No, *you* did this!"

I shoved Lyra's shoulder when she reached for my arm. "Whoa, Sterling!" she exclaimed.

"*You give me one good reason not to shoot you now!*" I shrieked.

Draven's gaze darkened under his brow as he dipped his chin. He eased Lyra out of the way and stepped forward until the barrel pressed against his chest.

"Do it," he threatened. "'Cause last I checked, I was a lab rat burning somethin' else."

I pushed the pistol deeper, my fingertip sweating over the trigger. I was one twitch away from blasting him to kingdom come.

"My sister is gone, my other sister might've burned alive, and now you still expect me to give you immunity? After I just lost *everything*? Do you even know what it's like?" Spit flung out of my mouth. Scum like him only knew how to *take*.

"Shoot me then!" Draven roared, his fangs bared and his claws readied. "I don't care what ya do to me, but you ain't gonna treat me like I don't know what loss feels like!"

"Sterling, back off!" Lyra shouted.

"I lost my parents, my home, *and* my human life! They stole my freedom at fourteen! And I almost lost my sanity," Draven yelled, his voice full of gravel.

The steel was clammy in my hand. I focused on the sharp fangs that revealed themselves each time his jaws parted. "How did they know where I lived?" I croaked, tears flooding my vision. "They took Lyra and me from the warehouse."

"Ya can't hide from the Nightshades. It don't matter who you are. Your whole family was in danger the minute Briar got in their crosshairs. From the moment she met me." Draven's voice shrunk with defeat as his shoulders slumped. He wasn't balking at my gun. His lips curled with disgust as he admitted the peril he'd caused Briar. He became a silhouette behind the watery curtain in my eyes.

Between losing Cyrene, my sisters, and my house, I wanted to flip my pistol on myself. I let my arm flop to my side and turned my back, shuffling to the debris and falling to my knees.

"Give 'em space," I heard Draven tell Lyra, who was probably poised to follow me. My eyes remained glued to the rubble, watching my memories float away on the thin smoke that still rose from the smoldering remains.

Stupid, stupid girl, I thought. *Don't you realize the law exists for a reason?*

Unlike Briar, I understood the dangers of the Vampyres' world. But I didn't know that breaking curfew one time would lead to a domino effect as fatal as this.

About ten minutes passed before shoes padded through the soft grass. Lyra stood over me.

"It's time to go. We all have people to call, so... I figured we'd go to my place. I still have my cellphone there." Lyra spoke quietly, like the other officers and paramedics had after I'd witnessed Cyrene's death. As if speaking too loudly would make me break. She offered her hand to help me stand, but I rose to my feet unassisted with a grunt.

I had showed enough weakness. I'd rather see Lyra's face twisted with disdain or annoyance than pity.

Draven was already waiting by the car, peering vacantly at the leveled lot as he waited for us to get in.

❋

Lyra's place was in a serene Nocturnal Zone—a small strip of six townhomes, several covered in vines. The chrome Corvette stood out against the ordinary trucks and cars in the neighborhood. I hoped we wouldn't stay long.

I lagged behind as Lyra dug through a flowerpot at her door for a key. I examined her second vehicle, a pickup truck that shined as if it had been through the car wash yesterday. I scanned everyone's front doorstep, surprised to see the same decorations that humans would have. I expected human skulls or overgrown weeds, but everything was kept with care, dignity, and taste.

Once we stepped inside Lyra's home, I was shocked further.

It was an open layout with abstract paintings, polished concrete floors, exposed brick and piping, a cozy leather sectional, and a large flat-screen TV. Unique pendants resembling stars lit the kitchen and living room while a chandelier made of criss-crossing bar lights hovered over the dining table.

I expected no furnishings since all Vampyres needed were blood bags to drink. Maybe one chair to sit in.

What stood out the most were the pictures of her and her late husband across the fireplace mantle. They were arranged chronologically, from the time they were teenagers to when they joined the force together, got married, went on their honeymoon, and several other vacations.

"Make yourselves at home, I guess," Lyra said, her voice echoing through the apartment. It was furnished, uncluttered. Some of the larger walls still remained bare, and I wondered what used to rest on them when I noticed pin-sized nail holes.

Draven shuffled to the kitchen, plopping in a seat as Lyra searched for her phone. I ran a finger over her mantle and checked for dust. To my surprise, there was none. Not like the strings of lint accumulated on the ceiling fan blades. The fireplace was immaculate, like a shrine.

I chewed my bottom lip and slipped from the living room before I accidentally messed something up. I joined Draven at the dining table, sitting three seats from him. I clasped my fingers together, blowing air out of my ballooned cheeks.

"Did Lyra say who she needed to call?" I asked.

"I guess the chief." He braced his forearms on the table and cracked his neck.

I released a strained exhale, hoping he was wrong. "Are you calling somebody?"

"My friend. I gotta let him know I'm fine so he don't do nothin' stupid to keep his promise." Draven ran a calloused hand over his face with a sigh.

"Who's that?" I tilted my head.

"Nobody," Draven said tersely.

The clacking of Lyra's shoes grew in a crescendo as she returned to us.

"Chief Duncan knows I'm alive and believes my story about getting caught up with a dealer. I said they got away when he started asking too many questions." Lyra presented the phone to us, moving it side to side. "Who's calling first?"

"I need to see if Astoria is somewhere safe," I said. Luckily, I'd made everyone memorize each other's phone numbers. I just hated that it became useful under these circumstances. I glanced at Draven and he gave the subtle nod of approval for me to go first. Lyra handed me the phone and my thumbs froze over the dial pad.

"We ain't got much time, man," Draven griped. I nodded and held my breath as I dialed Astoria's number.

I didn't hold it for long, though. Her phone went straight to voicemail. I felt heat rise in my face and wriggled in the seat with growing panic. I dialed again.

Again.

And again.

"Alright, brother, I'm sorry but I gotta call my friend." Draven's Vampyric strength was the only thing that allowed him to snatch the phone from my iron grip. His jaw muscle twitched as he stood from the table.

Lyra eased into the chair across from me and reached to touch my hand. Despite her icy skin, the gesture made my own frigid heart crack a little.

"I can't lose her too." My voice was coarse.

She kept her tone soft. "There's still hope she's okay. Didn't you say she was in school?"

"Yeah..." I whispered, dropping my gaze to the table.

"Well." Lyra laced her fingers around mine. "Maybe she's in class. Or... maybe she left her phone at home and it got destroyed in the fire."

"Or maybe they took her or burned her inside with everything else. Her car was scorched." I sighed, looking down at our hands. For the first time, her touch didn't trigger my acid reflux.

"What did they teach us at the Academy?" Lyra tilted her head expectantly. Textbook fonts flowed through my mind, as if I had the pages right before me.

"In the event of a missing person, always check hospitals and City Hall for any changes in species registration. Always assume a runaway first, abduction second, and homicide third. If the case has escalated to abduction or homicide, assume the former until irrefutable evidence presents itself to state otherwise."

"You remembered that verbatim?" she asked, blinking rapidly with an incredulous chuckle.

"Why are you so surprised? You had to remember it too in order to recognize it was verbatim in the first place." I loosed a soft chuckle, then let go of her hand and pushed up from the table. I approached the window and peered outside.

Lyra inclined her head. "Well, did you find a body?"

"No." I slipped my hands in my pockets with a pinched brow. I didn't check every nook and cranny of the rubble. Who said she wasn't there or that her body was elsewhere?

Lyra stood, the chair scraping loudly against the floor. She leaned against the wall next to the window, twirling a finger around the end of her braid.

Her gentle whisper smoothed my ruffled feathers as she said, "Then as far as you're concerned, Astoria is still alive and can still be saved."

32
DRAVEN

I stood on Lyra's back porch as I waited for Caspian to pick up. I could hear Sterling and Lyra's hushed voices inside and raised my eyebrows with intrigue when for once, his attitude wasn't like that of a python. To hear him nearly cry over his family... I guess the guy had a heart after all.

I dialed Caspian's phone back to back. He never kept a voice-mail—none of the Nightshades did. And it was past Gloaming, so it was possible he was doing official business.

Then it hit me. Sterling could be a target with the police since he missed his Check-In. Maybe the arson would delay them from hunting him down. But the cops could also be on high alert looking for an officer in danger.

I gave up after five calls and went back inside, extending the phone to Lyra. She and Sterling were still sitting at the dining table.

"Did you get in contact with whoever you needed to?" she asked, glancing down at the phone screen. I shook my head. It was risky, using a cop's phone to contact my friend. Although I didn't have much choice.

"I'll try again later, if ya don't mind," I said, stuffing my hands in my pockets. I looked around her townhouse. "Nice place ya got here."

"Thanks," Lyra said tersely, then took her phone to the kitchen counter and plugged it into a charger. Sterling followed her. I assumed he tried to reach Astoria as he leaned over the counter pinching the bridge of his nose. I could hear the quiet buzzing of the dial tone while he waited.

Sterling set the phone down and buried his face in his palms with a sigh, slowly shaking his head.

"What did we say?" Lyra asked warily.

"I know, I know. You're right." Sterling returned to the dining room table.

"I wasn't gonna say this, but... I think once you reunite with Briar and Astoria, y'all should get out of town," I said.

Sterling loosed a short, dry laugh. "My house is in *shambles*," he hissed. "Why on earth would I stay here anyway?"

I bit my tongue. The humanity he'd showed earlier instantly faded. I remembered that every second near him was another second I fought the urge to claw his face off. If I didn't care about Briar, I would've done it a long time ago.

"Do you boys ever get along?" Lyra asked with an exasperated sigh.

"No, and we don't need to be friends. We just need to get him to his family and never speak to each other again," I said. I dreaded the moment he saw Briar. I wondered exactly how deep that hatred ran in his veins. Would he abandon his own blood because of it?

I shuffled to Lyra's front windows, peering into the trees lining the street and the twilight sky.

"I'll find you, Briar," I whispered. "Just hold on a little longer."

Lyra's phone buzzed. I whirled around and locked eyes with Sterling, who jumped out of his chair and raced to the counter. By the time he took a step away from the chair, I was already at the phone and inspecting the caller ID. His face reddened with a glare as I stuck my tongue out at him and answered.

"Who is this?" the gelid voice demanded. A voice I knew all too well.

"I hope ya didn't have a funeral for me yet," I quipped as I pulled the sliding glass door to step outside again.

"Draven?" Caspian's ordinarily greyed tone filled with color for a moment. "Is that really you?"

"It's me, man." I eased into Lyra's metal rocking chair.

Caspian's voice seemed to drop lower. "Well, what's going on? Are you okay? Everyone is going crazy over here."

"I was hopin' I'd meet you somewhere to catch up. I ain't too comfortable talkin' on the phone like this." I peeked through the slats in Lyra's fence to check for neighbors, but everyone's patio was equally blocked off.

"Yeah, that's a good idea. Meet me at St. Brine's Bibliotheca in thirty minutes," Caspian said.

I considered the location. It caught me off guard, but it was somewhere none of the Nightshades would suspect either of us to be.

"Alright," I said. "I'll be there."

"Yep," Caspian replied stiffly before he hung up without warning. I imagined him at the King Estate, with Larkin or Wraith slithering nearby. After I was sent to White Fang, Caspian had been probably put under the microscope just for being my friend. They might've suspected he was just as corrupted as I was.

I went inside and plugged Lyra's phone back in.

"So?" she asked as she reached in her fridge for a blood pouch. She tossed one to me and I caught it out of reflex.

"I think this is where I split up with y'all," I said, quickly drinking it down and tossing it in the biohazard trash. I shuffled toward the front door, twirling my keys around my finger.

"What did you just say? No! You promised you'd lead me to Briar!" Sterling shouted, storming into my path. He grabbed my arm and stopped me mid-stride. I stared at him, looking up from under my brow with malice as I stifled the urge to rip his arm off. The heat in my arm increased until it scalded his palm, and he jerked away with a pained hiss.

"First, don't touch me," I growled. Sterling took a wary step back, his hand twitching ever so slightly to reach for his useless gun.

"Second, I'll take ya to her as soon as I find out if my friend ran into her. She's somewhere around Neoterra. It's just a hunch ya gotta let me follow." I took a deep breath, feeling the temperature drop on my skin. I guessed that whatever was happening to me was controlled by my temper.

Sterling's shoulders slumped forward.

"I can't believe I'm putting my trust in not one, but *two* Vampyres," he grumbled under his breath.

"You're welcome to trust neither of us and find Briar yourself," Lyra said plainly. "I've been over it a long time ago." Sterling barked a scornful laugh and stomped to the back porch. I smirked at her before I left.

Lyra seemed to have a bottomless pit of patience for Sterling despite his bigotry. I guessed every essential worker had to when they were forced to integrate with the other side.

I caressed the steering wheel of Mr. Moses' car for a moment, savoring the moment of solitude from the two of them and the insanity of everything else before driving off to St. Brine's. The blood bag had satiated my hunger, but I still ached for a toothpick or a cigarette.

Or Briar's lips.

I kept the car's top down until I drove deeper into the city. I kept the radio silent and let the wind blow against my face, fresh and earthy like a dewy morning.

My enjoyment was cut short when I had to raise the roof of the car again. I couldn't risk my face being seen by bystanders, with or without the haircut. The tattoos alone served as identifiers.

The closer I drew to the library, the more dread I felt. I wanted to feel excitement to see my old friend. I hoped he'd kept his word and tried to fulfill his promises. But I couldn't turn a blind eye to the fact that Caspian was always the most loyal Nightshade out of everyone.

Uriah took Caspian in when his own father wouldn't accept him.

So why on earth would he ever turn his back on him?

*

St. Brine's Bibliotheca was a magnificent piece of architecture, but of all places in this entire city with hundreds of thousands of occupants—Caspian chose here.

Cypress Hill University was only for Sun Dwellers. The campus was desolate, the students long gone to their dorms for their Check-Ins. The more I ruminated over it, the more I feared another trap.

I sniffed the air, my eyes darting in every direction for Nightshades lurking in the bushes. Most importantly, for Uriah, Wraith, or Larkin hiding with their paralytic darts. I heard chirping to my left and cracking twigs to my right—and I crouched low, ready to pounce at whatever was behind the leaves.

"I hope you didn't come here thinking I'd set you up." Caspian's voice appeared behind me, from the direction of the chirping. I spun around, the breath nearly snatched right out of me as I expected ten others to be with him. I straightened with a stiff laugh.

"I ain't tryin' to offend ya, but it did cross my mind."

"Has it been that long?" Caspian tilted his head slightly. "Have you forgotten our friendship?"

"A lot can happen in a few weeks, man. A lot *has* happened." I put my hands in my pockets and wandered in circles near the library's concrete steps, still monitoring the black spots the street lamps didn't touch. Caspian sat on the first landing of the steps.

"Why don't you sit down?" He gestured to the stairs around him.

"I'm good, man. Listen—" A glimmer from the lamp above caught on his foot, revealing fresh blood on his boot. I didn't acknowledge it. There was no telling what Uriah had him doing at this hour.

"Have you seen Briar at all? What about her sister?" I wanted to ask one question at a time, but I didn't have the patience.

"I met Astoria here. She's a sweet girl. It took a lot to get her to trust me enough to let me help." Caspian clasped his hands in front of him, bracing his arms over his knees. "She's doing better now."

"Sweet girl, huh?" I teased with a grin. This was the first time I ever saw color touch Caspian's pallid face. He chuckled and waved his hand dismissively. I snickered, then cleared my throat.

"Did you guys find Briar?" I looked around the campus once more before finally taking a spot on the step above Caspian.

"Yes, but... Astoria's hurt. She was in the hospital from the fire but she's out now." Caspian's knuckles tightened, his face hardening with an icy wrath as if he was replaying the memories for the hundredth time.

"How bad is she? How did you find out about the fire?" At least I could tell Sterling his sister was alive... but I dreaded what condition she was in. I worried that Caspian had done it himself— sanctioned by Uriah like Arlo's home—all in the name of keeping his loyalty apparent to the Nightshades.

"She only had a couple first- and second-degree burns. Most of the damage is from smoke inhalation, but the doctor said she'd make a full recovery with time." Caspian gazed at his shoes as he spoke. I blinked, surprised to see him so bothered. While I was in Hell at White Fang, I guess Caspian had had his own demons to battle.

"So where are they?" I asked after a beat of silence.

"Astoria and Briar are at my place," Caspian sighed. He sprang to his feet and brushed off his pants. I quickly rose with a frown.

"What do ya mean *your* place?" I narrowed my eyes. Caspian smiled thinly, glancing back at me over his shoulder as he jumped onto the brick railing. In a moment, he'd launch onto a nearby dormitory roof, and then he'd be lost to me once again until I got to a phone.

"The Nightshades might've been the only family I ever had, but when you've been betrayed once before, you tend to make backup plans." Caspian tucked his hands in his trench coat pockets and bent his knees slightly. "They threw you away like you were nothing. If I make one mistake, they will do the same to me. But at least I'll have my own sanctuary to run to."

"Ya haven't been living at the King Estate this whole time?" I took a step forward, hoping to catch his hem before he jumped. "Where? I need to see Briar, and Sterling is desperate to see both of them."

Caspian laughed so loud the breeze carried it across campus, triggering a few amber lights in windows across the courtyard.

"Sun Dwellers in my home? Not a chance. Astoria's the only one that gets a pass. I've bent enough rules for you, Draven." Caspian's eyes darkened. "She probably would've been better off—their house still standing—if I hadn't reached out to her to find your girlfriend."

"The Nightshades would've burned it down regardless," I snapped, taking another step. "Her family became a target the second they found out about Briar's blood type." Caspian straightened, then dropped back on the steps.

"Not necessarily. Maybe if you hadn't scorned Delilah, Astoria would've been fine. Maybe you and Briar would've been too." Caspian tilted his head slightly, scanning me from head to toe. "Tell me... how much *more* of a freak of nature did White Fang turn you into?"

I struck his jaw and listened to it crack like thunder. Caspian stumbled down a couple of stairs and caught himself. He sucked his teeth and hissed, revealing blood-stained fangs. His jaw was unhinged from its socket and he forced it straight with another crack.

"Don't," I growled with warning, my eyes burning. I inhaled deeply, trying to calm down before I reached the point of no return. "Just tell me where they are."

"If I tell you, then everything will fall apart." He spat blood into the bushes and looked at me with wild, desperate eyes.

"Caspian, *please*." I balled my fists and held my breath, but smoke was already rolling off my shoulders and a beam of light from the bell tower began sweeping over the campus. Caspian's eyes widened at the smoke, and he jerked backward to dodge the light.

"We need to get out of here," he said quickly, then sprinted through the grass. I flashed through the yard behind him before the beam could touch me. An automated lockdown announcement rang around the campus, but we were already off the premises. Caspian leaped over a wide alley and skidded across the roof, kicking pebbles over the edge. I followed, leaving a shallow crater in my wake.

"I should get going. I need to check on Astoria and get back to my assignment," Caspian mumbled.

"I need to see Briar," I insisted.

He held up an index finger. "One condition."

"Shoot," I said quickly. If only he'd said this from the start, before I started to haul punches.

"*You* can see them, but not a word to anyone else about where I live. As far as their brother goes, he can meet them at a neutral spot. He's not coming anywhere near there—or his Vampyre partner," Caspian said firmly.

"Fine! You have my word," I replied, and held out my hand. Caspian hesitated, but dapped me up before we left. I could've sworn he flinched, as if bracing to be scalded.

✳

I drove behind Caspian to keep my scent out of his car.

The further north we drove, I realized he'd bought a place in the Nocturne District. The method to Caspian's madness started to make sense, though. Uriah always felt like the Nocturne District was beneath him and the Nightshades as a whole. None of the clan members would go to the place the Crimson Daggers, White Fang, or anyone else would grovel if they didn't need to. They were considered swine, but Caspian was fine with hiding in the mud.

I parked next to Caspian and carefully observed the Vampyres roaming the apartment complex. They stared at the chrome paint of the Corvette, ogling it like fresh meat.

"Do ya think Briar can come down here?" I asked as I locked the doors three times. Caspian laughed softly.

"No one's gonna mess with your car," he said, as if he could read my mind.

My heart fluttered with both fear and excitement as the clock counted down to the moment I'd see Briar again.

Part 3

Rebirth

33
BRIAR

The porcelain tile floor was cool against my cheek. Muffled thuds and shouting punctured through the music, but I was too busy staring at the recessed lighting above. The bright yellow star beamed down like the sun, burning into my retinas and turning teal with every blink. I didn't care what the noises were, I was too mesmerized by the rainbow bokeh circles every time I closed my eyes.

I flinched at nails digging into my shoulder, shaking my limp body. A face eclipsed the light—he had aureate skin, an artistically chiseled face with high cheekbones, a strong jawline, and alluring lips I couldn't take my eyes off of. I giggled, reaching to trace the curves of his face. I tried to remember where I'd seen him before.

"Briar?" His voice was rough, but rich, like the taste of aged bourbon with a smooth finish that still stung the back of my throat. I blinked. How could a man like that already know me?

"Agh, of course she drank all of my wine." Another voice, honed from steel, dragged from the sink.

"What's wrong with her? I've never seen her like this before!" A woman, young with a shrill, lilting voice. I guess she referred to me, but I was too busy floating on cloud nine, staring at a model with neck tattoos, to care.

"She's fine," the taut voice answered. "Alcohol just doesn't mix well with Vampyres, *especially* fledglings."

"Briar, why would you do this to yourself?" the bronzed statue said to me, and I squinted before he grabbed my wrist and hauled me toward his chest. My head hung backward, then snapped forward like a rag doll.

"Where do I know you from?" I pressed my nose against his shirt and inhaled smoke, wood, and mild sweat.

"It's *me*. Draven." His tone roughened, almost with irritation. I blinked, pulling away from his chest and focusing more intensely on his face.

"Draven? Seriously?" Tears welled in my vision and everything began to ripple. I hooked my arms around his neck and wept, slurring unintelligible words. My head swam. I cracked my heavy eyelids open to see Draven lifting me off the floor. He carried me down Caspian's short hallway and I tightened a fist around his shirt with a quiet whimper as he lowered me to the bed.

"My head hurts," I whined. "Please don't go." He gently pulled my hand from his shirt. I turned on my side and curled into a ball.

"I ain't, I'm just gettin' ya some blood, okay?" Draven whispered, then disappeared through the doorway. The room spun and the bed rocked like a boat every time I closed my eyes. I was about to slip into a dream when the mattress dipped next to me. I raised my heavy head, sniffing the air as Draven extended an opened blood bag toward me. I took the pouch and lay down, letting it hang from my lips like a baby bottle. The throbbing behind my eyes subsided almost instantly, leaving only exhaustion behind.

"Please stay," I whispered, stretching out my hand across the comforter. Draven gave a half grin, revealing one deep dimple. He leaned forward, pressing soft lips against my forehead. He paused an inch away from my skin and whispered, "I'm not going anywhere."

The bed groaned as Draven lay down and wrapped strong, warm arms around me. I buried my face in his chest. I'd never known what safety felt like until that moment, and I only hoped I'd remember it in the morning.

✳

Caspian wasn't kidding about sleeping spells as a fledgling. I wasn't sure if it was the alcohol that triggered it, but it was the best sleep I'd had in years.

I awakened to the deep, resonant sound of a steady heartbeat. I lifted my chin ever so slightly, careful not to stir Draven. The sun scorched my back as it poured through the window. The light gave the bedroom a soft white glow. There wasn't a single burn on Draven's face or arms, and his body carried the warmth of a human. With a new clarity, I observed the curves of his face. I was worried I'd never see him again, yet here he was, peaceful as if sleeping. Heat rose to my cheeks as I pulled away, the pain in my back intensifying. Draven roused in a jolt.

"Whoa, calm down," I said around a yawn, and rubbed my eyes. I tried to swallow to relieve the dryness in my throat.

"I felt you move and thought something was wrong." Draven held his head with a wince.

"No, I just needed to get away from the window." I placed a reassuring hand on his shoulder. "I thought Vampyres don't sleep?"

"Right, of course," he breathed, and gave me a relieved smile. "We don't. I just close my eyes and try to relax sometimes. Are you okay?"

"Yeah, I can feel the burns letting up already," I said. I stretched and stood to draw the curtains. I rubbed my arms and sucked my teeth until the pain and redness faded.

Draven scooted back to lean against the headboard. "How are you feeling?"

"A lot better than whatever I was feeling last night," I said with a short laugh. The only thing that made the hangover worth it was blocking the desire to drain my sister dry.

"Why would ya do that to yourself?" Draven began to straighten out the covers. We slept on top of the comforter, but it was still wrinkled with our bodies' outlines.

"I didn't know I was going to get that bad. It wasn't the first time I've drunk alcohol." I rolled my eyes as I reached to straighten my side of the bed.

"It's sorta common knowledge that Vampyres shouldn't drink," he said. I shrugged.

"Well, I just wanted a distraction. I didn't know it was going to put me on the floor." I shrugged again, tucking my hands in my back pockets. I didn't want to admit I'd fought every urge to kill my own sister out of gluttony, or that I wished to forget about Moses.

"Briar, come on. You can talk to me. If there's anyone who can understand what you're going through..." He rounded the bed, caressing my cheek before trailing his hands down my arms to meet my palms. He intertwined our fingers. "It's *me*."

My throat tightened. I stared at the ceiling to resist the tears, wrestling with the urge to blink. I'd had enough of crying and being helpless, even in a moment of privacy. I was sick of being vulnerable. Most of all, I was sick of feeling like an addict. Like Vivian.

"Cass shouldn't have left Ria here. If that wine wasn't in there, those blood bags would've been gone, and after running out of those I would've—" I pulled my hand from his to cover my mouth and keep the words from escaping.

"I know... but try to understand ya still got a month or two left to adjust, alright? Ya can't go on tryin' to starve yourself to be like me. I've been a Vampyre for over a decade. The only way out of the fledgling phase is through," Draven said quietly. "Besides, starvin' yourself only makes it harder to control."

I nodded and stood on my toes to curl my arms around his neck. He lifted me up and I wrapped my legs around his waist, burying my face in the crook of his neck.

"I'm so glad you're safe," I mumbled against his skin.

"I'm glad you are too," he murmured, cupping his palm around the back of my head as he wrapped the other around my waist. I pulled back, staring at his lips for a moment, but instead loosened my grip. Draven did the same, allowing me to slide back to my feet. I let the space between us grow as I headed for the door. The more

I thought about our last moments together at White Fang, how he was willing to sacrifice himself for my escape, the more I thought about my ultimate betrayal—Moses.

Draven gave me a solemn grin as I held onto the doorknob. There was so much I wanted to share with him, but I feared the truth would come out. I didn't think I had the strength to handle Draven turning his back on me. Especially now, when I needed him the most.

"You'd tell me whatever's botherin' ya, right?" Draven asked. I gave him a small smile and nodded, but I couldn't bring myself to say it verbally.

There were no witnesses that day, and Draven hadn't seen Moses in years. But...

Why did I feel like the ravens had told him?

※

Astoria was gone. I fell into a flurry of panic for about ten seconds before Draven pointed out a note on Caspian's refrigerator, stating she was out buying clothes for us. I was still wearing old rags from Moses' home and Draven looked somewhere between a doctor and a patient escaping an asylum.

Draven walked across the living room and peered through the sliding back doors that led to the balcony. The sun didn't bother him, and I wondered if he'd noticed it yet.

"Have you been outside during the day yet?" I asked as I inched toward the refrigerator.

"Yeah, it's... I don't know," Draven sighed. "I always thought I'd be happier."

"I guess it makes sense why you're not. It's not like we can chill at the beach right now," I grumbled as I swiped yet another blood bag. I bit my lip, telling myself for the millionth time it'd be my last one. I didn't want to keep cleaning out Caspian's fridge. I certainly didn't want him to kick me out for taking all his blood. It was bad enough that I drank all the wine.

"I didn't think it'd take being a guinea pig to be able to walk outside again." Draven loosed a dry laugh as he turned away from the window. "Or that it would take the blood of the woman I care deeply for to do it."

"Happy to oblige," I said flatly and saluted him before drinking. I tried to at least do it slowly. Perhaps that was the first step to self-control. Draven chuckled and settled into a chair.

"I had to work with your brother and his partner to get back here. He's looking for you," Draven said. I laughed with a snort, peering down at the half-empty blood bag.

"Trust me, Draven, he does *not* wanna see me." I ran my tongue over my teeth and stopped at the edge of a fang.

"I think he's trying to come around," Draven said, a flare of hope in his eyes. I wanted to laugh more—at the impossibility of it. He grinned and held out his arms with a shrug. Maybe he wasn't joking, but the thought of Sterling ever being tolerant of Vampyres was equivalent to time travel becoming real.

"Well... I don't think I gotta tell you that White Fang is looking for *both* of us, probably more for revenge than science. The Night-shades too." Draven crossed an ankle over his knee. He spoke with a tone so bland it sounded like we were talking about the weather. I drained the rest of the blood and tossed it in the biohazard trash, then grabbed a kitchen knife and observed my reflection in the blade. I looked up at Draven with a hardened jaw.

"Let them come. We'll be ready for them."

34
CASPIAN

I COULD FINALLY BREATHE.

I left my apartment with Briar under Draven's care. He was more than strong enough to handle her if she fell into a frenzy and tried to hurt Astoria. I didn't have time to focus on them *and* my duties for the clan, nor did I need the distraction.

The Nightshade bar was bustling with patrons, but the VIP lounge was all business tonight—no pleasure. Uriah ordered everyone to receive numbers on a sheet of paper from the security guard at the door. He made us state our names to find us on the list, then grab our number on the table accordingly. It obviously wasn't random, but I couldn't figure out its true purpose.

I took my number—four—and sat at a rounded sectional toward the back with a glass of the same wine Briar had downed. It had sat in my cupboard for months, but just out of the principle that she'd opened it before its time, I wanted to taste it. I was sure it wasn't her fault—a fledgling had little impulse control for anything—but how long before blaming it on that phase would it become a crutch?

I leaned my head back and stared at the ceiling covered in human skulls and nightshade flowers, wondering what Astoria was doing.

Wraith's voice cut into my thoughts. "Long time no see, Ghost Boy."

"When will you use my actual name?" I lifted my head and swirled my wine with a look of boredom. Wraith shrugged.

"Casper seems more fitting." He grinned.

"Well 'Caspian' is what's on my birth certificate," I seethed before taking a sip. Wraith took a seat next to me without invitation, and his brother settled on my other side shortly after. I groaned under my breath. They'd hardly acknowledged my existence when Draven was still with us. Now, I could never be left alone.

I realized I had been spending the last few days—maybe weeks—contemplating if this was a family I even *wanted* to be around anymore.

"My, Caspian, you look rather... *handsome* tonight." Delilah approached our table wearing a white silk dress with fine glitter and sleeves that tapered to a loop around her middle finger. The white contrasted against her skin like the full moon against a starry sky. It flowed and sighed behind her like a wedding dress, and her locs were styled in an updo crown braid. A pearl necklace rested gracefully across her collarbone. I scanned her from head to toe with a stiff nod. She always dressed to get attention, but never got it from the one she cared about.

"And you're gorgeous as always," I said flatly, then decided to stab—

"Too bad Draven isn't here to see you. Not that it would've mattered anyways."

"Oooh..." Larkin winced from second-hand embarrassment as his brother laughed at Delilah. Her smile transferred to a sneer.

"He would've if he knew what he was throwing away," she said, then sat next to Wraith.

"I think he knows." I smirked coldly. Delilah hissed, lifting her cocktail to her lips while Larkin continued to chuckle. An uncomfortable beat of silence followed, with only the bar's music replacing it.

"How was your little bonfire?" I asked finally, wishing I could wring her neck right in front of everyone. Delilah smiled deviously as she crossed a graceful leg over the other. Her leg emerged through the high slit of her dress and Wraith didn't waste a second to ogle her. I averted my gaze, focusing on the wine as my rage simmered.

Every time I looked at her, I imagined burning her alive just as she tried to do to Astoria, or torture her slowly for all the dirty things she did to Draven, Briar, *and* Astoria. She was the catalyst to all of our sorrows. The second I'd made that promise to Draven, I should've known Hell would have broken loose.

I was only one Vampyre, surrounded by hundreds of Nightshade loyalists. Even if I were a reckless idiot with a death wish, I wouldn't be able to lay a hand on Delilah sitting between Wraith and Larkin. At the very least, I wanted the option to drag her down with me.

Other Nightshades poured into the VIP lounge. Uriah sat at a table, playing cards in a circle of Nightshades while a woman sat on his lap, giggling and whispering in his ear. But I also noticed they each shared another crest on the side of their necks—a set of four fangs yawning over an ace of spades.

White Fang is here? In the VIP lounge?

"What's wrong? You look like you seen a ghost," Larkin teased.

"I'm just wondering when this meeting will start." I set my empty glass down just as Uriah eased the woman from his lap and clinked his glass for everyone's attention. The VIP lounge died down, but the booming bass from the main clubroom still reverberated through the space.

"Good evening," Uriah announced. "Everyone should have a number in their hand. There will be assigned squads of four or five people as we enter the new phase. If you have an even number, it'll be four people. If it's odd, obviously five." His bright red eyes scanned the crowd and stopped on me. If I didn't know any better, his jaw feathered under the strain of gritted teeth.

"Find your matching numbers and the security guard will give you the assignment—a list of names and their addresses."

He didn't have to say the rest. We all knew it was a hit list. Of whom, at this scale, was the real question.

I turned the small piece of paper over in my palm. Four. I hated working with a team. Dealing with Draven was wasn't too bad. He didn't talk much, and we always agreed on strategy without discussing it most of the time. But at least my number was even... one less squawking mouth.

"Whatcha got?" Wraith craned his neck to see the paper in my hand. "Oh, nice! Me too!"

"What?" I snapped, a little more roughly than I intended, and wanted to spit out the bitterness as he held up the same number.

"Aye, the Kline brothers are back in business!" Larkin exclaimed, also holding up a four. They gave each other a quick dap.

That's three in a squad. The fourth one statistically can't *be this bad.*

"Pretty sure Uriah did this on purpose. He wanted his best to work together," Delilah crooned as she stood and dangled her paper in front of our faces.

Whatever little warmth I possessed in my body completely vanished. I caught myself staring at her maliciously from beneath ivory brows as Wraith and Larkin jumped from their seats to celebrate her assignment. The loud din in the lounge faded to muffled ringing, as if a gun had been shot right next to my ear. All I could hear was my heartbeat gradually speeding up as I glared at her. I leaped from the couch and barreled through the crowd to the security guard at the VIP entrance.

"What's your numb—"

"Four," I growled, and snatched the paper when he pulled it out of a briefcase. I stormed back inside, stopping in the middle of the lounge to collect myself. I straightened my blazer and took a deep breath, hoping for a little patience as I glanced down at the list and only saw four names. I wondered if everyone's list was this short.

I took a second glance at the names and blinked rapidly.

"Hey." I took wider strides to approach the three others. "I think these are cops."

"Okay, so? Uriah said we were going into the next phase anyway.

That makes this even more fun." Larkin shrugged. Wraith picked at his shark teeth with a toothpick before flicking it to the floor.

"I'd take any opportunity to bleed a pig," he said, then leaned forward slowly with his elbows on his knees. "You got a problem with that?"

"No," I said firmly. "Is Uriah planning to start the war so soon? If not, this isn't smart."

"You wanna tell the boss man that?" Delilah tilted her head slightly and gestured toward Uriah's table. "Draven never got it through his thick skull that it was a bad idea to tell Uriah about *his* bad ideas."

I laughed wryly. "I suppose you're right."

"Well, let's blow this joint and get working." Wraith stood and leaned backward, his body cracking. I felt a gust of wind from behind me, but I didn't turn to see who was running around in this confined space.

"Oh, hello, sir." Delilah and Larkin quickly stood and I whirled around.

"I just wanted to give you guys an extra assignment before you left." Uriah's metallic arm whirred and groaned before he folded it with his fleshed arm.

"For sure, we're up for anything." Delilah put her hands on her hips. I remained silent, waiting.

"You guys are aware of the tragedy at White Fang, correct?" Uriah asked as he lit a cigar. Wraith and Larkin shook their heads, and Delilah hesitated before she gave the same response. Uriah took a couple puffs before opening his mouth to speak.

"I can brief them on that," I finally cut in. Perhaps I could shape the story in my favor a bit.

"No need," Uriah said curtly, "Draven, Briar, and her brother Sterling Shaw escaped. Draven not only escaped, but destroyed the *entire* compound. They have bounties on them, but White Fang wants them alive. They decided that Draven's experiment was a success."

All three of their jaws dropped.

"He's immune to sunlight?" they asked in unison, a tinge of fear across their faces.

"By their calculations, yes. They had a sample of his new DNA and his cells were intact when exposed to UV rays, plus some other scientific mumbo jumbo. They were able to make a couple more serums, but they need more of his blood." Uriah's eyes shifted between the four of us as he spoke.

"How did he manage to destroy the whole place?" Wraith squinted as he tilted his head and folded his arms.

"Draven developed some sort of fire ability and burned the whole place down." Uriah slid a narrowed gaze in my direction. "You think you can handle capturing him and bringing him back? White Fang's alliance is vital in this upcoming war and they're trying to blame us for his escape, and maybe he still trusts you to let you get close enough."

"Of course. The Nightshades will always come first," I said, curling my fingers into a fist. I raised my chin, but the pit of my core hollowed out.

"What I tell ya?" Wraith elbowed Larkin and Delilah. "He's the coldest monster I've ever seen."

35
CASPIAN

By the time I left with Wraith, Larkin, and Delilah, the air was drenched in petrichor and the sky was stained sepia. I raised my face, allowing a couple raindrops to hit my cheeks. I inhaled deeply, but the earthy scent didn't do anything to relieve my head-ache. Instead, it intensified at the sound of the sociopathic trio's guf-faws as they poured from The Nightshade and stood next to me at the curb.

"Becoming one with the earth, huh?" Larkin hooked his arm roughly around my neck, leaning all his weight against me, and poised to ruffle my hair with his knuckles. I shoved him away with a hiss and raised my hand to flag down Hartley. He flashed his head-lights in acknowledgment.

"You can never take a joke, can you, Caspian?" Delilah asked as she rolled her eyes. I flashed a scowl at her before I looked down at my shoes.

"I guess I have different humor." Or none at all.

Hartley pulled up to the curb and stepped out to open the back door for us.

"Shotgun!" Wraith announced before jogging to the passenger seat. Larkin climbed in first, then Delilah, and finally—with every bone screaming to go the opposite way—I moved into the back seat.

"Where to?" Hartley looked in the rearview mirror directly at me. I opened my mouth to speak, but Wraith tapped his arm and waved his finger at the street ahead of us.

"Take us back home, we need to get ready," Wraith demanded. I sighed, turning to mentally escape through the window. The sooner we completed the mission, the sooner I could get away from them.

✳

We went to Uriah's small armory beneath the garage. We were gathering suppressors, rifles, and anything else we would need for the first target on our list—Amanda Calloway, fifteen years loyal to the force, but even more loyal to the bribes she received from both the Nightshades and other lower-level Vampyre thugs. I'd never particularly cared for the police, but I didn't hate them at the level Draven, Wraith, and Larkin did. I only appreciated how the superior officers were able to keep quiet about us when we needed it. But for them to agree to such vile acts eased whatever qualms I had about this mission. I viewed it as doing Neoterra a favor by ridding them of corruption.

Larkin gathered his favorite knives while Wraith and Delilah debated their preferred weapons. I remained silent, scanning the pegged walls of rifles, shotguns, and pistols like the shelves of a grocery store.

"These are all too loud and flashy," I said. The armory went silent.

"What do you suggest then, genius?" Wraith sucked his teeth and squinted his eyes.

"Larkin's poisons and maybe the bows. We don't need gunfire to alert the neighborhood. Even the suppressors aren't good enough." I ignored his snarky response and kept a matter-of-fact tone as I reached for a longbow off the rack. I loaded a small pack of arrows and slung the strap across my chest.

"He's got a point," Delilah said, and grabbed a crossbow. Despite her concurrence, I cut my eyes at her. The sheer sound of her voice dug under my skin.

"We'll pack some just in case anyway," Wraith insisted with a dry chuckle as Larkin gathered a wallet full of his toxic darts. I eyed him cautiously, remembering those were the same darts he'd used against Draven. The difference between my friend and me—I'd never turn my back on these people.

"Let's get going," I said, and stalked to a heavily tinted van, hopping in the driver's seat. I knew I would be vulnerable as a driver with the three of them surrounding me, but I didn't want to risk Wraith or Larkin drawing attention behind the wheel.

Or driving *me* into a trap.

I watched Wraith, Larkin, and Delilah huddle together. Between the van's rumble, the thick bulletproof glass, and the radio I couldn't silence from electrical issues, I couldn't hear what they were whispering. Larkin's eyes shifted in my direction briefly. I tightened my grip on the steering wheel and held my breath. I didn't doubt they were plotting my demise right in front of my face and assuming I was too stupid to come to that conclusion. Regardless of their intentions, I double-checked the two silver-tipped daggers tucked in my internal waistband holsters.

They piled into the van without another word. I didn't react or question their little meeting. Wraith turned the radio to a station he and his circle preferred, and I pulled out of the garage. The windshield was immediately pelted by sheets of rain. I flicked the wipers on and pressed forward. The rain was an inconvenience, but it would serve us well for a mission like this.

I drove carefully since the tires barely had any tread. Lights from other vehicles stretched and smeared through the windshield. The storm deepened the further I drove into the city.

Amanda Calloway lived in a Nocturnal Zone. It was a rough neighborhood with mostly overgrown lawns, chain-link fences that leaned from soil creep, and deep cracks interlaced across the driveways. Her house was the only one with a patrol car parked in its driveway and I kept driving past it when the GPS announced we had arrived. Wraith was in the back seat chewing on the stick of a lollipop he found somewhere in the van, and Larkin was counting the poisoned darts in his wallet. Delilah was on her phone the entire ride and only looked up when I decelerated.

I parked one street over, next to a house with a "For Sale" sign.

"Alright, we're here. We're gonna make this quick." I twisted in my seat. "That means no stealing or touching other things. No graffiti or spitting or defecating on the property, *Wraith*—and no torture. We're not trying to leave any evidence."

"Who died and made you Alpha?" Larkin scoffed.

I pinched the bridge of my nose. "Nobody, but while you're thinking you're defiling a police officer's house for fun, you're leaving the Nightshades vulnerable. The officers will only go so far to cover our tails if we're picking off their own people," I said through gritted teeth.

"He's... not wrong." Delilah tucked her phone back in her pocket. I slid my gaze toward her before turning my head in her direction.

"Why are you agreeing with me so much? Scared I might spill about your little rogue mission?" I laced my tone with venom, and she frowned like I was speaking a different language. "Don't play dumb."

"Oh that wasn't rogue," Wraith chimed in with a laugh. "Uriah called that in when we got news about Sterling and Draven's escape. Oh, by the way... you wouldn't have had anything to do with that, would you?" He pointed the lollipop stick at me.

I ignored him and grabbed the longbow before jumping out of the driver's seat. I dropped into a puddle as the cold rain soaked through my hair, and ran down my leather trench coat and combat boots.

"Not gonna talk?" Wraith demanded as the three of them followed me out of the van.

"We're not here to *talk*," I barked with a leer, and Larkin elbowed my chest, throwing me against the van. Lightning flashed and glinted off the needle between his fingers. I slumped forward, pretending to rub my back with a wince before snatching one of the daggers from my waistband and slashing it deep across Larkin's throat without hesitation. His hand shot to his neck, blood spurting past his fingers faster than he could heal. I snatched the pistol from his holster before he staggered backward, a thick gurgle in his throat.

Delilah gasped as Larkin collapsed onto his back. I stood there with a blank face, watching the blood mix with the rain pooling around him.

"*Lark!*" Wraith shrieked, then lunged at me with a bulleted fist. I ducked and his knuckles clanged against the side of the van with a force that nearly knocked it on its side. Lights began to turn on in nearby houses.

I jumped on the van's roof and searched for Delilah, but she was nowhere to be found, as usual.

Wind shot out of my chest as I flew off the roof with a backflip and landed on my feet clumsily. I fell to one knee, bracing one arm on the ground and extending the other with the pistol I'd stolen. Wraith took my place on the roof with a wild look in his black-and-red eyes, every sharpened fang bared. There was pain—a kind I'd never seen cross his face before—as he pointed two pistols in my direction.

"You..." His chest heaved as his face wrinkled in anguish and rage. "YOU KILLED MY BROTHER!"

His distress brought a sardonic smile to my face.

"He had it coming," I said with a shrug, "You do too."

Wraith roared and rained down bullets. I flashed forward, ramming my shoulder into the van and this time knocking it on its side. Wraith was flung off, and he shouted in agony when the van pinned his legs down. His pistols shined under the street lamp ten feet from us. As he wriggled beneath the van—probably weak from a lack of blood—I kicked his weapons into the storm drain.

I prowled back to Wraith with a subtle smirk and pointed my gun at his head.

"I'll find you, Caspian. I'll never stop until I do!" He shouted with all his might, drowning out the thunder that broke through. "You're *dead*!"

"I hope you do. I'll enjoy breaking you," I challenged, and holstered my gun. I kicked a puddle into his face and dragged Larkin's body next to him. I smiled at Wraith.

His screams became a symphony while I pulled his brother's head from the rest of his body, ensuring he'd never return.

✳

With Delilah nowhere to be found and the surrounding houses stirring from the commotion, I had to leave the neighborhood as soon as possible. I left on foot, hopefully leaving Wraith to get arrested. Odds were he'd still go free since no police officers had been picked off yet, so I had little time to put distance between us.

Blood pounded in my ears as I jumped across roofs and treetops. Car alarms blared, club music pounded through brick walls, and distant cries told of victims being mugged or carjacked. It must've been a full moon beyond those clouds in the black sky, because lunacy dominated the streets tonight.

I ran until I cut through an alley. I pressed my back against the wall, sliding to the concrete with heaving breaths. I buried my face in my hands, my entire body trembling violently.

What have I done?

I'd destroyed everything I built. The trust, the control. My home.

There was no way I could ever return to the Nightshades.

I let them get to me. I let my emotions drive my actions.

"You look like you've had a rough night, son."

I snatched my gun from the holster, racked it and shot to my feet. I pointed the barrel in the voice's direction. Then every joint locked in place and my breath caught in my throat.

The demon I'd been running from for as long as I could remember stared back at me. He had a face like mine, aside from the long scar carved along the left side of his face from his hairline to his chin—a scar *I* gave him when I refused to join White Fang—

"Father," I croaked. My throat and chest were caving in. I tightened my grip on the gun, my finger quivering over the trigger. But it seemed I couldn't regain that control over my body yet. Cyrus smiled as he extended his arms to his sides. His milky blind eye and his clear, piercing scarlet one fixed on mine.

"Is this how you're gonna treat your own blood?" He raised his eyebrows, but the menacing smirk never faltered. "If you're gonna shoot your old man, go ahead. Be a man and shoot."

My fingers ached from how tightly I grasped the gun. The freezing rain numbed the rest of my body, and short puffs of smoke left my lips as I resisted hyperventilating.

"What do you want?" My voice sounded as if I swallowed gravel.

With his arms still extended, Cyrus shrugged and said, "I want us to have a heart-to-heart."

36
DRAVEN

CASPIAN WAS GONE ALL LAST NIGHT AND AFTERNOON. WHILE I wanted to be concerned for his safety, I figured whatever the Nightshades had planned, it was keeping him busy. Better he found out information that could help us.

Astoria returned with bags of clothes for the three of us to wear, as well as extra toiletries. It took about two hours for all of us to get ready. Briar insisted she took the longest time in the bathroom, but I was convinced I took the title. I couldn't remember the last time I had a long, hot shower without Keepers monitoring me or the water pressure feeling like it was slicing through my bones.

Regardless, I let Briar have the win. I was just glad to see her swaying to music and playing with her makeup again. Although... something was still off. She didn't smile when her favorite songs came on. She only silently mouthed the lyrics, like they were text-book passages she had to recite while she put on mascara.

I was lounging on the couch in a black hoodie and navy joggers, watching Astoria rummage through Caspian's kitchen with one idle hand fidgeting with a lock of her long hair. Her eyes lingered over the empty cabinets with a sigh. When Astoria finally opened the fridge, she instantly closed it like a monster hid in it. Only two blood bags were in there, and I assumed that was what startled her. I guess it was easy to forget she was staying in a Vampyre's home until she set foot in the kitchen.

I rose from the couch and pulled the hood over my head.

"You must be starvin', huh?" I asked her. Astoria flinched at my sudden appearance and gave a sheepish smile as her eyes blinked rapidly.

"A little. I'm fine, though. Really." She waved her hand dismissively.

"I promise you, it's no big deal for us to find you somethin'," I insisted. "Caspian ain't gonna have anything in here for ya."

I heard the light switch click and heavy footsteps drag from the bathroom. I felt heat rise to my cheeks as I observed Briar from head to toe. Her face glowed like the full moon with her cherry blossom eyes glistening like raindrops on flower petals, contrasted by dark liner and lashes, matte mahogany lipstick, and red smokey eye shadow. Briar's pixie cut was somewhat longer than when she first arrived at White Fang, with the pink dye nearly gone and the natural black hair becoming more dominant. Without the dye, it was even more apparent she and Astoria were related.

I ogled at the once-frail frame now filling out the curves of her ripped jeans. She raised her eyebrows and tucked her hands in the pockets of her cropped, grey denim jacket with her thumbs hanging out. She wore a graphic tee with her favorite band—a thoughtful touch on Astoria's part. I whistled and she tilted her head with an amused grin.

"You look amazing." I leaned against the wall and folded my arms with a flirtatious smile. Briar rolled her eyes with a laugh.

"Thanks. I'm just glad Astoria didn't forget my style." She winked at her sister, who giggled with a playful bow.

"Are y'all ready to see your brother?" I asked them. Astoria nodded eagerly, but the smile ran away from Briar's face, replaced by unease. She shrugged, throwing the hood over her head and walking out without another word. Astoria followed behind her, and I used Caspian's extra key to lock up.

Caspian's neighbor poked her head through her door and quickly shut it when I glanced over my shoulder. My skin crawled, but I kept my focus on reuniting the women with their brother and jogged down the stairwell to catch up.

Astoria and Briar waited by the front door, observing the parking lot. Vampyres shut into their homes to abide by the curfew. It was still strange to step outside without pain from the sun. Nothing stood in my way to walk among the humans anymore.

The sports car chirped when I unlocked it. The roof was already arched over the seats, providing instant shade. I glanced back at the women. Briar gaped at the car, and Astoria's face lit up before she ran to the back seat like a child.

Briar remained inside the building, avoiding the shaft of light pouring through the door's window. I stepped out of the car and rested my elbows on the roof. I jerked my chin to the left, urging her to come. Through the glass, I could see Briar's lips part. I imagined her taking a deep breath like she was about to dive off a cliff into the ocean. She swung the door open and darted for the car in a flash.

"Where'd you get a car like this?" Astoria beamed as she traced her hands along the leather seats.

"It was an old friend's. He, um... died recently." I glanced at Briar and she briefly met my gaze before looking down at her lap.

"Oh... s-sorry." Through the rearview mirror, I saw Astoria shrink in her seat.

"I hadn't seen him in years. I'll, uh... get over it." I pulled out of the space and drove carefully through the apartment complex, waiting for Briar to comment.

She didn't.

⁕

The traffic was heavy during the usual lunch rush—a night and day difference compared to Eclipsis. We were silent as the vehicles waited at a stoplight that only allowed five to go at a time. Briar leaned against the window, but hissed when the light burned her face. She reclined her seat to lie down instead.

"Where's Sterling staying?" Briar asked in a tight voice, still reeling from the burn.

"With some other cop named Lyra." I didn't know how to feel about Briar ignoring my reference to Moses' death, or about how she wouldn't come forward about killing him.

I wanted to give her the benefit of the doubt. I wanted her to know that I wouldn't leave her if she admitted it, because every fledgling had their fair share of regrets. I had plenty myself, and even more since maturing to a full Vampyre.

Astoria snored lightly, leaning against the window. Maybe Briar didn't want Astoria to hear it.

"Great," Briar said flatly, then closed her eyes and tugged her hood further down her forehead.

"She won't care that you're unregistered or anything. She ain't exactly the by-the-book type," I promised.

"And somehow that doesn't make me feel any better," Briar grumbled. I guess that was fair. No matter what Lyra said or did, it would be nothing compared to however Sterling reacted. As much as I hated to admit, though—

"Sterling helped me break out of White Fang. I wouldn't be here if it weren't for him and he never stopped searchin' for ya either, so… it probably ain't gonna be as bad as ya think." I didn't want to get Briar's hopes up, but I hated how ashamed she seemed now. It reminded me of my own shame every time I looked in a mirror.

"You don't know him like I do. He arrested our own mother for drug possession. I'm sure he's capable of worse." Briar turned on her side in the seat and clung to whatever sleep she had left before her Vampyrism took hold completely.

Once we arrived at Lyra's quaint townhome, I woke both of them up. Sterling was already bustling out the front door, with Lyra tugging at the back of his shirt to slow him down. Astoria bolted out of the back seat and ran to Sterling, and they collided in a tight embrace.

"Drive off," Briar whispered as she gaped at her siblings in horror.

"Are you serious?" I frowned.

"I can't do this, Draven," she snapped quietly.

"Well, I ain't driving away. That's just wrong." I reached for her hand. "Briar... I'll be right next to you the whole time, I promise."

Briar closed her eyes, and stepped out of the car. She held her chin high as she approached Sterling. The bright smile he had for Astoria remained for Briar, until their eyes met. I watched every individual muscle in his face loosen then twist into disgust, fear, and anguish.

"No..." Sterling's breath hitched. His hand flung to his chest as if his heart was beats away from giving out. He staggered back and Lyra held her hands out, preparing for him to faint.

"What have they done to you?!" he exclaimed.

Briar's lips parted slightly, her head tilted while the glazed sclerae of her eyes reddened. Sterling grabbed her face. His forehead crinkled and his lips curled back as he observed the rose-colored irises and the burns that crept along her cheeks under the sun. Briar gritted her teeth when he forced a thumb under her lip before shoving him away. I took a step closer to her side, reminding her of my presence as he descended into madness.

"I'm fine, Sterling." Briar lowered her gaze, pulling her hood back over her head. She spoke low enough to hide the crack in her voice from human ears, but not from mine.

"No, no, no. You're *not* fine. You're one of *them* now. What am I supposed to do now? You're... God, they turned you into a monster!" Sterling cried.

Briar snapped her head upward and clenched her fists, her eyes hardening to ice. "A monster, huh?" She scowled. I could've sworn her eye twitched.

"Briar—" I placed my hand on her shoulder to calm her down, but jerked it away when I felt heat emitting from her skin.

"Briar, please calm down!" We couldn't have another White Fang incident. If Sterling could just shut his big, fat mouth—

"I told you not to hang with them, Briar! You play with dogs, you're bound to get bit!" Sterling shouted, his voice turning shrill.

"A monster, huh?!" Briar repeated, her voice rising. Black veins with glowing embers like lava crawled from her neck to her face. "I'll show you *a monster*!"

Briar lunged forward. I hooked my hand into the back of her hoodie, but my claws ripped through it like paper. She was already writhing in the grass—her brother screaming, Lyra watching with contempt, and Astoria begging for her to stop.

Briar latched onto Sterling's neck. I dove between them and forced Briar away from him before she could kill him. He clasped a tight hand over his neck while blood spurted past his fingers. He lay in the grass, gawking at the sky with gasps and burbling noises. Briar spat his blood on his face as I yanked her away.

"Who's the monster *now*?" she lilted, then flipped her middle finger at him with wild, maniacal laughter.

Astoria knelt next to Sterling, holding her hand over his to help keep pressure on the wound. Her brutal cries shook her body. I glanced at Lyra, the only other calm person in this scuffle. She gave me a reassuring nod and waved dismissively as the distant police sirens grew louder.

A neighbor must've called for the disturbance.

Briar didn't wince at the sun while I led her back to the car by her hood like a rabid dog on a leash. She kept licking her bloodied lips and spitting obscenities at him. This wasn't the same woman I met at The Nightshade or danced with at The Hole, or the woman I suffered with at White Fang. Whoever this woman was had just ruined her own brother's life forever, without a single shred of remorse. Assuming he survived the bite in the first place.

For the first time since I'd known her, Briar *scared* me.

37

STERLING

Ringing in my ears drowned out every scream, shout, and cry. I tried to breathe, but all I tasted was copper. I felt like I was drowning, sinking into the depths of the ocean. I tried to focus on the cool, damp grass from last night's rain beneath me. Astoria hovered over me, her hot tears dripping over my face and her mouth moving a mile a minute as she yelled at Lyra.

I was shivering and sweating simultaneously when foreign faces hoisted me onto a gurney. Figures ran back and forth in my peripheral vision.

Lightning strikes exploded through my body with every miniscule movement as the gurney rolled over uneven pavement. I cried out, but it was only a gurgle.

The sky soon turned into a metal roof with dull square lights.

Then it became black.

The last time I saw the grey crash rails against these dull beige walls was when I was forced to go to the hospital for a concussion after Cyrene's death. I never thought I'd return within the same year.

My eyelids were heavy and gritty with each blink. My mouth felt like I'd gone days without water, tinged with a horrid copper taste. There was a small plastic cup on a tray at my bedside, but when I reached for it, silver handcuffs held my wrist back just inches away. Inflamed red bands stained the skin around my wrists.

"What's this?" I croaked to myself, then flinched when Lyra rose from a chair in the corner of the room. I didn't realize she was there until the cushions sighed. Her movement was otherwise as silent as an owl's flight.

"Stage one." Lyra drifted toward my bed with her hands halfway in her pockets. There was something cocky about her subtle grin. The way her chin pointed upward and her head tilted to the side as she peered down at me.

"Stage one of what? *Cancer?*" I sneered.

"Worse." She handed the paper cup to me. I grabbed it, smacking my lips for glorious water until cinnamon drifted up my nostrils. I frowned and looked down to see the thick, dark carmine liquid in the cup. My mouth went from bone dry to coated in saliva. I hissed and threw the cup across the room, striping the far wall in red.

"What do you think you're doing?! Is this some kind of sick joke?" I snapped. Lyra sighed and sat on the edge of the bed. I could hear her heartbeat thrum while someone else's flatlined somewhere down the hall. I gripped the railings of the bed tightly.

"Let me guess. You can't remember what happened yesterday, huh?" Lyra flipped her fishtail braid over her shoulder.

"No! Quit playing games, Lyra!" I yanked at the chains. She didn't flinch at my spastic movements. Instead, she shrugged.

Everything was pointing at the one answer I couldn't accept. I had to be delusional, suffering from yet another concussion.

"You're one of us now. The best part? Your sister introduced you to the family." She smiled sweetly.

"You're lying," I said, and shook my head in disbelief. Briar wouldn't—*couldn't*—have done this to me. It had to have been Lyra or someone else, like the nightmare I had weeks ago.

"What goes around... always, *always* comes around," Lyra intoned as she leaned over me and pulled the red chord.

Then the memories came barreling back like a freight train.

No, no, no. You're not fine. You're one of them now. What am I supposed to do now? You're... God, they turned you into a monster!

I'll show you a monster!

"BRIAR!" I roared and threw my head against the headboard, arching my back and pulling against the handcuffs. Lyra laughed at me as I tried to break free, disregarding the cutting sensation of the silver. Nurses flooded into the room and Lyra rose to get out of their way. One plunged a needle in my arms, turning my body into lead.

⁂

They took me to a padded room with a single bed, a chair, a large display window, and a heavy metal door. My eyes were still crusted from earlier and my head swam when I lifted it from the thin pillow. I sat up and looked down at shackles around my ankles instead of my wrists, a strange white circle stuck to my calf.

"What—"

"Good morning, Mr. Shaw," a soothing woman's voice rang from a singular speaker in the ceiling by the door. "You may be confused, hungry, or in pain. This is completely normal while you go through stage one of the fledgling phase."

I slid off the mattress and padded toward the window to get a closer look at the doctor holding a small microphone to her lips.

"I am Dr. Nolan. We aim to make this a safe environment for new Vampyres such as yourself," she said. "The device attached to your leg helps us monitor your vitals at all times. Your program here will be six weeks, but your cooperation will determine whether or not you get released early. Some fledglings learn resistance sooner than others."

The shackles allowed me to reach the window and I placed my palm over the glass, snarling at the woman. Her hair was strawberry blonde, pinned up in a tightly braided bun. I pressed against the glass with all my might, and she remained unfazed.

"You still haven't had your first drink, Mr. Shaw. You will continue to be as weak as a human until you do so," she said plainly.

"Maybe I'm fine with that," I growled.

"You'll die of starvation." She kept her voice calm and even, and didn't flinch when I slammed my fist into the window.

"Let me out of here!" I screamed, then froze in place when Lyra appeared behind her. Dr. Nolan glanced over her shoulder, then stepped to the side to allow Lyra space to approach the glass.

"Traded your blues and suits for scrubs, huh? It's a good look on you," she taunted. I backed away from the window, reaching up to my hair and tugging on it while I paced as far as the shackles would allow.

"What are you doing here, huh? Haven't you done enough?" The metal scraped against the tile and the skin on my ankles went from chafed to healed, chafed to healed.

"I'm here to let you know Chief Duncan came to see you personally. Don't worry, I gave him the report instead since I was a witness." Lyra turned to Dr. Nolan and gave her a short nod. The doctor marched away, speaking to someone on a handheld radio.

"What kind of report?" I asked in a tight tone. Lyra shrugged nonchalantly and stepped closer to the glass.

"That White Fang attacked us and Turned you at the lab before some other Vampyre burned it all down," she explained. "He didn't seem too thrilled to hear that news, but I don't think it'll be an issue."

"You... you didn't report my sister?" I blinked with a dry chuckle.

"Why should I? She did you a favor. Maybe you'll be more likable." Lyra gave me a smirk and folded her arms behind her back. I sucked my teeth and threw my arm to shoo her away.

"If you're just here to rub salt in the wound, you can leave." I shuffled back to the bed. Every step felt like walking through thick sludge.

"Resist it as long as you want, but you're gonna have to come to terms with it eventually," Lyra said. "It's a part of you now."

I inhaled sharply to send a barrage of insults in her direction, but she was already gone. The door opened, more nurses pouring in. One held a tray of human food, another a glass of blood, and a third a syringe filled with a clear substance. Dr. Nolan stood where Lyra once was.

"It's time for your daily regimen, Mr. Shaw," she announced. I scowled at the nurses, growling lowly as a warning. They stopped halfway through the room, the nurse holding the syringe moving closer.

"Stay away from me," I said slowly through gnashed teeth. "I don't want *any* of this."

"It's Neoterra's law. You *must* finish the program before you're released to the public, Mr. Shaw." The nurse with the tray of food explained with a subtly quivering voice. "You of all people should understand that."

"If you fight us, you'll prolong your stay here," the nurse with the syringe warned as she inched closer. "And those who can't pass the program after a maximum of nine months get sent to Black Bay."

"Get away from me!" I roared, and leaped from the mattress.

The nurse with the cup of blood splashed the liquid on my face. The blood sprayed over my tongue and all my thoughts jumbled to pieces as I descended into a frenzy. My shouts became indistinguishable, feral snarls as I snapped my teeth at the nurses. While I was slowly gaining strength and lifting the three of them off the ground, I felt a piercing pain in my neck from the needle once again.

38
BRIAR

I was laughing wildly in Draven's car as he sped out of Lyra's complex before the police arrived. My heart bounced against the walls of my chest and my skin pearled with sweat. I hadn't felt so alive since the first time I broke curfew.

Draven caught the highway and bypassed most of Neoterra's inner traffic, then took an exit that led us back to the rural region.

I flipped the visor down and examined my face. My pupils were dilated so wide that only a thin pink ring surrounded them. Black veins spidered along my neck and cheeks, slowly fading to grey and blending into my skin as I calmed down.

Sterling's blood was still smeared around my lips and chin, crusting as the minutes ticked by. The metallic tang mixed with cedar and citrus burned my nostrils. Even as a fledgling, his blood didn't tempt me to insatiable hunger.

I glanced at Draven, whose gaze was fixed on the road ahead. The muscle in his jaw fluttered. He must've been clenching his teeth tight to trap whatever he wanted to say.

"What?" I raised my eyebrows, confused as to why he would be upset.

"What the hell was that, Briar?" he yelled, as if my voice had triggered the floodgates. I flinched from the boom of his voice and covered my ears.

"What was what, *Draven*?" I echoed his name the same way he spat mine.

"Your own brother!" He shouted.

"Sterling's dead to me!" My voice cracked.

Only the rumbling road noise filled the space after our yelling stopped. My throat tightened and I held my breath as my eyes burned again. I shrunk against the car door, watching the disgust contort Draven's face. For a moment, I wanted to throw myself onto the road.

I couldn't understand it. Sterling had given him a hard time from the start and I doubted he was easy to work with when they were tracking me down. He watched my own blood tear me down after I was missing for weeks. Sterling was too focused on what I'd become to embrace me like Astoria. Did Draven support him because he was a man, or was I truly in the wrong?

"He said hurtful things to ya, I know. But..." Draven squeezed the steering wheel with a soft exhale. "He never liked us, and definitely never wanted to *be* us."

"That's what makes it so *ironic*." I brought my fingertips to my temples and flicked them outward for further emphasis.

"It ain't funny!" Draven shouted so loudly, he jerked the car into the next lane. Luckily the roads were empty. He pulled over onto the shoulder with half the tires in the grass, dangerously close to a ditch. He twisted in his seat and extended his arm over to the back of my seat.

"I'm sorry for yellin'. While your brother is a jerk, he saved my life and... I understand him," he said in a softer tone. He ran a hand back and forth over his buzzed hair with a sniffle. "The Nightshades took me away after my parents died and Uriah ordered Wraith to take my humanity."

My heart shattered to a million pieces, and the furious veil lifted from my eyes.

While I thought I was serving poetic justice to my bigoted brother, Draven was reliving his own trauma right in front of his eyes. That was strike two.

What I had done to Sterling—allowing the anger drive my actions—finally hit me with a new clarity.

"I... I'm sorry," I whispered, curling my legs against my chest. "That wasn't the first time I lost myself."

If he was going to hate me now, I might as well see it through. I didn't deserve Draven's patience, support, or understanding—no matter how much I wanted it.

"I know," Draven sighed.

"He was nothing but nice to me and I killed him without a second thought," I mumbled against my knee. I ran it through my head a million times, tried to piece together how I'd tell Draven without breaking down.

"I know," he repeated, quieter this time.

But there was no denying the glistening sheen over his eyes as we drove further into the country.

※

We drove past my old house. I observed the pile of debris with a numb void in my soul. Not even the shed in the backyard survived.

I wanted to ask Draven where we were going, but instead he just pulled into the field behind the house and parked under the only oak tree at the center of it. He got out the car, slamming the door. He kicked the tree trunk and the roots broke through the surface bit by bit with each impact.

I quickly climbed out of the passenger seat and ran to him, wrapping my arms around his waist. I braced myself for him to lash out at me, to finally unleash the rage and sorrow he partially pent up in the car.

Draven's breaths shot rapidly through tight teeth, but he was losing momentum. He sank to his knees and stared at the mighty tree that now leaned with splintered bark. I kneeled behind him, burying my face between the solid muscles of his back. To my surprise, he didn't pull away.

"I'm sorry," I finally said. "First I thought you set me up and didn't believe you, then I left you at White Fang, then I killed... *him...*" I still couldn't say his name. "I never once thought about what you've been through. They took everything from you too, and all I've ever been was selfish. I can't take any of it back."

Draven leaned his head back, barely resting against the top of mine. "It wasn't your fault."

I tightened my arms around him with a whimper. There was

nothing in this world that justified Draven's level of patience with me. Maybe he was telling himself that too.

"I'll have to get over it." My heart splintered at the numbness in his voice. I crawled in front of him.

"You're right about everything. I shouldn't have done that to Sterling and he'll definitely never forgive me for it." I grabbed the hem of my shirt, balling it into a fist as I contemplated using the fabric to soak up my potential tears. "I just hope *you* will."

Draven's face hung low, but he lifted it again to give me a somber grin.

"I still love ya." Draven ran his hand through my hair, then down to my cheek, lightly brushing his thumb against my jawline.

"You love me?" I felt heat rise to my cheeks. No one other than my siblings ever shared those words with me. Not even Vivian. And hearing it from him after everything that happened... my soul shattered.

"I know fledglings who murdered their own parents while in a frenzy. I ain't no saint, either. The bodies I piled up..." He trailed off, staring vacantly across the field.

Draven had a million reasons to soften the blow of Moses' death, and I had a million reasons as to why he shouldn't.

He didn't give me time to respond before he swept me away in those arms of stone, held me against the tree trunk, and pressed his lips to mine. The guilt would never loosen its grip on me, but for the sake of this moment, I blocked out the thoughts.

And I fell to his mercy.

✳

The burns on my skin didn't start healing until Gloaming, but I noticed that being in the sun didn't hurt quite as much as before. I wondered if biting Sterling had anything to do with it, similar to how Draven received mine and gained abilities.

It didn't matter. Science had never been my best subject anyway.

Draven and I lay together under the protection of the oak tree's canopy with my head on his chest and his arm wrapped around me, drawing lazy circles over my arm. We watched the pale blue sky deepen to violet and magenta, the timid stars growing bolder.

"Let's get your bike back," Draven whispered. I snorted, brushing it off as a joke.

"I think I'd rather we revisit The Hole," I said. "Maybe listen to that angelic voice of yours again." Of all reckless things to do, why couldn't we just do the fun ones?

"If ya had the opportunity to face the people that tormented ya, wouldn't you take it?" I listened to the vibration of his voice through his chest, closed my eyes and tried to picture doing just that.

But I was a coward before, and I was a coward now.

"My bike was probably sold by now," I groaned.

"I highly doubt it. I can hear Wraith and Larkin fighting over it now," Draven said with a short laugh. I sat up and leaned back on my palms. I tugged on a few blades of grass as I pondered, staring at my reflection in the chrome of Draven's car. My hair was still cut short above my ears, tousled in small pink and black spikes. I didn't recognize myself. My cheekbones were higher, my jawbone was sharper, and my eyes protruded out of my sunken sockets.

I met my own sharpened gaze, a stranger glaring back at me in clothes I'd never owned until today.

I was still angry, I truly was.

I was angry before the Nightshades took me. At my life and the world.

But I was powerless. I always had been.

The only "strength" I'd displayed so far was against vulnerable humans—no, *Sun Dwellers*. It didn't count.

"Briar." Draven sat up and rested his chin on my shoulder. His breath tickled my ear as he whispered, "If you don't wanna go, we ain't got to. We can run far, far away from this place before Uriah destroys it."

Ever since I was taken to Uriah... I don't know. It was like my identity had splintered. I wanted to slash tires and bust windows and take down every Nightshade or White Fang Vampyre I crossed. I wanted to destroy Mundus Novus for creating laws that would separate me from Astoria despite our shared blood. But at the same time, I was terrified, I didn't have any fighting skills, and I wanted to escape into the world of yesterday when everything was simple.

"It's your choice," Draven said, his crimson eyes floating up to mine.

My chest ballooned and deflated as I mulled over the list of the Nightshades and White Fang's wrongs.

They kidnapped me.

Bled me.

Beat me.

Poked and prodded at me.

Forced me to transform into a killer.

Burned my house down and almost killed Astoria.
They've gotten away with too much for too long.

I stood and dusted the grass and dirt off my jeans. Draven rose as well and leaned against the hood of his car, folding his arms.

"Let's do it," I said, then hopped in the passenger seat. My hands were clammy but my heart was resolute. Draven's dimples tugged at his pearly smile as he rounded the hood and jumped in the driver's side. As he sped through the field and returned to the winding country road, dirt clouds followed.

I took one last look at the rubble of my home. It was just enough to remind me of Delilah's smirk—and awaken the craving for her head on a platter.

✳

Neoterra's lights shone more vibrantly than I remembered. Perhaps it was because I saw through the eyes of a beast, but I was able to lean back in Draven's car with the sunroof open and watch the city in awe. I wished we were safe enough to have the whole top down.

"We need to find Caspian," Draven said. "If I can convince him to ditch the Nightshades, we'd be a serious unit."

"Yeah, I don't think he's doing that anytime soon." I extended my hand above to feel the wind between my fingers.

"Maybe." Draven fell silent again and focused on weaving through traffic. I sat up once we started to hit a number of consecutive traffic lights. Despite marveling at colors I never thought could be so radiant, they turned my mind to the darkness.

"When you mentioned Uriah destroying the city, what did you mean?" I turned to Draven with a puckered forehead and propped an elbow on the armrest.

"He's plannin' a war. There were rumors about it years ago, but no one really thought he'd have the guts or the means to do it. Until... uh, he had me and Caspian assassinate Neoterra's top arms dealer." Draven sniffed and rubbed an eyebrow with a quivering chuckle.

"I could probably go for a smoke right now," he added with a grumble.

"I think I like you better without it." I shrugged. Draven rolled his eyes with a low groan. "So... what does he wanna go to war for?"

"Uriah's sick of how the Sun Dweller cops and politicians got everybody on curfew even though ain't nobody gonna go out during the day when their skin is on fire anyway," Draven said. "But... I guess Vampyres never really got a good rap anyway. Layoffs, unequal pay, lower employment rates, higher crime rates, whatever."

"Okay... and *why* do we care if he pulls it off? Uriah kinda has a point. I never liked the curfews as a human, much less now." I wrinkled my nose and cocked my head. "Not that we shouldn't kill him, though."

Kill. It rolled off my tongue too easily. My skin crawled.

"Uriah doesn't care about any of the Sun Dwellers or equality. He just wants to flip the script and treat them like cattle and also control other Vampyres. Of course, that's not the pretty speech he tells everyone," Draven explained. "I wouldn't be surprised if he was planning on turnin' against White Fang too once they give him what he wants."

I pursed my lips and tapped my palms against my lap to think. It was a lot to handle, something bigger than all of us.

"How big is your clan?" I didn't exactly want an answer, but I needed to understand what we were up against.

"Just in Neoterra alone? About two hundred." Draven gave me a sidelong glance. "And they ain't my clan no more, Sunny."

I rolled my eyes and leaned against the door, letting the cool air blow through what little hair I had left.

The skyscrapers and storefronts gradually switched for expensive Nocturnal Zone gated communities and subdivisions. The beach wasn't much farther from here, and all I could think of was the glimmering waves I saw in Uriah's backyard when I thought I could escape his mansion. I would've leaped right off that cliff if—

"Briar?" I flinched at Draven's voice despite its gentleness.

"Huh?"

"Did you hear anything I said?" The gentleness caught an edge. I shook my head.

"I said when we get there, you need to follow my lead. We're not there just for your bike, we need weapons too. We might be separated. Can you handle that?" Draven seemed to switch to warrior mode, preparing for battle.

"Can you handle that?" Draven repeated louder with more urgency.

"Y-yes! Yes." My blood ran cold as we crested a hill and the Mediterranean-styled mansion came into view.

The place where this whole nightmare began.

39

BRIAR

Draven drove past Uriah's house and followed the snaking road lined with bigger and bigger homes. He parked at an empty playground. The mirror-esque vehicle stuck out like a sore thumb, and I hoped none of his people would recognize it. He jumped outside before the engine fully fell quiet. I followed his lead without question.

Draven popped the trunk, revealing a metal baseball bat, a pistol, and a rusted machete. I crinkled my brows, glancing at him with a wary smile. Draven reached for the pistol, inspected it, then holstered it at his hip.

"Take your pick." He jutted his chin at the trunk. I poked my tongue against my lip ring as I scanned the remaining weapons. I picked up the bat and turned it over in my hands, measuring its weight.

"We're really doing this?" I whispered with a shaky breath. This was what I wanted, what I begged Caspian to let me do. I couldn't understand why I was still feeling anxiety.

"We're gonna be okay." Draven smiled confidently, seemingly sensing my fear. He shut the trunk and walked briskly downhill. I propped the bat over my shoulders, draping my arms over it for the majority of the walk back to Uriah's estate.

I flinched at a set of sprinklers cutting on at the opposite side of the street, then at a distant dog barking, and motion lights flicking on in a pristine house's driveway. I swung the bat back into my hand and held it at my side when the tension in my shoulders intensified.

A chain-link fence quivered and jingled when the dog jumped against it. Draven flashed forward and I followed suit to quickly leave the area. We crossed through a few unfenced backyards and stopped behind a line of boxy hedges. Draven didn't break a sweat, but I was still silently huffing as I separated a few branches to peer at the property beyond. I think the anxiety kept me breathless more than anything.

Sprinklers spritzed over Uriah's lush lawn. The rounded cobblestone driveway was damp around its edges. The garage door was down. I glanced at Draven to see what his next move was.

"It ain't gonna be long before someone senses us here, so move quick," he whispered, then hopped over the hedge. He landed with a soft thud, mine nearly silent. We crept along the other side of the bushes and avoided the light pouring from the garage windows. Draven pressed his back against the wall and craned his neck around the corner before he turned his focus to picking the side door's lock.

I took his place monitoring the front yard, peeking around the corner of the wall.

I heard the small click before the door groaned open. I whirled around and nearly stumbled over Draven's heels, eager to get inside. My lungs felt like they could only expand a half inch once I crossed the threshold and was greeted by an overwhelming number of cars and trucks inside. My knees locked in place. I gaped at every vehicle before I came back to my senses and searched for my motorcycle. Draven went straight for the back wall of weapons.

Voices on the other side of the garage door pierced the night air. I quickly tucked the bat under my arm as I ducked between a pair of vans. Draven caught up to my side and placed his index finger over his lips. We waited, listening.

A masculine voice—slick, ominous, almost maniacal—spoke with a raspy, seductive feminine one. A woman I could recognize anywhere.

Delilah.

I gripped the bat tightly, slowly rising to my feet. I was willing to throw my life away right then and there if it meant taking her down with me. Everything I'd personally gone through boiled down to her, not Uriah.

Draven quickly placed a hand on my shoulder and shook his head. I pinched my mouth, flaring my nostrils as I sunk back into a squat.

"When I see him again, I'm going to give him a slow and painful death." The man's words were heated, forced through the tight spaces between his teeth. "I don't care what it takes, he's gonna pay for Larkin!"

"Caspian could take you down in seconds. Oh wait, he already did once!" Delilah jeered. Draven's eyes widened, his lips stretching into a proud grin. If Caspian had killed Wraith's brother, then he was easily the Nightshades' enemy too. It was only a matter of finding him now.

"Maybe not if you didn't leave me behind," Wraith hissed. "Let's just get this dumb list over with."

A car door clicked open, then slammed shut.

"List?" I mouthed. Draven shrugged and slowly rose to his feet when the revving engine faded down the street. He went straight for the display of keys while I checked each row for my motorcycle.

And there she was, tucked away in the farthest back corner behind a lifted truck. There were small scuff marks on the black paint and one of the LED lights lining the tires had a dent in it. My cat-ear helmet was nowhere to be found. I groaned with disgust as I mounted it. They didn't even have the class to protect it with a tarp.

Draven tossed the keys to me and I caught them before realizing. I blinked at my hand, and he winked at me as he slung a rifle over his shoulder. He held a finger up before sifting through cabinets for ammo and a duffel bag. I twirled the bat around like a baton in one hand and kept my thumb on the key fob, waiting to activate my motorcycle. My gaze swept over all the beautiful cars in Uriah's garage, just begging to be smashed in. Draven walked up to me with another rifle in hand and leaned into my ear.

"I got what we need. Do whatever you want before I destroy this place... and be ready to drive as fast as you can," he whispered, sending chills down my spine. I smirked before I ran through the garage in a whirlwind.

I slashed tires with my claws, and cracked the bat across every windshield and side mirror I passed. I sprinted down the rows to scratch the doors from bumper to bumper, gritting my teeth at the sound. Draven stood at the center of the chaos, watching through the windows at the top of the garage door while I destroyed as much as I could in seconds.

The noise didn't seem to attract any attention, which made me wonder if anyone was home in the first place. Could Wraith and Delilah have been the only ones here? Did others have lists to take care of too?

Draven didn't seem too worried about whether or not we were going to be overrun by Nightshades. He walked to the side door and peeked outside. I followed behind him, rolling my neutral motorcycle through the doorway. I parked it on the side of the garage in shadow. Draven crept in a low crouch toward the backyard.

The pool cast teal glows over the veranda and the freshly cut grass. I remembered dashing toward the cliff that sloped down into the beach beyond, filled with the hope to escape, until Draven tackled me to keep up appearances with his clan.

I shook my head, dismissing the thought. Draven lifted his nose, his nostrils subtly flaring and contracting as he inspected the air. He crossed the wraparound patio and checked door handles until he ran into an unlocked set. I paused at the door, debating whether to wait by the motorcycle while he did whatever he had planned.

I didn't want to see this place again.

But now wasn't the time to be indecisive.

Rifle in hand, Draven snuck up the stairs. I raised my bat as if it would have any impact on a Vampyre.

This is so stupid.

With every step, I could feel my hair being yanked at the root as the Vampyres dragged me up the stairs to the study. I could still feel Uriah's ring crunch against bone when he struck my jaw as we drew near those lion statues. I didn't realize I was holding my breath until we approached the double mahogany doors.

Draven paused, staring at the handles as if they were coated in poison. I wondered how many times he'd approached these doors, anticipating the nightmare on the other side. Sweat beaded on his brow, drops slicking down the curve of his nose. He sniffed, took a step back, then rammed his foot into the doors. The door frame splintered as they blasted off the hinges.

Uriah sat at his desk, casually drinking a glass of blood. He wore maroon suspenders over a crisp white button-down with the sleeves rolled up.

"I figured that was you messing around in my garage," Uriah said coolly, swirling the remaining blood in the glass like wine. "It's been awhile, hasn't it?" I shrunk behind Draven, forgetting that I also had the strength of fifty men. All I could think about was being thrown to the floor, at the mercy of several Vampyres as they decided my fate.

"If you knew it was me, why didn't you try to stop us?" Draven puffed his chest and raised his chin in challenge.

"Everyone knows you've been at large. After what you pulled at White Fang... it was a matter of time before you came back here for unfinished business. I decided to let you have your fun." He cocked his head and set his glass down. He caught a glimpse of me and grinned with amusement.

Uriah rose from his desk. "I also wanted to thank you both for your incredible contribution at White Fang."

I stepped out from behind Draven with a scowl, despite my quaking stomach. I wanted to run, but I scanned him from head to toe, and remembered every sickening detail from when I first saw him. His salt and pepper hair gelled and combed in a wave with a flawlessly trimmed beard, the metallic left arm that whirred and clicked with life, and the soulless smile he plastered on his face when he seemed to have some sort of advantage.

"Fangs look good on you, girl. Say, rather than following this fool around, why don't you join us Nightshades? He's bound to lead you to your grave." Uriah clasped his hands behind his back.

"Why on earth would I go anywhere with you? You locked me up in a cellar and your goons—" I shook my head to reel back the rage he sparked within just by addressing my presence. I glanced at Draven. Wisps of smoke swirled from his shoulders and the top of his head while his breaths grew more turbulent.

"Because you're gonna wish you were in my good graces when the city falls down." Uriah's eyes flicked to Draven's hands when they became engulfed in blazes. I took steps back, watching in awe. Uriah didn't show a speck of fascination.

"You don't get to dictate anyone's choices anymore," Draven growled with a foreign voice like thunder.

"Okay, then. Show me what you got," Uriah challenged with a calm shrug. I searched his study for any indication of a trap. My breath hitched as I prepared a warning—

"Wait—!"

Draven hurled a fireball. There was a flash, and half the study was immersed in flames. Uriah didn't dodge, but instead emerged from the fire in a body covered in metal. His shoulders trembled with a low chuckle that rose to a guffaw while Draven gawked in horror.

I flew into a bookcase half a second before Draven and Uriah thrashed to the floor. Fangs were bared as they snarled like wild animals and went for each other's necks. I coughed from the smoke taking the air. I struggled to rise from the splintered wood and crumbled drywall.

Uriah was still in his metallic form when he held Draven in a headlock.

"White Fang might want you alive, but I don't agree. They gave me the serum, so what do I need to listen to them for?" Uriah said through gritted teeth, shoving his hand in Draven's mouth and pulling downward as he tried to snap his jaw.

Black dots filled my vision and the skin around my neck went taut before the room began to shake. Picture frames fell off the walls. The lights flickered as smoky shadows crept along the floor like fog, mixing with Draven's flames. The temperature rose, melting objects.

"Let him go!" I screamed, stamping my foot forward as I prepared to lunge. Uriah loosened his grip and took a moment to observe the study crumbling around him. His brows lifted, rippling his glistening forehead before he hardened into metal again. I leaped across the room, clashing into them both and knocking Uriah back just enough for Draven to get out of his grasp of steel.

Draven released a feral roar, his eyes burning white like stars. He released columns of fire from his palms. I dove to the side just in time to avoid most of the flames. I winced at the sensation of my jeans melting to my calf. I scrambled to the door, pulling Draven from the study as the ceiling threatened to cave in. Uriah laughed as we left, unbothered by the barrage of flames Draven had rained on him.

"Keep running, son! You won't get far! The whole city is after you now!" He sang his words between deranged chortles. "You better hope the Nightshades catch you before White Fang! You're gonna wish you were dead!"

40
DRAVEN

The wind slapped against my face as we zoomed away from the King Estate, making it nearly impossible to breathe. I pressed my face against the back of Briar's shoulder to get away from the wind and focused on my breaths. My skin still tingled as if I had been sitting under direct sunlight for hours. I clasped my arms around Briar's waist while she steered her motorcycle.

The sight of Uriah turning into a moving steel statue still clanged through me, and I couldn't help but worry about how far White Fang's capabilities stretched.

Uriah didn't seem to care that we'd burned down his estate either.

When my temperature dropped, her body relaxed. I hoped I wasn't burning her and she was just suffering in silence.

I inhaled the smoke clinging to her skin and clothes.

I didn't know what to do.

I didn't know what to do.

Briar skidded into the parking lot and I hopped off before she slowed to a complete stop. With Uriah still standing, we knew we had a long way to go to escape this side of Neoterra. We said nothing, focused only on getting away.

I vaulted over the Corvette's car door and immediately started the engine, then raced out of the lot. Briar followed closely behind, weaving through traffic whenever we got separated.

We had nowhere to go. I still had Caspian's key. But if Wraith was going after him for something he did to Larkin—and with multiple hits on us already—I didn't want to risk leading anyone there.

I changed course, heading further north toward the Nocturne District. I noticed Briar grimacing in my rearview mirror, and I hoped she trusted me enough to keep following.

There was only one place far enough to buy us some time to regroup. A place that Caspian and I had once agreed to meet if we ever got in trouble during a mission and had to lie low.

✳

The Nocturne District was once considered reprobate, but it looked like the police department had decided to try to clean it up. It always had a formidable reputation from years of violence. Ordinarily there would be someone crying for help from a robbery near the boardwalk. But this time the Vampyre patrons appeared less guarded, and music replaced the sound of sirens.

I felt guilty. Like I was supposed to hate Briar for what she did. But... wouldn't that be the equivalent of hating a child for hurting someone when you were the one who gave them the knife?

330

And it would've made me the biggest hypocrite on the planet.

I led us to the top floor of a parking garage at the edge of the boardwalk, closer to the ferry slip. The guttural rumbling of Briar's motorcycle rode the wind. I got out of the sports car and pressed my fingers over my lips, then touched the hood, saying goodbye to the only memory of Moses I had left.

"I'm sorry, Mr. Moses," I whispered. "You didn't deserve any of this."

Briar turned away to observe the dark, choppy waters ahead, probably to escape her self-loathing.

"Let's go," I said, popping the trunk and grabbing the duffel with weapons. I slung the bag across my back and mounted the bike behind her. Briar stared sullenly at the car before driving us toward the ferry slip.

We waited by the dock, with Briar hitting the kickstand on her motorcycle. She sat next to me on the weathered bench and leaned into my shoulder.

The briny air had a crisp bite to it. The waves rolled onto the shore, where a group of Vampyres danced to calypso music around a bonfire. It was a nice night despite the distant lightning flashes on the horizon. It probably wasn't going to be nice for long. The ferry floated in the distance with windows glowing like honey. I just hoped there was enough time for one more trip.

"What did I witness back there?" Briar asked, pulling a leg up to her chest to examine her calf. I caught a glimpse of the marred pants and the slow-healing blistered skin beneath.

"When did that happen?" I reached for her, but she flinched

away. "Please don't tell me I did that." Briar raised her eyebrows with a grimace, then lowered her leg.

"I'll be fine. You didn't answer my question." She poked my side.

"I ain't got an answer," I said, and ran a hand over my face, shaking my head somberly. I didn't think I'd ever felt so trapped in my life, even when I was a fledgling, or a quadriplegic in Uriah's basement, or a prisoner at White Fang.

"You... you were really shooting fire out of your hands, huh?" She picked at her nails.

"Yeah. And Uriah turns into some kind of indestructible metal." At first I'd thought he'd turned into steel or titanium, but he didn't so much as warp against my fire.

"And I... well..." Briar shrunk further against me, curling into a ball on the bench. "I don't know what I did in there, or if I was the one that did it at all."

"We'll have time to process everything on the way to Helios," I said. I'd experienced a new level of rage, but even then the mini earthquake didn't come from me. Whatever Briar did, it was the distraction that got me out of Uriah's grip.

I wrapped my arm around her and squeezed, cautiously surveying the Vampyres drifting around. So far, no one looked like they were affiliated with White Fang or the Nightshades, but I had to look for other rivals too. Uriah could start recruiting Crimson Daggers if he got desperate enough to catch us.

"I feel like I should tell Astoria before we go," Briar mumbled.

"There's no time. Plus... I think Sterling needs her more than you do," I said, and rubbed my thumb comfortingly against her arm as the ferry drew closer.

"I guess you're right." Briar scratched her head. "What about Caspian?"

"If he's under as much heat as I think, he'll be in Helios soon too." I hoped he hadn't change too much since this mess started. Caspian was as predictable as he was *un*predictable.

The ferry blared its horn when it docked. Briar put her motorcycle in neutral and rolled it toward the slip where we were first in line. I kept watch.

"Do you know how to ride?" Briar asked suddenly, staring out at the sea.

"Yeah, but I figured you would want a proper reunion with your bike," I said, glancing over my shoulder. I did a double take when I noticed a young guy resembling Oren Jacobs hanging out underneath the awning next to a smoke shop. With his back against the wall and his arms crossed, he narrowed his eyes at me. I was certain he'd been next on the chopping block when White Fang took him for testing, but I guessed he survived it.

Maybe they did something worse.

There weren't many people with curly, sandy hair and vitiligo skin like Oren.

I was certain it was him, and he wasn't backing out of our staredown.

"What are you looking at?" Briar started to turn, but I nudged her arm with my elbow to force her to look straight ahead.

"A potential problem." I shifted my weight on my feet, turning sideways so I could at least keep him in my peripheral vision. The last thing I remembered was him saying he'd heard I was a traitor, but that he looked up to me because of stories from my past. I didn't consider him a friend or an enemy at White Fang, just another face that would come and go.

The captain approached us from the apron leading up to the ferry. "Just you two boarding tonight?"

"Yeah." Briar handed him an old, wrinkly punch card from a small compartment in her motorcycle seat. The captain punched it without question and gestured us to the ferry. I hesitantly peeled my gaze from Oren.

We anchored Briar's motorcycle to a rack on the bottom deck, then sat on a bench bolted against the side of the cabin. I leaned over the edge of the armrest, peeking around the corner to see if Oren boarded after us. I didn't hear any footsteps shuffling across the deck, but I didn't see him standing near the smoke shop either. So far, we were the only ones aboard.

"What kind of 'potential problem' are we facing?" Briar cut in quietly. I turned away from the corner, slouching in the seat.

"I thought I recognized a guy from White Fang. He was a, um, volunteer from the Nightshades." I pursed my lips and knit my eyebrows together as I stared at a small speck of light at the far reaches of the ocean. A lighthouse the size of a pin. Like any potential problem, it was small until it wasn't.

She dropped her voice lower. "Is he a friend or an enemy?"

"He was neither. That ain't necessarily playin' to our advantage, though." I sifted through the contents of the duffel bag and reloaded my pistol. The ferry horn blared and the boat began to set sail back across the sea toward Helios. I felt Briar startle beside me.

I never knew her to be so apprehensive, but after everything we'd been through, I understood.

"Are you sure it was him? Wouldn't he have tried to stop us from boarding?" Briar stood from the bench and straightened her shirt.

"Not if throwin' us overboard is the goal." I grabbed her wrist. "Where are ya going?"

"Bathroom," she said curtly before pulling away.

"I don't think that's a good idea right now," I insisted in a harsh whisper. Briar put her hands on her hips and tilted her head.

"Why don't you come with me then?" she asked frustratingly.

"I need to keep an eye on the deck." I held the pistol discreetly between my knees, concealed in the shadow of the bench seat to avoid the metal glinting in the ferry's ambient lighting.

"I'll be quick," Briar groaned, then hurried off to the cabin inside. I sighed and peeked around the corner again to watch her disappear through the doors. I stood slowly, turning my back on her motorcycle. Despite the choppy waters, the boat remained steady—although the churning tempest remained in my chest.

I counted to sixty and restarted as each new minute began. After three minutes, I was tapping my foot. Once five minutes had passed, I took a step forward to charge into the cabin just as a draft carrying a foreign scent swirled from behind me.

"Draven Hawthorne... the outlaw, the traitor, the legend."

I swung around to see Oren standing on the edge of the ferry, gripping the metal railing with a smirk.

"So it *was* you at the boardwalk," I said stiffly, and waited for the moment to shoot. I didn't trust him or his intentions, but I didn't want to jump to conclusions either. Oren was just a kid caught up in something he couldn't possibly understand.

"Yeah, I'm surprised you remembered me. You didn't say hi." Oren dropped down from the edge and eyed Briar's motorcycle.

"That girl smells familiar. She was at White Fang, wasn't she?" He ran a hand over his curls before he slipped his hands in his pockets.

"Why? What do ya want?" I narrowed my eyes. "Did you do somethin' to her?"

"I'm supposed to kill you both. White Fang still wants you guys alive, but Uriah ordered a fatal hit on y'all." Oren pulled a dagger from his jeans and cleaned dirt from under his nails with the tip of the blade.

I chuckled and held up my pistol. "They sent *you* after me? You're what, one-fifty soakin' wet?" I took stride, circling him like a vulture without breaking the barrel's aim. "What did you do to her?"

Oren mirrored me, neither of us breaking eye contact.

"I don't mind a challenge." He stopped walking, closed his eyes, and tossed his dagger into the water. I frowned with a soft scoff.

Of course.

I let my pistol clatter across the bench and summoned the wrath that was rapidly building under my skin. The same wrath that drove me to burn White Fang's headquarters—but without completely releasing the reins.

My hands ignited. Oren's eyes flung open, glowing steel blue rather than dark cherry. He smirked as he twirled his index finger in slow circles. The ocean behind him opened its mouth to swallow us whole.

41
DRAVEN

Oren barely lifted a finger as the water twisted into a whirlpool. The ferry was put-putting forward and I doubted the captain had the slightest idea he was sailing us to our deaths. My eyes widened and the flames in my palms were snuffed out.

Pull yourself together!

I had to summon another emotion. One I never willingly partook in—desperation.

I shut my eyes tightly and swung my arm forward. Only a spark shot out. Oren mirrored my movement with swift confidence, sending a wave over the railing. I dove to the side and whipped my arm again as I fell on my back, finally catapulting a ball of fire. He held up both arms and blocked it with a wall of water.

"Briar!" I screamed, sending more blazes in Oren's direction.

I shut my mind off from questioning my power, Oren's skill, and what he might've done to Briar.

Oren leaped to the second level deck, and I darted inside the cabin to search for Briar. I staggered when the boat began to lean forward, but I trudged to the women's bathroom and kicked the door in.

Briar was on the floor, blinking wildly. She wheezed, but couldn't speak or move. It didn't take a genius to realize she was a victim of Larkin's poisons.

We needed to assume these serums and toxins were being mass-produced among the Nightshades *and* White Fangs. Uriah and Oren's abilities were evidence enough.

"I got you, okay? I got you!" I slid across the floor on my knees and scooped Briar into my arms before the boat jerked forward. The lights flickered and the ferry creaked and groaned. It was nothing but water through the windows, and I held Briar close to my chest as cracks splayed across the glass. I dashed across the cabin and searched for a lifeboat until a pillar of water shot through the doorway. It slammed into my chest, flattening us against the wall as the boat leaned into a ninety-degree angle, tilting backward into the whirlpool—and began its descent into the ocean's depths. I coughed violently, spitting up the water that went up my nostrils. Steam swirled from my shoulders, vaporizing the water left behind.

The wall of the bathroom tilted and became the floor. I flopped Briar over my shoulder and crouched, then launched upward. I caught onto the doorframe with my free arm, and started to pull us up.

Then the moonlight shifted.

I looked up to see Oren at the nose of the boat with a wide grin. He held up a fist while a tsunami-scale wave arched over his head. The wave froze in place, only a few drops escaping from it like rain.

"It's been an honor fighting you, Draven," he called, then splayed his fingers apart and leaped from the edge. He disappeared, and I watched powerlessly as the wave came crashing down.

⁕

My lungs screamed while I retched water, seaweed, and God knew what else. I opened my eyes and immediately shut them again when it felt like gritty glass sliced them to pieces. I slapped my face, knocking off sand. I crawled up the shore and rolled to my back, staring at the sky. It was still night, the moon only partially concealed by thin navy clouds. I jerked upright when I realized I was alone.

"Briar?!" I shouted, and forced myself to my feet despite the shifting ground. I sniffed the air deeply, trying to separate the smell of seagulls, fish, and seaweed from her rose scent.

"Briar!"

I climbed over the jutting rocks and ran along a pile of them leading into the water. I paused at the edge and examined the waves' violent crashes against the rocks, and remembered she had been given paralytic toxins. She couldn't respond even if she wanted to. She couldn't *swim* even if she wanted to.

And even if I could find her... I had no antidote for the toxin. The blood Caspian had given me helped metabolize most of it while I was in Uriah's cellar, but it wasn't enough.

I swallowed a knot in my dry throat. I beat my fists into my skull and bellowed her name into the night.

I heard a group of seagulls and crows squall, whipping my head in their direction. About fifty feet away, on the other side of the rocks, was a body. The short black hair with tiny pink spikes caked with sand—

I flashed over there without leaving a print in the sand, chasing the birds away. Briar was supine with grains scattered across her clammy face. I tapped her cheek rapidly. She didn't stir. I scrambled to the ocean's edge and cupped my hands, then carried the water back to splash her face.

"Briar, *please.*"

I grasped her face in my hands and kissed her forehead as a searing tear burned along my face and dripped onto hers. Black veins crawled up her arms, across her collarbone, along her neck. I reeled back in a frenzy. I didn't know what it meant, if she was dying or if her body was fighting the toxins. I checked her nostrils for breath, but I couldn't decide if it was the gentle breeze or from her lungs. I laced my fingers together and began compressions on her chest.

I counted to thirty, then tilted her head back and breathed into her mouth.

No response.

I did it again.

Nothing.

More compressions.

Breaths.

Again.

And again.

WAKE UP!

"I can't lose you too," I rasped, ramming a fist into the sand. I slumped over, pressing my forehead against hers as the will to fight leave my hands. The beach was empty on this side of the rocks and on the other side, no one cared to see who I was calling for.

My list of targets kept growing, but just when I thought I had the power to take on the Nightshades, they were getting stronger too. How was it that no matter how strong I got, I still remained weak?

I lay next to Briar, wrapping an arm around her waist. I buried my face in her neck and tried to make heat radiate from my body to hers, but I was exhausted from the shipwreck. I shivered and closed my eyes. I wished I could've gone back to that night at Caspian's apartment with Briar at my side, alive.

"Draven? From *the Nightshades*?"

My eyes flung open and I hovered over Briar protectively as I snarled at the woman standing before us. Tall and lithe with braids intricately twisted into a larger fishtail braid, she tensed and dropped her folding lounge chair and cooler.

"Who are ya?" I scanned her arms and legs beneath the sheer robe over her swimsuit and didn't see a single tattoo. She belonged to no one.

"Samara. You robbed me and my friends years ago at Sundance. I can't seem to get away from any of you people." She put her hand on her hip, curling her upper lip with disgust.

"If I robbed ya, why would ya approach me at all? There's plenty room on this beach." I wrapped my arms around Briar again, not caring if Samara stabbed me in the back.

"Because I know the girl you're holding and I wanna help her." Samara began gathering her things again. "If you care about her, follow me." She strutted across the shore, up through the dunes and across a short wooden plank that led to the barren parking lot.

This might be the miracle I needed. So I scooped up Briar's limp body and followed Samara to her purple off-road SUV.

✳

Samara took us to a part of Helios I'd never seen before. Far from the city, from any fields, and instead through a forest cut in half by a dirt path barely wide enough for her vehicle. Few patches of moonlight filtered through the thick canopy.

"I'm gettin' convinced you don't actually know her and you're just takin' me out here to try to get revenge over some orders I was followin'," I grunted as I shifted my weight across the back seat, Briar lying on top of me. The car's movement over the rough road rattled my brain when I leaned against the window.

"I guess that's just for me to know and for you to find out," Samara said, bracelets clinking as she drove. "I am a little salty you ruined my beach trip."

I didn't trust her, but I felt secure enough that White Fang's technology hadn;'t reach Helios yet. I could take her and anyone else that might be waiting for me at the end of the road.

"Yeah, sorry we decided to shipwreck when we did," I seethed. Samara's cheeks stretched outward and I imagined a smug smile plastered across her face.

She drove us to a meadow with a large log cabin at the center. There was a well toward the back, tamed bushes and trees artfully arranged among the wildflowers, and a dirt path that hardened to concrete as it led to a three-car garage.

"This isn't my house, so don't go thinking you can come back here and hunt *me* down," Samara said as the garage door rose and she pulled inside.

"Lady, I really don't care about you, the stupid hair salon, or this house. I just want Briar alive and well." I crawled out of the back seat awkwardly, then pulled Briar out.

"I suspected she was dealing with you when she worked with us. No wonder she's—" Samara's eyes widened, her nostrils twitching. Her russet skin turned ashen. "A Vampyre."

"Yeah. Long story. Can we hurry?" My eyes darted between her and the door leading to the inside of the house. She hurried up the brick steps and fumbled with her keys to get inside.

"Malachi! Azha!" Samara shouted through the house, which was filled with mounted deer heads, antler chandeliers, and paneled walls. Those names sounded familiar.

I paused near the dining table, eyeing the evergreen garland, the place mats and chargers, and the decorative vase. I debated shoving all of it on the floor and placing Briar there.

"What are you doing? Come on," Samara demanded, waving her arm through the archway. I followed behind her as she jogged toward a sweeping wooden staircase and rushed upstairs.

"Mars?" I heard a male voice ring from above.

"We need your help!" Samara shouted, and led me down a narrow hallway to an empty bedroom. I caught a glimpse of a man with short, dark wavy hair and rich umber skin poking his head out of a room on the other end of the hall. I eased Briar onto the bed, my only relief coming from her body being slack rather than rigid. There was still a chance she was be alive. Malachi came running to our bedroom, rolling his sleeves up.

"Briar?!" he exclaimed.

I studied him. His eyes were as dark as coals—undeniably human. He looked vaguely familiar, but I couldn't pinpoint where I'd seen him before.

"How ya know her?" I asked, suspecting an ex-lover.

"We were both prisoners at White Fang." Malachi didn't so much as look in my direction as he rushed to Briar's bedside.

"Ah." I knit my lips shut once I remembered.

Malachi placed the back of his hand over her forehead. I clenched and opened my fists at my sides repeatedly as I fixed my gaze on his movements. He pressed two fingers against Briar's neck, right below her jawline.

"There's a pulse, but it's very faint," he mused softly, then left the room just as a short woman appeared in the doorway. Her hair was jet black, styled in a short curly afro. Her face was frozen, her jaw set as if she had plenty to say but reined the words in.

"Ya know her too?" I folded my arms as I observed her scrutinizing Briar.

"Yeah. My husband and I..." She paused when she finally met my gaze. Her throat rolled with a hard swallow, but she kept her chin tilted and spine locked. "I remember you."

"Oh yeah?" I sat on the edge of the bed and caressed Briar's cold face. Samara stood stiffly in the corner without a word, as if she were the bodyguard for the married couple.

"You were there." It wasn't a question. *My* only question was in what circumstance did she see me? As a fire-breathing monster, or as a prisoner like everyone else?

"I'm assuming you're Azha." I said, recalling Samara using both of their names. Azha crossed the threshold of the doorway, entering the bedroom. As she stepped into the light, I could see her eyes were just as human as Malachi's and she had burn scars on her shoulders, on her upper arms, and across her chest.

"I am. And you're the guy that set the whole place on fire." She didn't question how I knew her name, only watched me like a hawk. I hesitantly gave her a small nod. There was a pretty high likelihood those burns had come from me, and she had a strong enough resolve to live with the scars rather than change her species to erase them. I averted my gaze, my gut twisting.

Malachi finally returned with a large suitcase and rolled an IV pole into the bedroom. He placed it at the head of the bed, then grunted as he plopped the suitcase on the foot of the bed. He opened it, revealing countless medical supplies. Among them, he set up a flat metal tray with tubes, needles, a cold blood pouch, and a saline bag. Once everything was laid out, Malachi took another moment to examine Briar's face.

"I've never seen anything like this before, but I'm going to start with giving her blood and fluids." Malachi's hands didn't stop working as he spoke. "Maybe it can help flush out whatever her body's fighting."

"Is there anything I can do?" I stood from the edge of the bed to give him as much space as possible, but I wanted to speed up the process. I didn't know how many minutes Briar had left, if any.

"Just let him work," Azha uttered.

Malachi double-checked the IV and grabbed a blood pressure cuff out of his bag, then moved to the other side to use her other arm. There was a moment of silence as he checked her blood pressure.

"Aren't Vampyres able to heal themselves?" Malachi asked as he deflated the cuff, glancing at Samara. He opened the pouch and propped it in the corner of her mouth. It dripped slowly, but didn't trigger a frenzied response. Not even a loopy one.

"Yeah, but—"

"It depends on the injury. UV rays and fire heal slower," I cut in. "And this... well, this is different entirely. She was poisoned."

"I overheard Dr. Ivanov talking about some Vampyres having a resistance to their sedatives. Hopefully Briar is one of them." Sweat beaded on Malachi's forehead and he swiped his forearm across it. "But I want you to know that if I can't save her—"

"Oh, you *will*," I interjected.

"If I *can't*," Malachi insisted, ripping his gaze from Briar to meet mine. "You need to understand I did everything I could and promise not to kill me."

"Whatever problems you people have with me, it better not effect what you do for Briar," I growled. Azha stepped between me and her husband. I chuckled as I examined her petite height paired with human eyes.

"What are *you* going to do?" I challenged.

"Try me and find out."

Azha didn't blink. Perhaps she had a trick up her sleeve, but the idea of someone her size and species subduing me was funny. I held up my hands in a nonchalant surrender before taking a step back and plopping in the desk chair.

Malachi checked her temperature. I understood it was important to check vitals, but it felt like a waste of time. Like stuff I could've done right on the beach myself.

"Her blood pressure is normal and her temperature is fine. So far, everything checks out. She's just... unconscious with weird veins." Malachi tucked away the medical supplies in his bag, but left the IV and saline bag alone.

"Looks like all we can do is wait for her to wake up," he said, then disappeared quickly through the hallway.

"Hold up—" I shot to my feet and Samara flashed in front of me. She crossed her arms.

"You said ya knew somebody that could help her!" I shouted. "He ain't done sh—"

"Give it time," Samara sibilated. Hot air huffed through my nostrils as my chest heaved and my jaw tightened. I balled my fists, my claws biting into my palms. I pushed past Samara and Azha, then paused in the doorway. I peered back at them over my shoulder.

"If Briar dies, I'm killin' all of ya."

42

CASPIAN

For the past year, my father hadn't stopped talking about how special my birthday would be when I turned six, how it would be the first stage of becoming a man.

When my birthday finally arrived, I was ecstatic. Maybe all the kids in the neighborhood would get invited for a party. Maybe there would be cake, ice cream, and games. Except... there weren't any balloons when I woke up.

The whole house was empty, and I sat upstairs in my father's library staring out the heavily tinted window. Children were playing tag in the cul-de-sac. I clung to the windowsill and imagined being with them, making friends. The smiles remained plastered on their faces, even when one of them tripped and fell. It made me want to go outside even more. It wasn't every day the Sun Dweller kids visited a Nocturnal Zone. Besides, all the Vampyre children in my neighborhood thought I was too weird to play with. At least the humans didn't know me.

The street lamps were turning on, which meant the sun wouldn't hurt as much. My father once said it was because Gloaming was approaching. Something about the sun getting weaker over time.

I pushed away from the windowsill and padded across the library to find my father downstairs, sifting through the starved refrigerator after being gone for hours. I flinched when he slammed the door shut and ran a hand over his face. He paused with his palm over his nose and mouth, sliding a sidelong glance in my direction.

"Happy birthday, Cass." His tone was even. He didn't smile until he heard the children's laughter outside. "You're gonna get a gift today, kid."

My eyes lit up with a wide grin. "Really?"

"But you're gonna have to do something for me first. Think of it as a rite of passage." I didn't know what that was, but I was willing to do it. It wasn't every day I got a surprise or a gift.

My father placed his large hand over my narrow, bony shoulder. He led me from the kitchen to the front door and opened it. A gust of chill, evening wind rushed through the foyer. Butterflies of hope fluttered in my stomach. Maybe he'd let me play with the other kids for ten minutes before they had to rush home for curfew. But when I observed the cul-de-sac, they were scattering to run home before they got in trouble—except one.

"You see that little girl over there? She's about your age, but as a Vampyre it's time you learn what it's like out here." He pointed at a little blonde girl in a dress and leggings. They were smudged with dirt, and blood blotted over one of her knees. She was rubbing the back of her hand over flushed, damp cheeks.

"She looks hurt," I murmured, rubbing my prickly arm.

"Yes. I want you to kill her." My father removed his hand to hold it behind his back. I gasped, my mouth gaping wide open. From what I understood, that meant making her go to sleep permanently and I thought only bad people deserved that. That's what he always said. Was she bad for being out so late?

"I can't!" I exclaimed. "Why?"

"You *can,* and you *will.*" He grabbed me by the ear and knelt in front of me, dropping his voice to a threatening whisper. "You're a Vampyre. There will be times when it doesn't matter what kind of person they are and you'll need food in the fridge. There will be times where we can't afford to go to the store for blood, but we need strength. Today, you will learn the real world."

My father shoved me outside and slammed the door shut. I shuddered and held my breath, puffing air into my cheeks. Crying always landed a big whooping, and that was the only way I knew how to control my tears.

I knew he wasn't going to open the door until I followed his orders.

I gripped the wrought-iron railing tightly as I descended the porch steps. My breath hitched into hiccups when I approached the girl.

"H-Hi, my name is C-Caspian. What's yours?" I asked as I my throat tightened. She looked up at me with sapphire eyes sparkling with her tears.

"Ella," she sniffled. "I don't know how to get home."

"My dad can help you." I stretched my hand out to her with every bone in my body screaming that this was wrong. Ella's skin was soft as powder. Dirt arched under her nails.

"Do you like board games?" I asked as I pulled her toward the house. She limped willingly behind me.

"Uh-huh." Ella's voice was a squeak. My father waited at the front door with a small smirk, the closest to a smile I'd ever see him do. The door closed behind us as she entered the foyer, unaware of what waited on her beyond it.

✳

"Where's your head?"

Cyrus torpedoed through my mind and everything came into focus through the window. I'd been staring at blinding headlights in a parking lot through the pane. I blinked and looked around at waitresses zipping by tables with plates of food. I'd forgotten we'd had gone to a local diner tucked away between a hardware store and a gas station. I'd stopped smelling the syrup, pastries, and beef when I fell into a pit of memories. By then, I could only smell Ella.

"Just reminiscing." My tone was low, with a subtle bite. I leaned back in the booth and picked up the menu. The words blurred together.

"I've done that lately myself. You know how deadly we both could've been together if you hadn't joined those swine?" Cyrus raised a glass of blood to his lips and forced a smile at a passing waitress.

"I see you're smiling more. It'd be safe to say that the White Fangs made you weak since your mantra was to never show vulnerability," I said, and placed my palms over my lap so the fabric of my pants could absorb the sweat.

Cyrus scoffed. I wondered if he'd crossed Briar's path and if he'd made her life miserable for entertainment. He opened his mouth to speak just as a waiter approached.

"Are we ready to order, gentlemen?" the waiter asked.

"Yes, it'll be one check." Cyrus ordered his food, then nodded toward me.

"I'll have nothing," I said, then handed the waiter the menu. I quickly hid my quivering hands under the table once more. The waiter hesitated, but took the menus without question.

"It'll be out shortly," he mumbled before hurrying off.

"I see you're still stubborn and full of pride," Cyrus murmured before taking another sip.

"Only when dealing with the likes of you." I scooted to the edge of my seat. "If this conversation is only going to be about getting me to join White Fang, then I think we're done here."

"I don't think you really have a choice," Cyrus said. I gripped the corner of the table mid-stance, then sank into the seat again.

"Oh?" I smirked with a dry laugh. "I always have a choice."

"You don't think I won't come after you? You will either join me by my side, or become my enemy. I don't mind killing you if I have to. You don't want that now, do you?" Cyrus tilted his head and narrowed his eyes, almost feral. I stood completely with a cool shrug, shoving my anxiety into its own compartment.

"I have plenty of enemies who haven't been able to kill me yet, so get in line." I reached in my pocket for my wallet and tossed enough cash on the table to cover his bill, then stalked away. I couldn't fully breathe until I got outside.

※

The sun was peeking above the horizon by the time I reached my apartment. Draven and Briar didn't have phones anymore and I'd forgotten to give them disposable cells while they were here. The apartment was empty, and I paced in the kitchen as I contemplated calling Astoria.

Where is everybody?

Everyone's scents had faded. They had been gone for hours now. I leaned over the counter and dialed Astoria's number, constantly shifting my weight while it rang. I looked around the kitchen and living room, soaking up my secret home as if for the last time. The clock was ticking on my stay here.

"Hello?" Astoria answered hoarsely.

My heart jumped with relief. I cleared my throat before speaking. "Hey, are you okay? Where are you?"

"Yeah, I'm fine. I'm still at the hospital." Her voice wavered with a sniffle.

"What do you mean 'still at the hospital'? When did you go?" I snatched my keys from the counter and flew out, already jogging down the staircase to get back to my car.

"Briar... she—" Astoria choked, and for a moment the only sound was a distant voice in the background. "She Turned our brother. She left with Draven. I don't know where they went. The nurses took Sterling to the Transition Wing, so I can't even see him anymore. I'm just waiting on the report."

The grey morning light gently burned my skin, like holding a hand inches away from a candle. By afternoon it'd feel like I put my entire hand in the flame.

I paused at the curb and tried to process what Astoria said while ignoring the pain.

I left for one night and Sterling was Turned into a Vampyre, Draven and Briar went missing, and Astoria was the only one left. *Alone*, with half the city searching for anyone with a blood type like Briar's. The statistical likelihood of Briar *and* Sterling inheriting the same blood type was already insane. A third relative? Impossible.

She did have a similar earthy and floral scent as her siblings, though.

"Are you there, Cass?" Astoria whimpered.

"Yeah, yeah. I'm here. Stay right there, I'm coming." I hung up.

The tires squealed all the way to the main road. I hoped that Sterling's partner Lyra was at the hospital too. Maybe she'd keep any hidden Nightshades at bay.

I put on brown-eyed contacts when I arrived, and took brisk strides inside. I went through security and straight down the hall, ignoring the admission desk. There had been a nearby wreck involving a bus, so no one stopped me while they dealt with the chaos.

The Transition Wing was in a restricted area, but I knew Astoria was probably waiting right outside of it. Her scent through the lobby was faint, but it intensified as I headed toward the unit.

Astoria was twirling a napkin in her lap and bouncing her leg as she stared at the double doors the doctor would appear from. I sat next to her and gently tapped her shoulder.

"Oh, you made it!" Astoria exclaimed and pulled me into a tight hug, hot tears instantly soaking through my shirt. My heart leaped and I froze, but then carefully wrapped my arms around her in return.

"What happened?" I whispered. I reached for the tissue on the end table next to me and passed it to her. She dabbed her eyes with a deep breath, then started to twist the new tissue instead.

"Draven took us to Lyra's place so Briar and I could see Sterling. He saw she was a Vampyre and started saying they turned her into a monster and she flipped out on him." Astoria kept her voice ten volume levels lower than mine.

"That's... well..." My voice trailed off as I imagined the events unfolding. Somehow, it didn't surprise me that Briar would do that. She was unpredictable and brash as a human. Every personality trait and flaw would be magnified as a Vampyre. But if her brother was as bad as they described... he had it coming.

"I'm sorry to hear that." I found the words and hoped they were good enough. I knew we weren't dealing with a death in her family, but to have a sibling change species status and be unable to see them without the threat of arrest or execution had to be similar. Especially for a girl like Astoria, who already despised breaking the law to begin with.

I was Vampyre-born and an only child, so I couldn't imagine the depth of her despair.

"I don't know what to do," Astoria breathed, bumping her head against the wall behind her. I twisted in the chair to face her squarely, leaning as close to her ear as possible.

"We need to get out of Neoterra," I whispered. "This place isn't safe for us anymore."

If I knew Draven at all, he and Briar got out and went to Helios. It was best place to lie low for the time being.

"What about Sterling?" Astoria whimpered softly.

"He's in good hands. The Nightshades can't hurt him in the Transition Wing, and by the time they release him, he'll be hell to deal with," I promised. I didn't know much about her brother, but from the things I'd heard from Briar and Draven, he sounded pretty easy to predict. Turning a man with combat training into the very species he despised was a deadly combination, but that was going to be Briar's thorn... not mine.

"I can't leave before the doctor comes out," Astoria said firmly, and clasped her loose fists in her lap.

"That's fine, but as soon as he's finished with the report, we're leaving before it gets too ugly," I insisted. Wraith and Delilah were probably risking daylight just to track me down. On top of that, with Cyrus failing in his attempt to recruit me to White Fang, things couldn't get much worse. I needed to tell Astoria everything, but now wasn't the time. I couldn't shatter her again like the news of Briar's transformation had after she survived the fire.

I felt like I was going to explode.

But I sat there with Astoria and slid my cold hand into her clammy one, and continued to be her anchor while she fought waves of tears in the lobby—all while my mind was plagued by the thought of losing my place with the Nightshades and of my father finding me.

I had to put up a front with my father... but if I were to be honest with anyone, it might as well have been with myself.

I was terrified of Cyrus.

43

BRIAR

The wind had stopped. Sirens and screams filled the streets as glass and dust sprayed from collapsing buildings. The road ran red while the sky was stained scarlet from fire and smoke. Helicopters flew above, weaving between the skyscrapers that were still standing. Until a missile threw one into the thirtieth floor.

I stood in the middle of it all, my clothes covered in blood. I didn't have a clue whose it was, where Draven was, or where anyone else was. Vampyres—both Turned and pure-blooded—rallied at the end of the street, emerging from the teargas and smoke as they carried flags and signs. They marched in my direction, eyes focused on whatever was behind me.

I whirled around and my breath caught in my throat. Tanks rolled over cars and corpses in the street, followed by *masses* of Onyx

Sentries that stretched along the road for miles. They were flown all the way from Mundus Novus itself.

Only then did I catch a glimpse of Draven's dead body moments before it disappeared under the tracks of a tank. Air rushed out of my lungs as I screamed without sound, and the Vampyre protestors ran around me like a rock in a river. I fell to my knees, gripping the front of my shirt as I waited for my heart to explode.

The bond that tethered me and Draven snapped. It was worse than watching my house burn down. Worse than watching Frankie implode. I felt the crushing pressure from the tank as if it were me underneath its tracks instead, and it was like being buried alive.

The second the opposing groups collided, the smell of gunpowder and copper singed my nostrils. I tried to block out the carnage by covering my ears. The ground began to tremble and crack as swirls of black fog and glowing magma seeped up from the depths, as if the war before me triggered the earth's wrath.

The same black fog curled and rippled around my body, absorbing the heat from the explosions, the gunfire, and the sun itself. I leaned back, peering at the enormous unkindness of ravens flying above my head. They blackened the sky. I rose my hand in the air, then slammed it against the concrete in a fist. Lava burst through and sprayed into the street.

It didn't care who it melted, human or Vampyre.

✳

I gasped awake to melancholy soft rock music and dirt in my mouth. I sat up rigidly, hacking up a lung while I tried to expel the dirt. I wiped my face and saw worms and roots poking in and out of walls of soil. I yelped with disgust.

"Stop, stop, *stop*!" A husky, angry howl.

Draven dropped from above and landed between my ankles. The impact sprayed more dirt over my tattered pants and stretched-out shirt. He dropped to his knees and grabbed my face, smashing his lips against my cold forehead and then my lips. I caught a glimpse of tears running down his cheeks before he clasped me tight against his chest. He shuddered violently. He didn't say anything, just rocked back and forth while I still sat there, dirty and confused.

I squinted at the light above, blinking wildly at the familiar faces peering down from the top of a deep hole that I quickly realized was my grave.

I examined my arms and touched my face, noting my skin lacked burns and boils from the sun.

"Your heart stopped for an hour," Malachi said, his eyes wide with horror as if I were a ghost. Samara and Azha poked their heads over the edge muttering in awe

"We thought you were dead," Draven breathed, and finally pulled away. "You... you healed yourself. No one's ever been able to do that against Larkin's toxins. And you're—"

"Not burning," I finished his sentence, turning my palms over in search of blisters. I released an incredulous exhale.

I was almost buried alive.

I touched my face, arms, and chest to ensure this was real.

I caressed Draven's cheek and felt the warmth beneath his skin. *Real.*

If my heart had stopped, and I woke up with sun immunity, maybe my body was resetting itself.

Maybe I was born again... but that didn't mean anything else was. Moses was still dead and Sterling had still lost his humanity.

Draven helped me stand. I wobbled and he scooped me up in his arms, then launched us out of the grave and flashed into a log cabin. He pulled a chair out from the dining table and eased me into it while the others filed inside.

"What are you guys doing here? How do you know each other?" The better question might've been what was *I* doing there, but the likelihood of Malachi, Azha, and Samara knowing each other was slim, especially since she was a Vampyre and they were humans.

"Well those two are married, and Malachi is my brother. They were both missing for months," Samara explained. I blinked, my jaw dropping. There was no chemistry between them whatsoever, but I guess Azha was serious when she'd said to never let White Fang find out about someone you cared about.

"Small world." I leaned into the chair, the wood creaking.

"What happened to Sundance?" I turned to Samara as I remembered how empty the hair salon was after I left Astoria at the hospital. In my earliest fledgling phase, I had high hopes of that place being my safe haven... and it was now gone.

"We got shut down shortly after you disappeared. I probably talked too much." She shrugged. "I came back here to get as far from the Nightshades as possible."

I raised my eyebrows. "Where's Jocelyn?" If the Nightshades had anything to do with their closure, I doubted it was peaceful.

"Everyone went their separate ways. We had a deadline to hit." Samara settled at the table and rested her forearms on its surface.

Azha and Malachi went into the kitchen. She eyed us warily

while he dug through the refrigerator. Unlike Caspian's, it didn't glow ruby from bags of blood—there were only two left—and was instead primarily filled with fresh vegetables, packs of meat, and varied juices and condiments.

I hope Caspian's doing okay... and that he's still keeping Astoria safe.

"So if you're related to Malachi... does that mean you're Turned?" I dropped my voice to a whisper. Samara bowed her head briefly, her long dangling earrings sweeping over her shoulders.

She shrugged nonchalantly. "It was my choice."

"Seriously? Even though it meant you couldn't be around your brother?" I tilted my head curiously.

Samara laughed and picked at her manicured nails. "They can't tell me to stay away from my own family. Before we got this house, it was just me and Malachi against the world. Before he met Azha and I found Sundance, we were homeless. It was getting too dangerous for us to survive, so I decided to get strong enough to protect us both." Samara's tone was casual, like everything was so simple.

"Why didn't he?" I dropped my voice low enough for human ears to miss.

"He's my little brother. It was and always will be my job to protect him, and I'll never forgive myself for failing them both when White Fang stole them." Samara glanced at the couple and I followed her solemn gaze to where Malachi and Azha were busily chopping vegetables and prepping pots on the stove.

I already understood Azha's distance. She wasn't chummy at White Fang. I didn't expect Malachi to be aloof though. They seemed more comfortable burying me than seeing me come back to life.

"Why don't you guys stay for a while?" Samara asked.

I shook my head. "I think we've stayed long enough."

I turned to Draven and rose to my feet uneasily. He quickly braced his hand at the small of my back until I found my footing. Judging by how heavily my head throbbed, I wondered how long it had been since I'd had any blood. Regardless, even with Malachi and Azha standing thirty feet away, I could smell what flowed in their veins. They were starting to look a lot less like friends and more like meals.

"Are you sure?" Samara asked as she stood with us. "At least take a shower, some clean clothes, and a blood pouch."

As much as I craved a nice hot shower and the blood, I didn't want to overstay our welcome. It didn't look like she had room to lend any blood either.

"Yeah, why don't you stay for dinner?" Malachi called from the kitchen, and I heard Azha hiss at him under her breath, "*Let them go.*"

"It's probably for the best," Draven said, pulling me closer as his arm curled over my shoulders. "Sorry I threatened y'all. I ain't the easiest to deal with under stress. Hard to trust folks too."

"No problem, we understand," Malachi said, dumping the sliced vegetables into a pan. The sizzle filled the uncomfortable beat of silence. Azha waved at us without looking in our direction.

"Glad you're better, Briar," she said flatly, then continued to cook.

"I'll see you guys out," Samara said, patting my shoulder. I couldn't wrap my head around Malachi and Azha's different behavior. We suffered through the same trauma under White Fang, yet they almost looked at me like *I* was White Fang.

Samara followed us onto the front porch and crossed her arms as she leaned against the banister.

"They might not seem like it, but they're relieved you're okay," she said.

I gave her an incredulous look. "Right," I mumbled, and scraped my shoe against the concrete walkway. "Well, thanks anyway."

"Of course. Be careful out there. I don't know what's going on with you, but you definitely have something that the Nightshades and White Fang would kill for," she warned. "If you guys ever need any more help, find me."

"Yeah... we will, thanks." Draven gave her a nod, and she waved. I returned the gesture, and we returned to the forest in silence.

✳

My nightmare kept replaying in the forest's stillness. The Onyx Sentries pummeling Vampyres was disturbing, but not as much as standing there, powerless, as Draven's body was crushed.

I wished I was back home, bored with my life at that stupid clothing store. I wished I was anywhere other than the city that had Vivian in it.

"Do ya remember anything?" Draven asked as he kicked a dead branch. It was getting easier to see the road beyond the trees.

"The last thing I remember was going to the bathroom on the ferry, and then I couldn't move or speak." I spoke numbly. Maybe that was why I couldn't do anything in my dream.

Draven clamped his lips together with a sigh. "I'm sorry," he rasped.

"For what?" I tilted my head and raised an eyebrow.

"Maybe if I'd followed you, none of this would've happened," he said bitterly.

"That's not true. The ferry still wrecked, so I don't think anything would've changed." I shrugged. Draven sighed and shook his head as his footsteps grew heavier. It didn't matter what I said, I knew he'd blame himself.

I wouldn't be surprised if he blamed himself for Moses' death and Sterling's attack, even though it was all my doing.

When the thick canopy started to thin out, I skipped between shafts of light, expecting pain. Draven ambled through, unbothered. I remembered that the sun didn't hurt when I woke up in the grave and followed his path. The warmth glazed over me, then disappeared.

I hoped the sun immunity was permanent.

"You apologized... for threatening Malachi and Azha?" I wanted to take my focus off the fact that I had *died*.

"I told 'em I'd kill 'em all if you didn't make it." Draven snatched leaves off a branch and started ripping them to pieces.

"Well I technically *did*, so why didn't you? Are all of your threats empty?" I blurted, then bit my lip with a cringe. I was glad he hadn't hurt them, I really was.

"Malachi did everything he could. They even gave you five blood pouches. It wouldn't have been right to take it out on him when somebody else put ya in that state," Draven explained calmly. "Not all my threats are empty. I got some I just haven't had the chance to fulfill yet."

I dipped my head and let the dead calm take over once again.

I tried to remember anything I could've done to wrong Malachi and Azha. While they had tried to save my life, they still didn't seem... relieved or anything. Something was off.

"They weren't the same as I remembered from White Fang," I said somberly.

Draven clicked his tongue and broke a thin branch before sticking it in his mouth like a toothpick. "Someone once told me that it don't matter who you were before. All anybody's gonna see you as... is a monster from here on out." The branch bounced between his lips as he spoke matter-of-factly. "You're one of us now, so get used to it."

His words stung. They implied that my own family could do the same. I expected Sterling to hate me after Turning him, but Astoria... I hoped she didn't.

"Malachi still seems close with his sister, though." I tried to ease the pain from the stake Draven's words drove into my heart.

"Yeah, maybe so. But if it came down to it, his wife would come first. Blood don't matter when your species changes." I stared at the fallen leaves in our path as my eyes burned. I poked at my lip piercing with my tongue to keep myself from talking more about it. He seemed to sense the topic needed to change.

"We need to regroup. We can get some cash from my bank. I'll get us a hotel and see if I can get a hold of Caspian."

Draven was focused, scanning left and right, above and below with each step, until he froze at the snap of a branch. I whirled around, sniffing the air like a wild dog for anyone that could've followed us.

I sighed with a quivering laugh when I noticed a raven flying out of a bush. Those blasted birds seemed to be following me. Draven chuckled, but the tension never left his shoulders. I hooked my arm through his as we continued toward the city.

I kept my head low with my eyes shut tight as I clung to Draven's side. I still braced for the scalding pain of daylight, even though the forest's beams yielded nothing.

I lifted my head and let go of Draven, slowing my pace to a full stop as I took in the warm rays without a tree's shield.

"What's wrong?" His eyes darted around the forest for enemies.

"It... it still doesn't hurt." I lifted my gaze to the heavens with a smile.

Draven grinned, his dimples deepening with pride to reveal his fanged teeth. I ran and leaped into his arms. He spun me around with a laugh and then set me down.

"Ain't it liberating?" he beamed. It wasn't often I saw a complete smile on his face.

I dreamed of a life where I could see it more often, because *that* was even more liberating than the sunlight.

44

DRAVEN

It was mid-afternoon by the time we reached the heart of Helios. We walked through the forest and along the shoulder of the highway for three hours. Briar didn't speak much after I'd ruthlessly responded with the cold truth of how people would view her from now on. I wished I had sugarcoated it, at least until later when she was less vulnerable. Even her newfound sun immunity didn't keep her spirits high for long.

I knew Briar was probably exhausted from lack of blood and her week in a coma, but we couldn't risk getting into a cab. We blended in with the Sun Dwellers at first glance, but the second anyone noticed our eyes, it'd be over. We needed contact lenses.

We kept our heads down as much as possible when the number of people increased. The roads had transformed from serene, narrow strips to three-lane beasts with crosswalks.

We stopped at the corner of an intersection and waited for the opportunity to cross the street. Next to us was a park with an empty playground and yellowed grass, where a small group of Vampyres were concealing themselves with thick umbrellas. They held handmade signs of varying colors in silent protest, demanding that curfews be lifted, families be brought back together, our species be treated with dignity, and equal pay. Some even declared that we weren't monsters, that we had medical conditions instead. They technically weren't wrong. We came into existence because of the Red Plague eighty years ago.

I never saw protests in Neoterra, and Helios always seemed like anywhere else—where everyone was satisfied with whatever side of the fence they were on.

A teenage boy broke from the crowd with a can of paint and began spraying "bigots" across a limestone monument of Eric Strickland, the city's historical founder. I grabbed Briar's hand quickly and leaned forward, poised to dart across the street—when I caught a swarm of police officers flooding into the park to break the protestors up. They howled in agony when the cops knocked their umbrellas away, exposing them to the sun and allowing the Sun Dweller officers to overpower them.

I gritted my teeth at the sight. It was harder to look away than to keep watching, fighting the urge to spray fire at the officers. What were those Vampyres thinking? What were they trying to achieve? It wasn't even a legal protest to start with, since it was hours before Gloaming.

"They're hurting them," Briar croaked. Gunshots rang and

bodies began to drop one by one. Every bystander outside screamed and ducked into whatever building they could.

Briar gaped in horror at the violence unfolding just a hundred feet from us. "They're *killing* them!"

The second the walk sign illuminated, I pulled her along the crosswalk with me in a near sprint.

I focused on the glass revolving door of the bank across the street. The gold trim glinted in the daylight. As much as I wanted to use the ATM, I didn't have my wallet with me. I couldn't remember the last time I had it. It was safe to say it was in the middle of the ocean.

We got trapped in the revolving door for two rotations, then staggered inside the grand lobby encrusted in black marble and jade. Four panicked Sun Dwellers piled in behind us, and the bank employees and patrons gasped at our clamorous entrance. I straightened my shirt, whispering to Briar to wait for me at the door. She looked rather homeless, and I didn't want any more attention on us than there already was. The four Sun Dwellers hung around the windows, peeking outside as the chaos continued. Most of them had their phones out, recording the violence.

I stuffed my hands in my pockets and approached the teller. Her shoulders hiked up to her neck and she took a half step away from the counter.

"Hey." I forced a smile to try to ease her tension, but kept my eyes low, glued to the counter. "I'm here to withdraw two thousand. I ain't got my stuff but I can answer the questions or whatever."

"What's your name, sir?" She hesitantly placed her hands on the keyboard.

"Draven Hawthorne. Born in Eclipsis, favorite teacher was Mrs. Hanson, and my first pet was a dog named Vinnie." The quicker I got through the process, the faster Briar and I could go to a hotel. I glanced behind me to see what she was doing, and her attention was glued to one of the televisions mounted above the tellers. The media was already covering the mayhem outside.

"And you wanted that in *cash*?" Beth asked with rapid blinks.

"Yeah, in all denominations if ya can." I smiled thinly, finally meeting her gaze so she knew I meant business. She gasped, but went right to counting. I leaned over the counter slightly to keep an eye on her quivering hands. This wasn't a robbery, but a police officer would easily believe a Sun Dweller's word over the likes of mine. She didn't press the panic button before her thumbs busily flicked over the crisp bills, but that didn't guarantee she wouldn't push it the second I turned my back.

And the cops right outside could be here in literal seconds if she did.

Beth placed the money in an envelope and grinned.

"I hope you have a good day, sir. Be careful out there." She clasped her hands on the counter. I dipped my head, then turned on my heel and whispered Briar's name to get her attention. I jerked my chin toward the door and she followed me.

Ambulances and police cars choked the traffic. Yellow tape barred journalists from the park. Everyone was too focused on the arrests, injuries, and deaths to notice me and Briar breaking curfew.

✳

The nearest hotel was next to Helios' City Hall. The parking lot was moderately full, without a soul in sight. I approached the sliding glass doors, searching for the sign that usually stated what patrons they allowed. I sighed with relief to see it was a Vampyre-only business. Maybe things were starting to look up.

I neared the receptionist desk while Briar admired the lobby's decor and upholstered furniture. I felt a little heat rise up my neck when she grabbed a set of glass coasters and examined them, wishing she could just stay *still* for a second.

I paid for our room under aliases, occasionally glancing back at Briar while I waited for the man to input the information.

"Do you need help with any bags?" The man raised the phone to call for baggage service, but I held up my hand to stop him.

"Ain't no need, thanks." I grabbed the plastic key cards and called for Briar before stalking to the elevator. She hurried across the lobby to catch up.

Briar leaned against the wall of the elevator and watched the numbers ascend with a blank expression.

"Are you okay?" I grumbled.

"Just thinking about the people at the park." Briar reached up to scratch her head with a small frown. "And I'm starving and need a shower."

"Well, I'll get ya somethin' in a bit," I promised.

I examined each number as we passed each door down the long hallway, illuminated by dim spherical sconces between each room. I stopped in front of our room number and swiped the card to enter.

There were two queen beds with comforters tightly tucked into the platform bed frames. A triptych of the beach hovered above the headboards and the nightstand positioned between them. Briar instantly disappeared into the bathroom and I waited to hear the shower cut on before taking her clothes and leaving the hotel room.

I padded down the hall to the laundry room and put a dollar in the machine. While the load ran, I returned to our room and went straight to the phone made of glass on the nightstand to call Caspian. I flipped through the menu for room service while I waited for him to pick up.

Briar started to hum softly, the sound growing into song just as Caspian picked up.

"Who is this?" He usually greeted with his surname, and for a moment I questioned if I had the right number.

"Draven." I wouldn't have been so honest if I didn't recognize his voice.

"*Draven?*" Caspian exasperated. "Where have you been, man?"

I laughed softly. "Literally everywhere. Ya disappeared on me too."

"Is Briar there?" I caught Astoria's voice in the background.

"Yeah, she is. We're in Helios." I glanced toward the bathroom and froze at the sight of Briar standing in the doorway, wrapped in a towel. Water dripped along her unamused face as she crossed her arms.

"Where are my clothes?" she mouthed silently. I held up my index finger and returned to my conversation. She rolled her eyes and disappeared into the bathroom again, shutting off the steam that rolled out of it. I completely lost my train of thought.

"That's crazy, cause we just arrived Helios too," Caspian said. "Where are you? What brought you here?"

"*Long* story, but can ya meet us at the Dogwood Hotel?" I asked. "I gotta go."

"Yeah, no problem."

Caspian hung up, and I jumped from the bed to rush to the laundry room. I threw Briar's clothes in the dryer, then hurried to the front desk to request a robe and blood be sent to our room. By the time I returned, the room service staff was already knocking on the door with an intricately carved gold tray holding wine glasses.

"I'll take some of this off ya hands." I grabbed the tray and robe from him, but he stood there until I passed a hundred as a tip. The man smiled eagerly, then rolled the cart away.

Briar was still in the bathroom when I stepped inside the hotel room. I held the robe to my cheek, marveling in its warm terry cloth.

"I got a surprise for you," I called. Briar cracked the door open and reached through, grabbing the robe. I hurried to the bed and carefully laid out the tray. She came out with the robe tied around her waist and pulled the collar to her nose with a pleasurable inhale.

"Thanks, it smells like lavender." She grinned as she hugged herself, then gasped at the tray of blood and snatched a glass. Only her feline grace prevented the red from blotting the white comforter. My heart vibrated at the near disaster, because it would've been my fault for having the stupid idea in the first place. She took the tray and set it on the desk next to the television, then lay among the six fluffy pillows.

"Ugh, this is paradise." She put her nose over the rim of the glass before chugging it entirely. I grabbed the other glass on the tray and plopped on the bed next to her, but I took small sips. "Even though hundreds of people probably want us dead, this is the safest I've felt in a while."

"Enjoy it while it lasts," I said. Briar puckered her lips ever so slightly to plant a kiss on mine. She caressed my face with a warm hand and pulled back an inch.

"We're gonna be fine. As long as we stick together, we can figure out how to make Uriah and White Fang pay," she said quietly, "Before they destroy everything." She had the same twinkle in those rose-quartz eyes as when they were diamonds—when I first saw her get lost in the music at The Nightshade bar.

We might be too late, I thought, and the grin on my face tugged inward. *If they're openly killing cops, the war has already started. And I don't think I can handle losing you again.*

I didn't have enough power to take on both clans. I couldn't even consistently control my power.

I kept my mouth shut. As much as I wanted to, I couldn't destroy Briar's hope. She needed to carry enough of it for the both of us.

45

BRIAR

THE HOT SHOWER SEARING MY SKIN AND VAPORIZING THE dirt from my pores was the type of cleansing I needed after nearly getting buried alive. The cozy warmth of the terry cloth robe combined with the rich blood lulled my headache to a low hum.

Draven eventually left me alone while he got my clothes out of the dryer. I let the pillows swallow me, sinking further into the bed like being engulfed in clouds. I closed my eyes to revel in it, only to remember the sterile cell at White Fang's headquarters.

And the scarlet staining the white walls as Frankie's body splattered in every direction.

My eyes flung open at the sound of a knock on the door, jolting upright. I set the glass down on the nightstand and crossed the room in a silent prowl. I didn't recognize the scent on the other side of the door and carefully stood on my toes to peek through the peep hole.

My heart paced faster, its beat rising to my ears—until I saw who was on the other side.

Caspian stood with a gaunt expression. I could see the top of Astoria's head behind his shoulders. I clutched the collar of my robe closed as I opened the door with a smile.

"You came!" I exclaimed with a bright grin. I wanted to hug Astoria, but her tight smile and creased forehead held me at bay. They stepped inside, both of them scanning the room in unison like a pair of cyborgs.

"We didn't really have a choice." Caspian flung his duffel bag on the spare bed. Astoria fidgeted with her hair, eyes bouncing between both beds, possibly stressing over being in a Vampyre-only establishment.

"Why?" I frowned, curling back into my spot among the pillows. Reality was drawing near like a bullet train, and I hoped my last dream would be pleasant.

"Well, I left behind quite a mess back home. I take it you two didn't do much better either." Caspian collapsed in the chair at their bedside, next to the blaring air conditioning unit. He leaned his head back with an exasperated sigh. Astoria rubbed her arm as she sat on the bottom of the other bed.

"Wow, you guys are here already?" Draven reentered the room with my clothes and tossed them to me. He kicked off his shoes and socks.

"We got here as fast as we could. I had to cash in a favor from an old friend to use his boat. You two wouldn't have anything to do with the ferry being shut down, would you?" Caspian squinted in Draven's direction.

"Probably," he responded curtly.

"How's... um... Sterling?" It didn't feel right to ask, but it gnawed at me more than the trials we would inevitably face.

"He'll be fine," Astoria mumbled. I nodded and accepted her terse answer. She didn't have to give me one at all.

"We brought the new clothes you two left behind," Caspian announced, pointing a lithe finger at the duffel bag.

"Thanks, man." Draven went straight for it, sifting through until he found a t-shirt and boxers. "Good ya brought weapons too."

"Of course I would," Caspian said as Draven vanished into the bathroom.

I yanked at the sheets, which seemed to be held down by anchors. I burrowed under them, dreading the conversation to come. For the first time in a while, I wished those glasses held wine instead of blood.

I lay there, staring at the ceiling in the dead quiet for thirty minutes.

The second Draven emerged from the thin cloud swirling out of the bathroom, he said, "What kind of mess did *you* leave behind, Cass?"

"I killed Larkin." He spoke as if he'd broke an antique vase. Astoria's eyes widened as her ivory skin turned grey.

"Alright!" Draven punched the air proudly, and I... well...

I buried my face deeper in the pillows to hide that I was also delighted.

"You... *killed* someone?" Astoria rasped. Caspian gave her a lazy smile with a menacing chuckle.

"Don't act so surprised. We're Vampyres." He rolled his eyes and moved the sheer white curtains to peek outside. "Not like you haven't *seen* me do it before."

"Hey, man, plenty of Vampyres have never killed someone," I cut in. I had no idea if that were true, but it seemed likely since blood was accessible in the grocery stores and the fledgling program had been implemented in the hospitals. I just hated not being part of that category myself.

"Like you, Briar?" Astoria asked pointedly. I propped myself up on my elbows and only stared blankly at her. I couldn't lie to her, but I wasn't ready to admit the truth yet either.

Did she already know about Moses, or did she say that because I'd *almost* killed Sterling?

Draven cleared his throat, possibly to dilute the tension that had rapidly become tangible. "What's the game plan, guys? Are we gonna keep running or try to figure out how to take Uriah down?" He sat on the edge of the bed and clasped his rough hands together as he leaned his elbows on his knees.

"Take Uriah down," I demanded. It was the obvious choice. Why run when the problem would *never* go away? "Teach me how to use a gun or something and I'll do whatever it takes."

"Run," Astoria whispered, rounding her shoulders forward as she wrapped her arms around herself. My sister and I turned to the men, waiting to see if the vote would be split between us.

Draven fixed his gaze on Caspian with a tight jaw and resolute expression. "I'm sick of Uriah dictating my life. I say we fight, even if we die tryin'."

Caspian's blank mask slipped, revealing weariness beneath. He flopped his head back on the chair's headrest before lifting it again.

"I guess we fight, then. With Wraith, Uriah, White Fang, and my father hot on our trail, we might need more than three of us. It doesn't help that Briar doesn't have her self control yet either... no offense," he droned.

I shrugged. I wasn't going to get offended by the truth. Any enemy of mine could probably sense I was a fledgling and throw a bag of blood into the bushes to distract me.

And I'd go, even knowing it was a trap.

I shuffled to the duffel for a fresh set of clothes. Suddenly I didn't feel comfortable being in the robe. I needed to be ready. Maybe I'd even sleep in my boots.

If I could even sleep anymore after dying. Real, physical exhaustion hadn't visited since. I really hoped that nightmare wasn't my last dream.

In the bathroom, I changed into a black long-sleeve and jeans, then took a moment to examine myself in the mirror. My light pink eyes—mirroring the same color hair I'd kept dyed for years—seemed like a sick joke at this point.

Draven had fire, Uriah had metal, but what did I have other than a bottomless pit of cravings and murder? Me, the one with the blood type so rare that it leveled up everyone's strength other than my own. Me, the one who'd finally become a Vampyre, one with the freedom to walk in the day and the night, but was still somehow weaker compared to the rest.

I loved Draven and my family—and I was beginning to consider Caspian as a brother. I was willing to die for them, but if our fates looked anything like that dream I'd had...

I had nothing to offer but to stand as a witness to their deaths.

*

Draven, Caspian, and I sat in silence while Astoria finally slipped into a fitful slumber. Every once in awhile she'd toss and turn or whimper and Caspian had to nudge her awake for a reset. If there was a fly on the wall, we'd either look like wolves surrounding a lamb or lions guarding their young. Draven and I never moved from our bed, only stared at the muted TV screen with our ears focused on the hallway beyond. He'd grabbed a pistol from the duffel bag and kept it near him.

Astoria was more restless as Gloaming approached. I guess her sleep schedule had turned into mine when I started breaking curfew as a Sun Dweller. She yawned and smacked her dry lips as she forced herself to sit up, hair disheveled.

"Did you sleep okay?" Caspian asked, gently. I glanced at Draven with a small grin, pleased to see how caring his friend was toward my sister. She never had anyone show that much concern for her well-being beyond me and Sterling.

"A little. I had a dream about our mom." Astoria rubbed her eyes and turned to me. "We should go see her one last time, just in case we die in all this."

I recoiled, but understood. Astoria had a point, but I never intended to let Vivian see who I'd become. All she ever did was criticize the very breath I took. I could hear the remarks she'd make if she saw me now.

The only thing keeping her safe would be the plexiglass that divided us.

No. Self control. You can't keep setting off every time someone says something you don't like.

"Fair enough," I responded through gritted teeth. Draven cupped his hands around mine. The callouses were grounding, keeping me in the present before my mind spun in a vortex, as it always did when Vivian became the subject of conversation.

"We need to stick together," Caspian announced. "If we keep getting separated, then we might not be so lucky finding each other next time."

"Agreed," Draven replied, and started packing whatever supplies the hotel had provided just in case we didn't return.

"Our mom is in prison, so you can't bring that," Astoria warned, placing her hands on her hips.

"No worries, one of us will wait outside for y'all." Draven looked at Caspian, who responded with a short nod in some secret communication they'd established. I chewed on my thumbnail as we filed out the door.

✳

Astoria was tense the second we left the hotel. With daylight savings time around the corner, the days were growing shorter, and it wasn't long before Check-Ins would shift earlier. For now, though... there was still time before she was technically breaking curfew. It wasn't the first time she'd broken it, but I didn't think she'd ever shake the fear of legal trouble.

As usual, passing Vampyres ignored Astoria's existence. Even the cab driver when we piled in the back seat, Caspian sitting in the front. I assumed our Vampyric scents masked her human one, or maybe everyone assumed she was a hunted victim waiting for her demise and looked the other way.

Or maybe no one cared in Helios either.

We stood at the edge of the long, dirt driveway, marveling at the building's architecture and might as we always did.

My mouth had long gone dry, the headache had since returned, and the warmth had been sucked right out of my bones the minute we left the hotel room.

The four of us walked down the path with Astoria leading the way, Caspian hanging right behind her like a shadow, and Draven slowing down to match my pace as I stalled nearing the gatehouse.

I froze when we finally approached the correctional officer sheltered in the spherical glass. He took our information, reminded Astoria what time it was, and allowed us to go inside. Caspian insisted on waiting at the bench near the front doors to keep watch of our stuff.

I wished I could've had that role, but I would've never heard the end of it if I didn't talk to Vivian one last time.

If it was the last time. I hoped so, even if we survived our enemies.

Draven, Astoria, and I were patted down when we entered, then escorted to the visitor room. We picked a booth, and Astoria took her place in the metal chair. I remained standing despite a second chair being available, and shrunk next to Draven when our mother approached.

Vivian's once sallow skin was now full and supple, her cheeks rosy. Her brassy hair more like honey now, shining under the fluorescent lights. I expected a different colored set of irises, but they were just the same—the stormy grey I had inherited.

"Full house today, I see." She eased into her chair on the other side of the plexiglass, the fabric of her black jumpsuit zipping as usual. She did a double take when she saw me standing next to Draven.

"You've gotta be kidding me, Briar." Vivian gasped. "You changed your whole species for some thug?"

Draven loosed a wry laugh.

"I don't remember ever meetin' ya," he said as he crossed his arms and raised his chin defiantly.

"You're not the type of man I envisioned Briar being with." Vivian's eyes scaled him from head to toe, lingering longer on the exposed arm and neck tattoos and the buzzed hair. "You look like you belong right in here with me."

"Mom!" Astoria snapped. "Stop it!"

"Don't you realize you're not allowed to hang out with Vampyres? Have I taught you nothing?" Vivian sneered.

"Actually you *haven't*. Unless you count how to use drugs and beat your kids." I watched Vivian's face contort in a scowl.

"When are you going to get over my mistakes? I'm already paying for them in here." Vivian's words sped up as her rage roiled.

"Why did we come here again, Ria?" I looked down at Astoria with a hand on my hip, ignoring Vivian's remark. It didn't matter that Vivian was atoning for her sins in Black Bay Prison. Every time she opened her mouth convinced me she hadn't changed one bit.

Astoria huffed and shook her head, turning her focus back to Vivian.

"Mom, we're in a lot of trouble." She dropped her voice to a whisper. "We came to tell you we love you just in case you never see us again."

Vivian frowned, but the tightness around her eyes and jaw loosened.

"What kind of trouble?" Vivian leaned closer to the plexiglass. "Are your lives in danger? What did you do now, Briar? *He's* got something to do with it, doesn't he?"

I rammed my fist into the plexiglass, and Draven snatched me away from the booth before the warden could reprimand me.

"Why are you *always* blaming me?!" I yelled, tugging against Draven's grip.

"Briar, *breathe*," he demanded, then stepped into my line of sight so I couldn't see Vivian anymore. He grabbed the sides of my face and tilted my head to meet his gaze.

"Don't stoop to her level. She's tryin' to get a rise out of ya," he said, then began inhaling through his nose and exhaling out his mouth. I mirrored his breathing, shutting my eyes to imagine I was elsewhere.

"Ya feel better now?" He angled his head with a soft grin.

"Yeah, where have you been all my life?" I asked with a short laugh, then walked around him.

"Searching for you," he quipped. I blushed moments before my face went cold at the sight of Vivian again.

Then we were thrown across the room in a violent blast of heat, dust, and debris.

The air smelled of burnt plastic and sulfur. I coughed violently. My ears rang. A klaxon blared in tandem with piercing shrieks.

"*Draven! Astoria!*" I cried. I tried to sit up, but concrete piled on top of me.

Strobe lights flickered. Through the flashes of black and white, I could see bodies lying still. Frantic wardens and inmates scattered. Then armed gangsters poured into the prison.

———◆◆———

Enjoy a Sneak Peek of

The Oleander

Final Installment of the "Until Equinox" Trilogy

———◆◆———

It was *always* me and Caspian on our missions as Nightshades. There were two bodies accounted for, and he was more than capable of taking care of himself.

Now?

I had Briar as a fledgling at my side, her insufferable mother in my arms, and her frail sister trailing closely behind Caspian, who was trapped in a vicious cycle of healing, burning, and fighting to keep consciousness. Five people stuck out a lot more than two. The weight on my shoulders crushed me.

To have so many lives in the palms of my hands—lives I *cared* about—distressed me to levels beyond comprehension.

Only the sound of birds chirping and the occasional whimper from Vivian circulated the woods.

Until a quiet thud prompted us all to turn and see Caspian sprawled on his back. Icing on the friggin' cake.

"Cass!" Astoria gasped and dropped to her knees, placing her palms on either side of his face. "What's wrong with him?" she whimpered, and drew another sharp inhale at sight of the burns across his formerly immaculate skin.

"He can't be out here like us," Briar explained with a subtle tremble in her voice, chewing on her thumbnail. Her forehead wrinkled before she snapped a bunch of leaves and laid them over Caspian's face and hands.

"I don't think we can find Samara before our time runs out," she said.

All good points, and all points that added more stress. The scenarios kept getting worse.

Onyx Sentries could arrive at Helios at any moment and make it impossible to leave the island, and Samara and her family could refuse to help us, leaving Caspian to risk potential death and Briar's mother still helpless.

In the thirteen years I'd known Caspian, I never once saw him in such a weakened state. I kept quiet while the others panicked, despite every alarm blaring in my mind as my thoughts ran a hundred miles a minute.

With a deep inhale, I lowered Vivian to the ground, and rubbed the back of my neck before shifting my focus to Caspian. I crouched next to him and lifted one leaf to see if it had helped. Only a quarter returned to normal, the rest still riddled with second- and third-degree burns and blisters. It was a slow rate, but at least he was healing. That was a good sign.

"We need to help him! Why are we still standing around?" Astoria exclaimed, and Briar shushed her with an index finger over her lips.

"Let us think, Ria!" she snapped.

Astoria hardly blinked as she watched Caspian's chest rise and fall with ragged, shallow breaths. Tears glittered along her waterline until she briefly closed her eyes and let them fall. I lifted my chin, squinting at the sky between the intertwining branches and leaves. The sun was still strong.

"We could look for shade until sunset and hope for the best. The best-case scenario... he gets better before the morning and we find Samara while it's still dark." I didn't trust myself to make the right decision. Had the roles been reversed, Caspian would've had the most efficient plan to solve our problem. But these were the cards I was dealt, and the best way I knew how to play the hand.

I wasn't comfortable with how heavily we depended on Samara, Malachi, and Azha agreeing to help us.

I turned in small circles, observing the surrounding woods. The sparse canopy grew denser going west. I passed over Vivian and hoisted Caspian over my shoulder, then began a brisk walk in that direction with Astoria hot on my trail. Vivian was smart—she kept her mouth shut long enough for Briar to decide to help her before changing her mind.

As the air went from humid heat to a damp chill, the woods transitioning to a misty maple and sweetgum forest. I followed the winding estuary cutting through the trees until we reached a cave. There, I eased Caspian over a bed of dead leaves and twigs, completely out of contact with the light beams cracking through. Briar did the same with Vivian, but with a lot less grace. She let her flop on the ground like she was too heavy, which was impossible. Fledgling or not, supernatural strength always manifested early.

But again, I stayed silent. Their beef was not my own, although her crass mother did say my tattoos made me look like an inmate.

Vivian hadn't even seen the Nightshades' clan insignia on my chest yet.

"So this is how you kids handle these things? Live on the run and hide in strange caves that might have bats in them?" Vivian said scornfully as she rubbed her tailbone. Briar squatted in front of her with the same wild spark in her eyes before she attacked Sterling. I bent my knees and inched forward, poised to separate them.

"Like you? Selling yourself on the streets for a thirty-minute high? Running off in the middle of the night, breaking curfew, and getting our dad killed looking for you?" Briar's tone was light, but lethal. "If you don't like how we're handling things, I'm happy to take you back to Black Bay."

"Black Bay is in ashes," Vivian responded without an ounce of fear in her voice, but her skin blanched. She didn't defend herself against Briar's allegations, and my heart sank at the thought of it being true. It wasn't Vivian's nature to stay silent otherwise.

"It's not the only prison that exists in the country." Briar's gaze locked on hers, as if she'd pounce at the slightest movement.

"Drop it, Bri," Astoria demanded, placing her hands on her hips. Briar cut her eyes at her sister, then at me. Maybe she expected me to say something in her defense, but my lips only parted without sound. She stalked to the edge of the cave, leaning against its vine-covered threshold. My shoulders relaxed when she moved away from Vivian, but the tension in my neck remained.

I sank next to Caspian to monitor his condition. He needed blood, but we were far from civilization, and I doubted Vivian or Astoria would donate. I didn't know how deep Astoria's attachment went with him.

"Why isn't he healing?" Briar frowned.

"He is, just at a slow rate. Vampyres don't do well with sunlight or fire. That's why Uriah always used it against his rivals. It's actually ironic that I can control it." I loosed a wry chuckle, and looked down at Caspian somberly. At this rate, he wouldn't be functional until tomorrow night—time we didn't have.

"Is there any way to make it faster?" Astoria asked, zipping her opal pendant across her gold chain necklace.

"Sorta..." I pressed my lips in a thin line and eyed Briar warily. "Blood helps us heal faster..."

"There's no shot in hell we're Turning Astoria," Briar spat.

Astoria didn't let me respond to her sister or take a breath before asking, "Can I give some to him without getting Turned?"

I blinked, taken aback by the blitzed responses from both siblings.

"Uh, well, hold on—"

"I'll step outside," Briar said, as if she foresaw the alternative. "I want him to be okay too. But I don't wanna risk attacking Astoria if she can help him."

"*How?*" Astoria demanded with more irritation.

Briar shrugged. "Cut your hand, let him drink that way."

"Oh, no, Ria don't do that for some boy that could be dead,"
Vivian condemned. "You'll scar up your pretty little hands!"

Briar growled and jerked forward before I flashed at her side and
caught her arm.

"Ignore her!" I shouted.

I shot a dark look toward Vivian.

"Not another word," I added through clenched teeth.

God, my head hurt.

I squeezed Caspian's shoulder when I didn't see his chest move.
He wheezed quietly. Good enough.

"Are ya willing to do it? He needs blood regardless." I narrowed
my eyes at Vivian. I didn't mind *taking* it from her instead. I was
sure the only one here that'd have a problem with it was Astoria.

"Yeah, you'd think a concerned mother would do it in place of
her daughter," Briar mumbled under her breath.

"I'll do it, I don't care." Astoria held out her slender, pale palm.
Vivian rolled her eyes with an exasperated sigh.

"Thanks," I muttered, and ignored the bitter taste in my mouth
as I elongated the claw of my index finger and dragged it across Astoria's palm. She sucked her teeth with a grimace, and clamped her fist
to keep the blood in place until she returned to Caspian. Her breath
tremored before she held her fist an inch above his lips and allowed
the blood to drip.

A gust whistled past the threshold of the cave, and Briar was
gone.

"Yell out if he wakes up," I said, and hurried after her. "Briar!"

Stepping outside didn't mean leave, *right?*

I tracked the small frame already a half mile away, trudging through the bushes. I broke into a dash, catching up in seconds.

"Hey, why'd ya go so far?" I reached for Briar's shoulder. "Where are ya even going?"

"I don't know, I was gonna keep going until I couldn't smell Astoria anymore." Briar rubbed her nose with a sniff. Her fangs extended, peeking past her lips with every word.

"Ya don't think you could hold back?" I raised my eyebrows.

Briar laughed dryly. "Do *you?*"

I had to calculate my response.

"I... I ain't expecting it yet."

"Well... you didn't have to follow me. Aren't you worried Caspian can wake up in a frenzy too?" Briar peered over shoulder, toward the cave. I shook my head with a shrug.

"Vampyre-borns ain't typically prone to frenzies."

"But the Turned are? You mean I'm still a risk after I'm out of the fledgling phase?" Briar's tone rose in a crescendo, and I gripped her shoulders with a gentle squeeze.

"No, that ain't what I'm sayin'," I countered. "It depends on the person. Some of us have less resistance than others even after maturing. For example... your Ma... if she was an addict before, somebody like her could be prone to frenzies well into Vampyrehood. A disciplined athlete or a soldier might not be. It just... depends."

Briar was silent. She stared bleakly at a lost twig, then her face returned to the pensive frown she'd been keeping since her brother's attack.

I guessed she'd have chosen differently at White Fang if she'd known.

Astoria called for me. At the very least, her tone didn't sound panicked.

"Let's head back." I held out my hand, but Briar didn't take it, instead shooting off in a blurred sprint. I waited a couple seconds before I followed, feeling the sting of her rejection.

⸻ ••• ⸻

Thank you for reading!
If you enjoyed this book, please consider leaving a review on Amazon and/or Goodreads. Reviews are golden for indie authors and they encourage more exposure. It would be very much appreciated!

⸻ ••• ⸻

AUTHOR'S NOTE

Looking for the next book? If you'd like signed copies with extra goodies like bookmarks and stickers, you can find them on my website: *www.taliawall.com/book-store*

If you are interested in monthly updates for upcoming projects and events, you can also sign up for my newsletter on my website.

ACKNOWLEDGMENTS

First, I want to thank God for giving my full imagination back. When I wrote *The Nightshades*, I expected another burnout. With the flooding amount of ideas that returned instead, I know I regained a piece of myself I once lost. I will never stop thanking Him for that.

I want to again thank my husband and the rest of my family for always being in my corner, no matter how dark it seemed. They always helped me stay encouraged and focused on the light at the end of the tunnel.

I give thanks to the beta readers and editors' support. This second round in the process was a lot less daunting than before. *The Bleeding Hearts* was more challenging with the introduction of more point-of-views, and I appreciate all the feedback to make the story as seamless as possible.

Finally, I once again give thanks to my readers. Your enthusiasm and appreciation of my storytelling motivate me to keep writing and publishing more content rather than letting it collect digital dust. Thank you for continuing to stay with me during this journey. I can't wait to bring you more adventures!

About the Author

Talia spent most of her life in North Carolina and had the lifelong dream of becoming an author since she was five. She not only loves to write but also to draw and paint. She has a loving husband and Persian cat named Thor who often interrupts her writing sessions. She writes young and new adult, paranormal, urban fantasy, and dystopian genres with the intent to send powerful, relevant messages and warnings through fiction.

Social Media Handles

TikTok | Threads | Instagram
@fromdreamstopaper
Website:
www.taliawall.com